"Seize the Moment."

Diana's words were a mere whisper, drawing Ben's attention to her face. Despite her dangerous act of sliding into the pool when she'd only just learned to swim, Ben felt his lips ease into a smile.

"Is that an excuse for almost drowning yourself, or an invitation?"

Her dark eyes widened and her full lips parted. They were impossibly tempting, and he suddenly became aware that he still held her cradled in his arms.

Diana's heart was full of conflicting emotions. She felt his arm tighten around her waist, drawing her toward him. She knew exactly what he was asking her, what he wanted to happen.

Her lips softened automatically as Ben's mouth covered hers. He tasted of salt and his lips felt like velvet. She felt their bodies meet, seem to meld...

DESIRE'S MOON

Nothing sedu

Diamond Books by Elane Osborn

SKYLARK
DESIRE'S MOON

DESIRE'S MOON

ELANE OSBORN

DIAMOND BOOKS, NEW YORK

DESIRE'S MOON

A Diamond Book / published by arrangement with
the author

PRINTING HISTORY
Diamond edition / November 1991

ISBN: 1-55773-612-X

Diamond Books are published by The Berkley Publishing Group,
200 Madison Avenue, New York, New York 10016.
The name "DIAMOND" and its logo are trademarks
belonging to Charter Communications, Inc.

PRINTED IN THE UNITED STATES OF AMERICA

10 9 8 7 6 5 4 3 2 1

Prologue

THE GROVE BECKONED. The call of the midnight pool drew her through the forest. And again, the dream began.

Once more, Diana McKenzie found herself garbed in the short white tunic of the Roman goddess she had been named for, walking through the velvet night with the lithe grace of a woodland deer, her sandaled feet cushioned by soft moss beneath the leafy canopy of trees that surrounded her like old friends. She had slipped into this world hundreds of times before, drawn by the serenity and the aura of power emanating from the grove she knew lay ahead.

Tonight, however, there was a different feel to the air, a shift in the breeze that made the hair on her slim arms stand on end. In her dream role as the goddess of the moon, Diana knew there was nothing for her to fear in the darkness, yet some sense of foreboding made her move with deliberate care.

Within seconds the trees thinned. Moonbeams filtered through the leaves to dance brightly along the curve of her silver bow. With the sharp eyes of a huntress, Diana spied the dark pool ahead, between a gap in the trees. Yet, as she neared the clearing, her footsteps grew ever slower. Finally, she reached the towering cypresses that encircled the pond like tall tapering candles. She stopped and scanned the grassy shore.

Everything appeared identical to her previous visits to the midnight glade. The pool was perfectly still, mirroring the round, opalescent moon and sparkling stars in the sky above. Across the water the opening to a small cave gaped darkly. The two slender trees that stood like sentinels on either side of the grotto remained motionless. Still she hesitated, sensing a disturbing shift in the atmosphere. Yet, the grove beckoned.

Diana felt herself drawn forward, onto the grass edging the water. She dropped her bow to the ground, then slid her quiver off her shoulder and let it fall as well, arrows spilling out to lie like shafts of moonlight on the grass. Staring at the dark water, Diana unfastened the silver thread that encircled her brow and held her midnight hair in a loose knot at the nape of her neck. Her black tresses fell in tumbling waves to the hem of her short tunic, forming a dark curtain around her slender body.

The cord at her waist fell away with a mere touch, and when she shrugged, the draped neckline of her tunic slipped off her shoulders so that the white silk slid down her body and dropped in a gossamer mass at her feet. Diana stepped over the material, then bent to untie the thongs wrapped around her ankles and released her feet from her sandals.

As the last bit of leather and thong fell onto the grass, Diana's senses once again issued a warning. She straightened, like a deer poised for danger, to search the grove once more, her heart beating rapidly, her eyes and ears alert. Silence filled the grove. She saw nothing but the trees, the cave, the night sky above, and still water below, calling to her, coaxing her to the pool.

A quick shiver tightened Diana's muscles, as if to shake away her baseless misgivings; then she stepped forward at last to obey the call of the water. The warm liquid caressed one foot, then the other. Soft sand cushioned her steps as the depth of the pond gradually increased and the water's gentle touch slid up her calves, then grazed her thighs.

Tiny waves were lapping at her waist when some deep-felt instinct made her stop moving. The ends of her hair floated like dark waterweeds around her as she listened. She heard nothing, yet still she tensed. Then she turned so abruptly that the curtain of hair cascading down over her left breast whipped through the air, tossing droplets of water into the pond as it swung over her shoulder.

Diana was aware that her exposed breast shimmered white in the moonlight, but she made no attempt to cover herself as she stared at the tall, broad-shouldered figure of a man standing on the shore she had just vacated, bracketed by cypress trees. Moonbeams glanced off his unclothed form, clearly defining his lean, powerfully built body. But it was his eyes, glinting like darkest obsidian, that caught and held Diana's gaze.

For several seconds she found herself unable to do more than simply stare into those black depths. Then, as the man stepped forward, sending powerful ripples out as he placed his foot into her pond, Diana grew hot with rage at the man's audacity. Still staring into his insolent eyes, she became aware that he had placed his other foot into the pool, that he stood there as if claiming it, and everything in it, for himself.

For the next several moments, a swirl of conflicting emotions held Diana motionless. Shame battled outrage as she thought of those dark eyes watching her as she disrobed; fear warred with wrath as she contemplated his threat to her place of power. Her muscles tensed as fury coursed through her veins. She knew what must be done. The man, whoever he was, must be punished for violating her grove.

Determined to destroy him, to rid herself of his disturbing

presence, Diana cupped her right hand and grabbing a handful of water, flung it in his face.

The man neither blinked nor flinched, just calmly stepped toward her again. The goddess stared at him a moment longer before she began to back away, feeling the water rise around her as she neared the center of the pool. Her mind raced. This was all wrong. The water she had thrown in his face was to have turned the man into a stag; instead, he continued to stalk her, defying her magic.

But he would not capture her. The pool was small. The water tickling the base of her neck told Diana that she had already reached its center. Behind her lay her cave, only yards away. There she would be safe.

Even as her thoughts raced, her gaze remained ensnared by his and she saw him move ever closer. Now she pulled her eyes from his, turned, and prepared to spring forward and swim to freedom. But as she pivoted, she felt her wrist trapped by strong fingers that jerked her back. She whirled to face him, only to find her attention once more captivated by his glittering dark eyes.

She stared at him until she managed to wrench her gaze away, to see the lean brown fingers encircling her pale flesh. The power of the man's hold sent lightning-like tingles dancing over her skin, up the length of her arm to render it weak and useless. Her knees buckled slightly and her heart raced.

Terror rippled through Diana in the wake of this sudden loss of power. Then anger returned, bringing renewed strength to her limbs, along with a determination to face and best this strange man. Diana lifted her eyes to his, certain she had regained her sense of control, only to find it slip away as she found her attention captured once more by the compelling glow in his dark eyes.

The man stood only inches away from her now. Diana could feel the heat of his body radiate toward hers, warming her flesh but doing nothing to ease the deep chill that gripped the center of her being. As she stared up into his eyes she found it difficult to breathe, and when she saw that he was bending forward, she discovered that she was unable to move, forced to helplessly watch his eyes come ever closer to hers.

She was unmindful of his intent until the moment that his mouth hovered a breath away from hers. Stunned by the audacity of this move, Diana gasped, a soft sound that was silenced when his firm lips took possession of her mouth. Despite her confusion she realized his kiss was warm. His lips moved with a deliberate slowness that elicited a foreign sensation in her stomach, like ice melting in the sun, as the lightning-like shivers that had affected her arm when he grabbed her wrist now raced the length of her body.

Fear filled Diana's mind. She willed her arms to move, to push this stranger away, but her limbs would not respond. Her eyes, wide with impotent anger, stared at the night sky above, at the tiny stars winking as if mocking her predicament, as if the gods in the heavens were pleased.

Her fury grew, but still she could not move. He was touching her now. His strong arms encircled her slender form, pulling her against his lean body. His mouth closed more firmly over hers, and she found that her anger was no match for the strange sensations coursing through her.

Responding to the pressure of his commanding kiss, Diana felt her lips soften and part, allowing his tongue to slip past her teeth, then caress the inside of her mouth. The warmth in her stomach coiled and spiraled lower, awakening a strange, nameless need along with a deep, uncomprehending fear. Fury flared in her mind still, but her body was limp, completely powerless in the wake of the potent sensations washing through her. A roaring sound filled her ears and the earth seemed to shudder beneath her feet as she surrendered her will to the demands of her body and let her eyes fall shut.

Diana McKenzie opened her eyes to total darkness. No longer did warm water caress her limbs, nor did forceful arms hold her captive. Instead, heavy blankets weighed her down as she lay on a bed that swayed and rocked to the rhythm of iron wheels clacking on steel rails. The wail of the train's whistle rose to echo in the night.

She knew where, and who, she was, but her strange dream had not left her completely. Her lips still tingled and throbbed as if a phantom mouth still claimed them, and her body was awash with a heated flush that urged her to throw off her blankets and pull herself into a sitting position.

Diana did just that, leaning against her pillow and rubbing her eyes, but when she removed her hands and opened her eyes again, it was to the same blackness that had greeted her moments before. Remnants of her dream still shimmered like a mist before her, confusing her newly awakened mind. Twisting around, she ran her hand along the bottom of the window until her fingers found what she sought. Pulling the cord, she raised the shade, then stared out into the night.

In the sapphire sky beyond the window a threadlike crescent shimmered in the sky. Tomorrow night there would be no moon at all. Tomorrow night she would be at Sutro Heights.

Diana took a deep shuddering breath as the dream receded and reality became firmly fixed in her mind. She was on a train, just hours away from Oakland, California. A ferry and a carriage ride would take her to her final destination, south of San Francisco, to the estate of the mayor of that city.

A tingle of excitement tempered by apprehension slithered down Diana's spine. So much waited for her in San Francisco. It had all seemed so exciting as she packed to leave Philadelphia, thinking she was at last leaving her past, and ready for the future she had prepared so long and hard for. But one last part of her past lurked there as well, and that element was undoubtedly the cause of the dream that had disturbed her sleep for the third night in a row.

It was her long-anticipated reunion with her father that was most likely behind these disturbing dreams, for she could still remember hearing Daniel McKenzie's deep, melodious voice recounting numerous stories about her namesake, the Roman goddess Diana. It had seemed reasonable for these bedtime stories to become dreams in which the goddess took on Diana's own angular features and dark blue eyes.

Then her father left. The dreams remained, but as Diana matured she had drawn strength from her association with a deity reknowned for her prowess in what was considered a masculine endeavor. The grove and the pool had become almost real places to her, so often had she visited them in her dreams.

As the train rocked around a curve, Diana shivered and drew the blankets back up to her chin. Once again she thought of the dream, still hovering on the edges of her mind. Not until the last three nights had she ever encountered anyone else within the circle of cypress trees.

Diana had made a point of tracing every element of the goddess's story, delving into the older mythology of Artemis, the Greek deity on which the Romans had patterned their goddess of the moon and of the hunt. She knew that Artemis had discovered a man named Actaeon spying on her as she bathed, and that she had dashed water on him, turning him into a stag to be destroyed by his own hunting hounds. So, if she was indeed a goddess in her dreamworld, why had she been unable to destroy the man who invaded her glade?

Another shiver rippled through Diana as she remembered

how the man had taken control with relentless ease, and how she had responded so passionately to his touch.

Passion had never been part of her life. She had not, of course, reached the age of twenty-two without some knowledge of the forces that drew men to women. She had seen passion, even lust, in the eyes of more than one man, but had never felt any answering spark.

And that was just as well. Her life had been full of more important things. Her studies in Latin and Greek, mythology, geology, and history—all to prepare her for her career as an archaeologist—left her with no time for men beyond the time she spent discussing these subjects with them. So why should she react like this to the stranger who had invaded her dream sanctuary?

The question echoed in Diana's mind for a moment, then she smiled and shook her head. There was probably no reasonable cause for this. She had never been one to look for signs and portents in dreams, and, she reminded herself, now was not the time to begin to do such irrational things. She had her father to question about his ten years of silence, and a career to launch. She could not afford to waste any more time worrying about dreams. She needed sleep. The dawn would bring far more important issues to address.

Diana's sigh hissed into the silence as she rolled onto her side and forced her eyes to close, waiting for sleep to claim her once more.

_____ *Chapter One*

"WELL, DIANA, we're nearing Sutro Heights. I can smell the sea."

Diana glanced over to see her companion lean toward the open window and peer out into the foggy morning. The face beneath the broad-brimmed black hat was comfortable-looking, as if the woman was pleased with how the last fifty-odd years had treated her. A smile curved the thin lips, and small lines fanned out from the dark brown eyes that turned suddenly to Diana.

"Go ahead," she urged. "Take a deep breath."

Diana did as she was bidden, leaning toward the open carriage window, drawing in the moist air that drifted by in shreds of gray, smelling and tasting of salt. Her own lips curved into a smile as she turned to the woman opposite her. "It smells wonderful, Dr. Merritt—so clean and invigorating. I've always longed to spend some time near the ocean."

Emma Sutro Merritt sat back and gave a straightening tug to the front of her black jacket. It was similar in cut to the pale beige one Diana wore over her high-collared ivory shirt and matching beige skirt. Both costumes were no-nonsense attire befitting women who knew their own minds. The ladies' choice of hats matched their suits as well. A black one sat atop Emma's gray hair, a tan one on Diana's thick black tresses, both wide-brimmed creations unadorned except for the grosgrain ribbon surrounding the crowns.

They had commented on the similarity of their suits when they met at the ferry landing that morning. During the long ride that took them up and down the hills of San Francisco, to the near wilderness on the southernmost edge of the city, they had discovered they shared more than just a similar taste in clothing. Both were women with careers. Emma had been a doctor for years, and Diana had just finished her degree in archaeology and was ready to pursue that following.

"Oh, we can't have you getting into the habit of addressing me as Dr. Merritt," Emma said with a smile. "My husband, George, is a physician also, so the title Dr. Merritt causes all sorts of confusion when we're both present. Please, just call me Emma."

Diana nodded. "All right, Emma, and before we arrive at your father's house, let me tell you once more how much I appreciate your taking the trouble to meet my ferry from Oakland and to accompany me all the way out here."

"Don't be silly." Emma held up a black-gloved hand. "It's the least I could do. I don't take patients on Wednesdays, anyway, so there was no problem getting away. I use the day to come to the Heights and see to Papa's business matters." Her smile took a rueful twist. "He's so busy being mayor of San Francisco that he's losing track of things at his own little kingdom out here."

The woman's words sent several disturbing emotions whirling in Diana's breast. A guilty voice shamed her for taking up this woman's valuable time, and a worried one whispered that she should have learned something about the place she was visiting before setting off so quickly.

Diana ignored the first voice, telling herself that this woman's assistance was necessary, both to help her put the past to rest and to open up her future. She quieted the second voice by using this opportunity to try to learn something about her destination. "Kingdom?" she asked.

Emma rolled her eyes and smiled. "Well, that's what I call it. Papa has created his own little wonderland out here on the edge of the world. I'll give you a quick look around this morning before I dig into Papa's things, and perhaps a longer tour before dinner. But I'm afraid you'll be on your own for most of the day."

"That will be fine with me," Diana replied. "I'm accustomed to amusing myself."

"Well, there's plenty to explore here. You can start with the gardens. In fact—" The woman paused as the carriage lurched forward slightly. She glanced out the window then turned to Diana. "We're almost to the front gate now. If you'd like, I can have the driver let you out and you can take your time wandering up to the house while I have your luggage brought up to your room, and get a start on Papa's correspondence. That is, if you aren't too tired for a little hike."

Diana was most certainly weary. Her strange dream had stolen sleep from her for three nights running, and the swaying of the carriage had made her sleepy. But that was all the more reason to take some exercise. She hadn't dared to ask if her father had arrived. If he was already there she wanted to have her wits about her when they finally met.

"Actually," she replied, "I think a walk would be perfect."

"Good." Emma nodded briskly, then leaned her head out the window to shout for the driver to come to a stop at the gate. She turned back to Diana as the carriage swayed to a stop. "It's a little misty this morning, but the wind isn't up yet so it shouldn't be too cold. And you can't get lost if you stay on the main path. Come, I'll show you."

The driver opened the door as Emma spoke, and she

preceded Diana out of the carriage. When Diana joined
Emma on the hard dirt road, she turned her attention to the
small woman as Emma extended one arm with a flourish
and smiled broadly. "Welcome to the wonderful world of
Sutro Heights."

Diana shifted her gaze to look in the direction Emma had
indicated and felt her jaw go slack. A huge gothic archway
soared above the road in front of the carriage, supported by
two square towers topped by cupidlike statues. Diana stared
at the Grecian urn sitting atop the peak at the gate's center,
then lowered her gaze to the lions reclining on either side
of the portal.

As Diana continued to stare, a man dressed in a dark
uniform and tall cap swung the double gate open to reveal
a wide, gravel-paved avenue stretching forward toward a
thick stand of trees. Both sides of the driveway were bordered by a row of palm trees that rose to a crown of spiny
fronds softened by the mist swirling above them.

Diana turned to Emma. "This is amazing."

Emma smiled. "My father is very proud of what he's
done out here. This whole area was nothing but sand dunes
when we bought Sutro Heights years ago. People thought
he was crazy back then, planting strange trees and importing
copies of famous statues, but now they come out here by
the hundreds to see the marvel Papa has created. This is
my favorite time of day for a stroll, with the fog swirling
around the statues, making them look almost like they are
moving. Later, after the fog burns off and all the tourists
arrive, I find that some of the magic disappears."

Emma's lips curved in an embarrassed smile, then she
turned to mount the carriage steps. She paused at the top
step and swiveled toward Diana. "Just follow Palm Avenue
here. It will lead you through the main body of the garden
and bring you right up to the house. Take your time and

look at all the statues and flower beds. I didn't have time for breakfast this morning, did you?''

This abrupt change of subject took Diana by surprise. When she shook her head, Emma smiled. "Just as I thought. I'll arrange for a little brunch to be served to us when you arrive at the house.''

Moments later Diana watched as the carriage rattled down the broad path; then she crossed beneath the arch herself, and felt suddenly like Alice stepping through the looking glass. A second ago she could smell only the ocean. Now her senses were overwhelmed by the scent of pine mixed with the aroma of roses and honeysuckle and other flowers she couldn't identify.

The world she entered was just as varied as the plants surrounding her. She spied a winged griffon, stiff and marble-white, perched above a bed of flowers near a building she took to be a conservatory rising above the trees.

Diana took a deep breath and stepped forward. The gravel crunched beneath her booted feet as she walked, noticing yet another statue. A replica of a full-sized stag lay in a reclining position atop a short, broad pedestal against the dark green backdrop of woody veronica. Its pale white antlers twisted upward to blend with the overhanging branches of a cypress tree.

A slight chill raced up Diana's back. For one moment the mist darkened and instead of the statue of the stag, Diana found herself staring at the tall, powerful man who had invaded her sacred dream.

A rustling noise made Diana blink, then smile, as a squirrel dashed out of the bushes and up a tree nearby. She watched its bushy tail disappear into the foliage, glanced back to see the white stag in its place once more, then turned and continued her walk.

The dream had meant nothing, she told herself again. It had only been the product of exhaustion and excitement over the step she was taking. If the dream had not continually robbed her of sleep, she would not be seeing things in the mist.

Her heartbeat had just begun to return to normal when another statue appeared through the slender branches of a large pine.

Even without the name "Diana" carved in the pedestal, Diana would have recognized the goddess. She had seen photographs of this particular statue, and knew that the original carving stood in the Louvre. But Diana was personally familiar with this rendering, for a much smaller version was carefully packed in her luggage.

She'd had the small statue ever since she was twelve. It was the last present she had received from her father, purchased in Paris on his way to Pompeii. This statue matched hers in every detail, except hers was made of silvery pot metal, and this one glimmered white against its backdrop of cypress trees.

The goddess was garbed in a short, flowing dress, and her left hand rested on the antlers of a small stag, while her right reached for an arrow in the quiver on her back. Around the statue the gray mist swirled, encircling her head like a crown or a halo. As Diana stared at the stone figure, it seemed to shimmer in the morning mist, to call her forward with a promise of power, of secrets only she could impart.

"They'll need to be painted, Mr. Abraham." Ben Potter's deep voice echoed off the glass enclosing the conservatory as he stared at the small cement forms of a deer, a racoon, and a fox sitting at his feet. The humid air in the glass building pressed around him, making his chest tighten with a familiar discomfort. He removed his broad-brimmed felt hat from his dark blond hair and fanned some movement into the stale air as he went on. "And not white. I need them to look lifelike."

The old gardener turned from his inspection of potted cypresses. His pale blue eyes were set in a narrow, leathery face, their expression doubtful. "I'll see if any of my lads have the skills that would allow for that, Professor, but I have my doubts. The group I have now can barely manage to paint the statues in the garden a simple white without spilling. I spent the entire morning supervising Diana's new coat of paint, seeing that they didn't stain the grass around her."

Ben sighed as he nodded his understanding. Good help was indeed hard to find— or at least, hard to keep. As he stared at the gray, featureless shape of the fox at his feet he found himself almost regretting the hasty words that had resulted in the loss of Laurence Brody. The man had been unreasonably slow at his work, but he had been a true artist.

"Young Jeremy does show some promise, though."

Abraham's musing voice made Ben glance up sharply. The old man's face had wrinkled into a mixture of hope and doubt that brought a reluctant smile to Ben's lips. "Well, send him down to me at the Baths, then. Counting today I have exactly eleven days to produce the marvels Mr. Sutro has demanded."

The old man responded with a knowing look and a brief nod before bending to check the primrose growing at the base of a small white statue of Cupid. Ben tightened his jaw as he opened the glass door, and stepped into the morning mist.

All this work just to catch a thief. A thief *and* a murderer, Ben corrected himself. His eyes narrowed as he crossed the path leading to the front gate. Trapping Daniel McKenzie was well worth any amount of time or money as far as he was concerned, but he was well aware that there was no guarantee the man would fall into this snare, no matter how elaborate.

Ben gazed around the gardens that Adolph Sutro had

created, at the blend of yellow, red, orange, and blue flowers, some surrounding the freshly painted statues, others encircling huge Grecian urns. This morning their brilliant hues were softened by the morning fog, but they stood as mute testimony to the far-reaching vision of the man who had designed this garden. When he and Will had planned their exhibition here, they had no idea what they were getting into.

The British Museum was thrilled, of course, that Sutro was spending so much money to house their statues for such a short time, but then neither the curators nor Mr. Sutro were aware of the more sinister motives behind the Pompeii exhibit, as it was being touted.

Oh, it was well known that the British Museum had almost lost its newly acquired statue of Diana several months before, and that a guard had forfeited his life while preventing the theft, but the museum had been content to leave the investigation in the hands of Scotland Yard. Their line of questioning led nowhere, just like similar queries into more successful attempts in Paris and Milan, and had been shelved—officially, anyway.

Ben shook his head and frowned. Moving the statue so far away, with the plan of drawing the culprit into the open, had seemed such an intelligent, sensible way to handle the matter when he and Will laid out the plans to the Yard. But that was before they knew Adolph Sutro. Now matters were complicated beyond all belief.

It wasn't enough for the man to display the museum's collection of artifacts from Pompeii. No, Sutro insisted that they be presented in a manner designed to impress and educate the citizens of "his" city. So instead of planning out strategy for McKenzie's capture with Will, Ben found himself searching for someone with the talent to help him pull off the extravaganza that this simple exhibit had evolved into.

Aware that he was nearing the front gate, Ben slowed his steps, then stopped when he caught sight of a pale figure standing in the road. For a moment he was certain that some new statue had been placed there, so still was the woman that stood garbed in pale beige, her face as white as marble beneath her wide-brimmed hat.

She was staring up the rise where he knew the figure of Diana stood, her face tilting up so that the morning light fell on her delicately sculpted features. Ben studied the slender nose, angled jaw, and full, parted lips that somehow hinted at the same strength seen in the figure of the goddess she was gazing at. As he watched, the young woman began to climb the gentle slope to stand before the stone pedestal.

Aware only of the goddess looming over her, Diana's pulse pounded loudly in her ears as she approached and stared up at the unseeing eyes of her namesake. Namesake, or rival? A familiar blend of admiration and jealousy, undulled by time, twisted in Diana's breast. She had often wondered if her father's long silence was due to his fascination with this mythological figure. She knew of all his digs, his visits to Italy and Greece to search out the origin of this particular deity. She had read about them in long, dry documents, where once he had shared his excitement with her in colorfully written letters.

What had happened to the warm man who had read Virgil to her while her mother wasted away in the bed nearby? Why had cold stone statues and ancient stories become more important to him than his own daughter? Diana felt her throat tighten. She frowned and blinked against the ache in her breast, refusing to cry as she gazed into the statue's sightless eyes, as if the shimmering marble might somehow possess the answers she craved.

The portion of Diana's mind trained in scientific logic scoffed at such imaginings, but the portion raised on myths urged her to reach out and draw whatever power or strength she could from the figure before her.

Ben had moved when Diana had, sidestepping up a corresponding rise so that he could watch her face. Her expression, a combination of reverence and pain, struck a chord in his soul, a painful reminder of a wound he thought was long healed. He watched as she lifted a gloved hand to the statue in a motion that could be either a supplication, a threat, or both. For a second he remained still, curious to see her next move, until he recalled old Abraham's words.

"Stop! Don't touch that statue."

Ben's voice echoed loudly in the hush of the morning. Diana jumped, just as she had as a curious child whenever her grandfather's commanding voice rang out in his house filled with irresistible treasures. Startled, she turned, searching for the source of the deep voice. Forgetting that she stood on a hill, she took a step down that threw her off balance. As she stared at the ground and fought the pull of gravity, she heard heavy footsteps hurrying toward her. Before they reached her, however, she gained her balance, straightened, and found herself staring into a deeply tanned face shadowed by the wide brim of a dark brown hat.

She was vaguely aware of a powerful masculine figure, much taller than her own height of five feet seven inches, casually dressed in a collarless beige shirt open at the neck and tan trousers. She noticed these things out of the corner of her eye as she gazed upward, searching for signs of anger in the face beneath the hat. The features were indeed hardlooking, sculpted in sharp angles that included a wide jaw, narrow, high-bridged nose, and lips that were firm, yet full. The man spoke again.

"I'm sorry." His deep voice echoed in the morning, though not as loudly as before. "I didn't mean to frighten you."

Diana's heart raced and her hands shook slightly but she

managed to clear her tight throat and force a smile to her lips. "You didn't. Not badly, anyway. I shouldn't have trespassed, I suppose. I—"

"That's not why I yelled."

Diana thought she saw an amused glimmer in his shadowed eyes as the man drew a quick breath and nodded toward the sculpture of Diana. "That statue was just painted this morning. I didn't want you to ruin your gloves."

"Painted?"

This time there was no missing the humor twitching at the corners of the man's mouth before he replied. "Yes. Mr. Sutro likes his statues to look like marble, but the sea breeze keeps stripping the paint off their cement surfaces."

Diana nodded slowly, glancing back at the statue. She had known, of course, that this was a copy, but she had taken the liquid sheen shimmering in the mist to be caused by condensation on the marble. Now, as she examined it more closely, she could see that the surface had a rougher appearance, and that the white was far too dazzling to belong to natural stone, no matter how pure.

Embarrassed that she had been fooled, Diana turned back to the man, only to find that he had already begun walking down the slope to the gravel driveway. She watched as he strode toward the entry gate without a backward glance, then she, too, continued toward the Sutro's house.

While Diana strolled beneath the rustling, pungently scented eucalyptus trees and gazed at the other statues, she found herself thinking about her encounter with the roughly dressed stranger. She was haunted by the amused expression that curved his full lips. Just how long had he been watching her, she wondered, and what, if anything, had he seen of her thoughts as she stared up at the statue?

Her musings ended as she drew near the house. The name, Sutro Heights, had conjured up visions of the elaborate

Queen Anne styled mansions topping the hills above San Francisco that Diana had seen from the window of the carriage. This house was far more simple. Rising a scant two stories in front of her was a simple, rectangular, many-windowed affair painted a gleaming white. The only item of architectural interest was a structure that appeared to be a square water tower, also white, poking into the thinning mist above the house.

The entrance was situated between two identical statues of Venus. Diana glanced from one female form to the other before mounting the stairs, then pressed a button on the door. A bell chimed and she stiffened.

Was her father there already? Perhaps waiting for her on the other side of this door? And if he were there, would she even recognize him?

Before Diana had time to ponder another question the door was opened by a small man dressed formally in black who ushered her into a modest entryway, then led her to the dining room, where only Emma waited. Diana's anxiety over meeting her father faded as she enjoyed the promised breakfast while Emma told her how Adolph Sutro's love of nature and art had culminated in the creation of the garden outside.

"It was originally just to be a small, private affair, of course. But Papa loves to have company up to the house and to show off his handiwork. Soon word got around and we found that our private world had become public. Actually, Papa loves to have people come up and—What is it, Matilda?"

Emma turned to face the maid. The woman dipped her lace-capped head as she replied, "Your father is on the telephone, Miss Emma."

The woman nodded and turned to Diana. "Isn't that wonderful? Here I am nearing fifty and the servants still address me as they would a young girl. Listen, dear. I'm likely to be tied up with my father's business for awhile. Why don't you go to your room and get yourself settled. I'll fetch you for that tour I promised you in an hour or so.''

Diana sighed as she closed the lid on her single trunk, then glanced about the room papered with yellow roses on a gray background. Her clothes, most of them newly purchased with the not insubstantial inheritance left to her by her grandfather, hung in the oak armoire. Her hat and macramé purse lay on the silver satin quilt covering the four-poster bed.

Sunlight streamed through the white lace curtains onto the gray carpet dotted with yellow and white roses. A mahogany writing desk filled the space between two wide windows, and that was where Diana had stored her personal treasures.

With nothing else to do, Diana crossed to the desk and lifted the tarnished picture frame from its place next to the small statue of Diana and the stag. She stared at the photograph of her mother, trying to recall more about the woman than the illness that robbed her of her life while she was so young. Diana studied the faded sepia-toned features that could very well be her own, if it weren't for the hat, now terribly out of fashion, sitting atop the dark cloud of hair framing her mother's face.

A wry smile twisted Diana's lips. ''When,'' she asked herself, ''have you ever been concerned about whether or not you were dressed fashionably?'' ''Never,'' came the answer. Still, she had always wondered what her attitude might have been had her mother lived to influence her in that manner.

Diana returned the frame to its place on the desk. She knew her mother's presence in her life would have made little difference in many ways. Certainly none of the feminine talents mothers normally passed onto their daughters could have distracted her from her interest in archaeology. The fact that she planned to use the artistic talents inherited from her mother in order to break into that normally masculine profession was proof of this.

What would her father think? Diana stared at the statue of the goddess she was named for, and for the first time in her life she found herself wishing it were a photo of her father, something that would bring his face more clearly to mind. It had been so long, over seventeen years, since the last time she had seen him. Her memory of him had faded to a blurred image of a man with a dark mustache and light, warm brown eyes.

But now she would not need a photograph. If her father wasn't already somewhere in this house, he would be coming to Sutro Heights soon.

A mixture of joy and pain shot through Diana's breast. She opened the desk drawer, and pulled out a thick, dark blue velvet envelope embroidered with the words "PAPA'S LETTERS" in silver thread. From its satin-lined interior she drew a folded newspaper clipping. The paper crinkled as she opened it and read the headline: "ANCIENT ITALY TO VISIT THE GOLDEN STATE."

The article beneath was dated June 15, 1897. She knew the words by heart, yet she read each one carefully.

"The British Museum will bring a collection of statues and artifacts featuring items excavated from Pompeii and Herculaneum to our fair city late this summer. Mayor Sutro, in his continuing quest to offer educational experiences to the citizens of San Francisco, has ordered the construction of a special area on the promenade deck at the Sutro Baths in which to display these items. Included in the exhibit will be a recently acquired statue of Diana, Roman goddess of the moon, which is to be housed in a replica of the ancient shrine erected to the pagan deity in Italy.

"This display will run from August 13th through the 30th.

Daily lectures will be offered on the subject of Ancient Rome: Its Civilization and Customs, to be delivered by such noted authorities as Professor Benjamin Potter of the British Museum and archaeologists Justin Harrington and Daniel McKenzie. These and other dignitaries will be staying at Sutro Heights, guests of the Mayor, for the length of the exhibit.''

Diana stared at her father's name for a moment, then glanced at the two pieces of paper that lay within the folds of the clipping. She didn't have to open them to remind herself of their contents. One was a draft of the letter she sent to Sutro Heights, in which she had forged her father's signature to a request that Sutro include McKenzie's daughter, Diana, in the invitation to stay at Sutro Heights. The other was the reply from Emma Sutro Merritt doing just that, along with an offer to meet Diana upon her arrival in San Francisco.

As Diana once again folded the clipping around the correspondence a knot of guilt twisted in her stomach. She had felt no such twinge when she sent that original letter. Until the long train trip out, she'd given little thought to how awkward this reunion with her father might prove. Now that she had met Emma, she began to regret the possibly uncomfortable position her actions might have placed these kind people in.

A knock at the door startled Diana. She shoved the clipping, the letter, and the telegram into the velvet envelope, placed them in the desk drawer, then hurried to open the door.

Emma stood on the red-and-brown-patterned hall runner. Like Diana, she had removed her jacket. The sleeves of her white shirtwaist hugged her plump arms. Gray hair, streaked with dark brown, framed her square face as she smiled at Diana. "Well," she said, "are you ready for that little tour I promised you?"

Diana nodded and stepped out to join Emma. "Good."
The woman spoke briskly as she led the way down the
corridor. "I'm afraid that I can only give you a brief over-
view, then let you explore on your own. I still have to go
through a shipment of books Papa recently received. Between his duties as mayor and the hours he spends interfering
with Professor Potter at the Pompeii exhibit, I know he
won't have time to see to them himself."

They went downstairs. Emma pointed out the parlor, then
led Diana down another long hallway. The door at the end
of the oak-paneled corridor opened to the outside. Light
spilled onto a set of stone steps. Diana followed Emma up
to a landing near the tower she had noted earlier. A semicircle of hard-packed earth curved in front of her, bordered
by a rock wall with the gap-toothed look of a Norman tower.

Each square section of wall held either a small statue or
a white urn filled with blooming plants. A stiff breeze blew
over the wall, ruffling the petals and bearing the scent of
salt and the sounds of crashing waves. Diana stared at the
horizon, where the brilliant blue sky met the deep green
sea, then glanced to see a wide golden beach.

"Come," Emma called as she stepped forward, "and
see my father's creations."

Diana followed, and as she neared the low wall, a sharply
pitched red roof came into view. With her hand resting on
the cool stone she saw a square building of enormous proportions and elaborate style. Sitting on a huge rock that
jutted out into the swirling sea, it soared eight stories high,
with round towers at each corner topped by pointed spires,
reminding her of a Bavarian *schloss* she had seen depicted
in a book of fairy tales.

Before Diana could pose a question about this structure,
Emma spoke. "That's the Cliff House. Inside it you will
find several restaurants and saloons, as well as billiard
rooms, parlors, and small music halls. You must visit it

while you are here. It's the perfect place to watch our seals.''

Diana turned to Emma. ''Seals?''

The wind had tugged curving tendrils of gray hair free of Emma's topknot. They framed her smiling face as she replied, ''The correct term, as Papa would be quick to tell you, is sea lions. They live out on those rocks for part of the year. It's more comfortable to watch them from inside the Cliff House, but if you look closely, you can make them out from up here.''

Emma pointed, directing Diana's attention past the huge building to the three cone-shaped rocks rising out of the sea. Seagulls and some larger birds wheeled above the largest rock and as Diana squinted she saw a brown, cigar-shaped form move against the rough gray surface. A moment later a hoarse bark floated on the cool breeze. Diana smiled, then shivered.

''That's what I meant when I said you'd be more comfortable inside.'' Emma's laughing voice drew Diana's attention to the older woman. ''It gets chilly up here in the wind. Let me show you one more thing, then we'll go back to your room to continue our talk.''

Emma turned and led Diana along the curving edge of the parapet. Diana stopped when Emma did, then noticed the strange structure below. The huge building was bordered by the sea and a tree-encrusted hill. Between these natural masses lay three arched roofs, formed of steel and glass, that reflected the sunlight like a thousand mirrors, making Diana blink.

''It looks like a huge hothouse,'' she breathed.

''In a sense, that's just what it is.'' Emma's tone held a hint of pride. ''Papa has many potted flowers and trees growing within the glass enclosure. You see, the Sutro Baths is not only the largest indoor bathing house, it also contains a wealth of fascinating artifacts, many of which my father collected himself. Hence its official name, The Sutro Baths and Museum.''

Emma's lips curved into the kind of sentimental smile a mother might reserve for a precocious child as she went on. ''Some people call it the world's largest curio cabinet. My father never does anything by halves, you see. Everything must be on a grand scale. He based his design on the ancient baths of Rome, expanding on the size, of course. There are a total of seven bathing pools inside, several of them heated to a very comfortable eighty degrees.''

The mention of pools, ancient Rome, and warm water had a very strange effect on Diana. One moment she was looking at the arching roofs, trying to imagine the interior of the building, and the next moment her imagination whisked her to her dream pool, where she stood entrapped by powerful arms.

Diana blinked and the image disappeared, along with the enervating warmth that had washed through her with the memory of her dream. A breeze brushed her burning cheeks, then a chill that had nothing to do with the temperature of the wind rippled through her.

_____ *Chapter Two*

DIANA RUBBED her hands up and down her upper arms as another gust of brisk air ruffled the black wisps framing her face. "The Baths sound marvelous. I'm looking forward to seeing them," Diana murmured.

"Well, you have plenty of time before dinner for a little—" Emma stopped as she noticed Diana. "Oh, my girl, you are half-frozen." Emma took Diana's elbow and urged the young woman toward the steps leading to the house. "Come, let's get you back to your room, and I'll finish explaining the routine around here."

Diana felt warmth seep into her form the moment she stepped into the house, and by the time she reached her bedroom, she was quite comfortable again.

"Ah, this is better." Emma smiled as she closed Diana's door behind them and walked to the windows. "I must warn you about the weather out here. As you just learned, even sunny days can be quite cool. And whenever the fog rolls in, you must take care to dress warmly. Mind you, sometimes even a woolen coat won't keep the chill from your bones, but it's better than nothing."

The woman turned as she finished speaking, her gaze resting on the small statue of Diana; then she glanced at Diana. "Am I correct in recalling that your father's letter

27

mentioned that in addition to your interest in archaeology you are also an artist?''

The rapid change of subject made Diana blink. "Yes," she replied. *Now is the time*, she told herself, *to explain about that forged letter*. "However," she started, "I wanted to speak to you about that letter. My father—"

"—won't be arriving for another week or so," Emma finished. "We received a letter from him to that effect just yesterday." She shook her head. "I should have told you about that first thing this morning, but we got to talking so furiously that it slipped my mind. It seems I'm becoming almost as forgetful as Papa lately."

The woman frowned, then gave Diana a rueful smile. "I'm doing it again. I was just going to ask you something very important and now I've—No, I remember now. About the art. If I recall, your father's letter mentioned that you were anxious to meet one of our other guests, Professor Harrington, about a position as an apprentice on his next dig. Wasn't there some mention of your abilities as an artist as well?"

Diana felt her face grow warm as she remembered this bit of self-promotion. At the time she wrote the letter, she was only concerned with making an impression on someone who could further her career. Now it sounded like pure boastfulness.

She was aware, in some corner of her mind, that now was the proper moment to admit to forging that letter, but her embarrassment, combined with the suppressed excitement in Emma's voice, coerced Diana into answering the woman's question. "Well, yes. My mother was a very talented painter, in her quiet way. I apparently inherited some of her talent. As I studied archaeology it became obvious from the unreasonable attitude of my professors and colleagues that men considered this following the exclusive property of the male sex. However, I learned that each dig needs an artist, to provide detailed sketches of artifacts as they are uncovered. So I studied art as well, hoping to use this talent to wedge my way into a career in archaeology.''

"That's a brilliant plan." Emma stepped forward and took Diana's hand. "Do you have any examples of your work?"

"Well, yes. I was hoping for a chance to show them to Professor Harrington if—"

"That's a superb idea." Once again Emma's words left Diana's sentence only half-finished. "I'm certain you shall have several chances to do just that in the next few weeks. But could you show me some of your work now?"

Diana nodded as she drew her hand from Emma's, crossed to the writing desk, and opened the drawer. The packet containing the draft of the forged letter seemed to mock her as she reached past the blue velvet envelope to remove the leather folder holding her sketches. She slid the drawer closed, then she stood biting the inside of her lower lip as Emma took the portfolio from her and began to examine the drawings within.

"You are very clever to anticipate masculine prejudice and plan around it," Emma commented as she stared at one drawing. "I had a difficult time getting men to accept my capabilities in the field of medicine, of course, so I know what you're facing. They seem to feel they deserve exclusive rights to certain areas of endeavor." The woman paused as she turned to the next sketch. "Your obvious talents as an artist, however, are sure to get you in the door; then, once you establish your abilities, the initial resistance to your female status should fade away."

Emma looked up, and went on more quickly, "But in the meantime, I know someone who is in great need of the services of an artist at this very moment. Would you be interested in some temporary employment?"

The question caught Diana off guard. She stared at Emma

mutely for a moment, marveling at the way the woman's thoughts jumped from point to point with such disconcerting speed.

With no indication that she noticed Diana's silence, Emma spoke again. "You would be working in your chosen field if you take this job. You see, Professor Benjamin Potter of the British Museum, the man in charge of preparing the exhibit to house the Roman artifacts when they arrive, is in desperate straits. The fellow he hired to do his painting and drawing just gave up and left him two days ago. Why don't you show these to him right now?"

Emma handed the drawings back to Diana, and without waiting for a reply, continued. "The promenade deck is something of a jumbled maze, so if you'd like I can telephone down to the Baths and have old Pete meet you at the entrance and escort you to the Pompeii display."

Diana barely glanced at the statue of her namesake as she hurried toward the front gate of Sutro Gardens. She had redonned her jacket and her hat in preparation for her interview with Professor Potter. Her pale, gloved hands tightened over her portfolio as she passed beneath the arch and turned left onto another wide street. She stared down the hill as her booted feet skimmed over the road.

On her right the Sutro Baths stretched out between the road and a tall rugged cliff. From this angle she could see that the huge building was a combination of gray concrete and arched windows with a curving glass roof topped by two small cupolas, reminiscent of something one would see in India or Turkey.

The entrance was purely of Greek design, however; square with a peaked roof supported by graceful white columns framing the double doors. Standing near the entry was an imposing figure dressed in a black suit. The man's heavy, square face beneath his black derby was well matched to his broad-shouldered, large-boned frame and fit perfectly Emma's description of the head caretaker who was to meet her. As Diana approached the man, his pale green eyes narrowed slightly, then his wide, sandy-brown mustache rose in a smile.

"You must be Miss McKenzie."

Diana returned the smile. "Yes, and you must be Mr. Martin."

"Pete. Just Pete, please, miss. And please come in. Miss Emma said you needed a tour of our facility."

Diana's fingers tightened on the edge of her folder again as she shook her head. "Not today, actually. Emma has sent me down to speak to a Professor Potter. She seemed to think I would have some difficulty in locating the area he's working in."

Diana smiled up at the huge fellow, tilting her head back so far that she could feel her hatpin tugging at the lock of hair it was fastened to.

"Miss Emma is probably right, too," he replied. "Oh, you'd find it eventually. After all, the exhibit in question is rather hard *not* to spot. But once people get inside, there is so much to look at that they sometimes bump into things before they see them. So, directly to the Pompeii exhibit it shall be. Are you ready?"

Diana nodded in reply, and the man took her elbow gently in his large hand. As Pete began to escort her through the double doors she noted that he limped slightly, dragging his left foot up to the right with each step. They moved slowly crossing a large room with walls nearly covered with paintings. Normally she would have welcomed the relaxed pace, even stopped once or twice to examine a particularly fine work of art. But today it was an effort to control her impatience and slow her steps to match his.

But when they came out onto what Pete announced as

the promenade deck, it was Diana's footsteps that slowed and finally stopped.

Now she truly did feel as if she were Alice, stepping into a wonderland. The interior of the building was unlike anything she'd ever seen before. High above her, sunlight filtered through the green glass and illuminated the open space below, a long, wide hall filled with statues, potted palms, and urns overflowing with brilliant flowers. Everywhere she looked she saw gleaming glass cases surrounded by women in plumed hats and gentlemen in derbies, small girls in short dresses and boys in knickers and caps, all staring in awe at the various displays.

"The actual Baths are to your left, past that railing." Pete's deep voice rose over the exuberant shouts and loud splashing sounds coming from the direction he had indicated. "Would you like to take a quick look at them?"

Diana felt a strong longing to do just that, but as merry as the laughter sounded, and as curious as she was to see the "World's Largest Indoor Bathing Pools," she forced herself to shake her head. "Not today, Pete. Perhaps tomorrow, when I have more time."

The man's pale green eyes gazed into hers a moment before he nodded; then he continued to guide Diana through the maze of display cases and statues. As she walked along, Diana couldn't help but glance at the glass boxes holding items as varied as butterflies on black velvet backing, a collection of coins affixed to a block of green marble, and a group of Egyptian carvings arranged within a tall rectangular frame.

Larger displays were open to the air, such as the brightly colored stuffed birds arranged in a leafy tree, a stuffed jaguar battling a huge snake wrapped around its torso, and an eight-foot gorilla grimacing in the most lifelike manner from atop a square of cement in the center of their path.

Diana was staring up at his vicious-looking teeth when

she heard a boyish voice call out, "Dad, hold up," and felt Pete come to a stop beside her. She turned as a boy of about twelve, dressed in a gray tweed jacket and knickers, hurried forward to come to a halt in front of the caretaker.

"Olson sent me to find you, Dad," he said. "He needs to ask you some questions about diverting water for the professor's volcano."

Pete nodded and turned to Diana. "Miss McKenzie, this is my son, Joseph. He helps me out after school and on weekends." He turned to his son. "Go tell Olson I'll be with him in just a few moments. I have to escort the lady here to the Pompeii exhibit."

Diana turned to Pete. "Is it much farther to the exhibit?"

The man shook his head. "No, actually. We just need to head toward the large bird cage, then turn to the right."

"Well, I'm sure I could find it on my own. Why don't you go see to this problem?"

Pete's eyes shifted from hers to where his son had disappeared, then slowly back to meet Diana's gaze. "I probably should. We don't have much time left on this project. If you're sure you can—"

"I'm sure," Diana broke in. "Besides, it wouldn't be a good idea for me to keep you from working on something for Professor Potter if I hope to get him to hire me."

Pete nodded slowly. "All right, Miss McKenzie. I'm sure you'll find it without any trouble now that you're this close. It's the only Roman temple in the place."

Diana smiled as she turned briskly and followed his directions. She came to an abrupt stop when she spied her destination rising above the promenade deck at the end of the building. Emma's words echoed in her mind, joking about the "grand" way her father approached everything he did.

This display before her was a perfect example of such excess. What appeared to be a stone hill with a broad, curving base rose far into the air. An exact replica of the Pantheon in Rome sat atop the mound of rock. The graceful white columns of the square vestibule and soaring circular rotunda that formed the main body of the building captured perfectly the grandeur of the ancient structure.

Diana squinted, searching between the columns for one of the workmen Emma had assured her would be in the area. Seeing no one there, she glanced around, but saw only other visitors.

Diana cradled her portfolio in one arm, pulling it closer to her breast as she wondered how to proceed from there. The chance to work on such an exhibit was not an opportunity to be missed simply because she couldn't find someone to let her in.

As she approached the hill, she saw that the rocks were actually formed by the clever use of paint. Her artist's eye marveled at the skill that had produced this sensational trompe l'oeil effect. Diana followed the curve of the mock hill until she reached the back wall of the building. There she discovered a neatly concealed set of stairs. Her booted feet echoed hollowly on the unfinished pine boards as she climbed.

Diana passed between two white columns, then hesitated a second before opening one of the double doors before her. She stood on the threshold a moment, narrowing her eyes to allow them to adjust to the relatively dim light in the room beyond.

Gradually, Diana's eyes grew accustomed to the gloom and she saw that she stood in a wide, shallow room lined on either side with several short pedestals. Between two doors at the far end of the room a wide altar was arranged above a set of steps.

As she stared at the altar, Diana felt the same sense of awe and respect that would have gripped her had she been entering the real Pantheon. It appeared to be carved of solid marble, but after seeing the artificial hill out front, she was certain that the marble veining was just an illusion. However, the brushwork here was far more delicate than the exterior work and would require closer inspection to reveal its secrets.

She crossed the room quickly. Even as she reached the top of the stairs she couldn't be certain whether she was gazing at a slab of real stone or not.

Engrossed in her study of the altar, Diana was unaware of any other presence, until a voice boomed out, "You there! What the hell do you think you're doing?"

Diana jumped, flinging her arms wide. Her purse slid off her wrist and her sketchbook flew into the air. She tried to turn toward the voice behind her, but only managed to twist her upper torso.

Her feet seemed rooted to the steps, causing her to sway. Unable to move in any direction, she lifted her eyes to the shadowed form framed in the wide entryway. She thought she saw him move as she opened her mouth to call for help, but before she could utter a sound she felt herself begin to fall.

Diana gasped, her body twisted around, then seemed to hang motionless in an impossible diagonal position for a second. When she felt herself begin to plunge downward, she stretched her arms out in front of her, hoping to break her fall.

Time seemed somehow to move more slowly, making Diana aware of each individual second as it passed. As she continued her descent, she heard an oath muttered, followed by the echo of rapidly moving footsteps. Unable to pull her gaze from the lowermost step, she watched it rise toward her with ever-increasing speed.

Her arms stiffened, braced for a collision with the step, but just as her outstretched hands grazed the wooden surface, strong arms encircled her waist and she was pulled to one side.

Diana's ribs felt as if they were being crushed in a vise as she fell upon a hard, masculine chest. All the air in her lungs was forced past her lips with a loud whoosh. Her first reaction was to push herself up, to disentangle herself from whoever lay beneath her, but when she tried to take a breath, she found that her chest refused to expand. Her eyes widened with panic as she fought to catch her breath.

A small, logical voice urged her to quit struggling. Forcing herself to relax, Diana lay with her cheek resting on the warm solid surface of the man's chest, feeling as if she were drowning, surrounded by air but unable to draw it into her lungs. Closing her eyes, she concentrated on the sound of her pulse pounding loudly in her ears, and on the softer echo of the heartbeat belonging to the man who held her.

Finally the tightness in her chest eased and air rushed into her aching lungs. Diana took another deep breath, drawing in a faint woodsy scent, then stared at the expanse of tan shirt so near her eyes, uncertain as to what she should do next.

Her hands were opened flat against muslin-covered curves of warm muscle. Slowly she pressed down, pushing herself upward, half-afraid she would find the man lying unconscious, or worse. Before she had lifted herself high enough to catch more than a glimpse of a squared-off chin, strong fingers clasped her upper arms. The man shifted Diana to one side, then rose to his feet, leaving her sitting on the floor while he stood in front of her.

"What the devil are you doing in here?" His deep voice, vaguely familiar to Diana's ears, echoed in the chamber. "This area is under construction. Didn't you see the warning signs?"

Stunned and still a little breathless, Diana could do noth-

ing more than stare at the man's scuffed brown boots. Then
slowly she lifted her eyes, taking in the rough tan trousers
that clung to well-muscled thighs above the tops of his boots.
Brown suspenders were fastened to the narrow waist of his
pants, and as Diana's eyes continued to sweep upward, she
saw that his shirt was collarless and open at the neck, dis-
playing a wealth of curling, medium-brown hair.

The man's sleeves were rolled up, baring tanned forearms, and his elbows were at right angles to his body, his
clenched fists resting firmly on his hips. When Diana lifted
her eyes past his broad shoulders to his tanned face, she
wasn't at all surprised to see the scowling face of the man
who had warned her against touching the statues earlier that
day.

"Well, what do you have to say for yourself? Do you
have any idea what kind of damage you could cause here?"

Diana gasped at the angry arrogance in his voice. Her
stunned mind reacted with instant anger bred of years of
defending herself against the dictates of males determined
to display their superiority. A quick retort leapt to her lips,
but her words were immediately silenced when the man
reached down, grasped Diana's wrist, and pulled her to her
feet. He then leaned close to her face and demanded, "Well,
do you?"

The sliver of light fell on his face. Diana found herself
staring into eyes that were such a deep, smoky gray that
they were nearly black, glimmering with a look of power
and control that was disturbingly familiar.

Diana's heart raced as she focused on those narrowed
depths, so very like the ones that had robbed her of sleep
for three nights. The angry words on her lips were stilled
by the nearness of those dark eyes and the feel of warm
flesh on hers. Her arm tingled from his touch.

The voice of logic screamed at Diana, telling her she was

being silly. Responding to its urging Diana lifted her eyes just as the man leaned closer. She willed herself to back away, but found that she could not move, but only stare, wide-eyed, as his face drew ever nearer to hers.

_____ *Chapter Three*

THE SLENDER WRIST beneath Ben Potter's fingers felt smooth and cool. He stared down into wide, midnight blue eyes set in a face as white as the finest marble, recognizing immediately the young woman he had encountered earlier in Sutro's garden. He had been beguiled then by her almost worshipful interest in the statue of Diana. But that was when she had been approaching someone else's property. Now she was trespassing in his domain.

His anger warred with curiosity as he studied the unusual creature before him. Her wide-brimmed straw hat had shifted to one side, loosening her thick hair so that it drooped slightly around her face and softened the angles of her sculpted features. Her lips, pale, almost bloodless, were parted in an expression of surprise, and her eyes gazed up at him with a mixture of fear and some other emotion he couldn't identify.

Then her expression began to alter slightly, becoming less frightened, more defensive, reminding him of a young girl who, finding herself with her hand in the cookie jar, was prepared to defend her actions, or to make up some lie to explain them away.

Sarah had worn an expression like that on more than one occasion, most notably the time he had found her in the arms of another man. Sarah had also been as fragile and defenseless-looking as a kitten, like this woman was, a kitten with deep claws capable of tearing the heart from a man's chest.

Ben's fingers tightened around the young woman's cold flesh and he narrowed his eyes as he spoke. "I asked you a question."

The harsh voice made Diana blink. The tingling sensation still danced up her arm, but his words reawakened her anger, returning strength to her limbs. With a quick jerk Diana pulled her hand from his, then gave voice to her anger. "Yes, I heard you. To answer your question, I was only examining the fine example of *faux* marble you have here. Now, why don't we talk about the kind of damage *you* almost caused, shouting at me and frightening me so that I lost my balance."

The man's light brown brows lifted slightly from their deep frown. "If you hadn't been where you had no business being, you wouldn't have jumped like a guilty child."

Diana knew that there was a certain amount of truth to his words, but she stood her ground and replied in an icy tone, "It just so happens that I was sent here to find someone. There was no one outside to help me, and I saw no signs refusing entry, so I came up here, hoping I could locate Professor Potter."

He held her gaze for a second before he asked quietly, "Benjamin Potter?"

"Yes."

His broad shoulders lifted in a shrug. "Well, you've found him. Now who are you and what do you want?"

Diana stared wordlessly at the man before her, trying to reconcile this rough-hewn, mannerless creature with the image she had conjured up of someone who would be employed by the staid British Museum.

Impatience colored his next words. "Look, Miss—

whoever you are. State your business. I don't have time to waste standing around."

Diana could only notice his hair, the color of autumn leaves, falling forward onto his forehead in a boyish manner that robbed some of the threat from his fierce scowl. She was appalled to find that this disparity awoke an almost irresistible urge to laugh. She fought the grin tugging at the corners of her mouth as she replied, "I—I'm sorry. I'm afraid you've taken me by surprise again. You aren't at all what I expected."

She was aware that some of the laughter bubbling in her throat had echoed in her words, and she saw some of the tension in Professor Potter's face ease as he lifted his head slightly. "What do you mean, not what you expected?"

"Well, knowing Benjamin Potter to be a scholar employed by the British Museum, I suppose I pictured someone older, with white hair. A bit stooped, perhaps."

Potter stared at her a moment longer; then his scowl eased. "And with an English accent, I suppose."

Diana watched his firm lips twitch into a slight smile. Her own mouth curved widely as she nodded. "Exactly. With just the barest hint of an intellectual lisp."

Once more the man stared into Diana's eyes a moment before shaking his head. A deep chuckle rumbled from his throat. "Well," he said, "I'm sorry to have destroyed all your illusions."

Diana found herself wordless again as she observed how very attractive the once forbidding features appeared now that he wasn't scowling. His lips were well formed, the lower one slightly fuller than the upper, and his even teeth gleamed white against his tanned complexion.

It was also obvious from his slowly lowering brows that he was again becoming impatient with her lack of response, so Diana forced herself to speak. "And *I'm* sorry for having trespassed, Professor Potter, but Emma said I should come down here immediately.''

The man continued to hold her gaze a second longer before speaking. ''Well, there was no harm done, to either of us or to the exhibit.'' He shrugged. ''However, as I mentioned, I have quite a lot of work to do here, so perhaps we could talk at some other time. I'll help you gather up your things''—he bent to retrieve her tassled purse as he spoke—''and then we can make an appointment to speak sometime when I'm not quite so busy.''

Diana turned from him, searching for the portfolio that had flown from her arms when he startled her. As she moved, she felt her hat shift sharply on her head. She lifted her hands quickly and stifled a moan of dismay as she discovered that the beige straw brim lay at a most rakish angle, and realized just how disheveled she must appear.

This had most assuredly destroyed the picture of professional competence she had hoped to portray. And there was precious little she could do about it, short of removing her hat and completely refashioning her hair, an action that would be most improper.

So, she contented herself with carefully drawing out the long pin that anchored her hat to her hair and placing the broad circle in the correct position atop her head, becoming aware, as she slid the pin back into place, that the professor had straightened and was watching her every move.

Actually, Ben wasn't watching Diana's hands at all. As he stood with her purse in his hands, he had allowed his gaze to wander up her graceful form past unfashionably slim but attractively curving hips. He had stopped at the center of her open jacket, where the action of Diana's raised arms had drawn the ivory blouse taut across her breasts, outlining their firm contours.

A slow heat spread out from the center of his stomach, a sensation that left him unaware of anything else until he felt the strap of Diana's purse begin to slip from his fingers.

Diana pulled gently on her purse as she puzzled over the strange expression in the professor's eyes and told herself that as far as interviews went, this one was not proceeding well at all. She frowned and glanced at her purse, making a show of dusting it off as she tried to collect her thoughts.

She had always prided herself on refusing to allow men to intimidate her, especially those in positions of authority. But somehow just being near Professor Potter seemed to cause her to act in a fluttery manner that was very uncharacteristic. Of course, between their earlier meeting, where she must have appeared quite strange staring up at that statue, and falling on top of him moments ago, she shouldn't be surprised that this encounter had started out so awkwardly.

Still, all was not lost. She had long ago learned how to present her artistic abilities in a businesslike manner. But when she looked at him, Diana found that all the well-chosen words she had been prepared to utter were obliterated from her mind. A warm flush heated her cheeks as she stared into those nearly black depths, and she found her mind so paralyzed by the confusing emotions coursing through her that she quickly looked away.

Seeing her leather folder near the altar, she decided that it was best to retreat and regroup before approaching this man about employment. Hurrying to retrieve it, Diana said, "Well, Professor Potter, this is obviously a bad time for you. I don't want to keep you from your work. When would be the best time to contact you again to show you my sketches?"

Diana grabbed the folder as she finished the question, then turned back to find the professor mounting the steps to tower over her. Before she could tuck the portfolio into the crook of her arm, a lean brown hand closed over one corner.

"Sketches?" Ben's voice rang with sharp interest. "You're an artist?"

"Yes, Professor Potter, I am." Diana looked up at him as the case was gently drawn from her fingers. She watched as he opened the cover and concentrated on the first sketch.

A bittersweet taste hovered on Diana's tongue as she watched the rich brown leather, scarred by years of use, held in this man's large hands. Ever since her twelfth birthday, when Grandfather had presented this to her, the item had represented his desire that she use the talents she had inherited from her mother. It was his wish that she engage in the gentle art of painting and follow the path he deemed seemly for a young lady.

But that was not the path Diana wanted to follow. Her father's stories of searching for the seeds of human culture had captured her imagination completely, and so the tug-of-war had begun. On one side stood her grandfather, a dominating personality who sought to influence her with a suffocating form of love, and on the other, her father's letters, which had continued to fuel her interest in archaeology and mythology. By the time those letters suddenly stopped coming, she had set her course and continued to fight the battle of wills with her grandfather, alone.

The soft, almost musical sound of thick paper bending drew Diana from her thoughts. She noticed that Professor Potter had turned to the next drawing, one she knew was among the best examples of her work. Using only her pencil, she had manipulated shades of light and dark to reproduce a statue of Faunus, the Roman version of the Greek god Pan. In depicting the half-man, half-goat she felt she had captured the proportions of the statue perfectly, down to the hint of mischief lighting the god's features.

Diana watched the professor's face closely, and felt a wave of pleasure course through her when she saw sincere admiration as he raised his head. "You're very good. Did you say that Emma sent you down to see me?''

"Yes. She mentioned you needed an artist, because the one you hired had left. I assume he was the one who painted the rocks outside and the marble in here.''

Ben nodded. "Do you think you could copy his work?''

Diana looked at the altar again and began to study the delicate brushwork until the professor's impatient words stopped her. "Not that. We don't need any more marble reproduced, thank heavens. What I need is something along the line of the technique used on the hill outside. You seem to do well with shading, but I've only seen what you can do with a pencil. How are you with a brush? Do you think you're capable of creating the appearance of rock similar to what Brody did?''

Diana shrugged. "Most likely. Once I get a chance to study his method more closely, I'm certain I could approximate it.''

"Good. Come with me, and I'll show you what we need done.''

His strong hand closed around Diana's wrist as he led her toward the door to the left of the altar. After a few turns they stepped into a wide corridor lined with arched doorways. Ben gestured toward one as he led her forward.

"When the statues arrive from the museum, most of them will be displayed back in the temple room, as we call it. These small areas will be set up to represent the various rooms in a Pompeiian home, with appropriate artifacts housed in glass cabinets against the walls—cooking utensils in the space arranged to look like a kitchen, for example.''

Ben stopped and turned to Diana as they reached a double door at the far end of the corridor. "In two of the rooms we'll need someone to reproduce a couple of the murals that were discovered when Pompeii was excavated. That shouldn't take too long. The major work I'm concerned about involves the shrine that will house the statue of Diana on the lower level, and the display in here.''

He swung open one of the doors as he spoke, then led Diana into a wide room that was as large as the temple chamber. A tall ladder led to a platform above her head. Below the scaffolding, in the center of the room, a concrete wall rose, curving out from the rear of the room. As Diana approached this, she noted that within the oval, bowl-like depression lay a miniature city.

Diana immediately recognized the town. ''Pompeii,'' she breathed. She stared at the tiny houses formed of pasteboard, amazed at the details that included clay urns sitting in square courtyards.

''It's wonderful, Professor Potter.'' Diana looked up as she spoke, and saw the man's tan grow a shade deeper as he frowned.

''Thank you,'' he replied. ''It's little more than pasteboard and lumber scraps. I do this sort of thing all the time at the museum in London. However, I am no artist. All the houses need to be painted to look as if they're made of rock, and the streets to look as if they are paved.'' He sighed and shook his head. ''And if that isn't enough, Mr. Sutro insists that this model demonstrate the manner in which the town was destroyed when Vesuvius erupted.''

Diana drew her gaze to the wall in back of the town where behind the wooden scaffolding towered an enormous conical shape. Its smooth surface was covered with smeared newsprint, except for the top. Here Diana noted that the now departed Brody had begun to work his magic, using various shades of black and gray to give the appearance of rough lava to the curved surface.

''Papier-mâché, Professor Potter?'' Diana asked as she turned to the man.

He nodded. ''Several layers of it over a chicken-wire frame.''

''I see. You mentioned some sort of demonstration?''

"Oh yes. The plan is for our volcano to erupt and rain destruction upon our little village several times a day to the amazement of all who watch."

Diana shook her head as she looked at the hill of paste and newsprint. "Impossible."

Potter chuckled and shrugged his shoulders. "That's what I said, until I learned more about Adolph Sutro. It seems that although the man has had little formal education, he is nevertheless an engineering genius. Years ago he saved the mining industry in Virginia City, Nevada, by designing a tunnel to drain away the water that was preventing the miners from delving deeper in their quest for silver. More recently, he conceived and built these Baths, and the same mechanism that allows him to fill the pools with fresh water daily from the sea will enable us to cover our little city and drain it as often as we wish."

"That sounds marvelous, Professor. However, Pompeii wasn't covered with lava, as a flow of water would suggest; rather, it was buried in volcanic pumice and ash."

Potter nodded. "Your education in the matter seems quite extensive. My compliments go to the instructors at whatever finishing school you attended." He gave her a tight smile. "And you're right, of course. It was the ash that destroyed the town and kept it hidden for so many years. We'll have a sign at the display to explain this. Also, we plan to color the water a dull gray and release it slowly, to make it appear that the town is being slowly engulfed by ash and pumice. Does that sound satisfactory to you?"

The man's assumption that she only possessed a finishing school education had stiffened Diana's spine. It always infuriated her when men figured that women had only been taught watercolors and French, along with a smattering of history perhaps. She knew, however, how pompous it would sound to correct him on this, so she simply nodded in reply to his question.

"Good." He paused a moment, then spoke quickly. "Well, this is the situation. We have a special paint for the houses and streets which is supposed to be impervious to water. What we need is someone with the talent to make them appear as if they are built of solid rock and wood. We also need the same type of magic worked on Vesuvius, although in that case we need the lower section to look as if it is planted with trees and grapevines. Do you think you can do the job?"

Diana met the questioning gaze in his eyes, waited several seconds until she had the satisfaction of seeing them narrow slightly with a hint of worry, then nodded.

"Do you think you can get this all done in ten days? Wait." He held his hand up. "Before you answer that, let me show you what has to be done downstairs."

As he took her elbow and led her toward the door, her lips curled into a wry smile. She couldn't remember ever being around so many impulsive people—first Emma with her mercurial mind jumping from one subject to another, now Professor Potter, commanding and arrogant and maddeningly attractive in spite of it.

Diana corrected this last errant thought; Benjamin Potter was handsome. The word *attractive* suggested that she found herself drawn to the man in some way, and that was certainly not the case, especially in light of his slighting remark about her "finishing school education."

When Diana realized that she was expected to follow him down a spiraling stairway, she brushed these thoughts from her mind as she concentrated on the task at hand, lifting her skirt free of her boots as she descended the ornate wrought-iron steps.

As Diana neared the bottom of the steps she found herself once more thinking of Lewis Carroll's literary heroine. But where Alice had gone down a rabbit hole into darkness,

Diana felt as if she were descending into a strange, outdoor world, one that had not yet been completed by the power that had conceived it.

Above her the ceiling arched, part of it painted the dark blue of a midnight sky. Lights shimmered out of small holes cut in the surface, and a larger, circular one glowed with the silver light of the moon in her dream. However, the walls curving around her had been painted in the same manner as the rocky exterior of the hill, and around its circumference several torches blazed, electric lights encased in flame-shaped bulbs. Two of these torches flanked an arched opening, and as Diana reached the bottom step, she saw that this led onto the promenade deck.

"This is another of Mr. Sutro's ideas." Ben's voice echoed in the cavernous room. "He has his own power plant on the premises, so he ordered electric lights to be placed behind the shapes of the stars and the moon." Diana shifted her gaze to meet his as he went on. "He wants our visitors to imagine how it felt to approach the shrine of the goddess of the moon in ancient times. You see, a recently discovered statue of Diana will be displayed in that grotto over there."

A strange prickling sensation crawled over Diana's skin as she turned and looked at the small, dark cave gaping back at her.

Professor Potter spoke again, but it seemed to echo from some distance as he continued to describe the proposed display. "Potted cypress trees will be arranged around the opening to the shrine, with small statues of animals peeking out between their branches. We need someone to bring the cement forms to life. Diana's altar and the rocks hiding the base of the trees will be real stones, but the rear of the cave will need to look as if it too is rock. The same goes for the archway leading to it."

"Well, what do you think?" Ben asked. But before she

could answer he continued. "I won't try to deceive you. I think it will be nearly impossible for anyone to finish all this work before the opening next Friday, but the job is yours if you want it."

The logical portion of Diana's mind took control, forcing her thoughts to the miniature city above. Not only would it require many hours to paint it in the manner the professor desired, but it would be backbreaking labor as well. She knew she could make quick work of the animals he'd mentioned, but creating the effect of rock on the volcano and the cave would most likely be very slow going.

However, if she could manage this, it would certainly impress Justin Harrington. Success here might be just what she needed to secure herself a position on his staff for the dig he was supposed to be planning.

She glanced back at the cavelike opening where the statue of Diana was to be exhibited, half-expecting it to shimmer to life as before. Instead, it just gaped blankly, an arch formed of wood and plaster that would require much reaching and stretching to paint. And, she reminded herself, she would have to duplicate Mr. Brody's technique. Failure to do so could put an end to all her plans.

Diana sighed as she met Professor Potter's expectant gaze. Slowly she shook her head. "Well, to be honest, Professor, I can't remember when I have received a more *tempting* offer." Diana paused, watching his brows lower to a disappointed frown, then let her lips curve into a smile. "So I guess I'll be forced to take the job. When would you like me to start?"

His full lips widened into a smile that made his teeth gleam brightly in the artificial moonlight. "Please, call me Ben. All the other workers do. As to when you begin to work, well, frankly I'd like to have you start right now. However, I guess we'll have to wait till tomorrow so you can make arrangements with Emma to stay at Sutro Heights.

I don't want you wasting time coming in each day from the city.''

Diana opened her mouth to explain that she was already staying in Sutro's home, but before she could speak, a raspy voice called out from the stairs above. "Ben? Are you down there?''

Ben shouted, "Yes, Will.''

"Well, don't move, then. We're coming down." Heavy shoes echoed on the iron stairs, all but swallowing the man's next words. "Where have you been anyway? Ian and I have been searching high and low for you. I've been up to the house, and learned the most interesting bit of news. You won't believe what Emma has done.''

Diana watched the newcomers descend the final curve of stairs. The man speaking was tall and lean, dressed in a brown tweed suit. The lower section of his narrow face was hidden by a pewter gray beard, and a brown derby sat atop his head. Another man stood behind him, a portly figure in a black and gray suit, sporting a wide, red mustache, but Diana barely noticed him. She kept her eyes on the first gentleman as he stepped slowly onto the floor of the exhibit, aware that he was staring at her through silver-framed glasses.

The man opened his mouth, but before he could utter a word, Ben spoke. "Let me guess, Will. Emma told you that she'd found an artist for us. Did she forget to tell you that she sent the lady in question down to talk to me?''

The man nodded then turned to Ben. "Well, you know how Emma jumps from one thing to another. She was in the midst of explaining the situation, apologizing for the fact that she had failed to mention that the young woman was expected, when her husband rang up on the telephone.'' He paused. "Am I to understand that you've already hired her?''

"I have," Ben replied. "And once you see her work,

you'll agree with my decision, I'm sure. Her examples are done in pencil only, but they demonstrate that she can handle the nuances of light well. I'm certain she can reproduce Brody's style."

"I see." The man nodded and the warm brown eyes behind the glasses turned to Diana. "Well, since Ben has forgotten his manners, please allow me to introduce myself. I'm Will Babcock, and I'm in charge of seeing to security precautions for the Pompeii exhibit. This fellow"—he pointed over his shoulder to the shorter, red-haired gentleman—"is Ian McRogers, my assistant. We're an informal lot, so just address us by our first names, Miss McKenzie."

Diana was aware that Ben had suddenly straightened and taken one step back as she nodded. "I'll do so if you will promise to call me Diana."

Will took her outstretched hand in a warm grasp. "Well, Diana, welcome to the madhouse. I suppose that Ben has rushed you willy-nilly through our exhibit here."

The warmth in Will's voice made Diana smile. She glanced at Ben to include him in the moment, only to find him staring at her with a strange, intense expression.

"Well, I must apologize for Ben. I'm afraid that was hardly a fitting greeting for the daughter of a man as distinguished as Daniel McKenzie, but he had no way of knowing who you were. As you must imagine, we have anxiously been awaiting your father's arrival. Do I dare hope that your presence means that he will be here soon?"

"No," she answered quickly. "In fact, my father—"

"You are Daniel McKenzie's daughter?" Ben's voice, sharp and loud, interrupted Diana's reply. His dark eyes held hers with an unspoken accusation. Feeling suddenly defensive without really knowing why, Diana rushed to reply, "Yes, I am, but we—"

"Why didn't you tell me this when we first met?"

"Because there wasn't—" Diana broke off from the reasonable explanation she had started. Resentment at Ben's sudden and unreasonable display of anger sharpened her tone as she began again. "Because you didn't give me a chance. I've hardly been able to complete one full sentence since the moment you startled me upstairs."

"Don't be ridiculous," he snapped. "You've uttered entire paragraphs."

Diana gave her head an impatient shake. "I've certainly not managed to convey anything of a personal nature. You wanted to know if I could complete your volcano and your city for you, and I can. Since you were more than happy to hire me without so much as asking my name, I fail to understand why you are so upset now."

"Your father—"

"My father, what?" Diana broke in quickly as her heart took a painful twist. She had no wish to discuss her father. "My father is an important man in this field? He wouldn't want his daughter dirtying her hands with paint and papier-mâché? Well, don't concern yourself about him. He doesn't care what I do. He—"

Again Diana stopped speaking, aware that she had already said more than she wanted. "I won't beg for the job, Professor." She swallowed as she straightened her shoulders. "If for some reason you feel that it would be uncomfortable to have me working for you, then perhaps it would be best if you found another artist."

Diana turned toward the narrow, arched exit. She had taken only two steps when warm fingers closed over her wrist. She turned, prepared to see Ben's scowling face, to find Will Babcock smiling down at her.

"I'm sorry," he said in a quiet undertone. "Please excuse Ben. He's very methodical when it comes to his work and doesn't handle unexpected developments well." Will paused as he straightened away from her and went on in a louder voice. "Emma mentioned that dinner was to be served soon, so I suggest we all go up and enjoy the meal. We can discuss your employment after we've enjoyed the wonderful food Sutro's chef provides for us.''

Diana gazed into the warm, almond-colored eyes behind the lenses and nodded. Out of the corner of her eye she saw Ben fold his arms across his chest as the older man took her elbow. She allowed Will to lead her toward the exit as he continued speaking. "You go back to the house and change for dinner, my dear. Ben, Ian, and I have a few things to finish here, but please tell Emma that we'll be up directly.''

From his place near the stairs Ben listened to his friend's words. Will's soothing tone annoyed Ben. His scowl grew deeper as he watched Diana turn without a backward glance and walk through the exit. Despite his anger and his deep distrust of the young woman, he found himself mesmerized by the way her beige skirt curved over her slim hips before it fell, draping in a soft bell shape that swayed across the floor in time to her brisk steps.

The cavern was soundless as he watched her disappear into the crowded exhibit area beyond. Ben said softly, "So that's what the daughter of a murderer looks like.''

_____ *Chapter Four*

"YOU WERE quite abrupt with her, Ben," Will began. "I'm not sure that's the best way to handle this situation."

Ben crossed his arms over his chest. "I'm in complete agreement with that, but I'm afraid that I was taken by surprise. I thought you said that McKenzie hadn't had any contact with his daughter in years."

"That's the information I was given—by a very reputable source, I assure you." Will shrugged. "I was so surprised when Emma told me the girl was here that a puff of wind could have knocked me over."

"Well, what exactly did Emma have to say about Miss McKenzie?"

"Only that she arrived just this morning. Apparently the girl's father wrote to Sutro several weeks ago asking if his daughter could join him on his visit here. But you know how Emma and her father are. The old man seems to be growing more forgetful by the day, and Emma has far too much on her mind, between her practice and overseeing things out here. And, since they have no way of knowing what we suspect about McKenzie, I really can't fault them for not mentioning it to us."

Will paused, then went on slowly. "I'm not all that certain that we have anything to worry about, anyway. There's

55

a good chance that the young woman knows absolutely nothing about her father's activities.''

Ben shook his head and released a mirthless laugh. "*No one* knows much about her father's activities.''

In the silence that followed, Ian McRogers stepped between the two men. "Well, I fail to see what all the to-do is about.'' His clipped British accent echoed off the walls as he turned from Will to Ben. "As I continue to remind you chaps, we aren't even certain that Daniel McKenzie is the man we're after.''

Ben and Will spoke at the same time. "*I'm* certain.''

Ian shook his head as he lifted his double chin. His dark green eyes narrowed. "Well, I am far from convinced. The Yard has looked into this matter most deeply and we feel that both Professor Harrington and Jean-Paul LaPierre demand equal scrutiny. Not only were they both in London when the attempt on the museum's statue was made, but our contacts in Paris and Milan revealed that all three men were in the vicinity at the time of those thefts.''

Ian paused for a moment, then continued. "I am aware that you've been tracking McKenzie for years and that you have valid reasons for suspecting him. I also appreciate the fact that you have listened to my advice in so far as ensuring that both Harrington and LaPierre were invited here. That is quite fair of you, considering the fact that Scotland Yard has no authority here in the States. I hope that since you've gone that far you'll at least consider the possibility that one of them might be your culprit. To fail to do so might prove fatal.''

Ben's stomach twisted into a painful knot. The man they were looking for was Daniel McKenzie. He was sure of it, no matter what Ian thought. He understood the man's doubts, of course. As an inspector with Scotland Yard, Ian had delved deeply into the string of robberies that had started two years ago with a simple theft of minor artifacts pertaining to the goddess Diana from a museum in Rome and had escalated with each offense.

But Ian had no personal knowledge of the men he suspected; Ben knew each of them, to one degree or another. "Ian, I've told you before that Jean-Paul LaPierre is nothing more than a collector with more money than brains. He would be incapable of planning such successful heists."

The inspector drew himself up to his full height. "May I remind you that the last attempt was *not* successful. The British Museum still has its prized statue."

Ben gave him a curt nod. "Yes, but it lost a valuable employee, if you remember. Or have you forgotten the knife that laid open old Albert's chest?"

Ian's red mustache twitched as he shook his head. "Of course not. That is one of the reasons I insisted on coming along on this plan of yours." He took a deep breath and blinked. "I've met LaPierre, and I agree with you that he's a silly man who seems incapable of such an act. However, he could have hired a professional to perform the robberies and the murders for him. And what about Justin Harrington? By your own admission the man is without scruples."

Ben's lips twisted in a bitter grimace. "He'd sell his own mother to a camel driver, but he's not a murderer."

"So you believe. I suppose you have proof that Daniel McKenzie is?"

Ben's mind raced back ten years. The room darkened for a moment and he could almost feel the walls closing in on him and hear Rob's tortured cries. Yes, Daniel McKenzie was capable of murder. In Rob's case it had been indirect, the result of greed and negligence. But a more concrete example of the man's disregard for human life existed.

"Have you forgotten Peter Vicini?" Ben asked.

"Peter Vicini died of exposure," Ian replied. "There was never any proof that McKenzie had anything to do with the man's death."

"Nothing to do with his death?" This time it was Will who spoke. His eyes narrowed as he stepped forward. "McKenzie chased Vicini into the hills above Pompeii then abandoned him to his death, all over some statue of Diana Vicini had uncovered and tried to secret away to keep as his own.

"It was McKenzie's job to reclaim that statue, as head of that particular dig," Ian replied. "I know you seem to believe that this fatal fascination McKenzie is purported to have with the goddess dates back to that incident, but I fail to see the connection."

"You'd see it if you had known Daniel McKenzie as I did." Will spoke these words in a quiet tone. "The man was an open book before that incident. Now he's a near recluse, living on that ship of his and devoting his life to the study of an obscure Roman deity."

Ian's features began to glow a dark red. "I have already conceded that you have good reasons for your suspicions. But I must reiterate: you are being quite foolish if you insist on focusing on McKenzie and ignoring the other two."

He cleared his throat as he finished speaking, then walked rapidly out the arched doorway. Ben watched the stiff figure a moment then turned to Will.

"He has a point, you know."

"Yes, he does," Will replied.

Their eyes met and again both men spoke at the same time. "It's McKenzie."

Ben's smile mirrored the one framed by Will's gray beard. A moment later he frowned. "So, what do you make of Miss McKenzie's sudden appearance here?"

"I don't know. It does seem to be a strange coincidence, but as you know, I've kept tabs on her over the years. I thought perhaps her father would come out in the open to visit her, but unless the people I have had watching her have been incredibly lax in their reporting, this meeting here will be the first time they've been together in seventeen years.''

Ben shook his head. ''I'm beginning to think the man is capable of walking down Main Street in the middle of the day without being seen. You said he and his daughter used to correspond. Is it possible that they've continued to do so and that he's sent her here to get the lay of the land before he arrives? Then he could strike without warning.''

Will pursed his lips. ''I don't know. The last three thefts have taken place on a night with a full moon, so I'm not looking for anything to happen before that time. We're almost two weeks away from that, but I would say that Miss McKenzie certainly bears watching.''

''Watching?'' Ben's eyebrows shot up as he turned sharply to his friend. ''Forget it. She needs to be barred from entering the Baths, or at least from coming into the display area again.''

Will shook his head slowly. ''We can't do that. If his daughter *is* involved with him, a move like that would definitely tip McKenzie off to the trap we've laid. Besides, the artifacts won't arrive till the end of next week, and in order to get ready for them you need the young woman's talents. You'll just have to watch her closely.''

Ben's jaw tightened as he shrugged. ''I suppose you're right.''

As Ben looked at Will the older man smiled broadly. Ben squinted suspiciously at his friend. ''Just what do you find so amusing?''

''Oh, nothing really. I was just thinking that if I were a younger man, watching Diana McKenzie closely wouldn't be such a dreadful hardship. And if I observed you correctly as you gazed after her when she left, I would say that the job won't really be all that hard on you, either.''

* * *

"I believe that I'd rather dig that tunnel under Virginia City all over again, with nothing but a tablespoon, than deal with those imbeciles down at city hall for one more day."

Diana watched Adolph Sutro, who was sitting at the head of the table, lower his coffee cup to his saucer. Small black eyes glinted out of a kindly face framed in old-fashioned muttonchop whiskers that nearly met at his chin. His bushy hair gleamed snowy white in the light from the crystal chandelier.

"Papa, you're exaggerating again," Emma admonished.

She had changed from her shirtwaist and skirt to a gown of lavender silk with widely puffed sleeves that ended at her elbow and a curving neckline that scooped modestly over the upper regions of her generous bosom. Her father wore a dark gray suit over a high-necked white shirt. Emma reached over to pat his arm as he turned to her.

"I am not exaggerating." He shook his head, then went on in a voice tinged with a slight German accent. "This mayor business is completely insane. I can make no progress with people pulling me in so many different directions. I tell you, my girl, I sometimes wonder how anything at all gets accomplished in this city."

Emma's smile widened. "The wheels of democracy move slowly, Papa. You can't run San Francisco the way you order people about out here."

Sutro shook his head. "If I ran my holdings the way San Francisco is organized, this property would still be nothing more than a windblown hill of sand. There would be no trees or flowers, not to mention the Baths and the—"

"All true, Papa," Emma broke in. "But you are the mayor of the city, not the emperor. You must learn patience."

"I should do that now, at my age?" He winked at his daughter, then took a bite of sponge cake.

Diana toyed with her own untouched desert. Despite the

tempting dishes placed in front of her during the meal, she'd been able to eat very little. A deep sense of guilt had formed a knot in her stomach that seemed to grow larger as the meal went on.

This phenomenon had started when she came down from her room wearing an ice blue dress similar in style to Emma's, one of the new gowns she had purchased before leaving Philadelphia. Both Emma and her father were perfect hosts, and as the meal progressed Diana found herself thinking about the uncomfortable scene at the Baths that afternoon and regretting the predicament she had put the Sutros in.

She was still angry at Ben Potter, of course. She was aware of him, sitting across the table from her, conversing with Emma as he ate his dessert. He had changed into a black dinner jacket and dazzling white shirt. With his neatly combed hair gleaming gold and bronze in the light from the chandelier, she had to admit that he looked much more like a university professor than he had this afternoon—and possibly even more attractive.

The muscles in Diana's stomach contracted again. She bit her lip to ward off the strange warmth she felt creeping through her, a warmth similar to the one that had assailed her when Ben had touched her this afternoon. Benjamin Potter was an arrogant, overbearing male, she reminded herself. His anger upon discovering her identity had proved that. His reaction had been completely unwarranted, considering that not once had he asked her name.

Diana sighed as she picked up her fork and began flaking off the edge of her cake. Admitting her relationship to the famous mystery man her father had become had always been difficult for her, especially when she had to face university students and professors who seemed to know more about her father's latest archaeological find than she did. Over time she had learned that not acknowledging any connection to the famous man was the simplest way to avoid seeing the veiled pity in their eyes.

She did not view this as a deceitful act—just a method of protecting herself from unnecessary pain. Given the chance this afternoon, she might have repeated this practice, but she would not have considered that a lie. However, she could not escape the fact that she *had* lied to the Sutros when she forged that letter asking them to accept her as a guest. And the more she thought about that, the stronger her feelings of guilt had grown, robbing the food of taste to the point that even the tempting dessert, topped with wild strawberries and whipped cream, made her stomach lurch and roll.

"You do not like sponge cake, Miss McKenzie?"

Mr. Sutro broke into Diana's musings. She forced a smile to her lips as she replied, "Yes, I do, normally. But I'm not very hungry tonight."

"She's probably tired," Will Babcock commented. "I understand her first visit to our little exhibit was quite an adventure. It seems Ben discovered her in the temple room, examining the *faux* marble Brody had created on the main altar. Unaware that Emma had sent her, he shouted at Miss McKenzie and startled her so badly that she fell down the stairs."

Diana felt a blush creep up her neck. Quickly she shook her head. "No, I didn't actually fall. Professor Potter caught me before I touched the ground."

It hadn't occurred to her until this moment that he hadn't simply caught her, but had used his body to break her fall. Once more her limbs grew limp, just as they had that afternoon, and a languid warmth seeped into them as she recalled lying atop the professor's solid chest, breathing in his woodsy scent.

"That's good." Once again Sutro's voice boomed down the table, drawing Diana back to the present. "Benjamin, my boy, you must be more careful how you approach artists such as Miss McKenzie,'' the man continued. "Emma tells me that the young woman can help us complete our little project on time. That is, of course, if she is in one piece to do so.''

Diana watched Ben glance toward the older man and nod. "You're right, of course.'' His smile tightened slightly as he returned his attention to Diana. "I'm afraid that I'm not an easy man to work for, Miss McKenzie. I've been told that I'm impatient, overbearing, and demanding.''

"But that is how one gets things done." Again Sutro spoke forcefully. "One must be bold if one is to fulfill one's dreams.''

Diana nodded in response to Sutro's comment. She had sensed a strong warning hidden beneath Ben's straightforward-sounding words. She longed to rise to the challenge his dark eyes delivered across the table, but before she picked up that gauntlet, she had an important matter to clear up.

The knot in Diana's stomach tightened as she turned to her host and spoke quickly, before she could lose her nerve. "I agree, sir; boldness is imperative if one wants to make anything of oneself. And knowing that you feel this way gives me hope that you will understand and forgive what I have to tell you.''

Diana paused, feeling many eyes upon her, and had to force herself to speak again. "I am sorry to say that the letter you received several weeks ago signed by Daniel McKenzie was a forgery. My father didn't write it . . . I did.''

Sutro's white brows dropped to a frown, but it was Emma who asked softly, "Why, Diana?''

Diana faced the woman. "Because I haven't heard from my father in ten years. When I learned he was to be a guest here, I decided that coming to Sutro Heights was the only opportunity I would have of reestablishing contact."

Emma leaned forward. "Ten years, Diana? What happened? Did you argue?"

Diana almost laughed at the woman's shocked inquiry, for she had no answer to it, only ten years of questions of her own, along with a deep ache in her heart that she had learned to hide beneath the veneer of the logical scientist she'd trained herself to become.

Tightening her hands in her lap and straightening in her chair to help herself assume this role, Diana said, "No, we didn't argue. In fact, until my twelfth birthday, I received correspondence from my father regularly."

Diana's chest tightened as the disappointment and pain she had felt that day crowded into her memory. "You see, my mother died when I was five. For the first three years of my life, she and I accompanied my father to various parts of the world as he moved from dig to dig. When Mama became ill with consumption, my father gave up archaeology to stay with us at my grandfather's home in Philadelphia." Diana paused, then continued her explanation. "Papa and Grandfather never got along well, I'm afraid, but when Mama died, Papa said it would be best for me to stay with Grandfather while he resumed his career."

"Couldn't he have taken you with him?" Sutro asked as Diana paused. "I took my children all around the world with me when they were young."

She shrugged in reply. "That would have been perfect as far as I was concerned, but Grandfather convinced Papa that it wouldn't be a good life for a *young lady*."

Diana was aware that a hint of bitterness had colored her last words. She didn't want emotion creeping into this tale; she wanted to tell it in as objective a manner as possible. She clasped her hands tightly and continued. "So, for the next seven years, while Grandfather saw to it that I received what he considered a proper upbringing, my father wrote often, sharing his adventures with me in his letters. He repeatedly made plans to return to Philadelphia for a visit, but each time something important, such as rumors of a fantastic find somewhere or the chance to field a new dig, interfered.''

Diana sighed to relieve the pressure that had continued to build in her chest, then spoke again. ''This happened again on the occasion of my twelfth birthday. He had written to me three weeks earlier, telling me he was to set sail in several days from Paris in order to reach Philadelphia in time for the party Grandfather had planned for me. Apparently, shortly after he wrote this, he was awarded a dig in Pompeii that was to begin immediately, so a letter of apology and a lovely miniature statue of Diana, just like the one in your garden, Mayor Sutro, arrived instead of Papa. That was the last contact I had with him.''

Despite her efforts to maintain emotional control, Diana's throat closed over her last words. She reached for her crystal goblet and took a sip of wine. The silence was broken only by a high-pitched ringing that echoed down the hall until Emma spoke. ''And you have no idea why this happened?'' she asked.

Diana started to shake her head, then stopped herself. ''Yes and no. I thought for years that Papa had just become so involved in his work that he forgot about me. Last year, however, I learned that during that dig ten years ago he became lost in the hills above Pompeii, and stumbled into Naples weeks later, very near death. To be honest, I've wondered if perhaps he suffered some kind of amnesia that wiped my existence out of his memory. That sounds quite melodramatic, I know, but that's why I've come here. To find the answers to this mystery, and to put it behind me.''

Diana's shoulders tensed as she saw an expression of pity fill Emma's dark eyes. Quickly she turned to the woman's father. ''I want to apologize for foisting myself on you,

Mayor Sutro. I realized the moment I arrived that what I had done was wrong. I started to tell Emma earlier, but—''

''—but I have a tendency to control the conversation,'' Emma finished. ''And now that you've met my father, you must see that I have developed this habit of interrupting out of self-defense. If I don't speak quickly when I see an opening, I don't get to say anything.''

Once more Diana's throat tightened as she observed the affectionate glances that passed between father and daughter, and she had to cough lightly before she could speak. ''Well, I want to assure you that everything else I told you was the truth. I *do* have a degree in archaeology, and it was *my* hand that drew those sketches.'' She paused to brave a quick look at Will, then Ben. ''I would very much like to work with you both, but if you would prefer that I leave, I will understand.''

''Don't be ridiculous, girl.'' Sutro's booming voice drew Diana's attention to his end of the table. He was going to continue when a uniformed maid stepped into the room and stood at his elbow.

When he turned his scowl to the young woman, she dropped a quick curtsy that set her white cap wobbling as she spoke. ''Telephone, sir. The man said to tell you that it is regarding city business.''

Sutro sighed, then nodded and lifted his hand with a slight wave. ''Tell whoever it is I will be a moment.'' His eyes shifted back immediately to Diana. ''Miss McKenzie, I want you to know that I disapprove of lies in any form. However, I understand the emotions that directed you to write that letter. Furthermore, it was very brave of you to admit your deception. I happen to think that courage is a virtue nearly as sterling in quality as honesty, so I say that we will be happy to have you stay with us and host your reunion with your father.''

He paused as he pushed himself back from the table and got to his feet. "As to your working on the exhibit, well, Professor Potter is in charge of that. I cannot speak for him; however, if he's anything short of a fool, I think he will beg for your help. Now, speaking of fools, I must go to the telephone and learn what is so very important that it cannot wait until tomorrow. There are times I regret having had the machine installed. I think people use the device just for the novelty of the thing."

Sutro nodded at her before leaving the room. Diana lowered her eyes to her lap where her fingers gripped her linen napkin. Several seconds passed before she was able to force herself to look up, across the table, at Ben. He gazed at her for a long moment, his features still and unreadable; then his lips twitched slightly. "I'm afraid that I've yet to find anything in life worth begging for," he said, "but I must admit I do need your help on this project."

Diana whispered, "It's yours."

Ben smiled then, but it was a smile that lacked the warmth and attraction of the spontaneous expressions that had crossed his features in the exhibit area, before he'd learned of her identity. "Good. As I mentioned earlier, time is growing short, Miss McKenzie. I'm going to change my clothes and go back down to the Baths to work. If you're serious about your offer, I suggest you change into something more suitable and meet me at the front door in twenty minutes."

This time Diana was ready to meet the challenge in Ben's eyes. She pushed her chair back from the table, but before she could stand, Will reached over and placed a hand on her arm as he spoke. "Ben, I don't think the girl needs to start now. After all, she just arrived today. Let her get a good night's sleep before you begin ordering her about."

"Thank you for your concern, Mr. Babcock. But it's only eight o'clock. I'm accustomed to keeping late hours, and besides, I'm anxious to study Mr. Brody's technique more closely so I can learn to copy it.''

The older man's hand slid off Diana's arm as she stood. "Well, the Baths close to the public at ten. Be firm and don't let Ben keep you down there past that time. I think it only fair to warn you that one of the reasons that Brody left was that Ben had worked him to a state of total exhaustion.''

"Nonsense. If the man hadn't worked so incredibly slowly, I wouldn't have been forced to push him so. And don't start in again about what a perfectionist he was. There are limits to how long one should fuss over something. If the Lord had worked as slowly as Laurence Brody did, the world would still be a ball of salt water. Miss McKenzie''— Ben turned to Diana—"twenty minutes.''

_____ *Chapter Five*

DIANA WATCHED Ben's broad back disappear through the doorway. She stayed at her place long enough to express her gratitude to Emma for understanding her deception and to give a quick smile to Will; then the blue silk of her skirt rustled as she hurried up to her room. Unwilling to take the time to call for a maid, she struggled to unfasten the tiny buttons that ran down the back of her dress, then quickly slipped into a sensible dark blue skirt and a fresh white shirtwaist with a high, curved collar.

She was waiting at the front door when Ben came down the stairs. He was dressed as he had been that afternoon, except that the ivory shirt and brown pants he wore tonight were smeared with several shades of paint. In one hand he held a small, square lantern and in the other arm he cradled a paint-spattered bundle of muslin.

As he crossed the entryway, Diana saw his gaze slip down her form in a searching look that made her face heat up and her muscles stiffen. Before she could form a satisfactory protest he asked, "Can you climb a ladder in that skirt, Miss McKenzie?"

The question puzzled Diana for a moment, until she remembered the scaffolding that surrounded the volcano. She nodded briskly. "I can if I'm careful. However, I do have a divided bicycling skirt I can change into if you wish.''

Ben shook his head. ''I don't want to wait for you to change, but that's the sort of thing you should wear after this.'' As he spoke Ben held the door open for Diana.

The blue of the sky above had taken on a deeper hue and the hill that held Sutro Heights threw a long shadow onto the gardens below. Blocked off from the rays of the setting sun, Diana was chilled by the cool, salt-scented air, which reminded her of Emma's warning to always take a coat. But one glance at her new employer told her it was not a good idea to ask him to wait while she ran back to her room for one.

They walked in silence for several minutes as they descended the gravel path toward the front gate. The scent of roses perfumed the air and their dark green leaves glimmered in the fading light. For several moments the only sounds were those of soft footsteps on gravel and the distant murmurings of the sea. Then Ben glanced over at Diana and asked, ''Had you planned on bicycling much while you were in San Francisco?''

Diana thought she detected a hint of amusement in the man's tone. ''No,'' she replied. ''I found that divided skirts were much easier to work in last year when I did field work in Wyoming, so I bought several to use on future expeditions.''

''Wyoming?''

There was no mistaking the derision in Ben's tone this time. Diana's muscles stiffened as she raised defiant eyes to his. ''Yes, Wyoming. It wasn't as exciting as working a dig in Italy or Egypt, but it was the only work I could find to complete my degree. Besides, tracing the culture of the Plains Indians proved to be most interesting.''

''Dusty work, though, isn't it?''

Ben's dry tone brought a slight frown to Diana's brow. ''Dust and dirt go with the territory, as you well know,

Professor. But they are simply a veil, concealing the mysteries that we archaeologists strive to uncover."

A moment of silence followed Diana's statement, then Ben's sharp laugh echoed off the trees that bordered the sloping path. "You're uttering romantic claptrap, Miss McKenzie. On-site work is hot and dirty, the hours are long, and those mysteries you speak about are nearly as rare as dinosaurs' teeth."

"Professor Potter, why don't you simply come out and say what you are thinking? I assure you I've heard it all before."

"What I'm thinking?" Ben stopped at the huge arching gate. He handed the lantern to Diana. "Here, hold this while I unlock the gate." He drew a key from his pants pocket and a moment later held the gate open for Diana and asked, "Pray, tell me, Miss McKenzie, just what do you imagine my thoughts to be?"

Diana shrugged as she crossed in front of him. "Oh, I would imagine you hold opinions quite similar to most of the men I've met, views that run along the lines of 'Women should be at home, minding the stove,' or 'Women have no business doing a man's job,' or, most insulting of all, 'Poor things, they just don't have the stamina for this kind of work.' "

Diana paused on the other side of the gate. As each phrase echoed away on the light breeze, she recalled the many times she had heard these things, and more. The old anger festering in her soul sharpened her voice as she spoke again. "Well, Professor Potter—"

"Wait just a second, Miss McKenzie." Ben's words rose over the clang of the gate. He took the lantern from her hand as his narrowed eyes met hers. "I refuse to be lumped in with such shortsighted fellows. My mother was quite well educated and had a career of her own, so I am fully aware of what women are capable of accomplishing."

He began striding down the hill toward the Baths while Diana stood, captivated by the sight in front of her.

The sun was a brilliant salmon globe resting on the horizon, setting the ocean in front of it on fire. Wisps of clouds in the sky formed streaks of rose and orange and pale lavender. Against this magnificent backdrop, the Sutro Baths glowed like a huge votive candle, and for a moment Diana could only marvel.

She hurried to catch up with Ben and said, "Well, Professor Potter, what kind of career did your mother have?"

"She was a nurse. My father was a doctor, and her help was invaluable to him. Besides helping him in his practice, she bore four children, ran a household, and served on the boards of several charities."

"But?"

Ben stopped in front of the entrance to the Baths. "But what?"

Diana forced a smile. "I'm waiting for you to finish your statement. I've heard this sort of thing before, you see. You're trying to assure me that you're more enlightened than most men, but the next thing out of your mouth is bound to be some disclaimer that your mother and others like her are the exceptions to some imaginary rule that says women should stay in their sphere and leave 'real work' to men."

Ben hurried through the doors, while Diana followed. He ignored her until they had crossed the picture-lined entry hall and were about to step onto the well-lit promenade deck. He stopped, then turned to Diana.

"You're right," he said at last. "I do think my mother was exceptional. However, I can't help but believe that if she hadn't overexerted herself she wouldn't have died at the age of thirty-five, leaving four children under the age of twelve to more or less fend for themselves."

Diana's solemn eyes met his, immediately recognizing

that this man bore deep scars from his childhood. She had heard that same defensive tone in her own voice more than once whenever she was forced to discuss her past. It was always an uncomfortable moment for her, hoping the other person would not notice the pain beneath her words and comment on it. She knew the kindest thing she could do was speak as if she wasn't aware of the wound this conversation had opened.

"Professor, I know that hard work can take a toll on anyone, man or woman. But it sounds to me like your mother led an active, fulfilling life. Now *my* mother died when she was only twenty-four, and as far as I know, she never did anything more strenuous than raise a paintbrush to a canvas. I have a feeling that your mother's life was far more satisfying. She was fortunate to be married to someone who allowed her to test her limits, to truly live."

Ben replied sharply, "Testing limits is one thing; pushing yourself beyond them is another." They silently wove their way through the maze of glass display cases and the people crowding in little groups around them.

It became obvious that Ben's wound was a deeper one than Diana had imagined. It had not been her intention to cause him pain, no matter how much she resented his overbearing attitude, so as the hill and temple came into view she sighed audibly, and tried to make her tone as offhand as possible. "I suppose, Professor Potter, that you're one of those men who feel we ladies need to be protected, that we lack strength."

Ben sent her a sharp glance. "And I suppose you are one of those women who insist that females are as capable as males."

The unmistakable sarcasm in his voice told Diana that he had buried his pain and had taken up the gauntlet again. A thrill of excitement tingled through Diana as she prepared to answer the taunting note in the man's words. "That all depends on which male and which female one is comparing," she said. Close by she spied exactly the example she had in mind.

"Look—over there by the fountain." Diana kept her voice low. "Which of those two individuals would you put your money on in an arm wrestling match?"

Diana watched Ben frown at the couple she had indicated. The puffed sleeves of the woman's brown jacket emphasized the thickness of her waist and the width of her hips. The broad rim of her matching hat floated a full six inches above the gray derby of her companion, a mustached man who was nearly as slim as Diana.

Ben's lips twitched into a reluctant grin. Diana watched tiny creases fan out from the corners of his eyes. "I'm not sure *I* would take that woman on," he said.

Before Diana had a chance to return his smile, all traces of mirth disappeared from Ben's features. "I suggest, Miss McKenzie, that we bring your example down to a practical level. I will admit that a female with that particular woman's Junoesque proportions wouldn't have any trouble performing heavy duties. However, someone less well muscled, yourself for example, would have more difficulty. Now on a dig—"

"Wait just one moment," Diana broke in. "You know as well as I do that common laborers are hired to do the shoveling and other heavy work on a dig. An apprentice, such as myself, would be assigned to jobs no more strenuous than sifting through layers of dirt. That may not be the most pleasant work, but it certainly wouldn't overly tax my strength."

When he opened his mouth to reply, Diana went on quickly. "Stamina is more important than strength, anyway. And it's a quality that women have in abundance, unless they are foolish enough to lace themselves into tight corsets. And as far as more strenuous work is concerned, there are ways of compensating for lack of muscle, such as the use of fulcrums and levers.''

They had finished rounding the base of the artificial hill as Diana finished speaking. "Miss McKenzie, I surrender. I'm sure that when you are on a dig, you will put all the men to blush with your displays of stamina. However, at this moment you are in my employ, and I would appreciate it if you would leave any heavy work to me or to my men. The job will be demanding enough, I assure you. I can't afford to have you injure yourself if I hope to complete this project in the time alloted.''

Ben's dark eyes bore into Diana's with such intensity that she deemed it best to swallow the retort poised on the tip of her tongue. He hurried up the steps and had disappeared when Diana reached the threshold. She noted that electric torches, similar to the ones she had seen on the Diana chamber below, cast dim lights onto the walls. She peered across the room and caught a glimpse of Ben standing at the doorway on the left of the altar.

With quick steps, Diana followed him to the long corridor she remembered from that afternoon, down toward the double doors leading to what she had come to think of as the Vesuvius room. Ben motioned her to join him at a table set underneath the scaffolding.

Several large tubes of paint lay on the table. Most of them were obviously unused, but a few of them appeared to be only half-full, their bottoms squeezed flat and curled up. "Brody ordered the paint," Ben said. "He used some when he started on the top of the volcano, but they are to be utilized to paint the city as well, which is what I would like you to start on tonight."

Ben pointed to a small canvas leaning against a wall, an unfinished painting of a stone house. "This will give you an idea of the look we want. As you can see, Brody applied the paint with a heavy hand, blending shades of gray, black, and tan to give the effect of masonry.''

Diana nodded as she studied the painting, then turned to study the city she was to complete. ''I guess I'd best work from the center out to the edges.'' She sighed. ''You were certainly telling the truth when you said there was a lot of work to be done here. This job alone will take days to complete.''

''Yes, but I'm sure that will be nothing to someone with your stamina.'' His mouth curved into a wicked smile as he thrust the bundle of muslin he'd been carrying into her arms. ''Here. Wear this to keep from getting paint on your clothes. If you need anything else, I'll be downstairs painting the sky in the Diana chamber.''

He stepped back as he spoke and lightly pressed a spot on the wall. A narrow panel sprang open. ''There are more supplies stored in this closet. You'll also find a ladder,'' he said, ''which leads down to the room where the waterworks are set up for our 'eruption.' Another door down there opens up to the shrine room. You are *not* to go down the ladder. But if you need me, you can call down and I'll hear you.''

Diana stared at his broad back as he reached the spiral staircase beyond the side door and began to descend, then shook out the material he'd handed her to find that it was one of his shirts. She shrugged into it. The hem of the garment nearly reached her knees and the sleeves hung several inches beyond her hands. With deft fingers she rolled the sleeves up to her elbows, then unbuttoned her own cuffs and shoved them up as well.

Clean brushes sat in a jar on the table, and a palette lay next to them. Diana squeezed several dollops of paint in various shades onto the oval board, then turned and stared at the little city before her. She would begin by laying a base color for the streets in the center quadrant, she decided.

She began blending the colors on her palette to a brownish gray.

As Diana leaned forward, her brush in her outstretched hand, a faint woodsy scent rose from the shirt she wore, bringing the man who had lent it to her sharply to mind, and making her heart pound with the same excitement she'd experienced during their argument on the way to the Baths.

Diana frowned and told herself that her heart beat faster in remembered anger, but she knew that wasn't true. Despite what she'd said to him, Benjamin Potter wasn't like any man she'd ever encountered. True, he seemed to hold the popular male attitude that women needed to be protected against overexertion, but she had to admit that not once had he suggested that she wasn't qualified to enter the field of archaeology simply because she was a woman.

It was to his credit, too, she mused, that he had left her up here alone to work, demonstrating a commendable respect for both her artistic talents and her intelligence.

But he *was* arrogant, she reminded herself as she studied the effect of the stroke of paint she'd just applied. Satisfied that she had the right blend of colors, she leaned forward again, then bit her lip as she considered the defensive response that Benjamin Potter seemed to evoke so easily in her, causing her to react with an irrational anger that was completely foreign to her.

She knew better than to respond in such a manner. At the university she had learned it was best to quietly defend her rights to an education and to a career, and had become so successful at blending in, that over time she had not only made her instructors and peers disregard her gender, but had gained their grudging respect, as well.

Something told her that the challenge she sensed in Ben Potter came from a deeper, more elemental level. At the university she had downplayed her femininity, sometimes almost forgetting herself that she was a woman. This didn't seem possible where Ben Potter was concerned.

Even when she was thinking logically, which she found strangely difficult to do when his dark eyes were holding hers, she found that this man made her uncomfortably aware of the womanly aspects of her personality. Something about him managed to evoke a degree of vulnerability she hadn't experienced since her eighteenth birthday, when she had made up her mind to take responsibility for her life. Leaning forward a bit further to apply her paint, Diana frowned as she considered how she should deal with her strange and confusing reactions to this man.

Two hours later, Diana's expression only reflected physical discomfort. She had unfastened the top button of her blouse as she worked, but this had only released the pressure at her neck. Her eyes hurt from squinting and her back ached from leaning forward for so long, but at least, as she was drawn into her work, Ben Potter had slipped from her mind.

With a sigh, Diana straightened and gazed contentedly at the portion of the small city she had brought to life so far, then turned to the table where she cleaned the brush with linseed oil. When the palette and brush were freshened, Diana stretched her sore muscles before removing Ben's shirt. After hanging it on a nail protruding from one of the legs of the scaffolding, she stepped back and glanced up at the volcano.

Now that she had spent a couple of hours creating the appearance of rock by dabbing shades of paint on the small houses, she had a fair idea of how to duplicate Mr. Brody's technique, but without a closer look she couldn't be sure.

Diana placed one hand on the ladder leading to the platform above, then lifted one booted foot to the bottom rung of the ladder and scowled at her skirt, as Ben's warning about avoiding injury echoed in her mind. She paused for a moment, then shrugged. Climbing a ladder wasn't going to put her in any danger as long as she took her time and was careful to keep her hem away from her boots. Placing her other hand on the next rung up, she began to climb.

Down in the small closet near the cavelike opening where the statue of Diana was to be displayed, Ben finished cleaning the dark blue paint out of his brush with hurried motions, fighting the tension building in him as he worked in the cramped area. A few moments later he took a deep breath, releasing the pressure in his chest as he closed the small door behind him and stepped into the relative spaciousness of the room beyond and looked at the portion of fake sky he'd just finished.

His arms ached, as did his back, and as he reached up to ease out the kinks in his muscles it occurred to him that Miss McKenzie must be suffering similar discomfort.

He hadn't planned on letting her work so long, but as usual, once he'd become involved in his work, he had lost all track of time. He shook his head as he thought of the young woman upstairs, and his lips curled into a half-smile. He suspected that even if Diana McKenzie *were* sore, she most likely wouldn't admit it. The young lady displayed a strength of will that he hadn't seen in many people, male or female.

And if the story the girl had recounted at dinner was true, this strength of will was the result of years of pain. Sympathy for Diana twisted in his chest as it occurred to him that her father's abandonment of her was most likely the source of her determination to succeed in an area dominated by men.

Again he shook his head. He was quite familiar with the desire to try to prove oneself in the eyes of another, along with the futility of such an endeavor. But this was something Diana would have to discover for herself. In his years of teaching mythology and history at Oxford he had found that the teacher only presented the information; it was up to the student to assimilate it. This was especially true when the lesson to be learned involved emotions.

Ben became aware of the slight throbbing sensation in his chest, a reminder of several old, scarred-over wounds connected with his own education in this area. The stirring of these old emotions brought a cramping to his muscles and awoke a twinge of resentment at the young woman who had brought best-forgotten memories to the surface.

Action, he had learned, was the best remedy for his rare moments of introspection. Ben marshaled his weary muscles and in moments he had turned the switch to extinguish the torches on the walls and the lights in the sky above, retrieved the softly glowing lantern, and begun climbing the steps.

Once he reached the top he strode quickly to the small side door leading to the volcano display. He went inside, half-expecting to find Diana curled up on the floor some-where, asleep. The room appeared to be empty. Yet he heard a scraping sound above him.

He lifted his head with a jerk, to see Diana descending the ladder. His eyes narrowed as he noticed that she held one section of her skirt with her left hand as she carefully lowered one foot down toward the rung beneath the one she stood on. Concern for Diana's safety collided with anger at her disregard for his instructions, and without thinking, he shouted, "Blast it, Miss McKenzie! What the devil are you doing up there?"

Startled, Diana jumped slightly. Her foot slid off the rung it had just touched. She gasped as she felt herself begin to drop, but managed to tighten her right hand around the rung it had been holding. She jerked to a stop with such force that her teeth clicked together and her thick topknot loos-ened, sending hairpins clattering to the ground below.

Diana dangled in the air a moment, her arm aching, her heart racing madly; then she clenched her jaw as she released her skirt and reached her free hand up to grasp the rung as well. When her boots found footing below, she took a deep breath and slowly the beating of her heart began to return to normal.

The calm lasted mere seconds. As anger began to surge through her veins, Diana turned her head with deliberate slowness and glared down at the man below. "What am *I* doing?" she demanded. "What are *you* doing, shouting at me like that? Have you already forgotten what happened this afternoon?"

Ben scowled up at her, his hands on his hips. "You have no business being up there. I told you I didn't want you doing anything dangerous."

Diana clenched her teeth together, swept her skirt into one hand again, then began to descend, speaking as she moved. "This wouldn't have been dangerous if you hadn't frightened me. If you expect me to finish your volcano, then you had better become accustomed to the idea that I'll have to spend some time up here to do so."

Diana reached the bottom of the ladder and turned to see that Ben stood so close that she had to tilt her head back to meet the anger in his eyes. "I fully expected you to have to mount the platform at some point, but only when I've arranged to have someone assist you in the climb."

A tremor raced through her. Her body was once more responding strangely to his nearness. The weakening of her knees frightened her and added an edge of sarcasm to her words. "Well, as you can see, that will hardly be necessary. I'm more than capable of managing the climb on my own."

Ben shook his head. "If I weren't in such desperate need of your talents, I would refuse your help completely. You are stubborn and dangerous."

"And you are overbearing and impossible to work with."

Ben grasped her upper arms. "What is wrong with you? I'm not trying to interfere with your work. I only want to be certain you don't fall and break your lovely—but stiff—neck.''

Diana was surprised at the honest concern she saw on Ben's face. She pulled away from his grasp. As she did so, she felt her hair loosen further, and before she could reach up, it tumbled down to float past her waist as the last hairpin clicked to a landing on the floor.

Diana ignored the black cloud curving past her cheeks. A strange expression mingled with the concern in Ben's eyes as he gazed down at her, an expression that robbed Diana of her anger and threw her emotions into turmoil.

Gathering her tattered shreds of will, Diana turned to focus on the miniature city of Pompeii. For as long as she could recall, only her grandfather had revealed this kind of deep concern for her. Unfortunately, the old man's overprotective attitude had threatened to smother the life out of her. It was this attitude that she had been fighting all her life, first in her grandfather's home, then at the university.

Ben's anxiety for her physical well-being filled Diana with a warmth she found dangerous, far more threatening than her near fall from the ladder. She wanted respect, not coddling. She couldn't allow herself to give in to the trap of looking for safety and security, to be kept from her path in life because she appeared to be weak and in need of protection.

Tears clouded Diana's eyes as she recalled all the battles she had fought over the years on this front. She blinked them back rapidly, then took a deep breath and faced Ben, hoping she could make him understand how important this was to her.

''Have you ever thought about what people were doing that last day in Pompeii?'' Diana's voice quivered slightly as she asked the question.

Ben's brows lifted in surprise at Diana's abrupt query.

''Well, I have.'' Diana took another deep breath. ''On

my eighteenth birthday I was reading over my father's letters, filled with childish self-pity, wishing that I could hear from him again. I came to the last letter, the one I had received on my twelfth birthday. In it he spoke of the things that had been found during earlier digs, mentioning bread that had been found in stone ovens, and pies that had been left on windowsills to cool.''

Diana glanced at the small city again. "As you know, disaster struck without warning. Many escaped, but thousands of people died in mere hours. As I sat on my bed that day, my father's letters in my lap, it suddenly occurred to me that disaster could strike anyone at any time. I realized that if some tragedy were to befall me on that very day, all I would have to show for eighteen years on this earth was a stack of letters, a few mementos of places my father had visited, and a heart full of unfulfilled dreams.''

She once more gazed out over the model of Pompeii as she went on. "The Latins had a saying—*carpe diem*—seize the day. I decided to make that my rallying cry, and I refused to dream any longer that my father, or anyone else, would come to make my life happy. I became determined to be responsible for that myself. Living life in such a way means taking risks, Ben.'' She looked up and held his gaze with her own. "It also means that when it is my time to die, whether I fall from a scaffold and break my neck, or pass away in bed at the age of eighty-four, I will take more than empty dreams with me.''

Diana's words echoed in the otherwise silent room as Ben noticed the mixture of defiance and anguish in her features and felt something soften in his chest. She looked like some lost child, with her hair tumbling about her delicate features. At the same time she was undeniably all woman—soft, seductive curves and parted, inviting lips.

He tried to fight his reaction to both her vulnerability and her allure, reminding himself that Sarah Wilson had possessed just such an appeal once.

A small voice in the back of Ben's mind protested this comparison. Sarah had been a consummate actress, something that he, in his youth and inexperience, had been unable to discern. Over the years he had gained the ability to recognize that the emotions etched on Diana's features were honest and completely without guile.

His blood still pounded with anger at her disregard for her own safety. Now it quickened at the lips that trembled so very slightly. He was familiar with the urge to comfort that he had developed in his role of older brother to three young sisters. The desire he felt now, to draw Diana's slender form to his, went deeper than that instinct. His desire grew until it was stronger than the whispered warnings in his mind.

Diana observed that his features were set in still, unreadable lines, and she found her hands tightening into nervous fists as she tried, unsuccessfully, to draw her gaze away from his.

"Your desire to be mistress of your own destiny is very admirable, Miss McKenzie," he said. "However, you don't seem to take into consideration that others may have different ideas. I have a saying of my own, very similar to yours, you see." He paused and bent forward. His fingers touched her jaw lightly as he spoke again. "Mine," he said huskily, "is *seize the moment*."

Ben's face was so close to Diana's that his breath caressed her cheek. Diana's heart raced and her mind urged her to turn and run, but she could not move. As Ben moved ever closer she was reminded once again of the dream figure in the grove, and just as in her dream, Diana found she was able to do nothing more than stand helpless as warm lips closed over hers.

The gentle pressure of Ben's mouth was oddly familiar,

filling Diana with a strange heat that robbed her of her last ounce of strength. The kiss intensified. Ben's lips moved firmly over Diana's as he slid his hand to the back of her head, tunneling his fingers into her hair. His other arm came around her waist and pulled her closely to his hard form. Diana's heart pounded wildly as first surprise, then anger blended with a strange emotion that seemed to prevent her from doing more than savoring the pleasurable sensations coursing through her.

But as Ben's words, "seize the moment," echoed over and over in her thoughts, anger at last broke the spell. Her mind flared with fury that this man would assume that he could simply "seize" her, without any regard for her wishes.

The heat of Diana's wrath gave strength to her arms. Pushing hard against Ben's chest, she broke his hold on her and pulled her lips free of his. She stumbled back, fighting the urge to slap his face; then, before he could say or do anything, she turned and rushed through the double doors, into the dimly lit corridor leading to the temple room.

Chapter Six

DIANA SQUINTED as she hurried through the dim corridor. Her footsteps slowed as she entered the temple room, but her heart still raced. She lifted her hands to her cheeks to find them still burning.

"Diana." Ben's deep voice echoed down the long hall she had just traversed. Diana hesitated a moment, half-turning toward the doorway she had passed through. Logic told her she should wait where she was, compose herself, and face Ben Potter. But logic had little power in the face of the irrational need to flee that gripped Diana, making her pivot toward the entrance to the temple and hasten across the room.

Once she had passed the threshold, her feet responded to the panic pounding in her breast, turning instinctively toward the stairs. She was down the steps and halfway around the small hill before she noticed that darkness surrounded her. She gripped the railing and took the final steps more slowly as she started at the shadows. What was it Will had said at dinner—something about Ben working long after the caretaker had closed up for the night?

An eerie glow shimmered down from the glass panels overhead, creating strange silhouettes of the palm trees and flower displays crowding around her as she left the stairs behind her. Her heart hammered against the wall of her chest, as she squinted in the half-light, searching for the path that would lead her to the front door of the Baths.

Some part of her mind shouted at her foolish pride and told her to wait for Ben to guide her out, but all Diana could think of was escaping the man whose words and actions had filled her with this disturbing and uncharacteristic confusion. Squinting into the shadows before her, she stepped carefully forward, willing her eyes to adjust to the dim light, commanding her heart to stop its mad racing.

She tried to tell herself that she was being extremely silly to react so strongly to a kiss, to a simple touch of lips to lips. Yet every time her memory recalled the way her body had nearly melted at Ben's touch, she could feel another blush rise to her cheeks and her knees begin to weaken again.

She could not understand these sensations. She had always managed to maintain dispassionate relationships with the men she came in contact with. Until she could understand her strange responses and bring her emotions under control, she did not want to see Benjamin Potter. More to the point, she didn't want him to see her in her present state of mind. If he was able to discern her confusion, he would undoubtedly draw some erroneous conclusion about its origin.

Diana searched for the wide avenue she remembered taking from the entrance to the rear of the building. After she took a few more steps, a shaft of light pierced the shadows ahead, as if to direct her toward her destination. With a sigh of relief, she quickened her pace. Then, once more, she heard Ben's voice calling her name.

Diana moved more rapidly, her boots echoing loudly on the boarded walkway, one footstep following the other in quick succession, keeping rhythm to her pounding heart. For several yards in front of her, she could see the path clearly, bordered by waist-high display cases that she was certain looked familiar.

Or did they? The promenade deck was full of display cases, lining paths that led in a hundred different directions. Still, she continued forward, certain now that she could hear the sound of heavy boots following behind her, not bothering to slow as the path was once more swallowed up in shadow.

She saw a glimmer of white in front of her too late to slow down. She gasped and cried out softly in pain as her shins slammed into something cold and hard with a sharp, square edge. Before she could catch herself, she fell forward, striking her head on what felt like a small tree trunk. Straightening and looking up, she gasped again and jumped back, away from the huge ape looming above her from atop a marble stand, its raised arms silhouetted against the relative light of the glass ceiling above.

Diana looked at the beast, her mouth dry and her heart frozen, until she remembered seeing the stuffed gorilla earlier in the day. As her heart pounded anew, Diana shook her head at her skittish fears and backed away from the display.

She narrowed her eyes, squinting so hard that they almost completely closed, but she could see only darkness directly in front of her. It seemed lighter off to her right. She moved slowly at first, until she saw a tall, narrow opening ahead that appeared to be filled with a pale silver light. Again she heard Ben call her name.

Like a racehorse responding to the sound of a gun, Diana began to run forward, her eyes on the rectangle of brightness ahead, her hair whipping behind her.

She had almost reached the opening when she realized her mistake. Her eyes widened as the shape of a mummy in its upright coffin loomed in front of her, and she ordered her running feet to stop. Her boots slid across the painted boards. She nearly lost her balance, but managed to remain upright and pull herself to a halt just in front of the eerie object.

For one long moment she gaped at the empty eyes of the wrapped skull, then turned away, glancing both ways. She felt sure that the entrance lay to the left. Diana hurried down the dark aisle, her breath coming in short gasps as her pulse pounded loudly in her ears.

One moment the path ahead appeared perfectly clear, then it was blocked by a tall, broad form, filling the aisle and causing Diana to come to an abrupt halt. A sound—a cross between a growl and a cry—echoed across the boardwalk. Her ragged breathing came to a stop every bit as abruptly as her feet had moments before, and for a second she could do nothing more than stare at the form blocking her escape as she shuddered.

As the hulking shape began swaying from side to side, Diana thought back to the stuffed gorilla she had just encountered. Her mind flashed to the display of stuffed birds she had seen in one area of the museum as Pete escorted her through, and the caged living ones in another section. Was it possible that Sutro kept other live animals in his museum?

Diana had no desire to learn the answer to this question. With a violent gasp, she leapt backward, and her fevered mind ordered her feet to turn and run. Somehow they obeyed, pounding loudly on the wooden floor, twisting and turning as she dashed through the dark paths. Diana had no idea where she was, or in what direction she was going. She only knew she had to keep moving, despite the nameless things that tugged on her skirts, and the vicious edges that scraped the backs of her hands.

Her mouth was dry; her breath came in labored spurts. A sharp pain pierced her side with each step, yet still she moved on, rushing from the echoing sounds behind her.

She was running too fast to stop when the dark form

stepped directly in front of her. Strong hands grasped her upper arms, and pulled her around in a tight circle. Her throat was too parched to release her scream, so she uttered a wimpering croak as she fought against the bruising grip.

"What the hell is wrong with you? Are you trying to ruin the place?"

Ben's voice, angry and rough as it was, sounded like choir music to Diana's ears. She managed to swallow, then to speak in a harsh whisper.

"I had to get away. He's after me."

"Who's aft—"Ben stopped and his hands tightened on Diana's arms. Then a deep chuckle reverberated through the darkness before Ben raised his voice and called out, "Pete! I have her."

As Diana's mind raced with questions, a shaft of light pierced the blackness and fell on Ben's features.

"Diana, I'd like you to meet the watchman here, Pete Martin."

Ben loosened his grasp on Diana's upper arms as he turned her around toward the tall, broad-shouldered man holding a lantern.

"We met earlier today." Pete's voice echoed loudly in the cavernous building. "Is she all right?"

"I think so, Pete," Ben replied. "Bring that lamp here, won't you?"

Pete's shuffling gait echoed through the cavernous room. "Certainly, Professor. What happened to the young lady?"

"Nothing, really. We were working late, and when I told her it was time to quit and go back to the house, I forgot to tell her that you turn out the lights before you leave. When I realized what time it was I ran after her, afraid that she would get lost in the dark, which is apparently exactly what happened. I'm glad you headed her off."

Diana glared at Ben, her mind protesting his blatant lie, but before she could say anything, Pete reached her side.

"Well I was glad to help. I couldn't understand what was going on at first." He turned to Diana. "I'm sorry if I frightened you by stepping in front of you, but you were headed right for the stairs leading down to the pool. I was afraid you'd come to grief if you fell down them."

"That was quick thinking, Pete." Closing his hands over her arms again, Ben said, "If you had kept running the way you were going, you would most likely be a crumpled heap at the bottom of a long marble stairway. What did you think you were doing?"

The harsh light from Pete's lantern etched deep lines in Ben's face, tight ones around his mouth that spoke of anger, and short ones between his lowered brows that spoke of concern. Suddenly self-conscious, aware of the long hair tangling wildly around her, Diana had to draw a deep breath before answering. "I . . . I became startled when I bumped into the stuffed gorilla. I was frightened and began running any which way. Silly, I know. I'm sorry if I caused you and Pete any trouble."

Ben released her arms and stepped back. "It could have been worse. You didn't hurt yourself, and I don't think you damaged any of the exhibits." He lifted his eyes and spoke to the caretaker. "Pete, I left my lantern in the volcano room. Will you light our way out? I believe we're done for tonight."

As Pete led the way, Diana recognized the shuffling sound of his limp that she had mistaken for the tread of some large beast. Her face began to burn again. The moment she and Ben stepped out the front door, her blush was cooled by a gust of moisture-laden air rushing up from the sea. Then, as Ben took her hand and led her toward the entrance to the gardens, lighting their way with Pete's lantern, a chill began to seep through her thin blouse.

By the time they neared the gate, only her hands felt warm. The right one had scraped along the edge of a glass case as she ran in the dark. A glance at it in the moonlight revealed a long, angry-looking gash along the back that throbbed with a feverish heat.

Her left hand was nestled in Ben's large one. Diana glanced at it, small and white within his grasp, aware of a strange tingle there that was both pleasant and frightening at the same time. He released her hand to open the gate, then took it again as he began striding forward, holding the lantern high to light the gravel path in front of them.

As Diana hurried at his side she concentrated on not shivering. She had displayed far too much of what she regarded as weakness already that evening, and she was determined not to add to that. So intent was she on controlling her response to the misty chill soaking into her bones that it was several minutes before she noticed that they were no longer on the main path leading up to the house. She slowed her pace, and when Ben turned to look down at her she asked, "Aren't we going in the wrong direction?"

"No. When I come in late like this, I use the back way."

Diana nodded numbly, then stepped forward when he did. The cliff holding Sutro Heights rose on their left as they followed a wide road that curved around it. The sound of a crashing wave made Diana glance in its direction, then stop and gaze at the sight before her.

Directly below sat the Cliff House, its arched windows glowing brightly. There was no moon tonight, but shreds of mist floating by its spires, glowing softly in the light of the star-sprinkled sky, made the building look more than ever like something out of a fairy tale. The loud hissing of the waves blended with the night, and suddenly the chill seemed to melt from her body and she wanted to do nothing more than stand and admire the magical sight.

"Quite a view, isn't it?" Ben spoke so softly that his words were nearly lost in the whispers of the swirling sea below. Diana nodded mutely.

A second later Ben's hand tightened slightly on hers and he spoke again, his deep voice brusque. "Come along, Miss McKenzie. It's late. You won't be much good to me tomorrow if you don't get some sleep tonight. And you have some more climbing to do."

Diana lifted questioning eyes to his. His white teeth gleamed in the dark beyond the lantern's glow. "There are some steps cut into the cliff." He lifted the light and let it illuminate the rock wall. Narrow steps twisted up the steep cliff between plaster statues of nymphs and woodland animals that dotted the embankment leading to the crenellated wall above.

"The steps will take us to the parapet." Ben's voice rose over the echoes of another crashing wave. Diana turned to him as he went on. "That's the area just behind Sutro's house."

Diana felt a twinge of regret at having to pull herself from the sight of the sea and the sky. She bit back her request that they stay there a few more moments and nodded. "I know. Emma took me up there today."

"Then you have some idea of the climb ahead of you." Ben spoke as he guided her forward. "It's not too bad, really. Just be careful not to trip."

Their feet echoed on the stone steps, slick with sea mist. Diana clutched Ben's hand, for the stairway was steep and narrow and in the uneven light it was hard to find the best footholds.

Her legs were shaking from the exertion of the climb by the time they reached the top. Her pulse pounded loudly in her ears, and she found it difficult to catch her breath as they trekked toward the water tower. She noticed a soft light falling onto her path and looked up to see that the top section of the tower was well lit. Puzzled, she slowed her steps as they neared the structure.

"Is something the matter?"

Diana realized she had come to a complete stop while looking up at the balcony that encircled the tower. Then she looked at Ben and saw no signs of his earlier anger. She wondered if the starlit mist might not have cast the same soul-soothing spell on him as it had on her.

The second that thought crossed her mind, she dismissed it as being illogical and fanciful, and forced herself to reply to his question. "The water tower," she said. "It's lit. Is it some kind of lighthouse?"

Ben shook his head and smiled. "No, it's an observatory of sorts. Sutro has a very nice telescope up there. Guests of the house are welcome to use it, Emma tells me, so whenever you have some free time you should go on up."

Diana felt a disturbing warmth seep through her body, a dangerous return of the weakening force that had gripped her in the volcano room just before he kissed her. "Well, I have some free time right now, but I think it would be best put to use by getting some sleep. It's been a long, eventful day."

As Ben noticed the wry smile set in the obviously weary lines of Diana's face he became aware of a twinge of guilt twisting within his stomach. Will had been right. Tomorrow would have been soon enough to have started Diana working on the exhibit. And it would have been safer. With other workmen around he doubted if he would have been tempted to draw her to him, to kiss her lips, to "seize the moment."

His face grew warm as he remembered the arrogant sound of those words. It was on the tip of his tongue to apologize for his actions, but as he took a deep breath in preparation for his speech, he drew in the scent of jasmine blended with the salt air. The flowery aroma brought back that moment in the volcano room, where Diana's face, softened by her remembered sorrow, and her dark blue eyes glittered with a determination to rise above her father's absence in her life, danced in front of him. He knew the words he was preparing to say would be a lie.

The only regret he could claim regarding that kiss was that Diana had obviously not found the same pleasure in it that he had. He knew the moment his lips touched hers that she was unpracticed in the ways of love, but instead of pulling back as any gentleman should have, he had pressed his attentions further, as if he were somehow compelled to draw her supple form to his, urging a deeper claim upon those pliant lips.

He realized now that her apparent willing response had been due to shock, a stunned reaction to his brash conduct, something he would have realized then if his senses had not been spinning out of control.

Ben watched the dark tendrils dancing in the breeze around Diana's pale features. His feelings of guilt increased. He had done her more than one injustice this evening, first coercing her into working late, then forcing his attentions on her.

But even as Ben berated himself for his churlish actions, he realized that knowing all this, he still—right this moment—felt the same desire he had experienced earlier to lower his lips to hers. He looked into her dark eyes, which mirrored the night, and fought this emotion, warning himself against making a fool of himself twice.

As he continued to study her eyes, still battling with his desire, Diana lifted her right hand to brush the wisps of hair out of her face. When he caught a glimpse of a dark line on the back of her hand, he reached out and grabbed her wrist.

"How did this happen?"

The brusque question made Diana blink. Only a moment earlier she had been certain that the harsh lines in his face had softened somewhat. Now another deep scowl creased his features as he glared down at her hand. "I think I hit it on the edge of a display case while I was running through the museum.''

"I'm sorry,'' he began, speaking in a near whisper. He opened his mouth to say something else, only to pause a moment before he went on in a firmer tone. "I'm sorry you hurt yourself. You should probably have Emma see to that cut.''

Diana nodded slowly. "I will. Whenever she comes up to the house again. I have some bandages in my room that will do until then.''

Ben seemed ready to reply; then he shut his mouth suddenly and nodded briefly before he spoke. "That's probably a good idea. You should get to sleep as soon as possible so you can be fresh to work tomorrow. Just be sure you clean this first. And you be sure you do a good job of it. If it becomes infected, you won't be much use to me.'' He paused, shook his head slightly, then spoke more softly. "Good night, Miss McKenzie. Sleep well.''

Her feelings were in an uproar as she entered her room and turned the key on the wall lamp to set the crystal globe glowing. She headed to the private bathroom and opened the little cabinet above the sink. As she washed the back of her hand with moistened gauze she questioned why she should feel so confused by this man.

It was time to be honest with herself. It was no longer possible for her to deny that she was physically attracted to him. Earlier in the day, before he had taken her into his arms and covered her lips with his, she had been able to convince herself that she had no interest in Ben Potter beyond seeing him as an employer who might help her further her career. But in the few moments she had stood pressed to him, her lips parting to receive his kiss, she had been forced to acknowledge that she was drawn to him more than she wanted to admit.

How she could have allowed herself to react in such a

manner to someone as arrogant and overbearing as Ben Potter was beyond imagining. Diana shook her head as she wound a strip of gauze around her hand, and before she realized it her memory began reliving every moment of that kiss.

Never before had she experienced such sensations, the pounding heart that sent heated blood rushing through her, the warmth that seemed to rob her limbs of strength, the taste and feel of firm lips on hers that made her hunger for more of the same.

These feelings had frightened her down in the Baths, and they frightened her now. Diana lowered her hand to the curve of the sink and studied the wide, dark eyes in the mirror. Terror stared back at her from those blue depths— fear of the unknown, of untapped emotions, of the loss of strength that had followed in the wake of that kiss.

Diana shook her head at her reflection. The pleasure that had coursed through her then and that vibrated weakly through her now was dangerous. She needed to have control over her emotions if she expected to face her father when he arrived. She would need it even more if she expected to be viewed as a capable person, well suited for a position with Justin Harrington, when he arrived for the opening of the Pompeii exhibit. Whatever attraction existed between her and Ben Potter would have to be ignored if she expected to carry out her plans.

No dreams visited Diana that night. After a restful sleep, Diana found that in the light of day whatever danger she had imagined that Ben presented seemed to dissipate. He was polite but distant at breakfast. The distracted way in which he responded to Will Babcock's questions indicated to Diana that Ben's mind was already down at the Pompeii exhibit.

Since Emma had left after dinner the night before, and

Mayor Sutro had departed Sutro Heights earlier for meetings in the city, Diana had expected the meal to be a silent affair. Will, however, had other ideas.

"I trust you slept well last night, Miss McKenzie?"

Diana looked up from her plate of ham and eggs. "Yes, I did, Mr. Babcock. And I thought we agreed that you would call me Diana."

The older man smiled. "It's a deal, but then you must remember to call me Will." At Diana's nod, his smile widened. "Well, I'm glad to know that your sleep wasn't disturbed last night. I was afraid, after hearing of your little adventure, that your dreams might have been invaded by visions of malicious mummies and man-eating gorillas."

Diana tensed immediately but he winked at her from behind his glasses.

"Sutro's little museum is a confusing place in the middle of the day when it's all lit up," he said. "I would imagine that it's something of a nightmare in the dark, especially if you don't know your way around."

The warmth in his tone made Diana relax and reply, "You're right about that. And now that I think of it, it's really something of a marvel that my dreams *weren't* filled with nameless horrors. I suppose there is something to be said for being totally exhausted when one finally goes to sleep."

"Aha. I thought so. Ben"—Will turned to his friend— "I warned you about working Miss— Diana too hard. She is not some—"

"Wait." Diana reached across the table to lay a hand on the older man's arm. "It wasn't Professor Potter's fault that we worked so late. He told me to stop when I got tired, but I became so caught up in what I was doing that I lost track of time."

Ben's eyes met hers. "Well," he said, "since you're rested and find the work so engrossing, I assume you're ready to get back to it. And, please just call me Ben.''

Diana nodded, and rose. ''I need to get a few things from my room, Ben. I'll meet you at the front door in a few moments.''

Diana mounted the stairs with ease, pleased with the freedom of movement afforded her by the brown divided skirt she wore. In her room she paused in front of the mirror to adjust the high lace collar of her ivory blouse. She wore her hair down today, waving thickly back from a center part and captured in a tortoiseshell clip at the nape of her neck. It was not as professional-looking as her normal upswept hairdo, but it had the advantage of being more secure. She didn't want it tumbling about her as it had the night before.

In the mirror, Diana saw her cheeks take on a deep pink glow as she suddenly recalled Ben's fingers curling into her hair as he deepened his kiss. Tightening her jaw she brushed the memory away and lifted her hand to her clip one more time. Satisfied that her hair would stay where it belonged and that she had her emotions well in hand, she threw her black coat over her arm and hurried down the stairs to find Ben and Will waiting by the open door.

The sky above was bright blue, but the morning breeze was cool enough to warrant slipping her arms into the sleeves of her coat as she walked between Ben and Will. Neither man spoke as they made their way down the gravel road. They took the path through the rose garden, with Diana walking between the two men, content to breathe in the flowery fragrance and to listen to the songs of birds in the trees blend with the sigh of the sea floating on the wind.

As they approached a small white building next to the gate, an old gentleman dressed in khaki stepped out and waved them over. Diana followed Will as he stepped off the path and approached the slender man who squinted at them beneath the wide brim of his hat. ''I was wondering when the professor will be wanting the stone animals,'' he said.

Will glanced back over his shoulder and when Diana heard no answer from Ben she turned also, just in time to see him pass through the arched gateway.

"Well, I'm not sure, exactly." Diana turned back to see Will shake his head at the older gentleman. "As you can see, Ben is slightly preoccupied at the moment. I'll ask him about the statues today, Mr. Abraham, and let you know. Are they in your way?"

"Not so's anyone would notice. I been storing them in the conservatory. There's already as much statuary in the place as there are plants, so a few more don't hurt any. I just didn't want the professor to forget we had them."

"Oh, I think he'd remember soon enough, especially now that we have someone to paint them and bring the creatures to life. This is Diana McKenzie, our new artist." Will turned to Diana. "This is Mr. Abraham, Diana. He's the head gardener here at Sutro Heights."

"I'm very glad to meet you, sir." Diana smiled broadly as she shook the old man's hand. "You have created a real wonderland here. I'm amazed at the variety of plants and flowers you have growing. Many are quite unfamiliar to me."

"Why thank you, miss. That's Mr. Sutro's doing. Always trying things people say won't work. Some of these plants have never been grown this far north before. I'd be more than happy to take you on a tour of the gardens some time."

"I'd love that."

Will quickly added, "After the exhibit opens, Mr. Abraham. Between now and then Professor Potter has first claim on Diana's time. And speaking of the professor, we'd best catch up with him. He's obviously got his mind on the exhibit already. When he gets like this he's perfectly capable of walking right past the entrance to the Baths and off the cliff into the sea.''

A horse-drawn carriage rattled past the gate as Diana and Will crossed beneath the white arch and started down the path. In front of them Ben walked slowly in the middle of the road, so deep in thought that the carriage sped by, just missing him.

''I hope you don't find him utterly impossible.'' The unmistakable amusement in Will's voice made Diana turn to find the man staring down the hill at Ben for a second before shifting his gaze to her. ''He really is quite a catch.''

_____ *Chapter Seven*

WILL'S WORDS ECHOED loudly in the early-morning hush. Diana stiffened and quickly looked down the hill toward Ben. When he didn't pause she turned back to Will and spoke in low, intense tones.

"A catch? Mr. Bab— Will, I want to make something perfectly clear. I am not looking for a husband. I came to Sutro Heights with only two objectives in mind. One, to see my father, and two, to speak with Justin Harrington about securing a position on his archaeological team."

"I see." Will inclined his gray head slightly as he took Diana's elbow and began guiding her down the road. Diana matched her stride to his energetic one and watched him closely. "I suppose it would do no good to point out to you that Ben is also an archaeologist."

The twinkle in his brown eyes made it difficult for Diana to keep from smiling. She shook her head. "I know he is, but I am not looking for the kind of position you are hinting at. And more to the point, I feel quite certain that Professor Potter is not looking for anyone to fill that spot."

Will sighed and shook his head. "Well, you are a very perceptive young lady then. Most women choose to ignore Ben's brusque manner and imagine that a wife is exactly what he needs. As you have apparently deduced, he's highly resistant to the idea of marriage.''

Diana watched the broad-shouldered form striding ahead of them, obviously unmindful of the people following him. ''I completely concur with his decision. It's my experience that men who are deeply immersed in their careers make for difficult husbands and disappointing fathers.''

Diana regretted these last words the moment she uttered them. In her ears they sounded bitter and self-pitying, and the last thing she wished was for people to feel sorry for her. She was half-afraid to look at Will, but she found that his expression was one of contemplation. His brows met in a slight frown as he spoke in a musing tone. ''You know, even though Ben is very good at what he does, he does have interests other than archaeology. He would make a very good husband and father, I think. I don't know if he told you, but he helped his father raise his younger sisters after his mother died.''

Will paused as he cocked his head to one side and glanced at Diana. ''I think he's only happy when he has someone to look after. His work demands attention, but not really his heart. He reminds me of a sheepdog without a herd.''

The teasing glint in Will's eyes was irresistible. Diana found herself grinning broadly at the old man and shaking her head. ''Well I like *that*. You seem to be suggesting that I let the professor look after me. Do you find me sheep-like, fuzzy-minded, and easily led?''

''Oh, no. Quite the opposite, my dear. You obviously have a mind of your own—a good one, too. But you must admit, you do have a tendency to get yourself into scrapes.''

The smile fell from Diana's lips. ''You must be referring to my escapade in the Baths last night. Let me assure you, that sort of thing has never happened to me before. I am normally quite composed and sensible. I don't know what got into me, but I assure you it won't happen again. Mr.

Sutro's museum is safe from anymore midnight dashes.''

Will placed a hand on her arm. "My dear, I know that. Please forgive an old man's teasing.''

"Of course. That is, if you'll forgive me for becoming testy. I tend to respond that way, you see, when it's suggested that I should be a good girl and think of marriage.''

"I promise not to suggest it again." Will gave her a solemn nod, then looked forward to shout at the man ahead of them. "Ben! Wait up, will you?''

Ben stopped abruptly, and looked at them with a mixture of confusion and irritation. Seconds later, when Diana and Will reached him, Ben asked, "What kept you two?''

"Mr. Abraham. He wants to know when you want the statues of the animals for the Diana exhibit.''

"I'm sorry. I didn't even see the fellow. I was trying to figure out just what we might be able to accomplish today.''

"Well, I hope you have made plans to give your new employee a quick tour of the area. Now, don't you scowl at me like that. You can't have the girl getting lost every time you send her out for something. Take a few moments and do it now, and you'll save time in the long run." Will smiled as he moved toward the entrance. "I'd do it myself, but I told the locksmith I'd meet him at the exhibit. He's probably waiting for me right now.''

With a wave of his hand, Will disappeared into the Grecian entryway. "The old man is right. You should be shown around. But it will have to be a quick tour.''

At Diana's nod, Ben turned toward the sea and stood next to her. "You know about the Cliff House over to our left, of course. The long, low building stretching toward us is a stable and carriage house. The structure to the left of the entrance to the Baths is a photographic studio, a popular attraction for the tourists.''

Diana had barely nodded when Ben placed his hands on

her upper arms and spun her around so that she was facing the opposite direction.

"Up the hill on your left is where the trains come in from the city. If you'll look up, you can see the top of a ferris wheel. Just beyond the train station lies a small midway with a few rides, a peanut stand, and a fellow who displays trained birds."

Ben took another deep breath at the end of this last sentence as he turned Diana toward him. "Have you any questions?"

Diana shook her head.

"Good. Now, just so that you don't believe that I am a complete ogre, I should tell you that I give all my workers an hour off for lunch. You will also have time off for dinner, but I'll need you to work a few hours in the evening in order to get all the artwork completed. However, in your free time you can explore all this, as well as the beach south of the Cliff House."

Ben smiled and shrugged. "Of course, now that I think about it, I'm afraid your free time won't amount to much. Are you sure you still want this job?"

It was on the tip of Diana's tongue to tell him that when he smiled he didn't look a thing like an ogre, but the surge of warmth rushing through her as she noticed his suddenly boyish expression served as a warning against saying anything so foolish.

Instead she replied saucily, "I have all that stamina at my disposal, remember? I have no doubt that I shall be able to complete my work and still fit in some time to see the wonders Mr. Sutro has wrought out here."

Ben's eyes narrowed slightly as if half-angered at her sarcastic reply, as he guided her toward the entrance to the Baths.

He was silent until they were standing beneath the glass roof of the promenade near a man selling picture postcards.

"Well, before I begin, I suppose I should ask you what you've seen already so my tour won't be repetitious and time-consuming."

At his mention of time, Diana saw his features tighten. She spoke quickly. "Well, actually, I noticed quite a few of the displays as I walked through yesterday. I really don't need you to take me through the museum; I can explore it as I wish on that generous lunch hour you mentioned. I'd just as soon get to work."

The blend of sincerity and disappointment in Diana's voice brought a smile to Ben's lips. But he asked, "What about the pools? Did you get a chance to look at them?"

"No." Diana glanced at the nearby railing. "I heard the splashing, though, and I know that they're over there." She paused as she turned back to him. "All I really need for you to do is show me which paths lead which way, so I don't feel so much like Alice lost in the looking-glass world as I make my way to the exhibit and back."

A strange glint in Diana's eyes belied her seeming disinterest in the pools and intrigued Ben. His lips twisted into a wry smile as he took her elbow. "No, you should see the pools first. Mr. Sutro is very proud of them, as well he should be."

After a moment's hesitation, Diana walked briskly next to him toward the splashes and shouts rising from beyond the white railing. Above their heads another glass and steel ceiling arched out toward a glass wall facing the ocean. Ben watched Diana look past the rows of bleachers toward the water shimmering within the greenhouselike enclosure.

"My word," she breathed.

"It is quite amazing," Ben said. He pointed to the pools, which were separated by raised wooden walkways. "Those are all heated to various temperatures, and range from two feet to ten feet in depth. The larger pool, the one angled around the others in an L shape, reaches a depth of some twelve feet down at the far end, where the slides angle into the water.''

As Ben finished speaking, a figure clad in a black bathing costume swung out over the water at the end of a set of rings. At the top of his arc the bather released his hold, did a somersault in the air, then plunged downward, sending a huge plume of white water surging into the air as he landed.

Diana sighed. "This is wonderful. No wonder Mr. Sutro is proud of his creation. Children must love it.''

A wistful note in Diana's voice made Ben look at her as he replied, "They do. So do the adults.''

"Only the ones who know how to swim,'' she murmured.

"Sutro is a much better planner than that. He feels very strongly that everyone should have access to the benefits of bathing in salt water. Those who can't swim can always splash about in the shallow end.''

"But then they can't use the slides.''

Diana's words were uttered in a soft voice that held unmistakable traces of both longing and disappointment. Ben watched her sadly gaze at the water and felt his heart twist as he wondered what her childhood had been like. From what she had said last night she had been raised by her grandfather, with no brothers and sisters with whom to run and play, laugh and argue.

"I take it no one ever taught you to swim,'' he said.

Diana looked up at him, her dark blue eyes shadowed with some unreadable emotion as she shook her head. "I visited an indoor pool with my grandfather once, and asked him to let me go into the water, but he refused. He said he was afraid I would catch a cold. Since my mother died of consumption, he always worried about anything that might affect my lungs, you see.''

Ben did see. He also saw from the defiant tilt of her chin that Diana would not welcome the words of consolation that were on the tip of his tongue, so he said, "Well, it's never too late to learn. Lessons are available here. When you have the time, of course.'' He gave her a wicked grin and went on. ''And speaking of time, I think we'd best finish up our tour and get to work.''

Something about Ben's tone gave Diana the uncomfortable feeling that he had discerned the pain she wanted so much to keep hidden. She tightened her hands into fists at her sides, then swallowed the strange lump that had formed in her throat. ''I think that's a good idea.''

She followed Ben as he led her along the railing above the pools, nodding as he pointed out the various oversized glass cabinets bordering their path. They stopped in front of an exhibit that consisted of a large stuffed sea lion sitting atop a rock while Ben explained that the seal, Old Ben, who had died of old age, had been a favorite of Sutro's.

''Sutro has a great love of animals, for everything in nature for that matter. Old Ben's passing disturbed the gentleman so much that he decided to have the old bull stuffed. He gave him a place of honor in the museum in hopes of inspiring a similar interest in his visitors.''

The only other stop they made was at the broad set of stairs that led down to the bathing pools. Diana contemplated the steep marble stairway bordered on both sides by planters filled with palms and other tropical plants, then remarked, ''It's a good thing you stopped me when you did last night. That would have been quite a fall.''

Ben's eyes narrowed. ''Yes, indeed.''

''Well.'' Diana took a deep breath, pulled her eyes away from his, and turned toward the Pompeii exhibit. ''I think I've seen enough to manage to get around on my own. As you say, I have my lunch hours to explore further. Shall we get to work?''

''We shall. Lead on.''

* * *

Diana straightened from her work several hours later and studied her morning's accomplishments. The little city of Pompeii was beginning to shape up nicely. Most of the center had been completed, and she had made good progress on the marketplace. Her next project was to be the huge oval amphitheater with its numerous rows of seats, but that would have to wait until she attended to the growling sounds her stomach had been making for the last half hour.

"Are you ready for lunch?"

Will's voice echoing from the door behind her made Diana jump slightly. She turned to see him holding a red plaid blanket in one hand and a wicker basket in the other. "I had the cook up at Sutro Heights send us down a picnic. I thought you might like to get out into the fresh air, away from the paint fumes, for a little while."

Diana gave him a wide smile. "Thank you, Will. Just give me a moment to clean up."

Moments later, brushes soaking and her hands scrubbed clean of paint, Diana removed Ben's shirt and hung it on its nail. She followed Will through the temple room and down the steps set in the artificial hill.

Instead of taking her out the front entrance, Will led her around the hill to a doorway that opened to a labyrinth of pipes and larger cylindrical forms made of metal.

"The boiler room," Will said over his shoulder as he led her forward. Diana followed him, smiling at the khaki-clad worker that stepped out of their path. The air was warm, moist, and heavy. When Will opened another door, she stepped out to a brisk, refreshing breeze to stand at the edge of a wide pool of calm water. On the other side of the cement enclosure a cliff rose above the frothing sea.

"We'll be going through that tunnel." Will stood next to Diana, pointing to the opening in the rocky wall that lay on the other side of the pool. "Follow me and watch your step."

Diana did as he instructed, tracing his steps across the narrow concrete strip that formed the pool's edge, then into the dark semicircle cut into the side of the cliff. The carved rock formed a rough-hewn dome overhead. Her black boots sunk into the coarse, damp sand beneath her feet with a soft hiss that blended with the other whispering sounds that filled the tunnel as she and Will made their way toward the arched opening.

As Diana walked silently next to Will, glancing at the rock walls and mentally mixing paint to approximate their gold and brown tones, she found the tightness in her shoulders relaxing. There was something warm and welcoming about the cavelike tunnel, despite the cool, moist air rushing past her.

"Watch your step here, now."

Will's words drew her attention to an opening in the tunnel wall. She stopped to see smooth wet sand below, then watched as white frothy water rushed into the opening with a loud roar. She stepped back as fine droplets of salt water splashed up into her face, then laughed as the water receded just as quickly, retreating with a loud hiss.

Diana turned to Will. "Thanks for the warning. Does the water ever fill the tunnel?"

"No, though at high tide one can get quite a shower standing in this spot. And it would be a very cold shower, my dear. The water out here isn't heated like some of the pools in the Baths."

Diana asked as they began walking again, "Do you use the pools often?"

"No. I've gone in a few times, but I'm not as fond of swimming as Ben is. I know that bathing in salt water is supposed to have all sorts of curative effects, but I find even the warmer pools too cool for my taste. Ben, on the other hand, seems to feel the colder the water he swims in, the better it is. He claims it builds stamina and character."

Will finished speaking just as they exited the tunnel. Diana blinked against the bright sunlight, then stared at the small crescent-shaped beach nestled within a rugged, rocky cove.

"Is that where we will picnic?"

"No." Will shook his head. "It's not as sheltered as it appears. The waves rush in, all the way to the cliff without warning sometimes. There's a little spot up here on the rocks that's safer."

Will began climbing a narrow, rugged path that led to the top of a flat oval area. Another, taller ridge blocked Diana's view of the Baths, but the scene in front of her more than made up for this.

Beyond the edge of the cliff, the sea rose and fell, dark blue beneath the paler, cloudless sky. Diana was only half-aware of the flap of the blanket as Will unfurled it. She walked right past him, drawn toward the ocean, coming to a stop when she noticed the rocky surface beginning to slope downward. She stood near the edge, staring out over the water, watching it rise and fall in the sunlight.

It was so unlike the pool she visited in her dream. There the power she sensed was quiet, hidden. A stiff breeze tugged at her skirts and loosened a few tendrils of hair around Diana's face as she witnessed the awesome force contained in the waves crashing onto the rocky face of the cliff below. Each surge of water rushed over the rocks at the base of the cliff, then drew back, leaving a different pattern of white foam spreading down the side like a lace curtain laid out to dry. Each roaring crash of wave against rock was followed by a sibilant whisper, so hypnotic that Diana jumped when Will spoke.

"Don't get too close to the edge, Diana. A sneaker wave could come in and pluck you right into the sea."

Diana turned to Will. "A sneaker wave?" she asked skeptically.

The older man paused as he opened the wicker picnic basket, his brown eyes serious behind his oval glasses. "Yes. Those are the waves that I mentioned to you before. They rush in with more force than normal, and they've killed many a casual hiker out here on the rocks. Please, come join me here. You should sit down and relax while you can."

Diana asked herself why it was she found it so easy to respond to Will's paternal concern, when such a request from Ben Potter would only have made her move closer to the edge of the cliff.

Because you don't behave rationally around that man, some portion of her mind replied as she sat down and turned back to study the sea. It was true; there was something about Ben that brought out the rebellious child in her, perhaps because she had never allowed herself to express insurgent emotions. Her grandfather's orders had angered and frustrated her—much as Ben's did—but because she couldn't risk angering the old gentleman for fear he would disappear from her life like her father, she had swallowed those emotions and obeyed his orders, at least while she was young.

She lifted a sandwich to her mouth and watched a flock of seagulls wheel around the rocks on the other side of the small cove, envying the ease with which they glided through the air, her heart beating with excitement as they turned and dove toward the swirling sea below.

"Oh, so you decided to take time out to eat today?"

Will's voice startled her. She glanced over and saw him looking up at the taller ridge behind them. She turned and let her gaze follow Will's.

Ben stood atop the crest staring down at them, then began to make his slow way down before he replied, "Yes. I've begun to think that perhaps you're right about pushing myself too hard. After I refused your invitation to join you and

Diana out here, I had second thoughts, and decided it was just the kind of refreshment I needed.''

Diana watched Ben hop from rock to rock with the ease of a mountain goat. She looked up at him as he reached the blanket. ''Is it quicker to come over the ridge than through the tunnel?'' she asked.

Ben shook his head. The tunnel would have been much quicker, and less strenuous—for anyone but him. He had actually tried to pass through it today; however, he had only gone in a few feet before he began to have difficulty breathing. Two steps later and he could feel the earth pushing around him, crushing his chest. Sweat had sprung to his brow, his breathing had become labored, and he had turned and dashed out into the bright sunlight.

''Ben was almost buried alive once. His best friend was.''

Will's voice made Ben blink. He saw Diana turn to him, her eyes filled with an expression of horror. He wondered just how she would react if she knew that it was her father's negligence and greed that had caused the accident that had cost Rob his life. It would have taken so very little to shore up that cave, but Daniel McKenzie was too anxious to locate a particularly fascinating artifact.

''Well, I'm glad you are finally heeding my advice.'' Will's voice, more animated than normal, drew Ben's thoughts back to the present. He lowered himself to the blanket as the older man went on. ''I keep telling you that you need to get out of that place from time to time. I've found that once one gets tired, the work pace slows dramatically, and mistakes crop up more often. Don't you agree, Diana?''

Diana was still trying to imagine what it would be like to be buried beneath tons of dirt. She replied, ''I suppose you're right, but I'm the wrong one to ask. Once I get started on something I become so involved that I completely lose track of time. By then I'm exhausted, of course, and

I'm *forced* to stop, or fall asleep on top of my work. I know better, but I seem to have little say in the matter."

Ben nodded as he took the sandwich Will offered and began to unwrap the linen napkin surrounding it. "That's exactly what I've been telling him."

"No, it isn't. You just insist that we will never have this exhibit completed unless we work around the clock. That isn't the same thing as becoming lost in the work you love," Will retorted.

The three of them ate in companionable silence. Ben finished his sandwich quickly, then reached into the basket and drew forth a handful of strawberries. These, too, disappeared, followed by a glass of lemonade poured from a large corked bottle.

Diana dined at a more leisurely pace, watching Ben grow more restless by the moment as he waited for the other two to finish eating. After several moments he picked up a small rock and tossed it out toward the edge of the cliff. It bounced once, then disappeared over the edge. She watched as he repeated the movement with another pebble. It landed at exactly the same spot before vanishing from sight. When this happened a third time, she glanced at Ben and remarked, "You have a good arm."

Ben smiled. "I played stickball constantly as a youngster in Chicago. When I moved to England I took up cricket. It gets me out of the museum—keeps me from becoming old and bent before my time."

Ben looked across the blanket separating him from Diana. Her eyes narrowed against the glare of the sun as she looked at the sea. She seemed very young with her hair down, curving back past her face, tied at the nape of her neck. It fell down her back in thick, black waves, and slender tendrils blew gently about her fair skin.

She should be wearing a hat to protect her face from the sun, he thought. He was doing it again, watching over her

like he would one of his younger sisters, when he should
be viewing her with suspicion. It had occurred to him last
night, after they had parted, that there still existed the very
real possibility that she might in some way be involved in
her father's nefarious schemes.

A voice in the back of his head told him this was absurd,
and for the most part, he agreed with this assessment. Despite Diana's attempts to speak about her father without
emotion the evening before, it had been obvious that
McKenzie's absence had caused her great pain. Unless she
was a very, very good actress, she really had not heard from
the man in ten years. Still, he would not feel he had done
his part in protecting the museum's possessions if he didn't
examine this possibility more completely.

"So, when do you expect your father to arrive?" His
question startled Diana; Ben could see that in the wide eyes
that turned to him quickly, and in the slight stiffening of
her lips before she replied. "I'm not exactly certain. Emma
told me that her father received a telegram from him a few
days ago, stating that he would be delayed, but that he
would arrive in time for the opening."

Ben nodded. "How do you think he'll take your presence
here?"

Diana's eyes widened slightly before she replied, "I don't
know. I'm not sure how I'll react when he arrives, either.
He will be a complete stranger to me. I don't even know
that I will recognize him."

"Do you think he will have changed so much in ten
years?"

Diana's eyes narrowed slightly. "It's been ten years since
his last letter, but seventeen since I saw him last. I only
have a vague memory of a thin man with a beard and light
brown eyes."

"No pictures?"

"No. My father hated cameras. As far as I know, he has never allowed his picture to be taken."

Ben was painfully aware of this fact. Due to this quirk of personality, Daniel McKenzie was able to slip into cities throughout the world unnoticed, leaving a trail of missing artifacts in his wake. Will and a few others had known the man years ago, but as Diana had obviously realized, people change over time.

He was also aware that the open expression he'd seen soften Diana's features as she gazed out over the ocean had disappeared, to be replaced by a smooth, emotionless mask. Only her eyes registered any feeling, a mixture of wariness and pain.

"I'm glad you mentioned this," she said finally. "That was a hole in my plan I hadn't considered. Now that I think of it, I guess I shall have to have someone point my father out to me." She shook her head ruefully. "At least I know what Professor Harrington looks like."

Ben frowned. "Justin Harrington?"

"Yes. I think I mentioned last night that he is the other reason I am here. I understand he's preparing for another dig, and I hope to convince him to hire me."

"You don't want to do that."

Ben's officious tone made Diana's features tighten. "Yes, I do. He spoke at the university last year, and I've also read all his papers. He's the foremost expert in Roman studies, which happens to coincide with my own interests."

"He's a fraud," Ben replied. "Whatever artifacts he is credited with finding have been uncovered by underpaid workers, who get none of the credit they are due. That goes for the secretary who writes his speeches and those papers, too."

Diana stiffened. "I don't believe you."

"I'm not in the habit of lying," Ben said. "But you don't have to take my word for it. Harrington is to be honored at a dinner at the Cliff House tomorrow night, and Sutro has invited all of us to attend. You should have ample opportunity to judge the man for yourself.''

''I shall do just that.'' Diana got to her feet as she spoke, brushed her skirt off, and turned to Will. ''Thank you for bringing me up here, and for the lunch. I believe that my hour of leisure is over, so I'd better get back to work.''

The older man squinted up at her. ''You didn't eat much—only a half a sandwich. Here, take this with you in case you get hungry later.''

Diana took the apple he offered. ''Thank you. And, yes, I will watch out for the waves in the tunnel.''

Without a glance at Ben she left. Ben waited until she was out of earshot, then he turned to Will. ''Well, I guess I managed to say the wrong thing again.''

Will shook his head. ''I get the impression that Diana would have found some reason to leave, regardless of what you said about Harrington. It was obvious that she was very uncomfortable talking about her father.''

''Ah yes, the mysterious Daniel McKenzie. I wonder if she has any of those letters she mentioned receiving from him.''

''I would be willing to bet she saved every one of them.''

Ben looked sharply at Will. ''Why do you say that? Miss McKenzie doesn't strike me as a particularly sentimental young lady.''

''Your powers of observation are failing you, young man, if you've missed seeing the pain she tries so hard to hide. Not only do I think she still has those letters; I've no doubt that she brought them here with her.''

Will was right. Ben scanned the rising and falling sea again, recalling the suppressed longing he'd observed in Diana earlier that day when they saw the pools. A girl who had been virtually abandoned at the age of twelve would save things like that. And although Diana did a good job of hiding it beneath her independent bravado, Ben was sure that twelve-year-old girl still existed in the outwardly practical Miss McKenzie.

"She's not Sarah, Ben."

Will's abrupt change of subject caught Ben by surprise. Will continued as he began to place the remains of their meal back in the picnic basket. "I know the way your mind works, my boy. I've noticed an expression on your face that I haven't seen since the first time we met, at Harrington's dig, when you introduced me to Sarah."

Ben picked up a small stone and threw it. "Then you're seeing things, old man."

The stone missed its mark, sailing silently through the air to vanish over the edge of the cliff. Will smiled. "Yes, I am seeing things, far clearer than you are. Considering what Sarah did to you, I can't blame you for not trusting the feelings Diana obviously stirs in your soul. I also can't help pointing out that the two women are very different. Diana might be ambitious, as Sarah was, but she is going after her goals on her own, not looking for anyone else to do it for her." He looked up as he finished repacking the picnic basket. "From what you've told me about your mother, I would say that Diana resembles her more than she does Sarah."

The old man was right, of course. Perhaps that was why, despite the comparisons he'd been drawing between the two women, Ben found his concern for Diana's well-being— along with other reactions he didn't want to examine at the moment—increasing with each contact.

"I suppose we might find some answers to our questions in those letters of hers."

Will's reluctant tone broke into Ben's musing thoughts. "That's possible. I doubt that they will tell us much, but we can't pass up the chance to learn whatever we can about the mysterious Daniel McKenzie. I'll keep Diana working late again tonight. That will give you the opportunity to let yourself into her room and read them.''

Will snapped the wicker basket closed. He glanced up, his expression unreadable, and gave Ben a curt nod.

Diana smoothed her paintbrush over the strip of sea green paint running along the front of the tiny town of Pompeii, then straightened slowly and studied the area depicting the wharf. Despite the tension in her shoulders and back, she grinned. The city was complete.

After lunch she had worked diligently, erasing the questions about her father that had been raised at lunch with each stroke of her brush, blending colors on the remaining buildings, then finishing the green fields at the foot of the fake volcano.

Dinner had been a simple meal of roast chicken and baked potatoes, during which she had listened to Sutro describe the machinations of city government. Again she found she had little appetite, but at Will's cajoling insistence she had forced herself to eat a little more than she had the previous evening. With her stomach uncomfortably full, she had found herself quite sleepy when the meal was over. The last thing she had wanted to do was return to the exhibit and the smell of paint, but she was not about to admit this to Benjamin Potter.

Leaving Ian and Will at the house to discuss strategy for guarding the artifacts once they arrived, Diana and Ben started for the Baths. They hadn't spoken at all as they walked toward the purple and orange sunset that decorated the evening sky. Once they reached their destination, Ben had again gone downstairs to finish painting the ''sky'' in the chamber below, leaving Diana to wonder how her aching muscles could bear any more stretching and bending. But once she began to work, she again lost all track of time, and succeeded in completing far more than she had thought possible.

Diana sighed again, letting some of the tension ease from her shoulders as they rose and fell, then stepped back to get a wider view of her handiwork, only to collide with a tall, solid figure. She gasped and twirled around.

Chapter Eight

BEN SMILED. "I startled you, didn't I?" His voice was deep; the words seemed to vibrate through Diana, robbing her of the ability to speak. When she nodded, he apologized. "I'm sorry. I guess I should have knocked."

He studied her then looked at the display. "You've done a good job," he said.

Diana watched him closely and saw his harsh features relax into an expression of pleasure as he continued to study her work. A sense of pride filled her breast, easing away the trepidation she had unaccountably felt. Then she saw the look of approval in his eyes as he gazed at her for several moments, and her stomach tightened with some emotion she could not identify.

"It's late," he said. "Almost eleven o'clock. Aren't you tired?"

His words, so simple and straightforward, eased the trembling in her bones. She must be more exhausted than she thought to respond to his presence in such a ridiculous manner. "I don't think I realized just how tired I was until I stopped working"—she paused as she rolled her shoulders—"or how stiff."

"Turn around."

Diana looked at him with a puzzled frown. Ben bent

123

toward her and spoke gently, as a father would to a small child. "Turn around."

Diana did as she was told. A second later she felt the warmth of his large hands on her shoulders, kneading her tight muscles firmly but gently. A tiny tremor slipped down her spine as she felt her tension ease, and as the massaging motion continued, a tingling sensation spread throughout her body and a strange lassitude robbed her limbs of strength.

"Is that better?" Ben spoke softly, but his mouth was so close to her ear that Diana jumped. Aware that she had begun to lean back toward him, she straightened and nodded.

"Much better. Thank you."

"What about your back, and your legs?"

Diana looked up sharply into his eyes, but saw only mild concern reflected there. "They're not too sore," she replied. "Nothing that a good night's rest won't fix."

Ben shook his head. "No. If you don't do something about those kinks tonight, you'll be too stiff to move in the morning."

Diana observed his hands, now resting at his sides. They had worked miracles on her shoulders and neck, leaving those muscles warmed and relaxed. The thought of allowing those hands to caress the ache out of her lower back and her thighs sent warm waves washing through her, a warmth that warned her of incipient danger and made her quickly lift her eyes to his.

"You're probably right. I'll take a hot bath before I retire."

"I have a better idea."

Diana's newly relaxed shoulders tensed. "And what is that?"

"A swim."

Diana looked at him uncomprehendingly. "In the pools

here in the Baths. Several of them are heated nicely, and I've found the exercise works wonders for stiff, overworked muscles.''

The glint in Ben's eyes held a definite challenge, and although a leisurely soak in a hot bath sounded far more soothing to Diana, she found herself nodding. ''That sounds fine, except I don't know how to swim.''

''During my three years of teaching at Oxford I gave instructions in swimming. If you like I can give you a lesson.''

Swimming lessons, Diana thought. Just this morning she had watched the people in the pools, wishing she could copy their competence in the water. She had always found it strange that in her dream she could swim with ease, whereas awake the thought of immersing herself in a large body of water awoke a strange sense of trepidation in her.

Mentally acknowledging this fear made Diana's muscles contract slightly. She was not, at this point in her life, going to back down from a challenge. She lifted her eyes to Ben's once more.

''Thank you,'' she said. ''I would like that. Just let me finish up here.''

Diana began to clean out her brush. As she ran the bristles over the rag, her thoughts flashed to the water she had gazed at this morning. A shiver raced down her spine. She stopped in midstroke and looked back at Ben, to find him lounging against the doorframe, watching her.

''I will need a bathing costume though, won't I?''

''Oh, yes. They are down in the women's dressing area, off that wide stairway I showed you this morning.''

''I see.''

Diana returned her attention to the brush and the rag. There seemed to be no way out of this late-night swim, unless she wanted to admit that suddenly she found the idea of all that water somewhat intimidating. Her lips tightened as she slipped out of the shirt she was using for a smock, and taking a deep breath, she turned to Ben. "I'm ready. Show me where to change."

"Pete has left for the evening, so all the lights are out. Let me guide you so that we don't have a repetition of last night."

Ben walked with Diana down the wide staircase leading to the pools and pointed to an opening on their right. "I'm not sure how the ladies' changing area is set up, but you should find a switch on either side of the doorway. Behind a counter you'll see the bathing suits and towels. I'll be waiting for you in the ladies' pool. It's the warmest one."

Standing in one of the many small, private changing rooms, Diana held up the black dress that she was expected to swim in and shook her head. The simple bodice had a square neck trimmed with white piping and short sleeves edged in the same white thread. Beneath the gathered waist, — yards of material formed the skirt. When she unfolded the dress, a matching pair of bloomers and two black stockings fell to the floor.

Several minutes later, having stripped off her blouse, her skirt, and all her underthings, Diana slipped the black costume over her head, then struggled to fasten the large buttons in the back. The clip holding her hair back had come loose, and fearing she might loose it in the water, she placed it atop her folded clothes on the bench at one end of the room and let her hair tumble down around her shoulders.

When she turned toward the mirror she almost laughed out loud at the figure that stared back at her. She had decided not to wear the bloomers and stockings, figuring that they would only make the process of swimming more difficult. So, with her bare feet and white legs sticking out beneath the hem of the skirt, and her long hair tumbling over her shoulders, she looked like a poor street urchin.

And inside she felt just like a youngster of perhaps ten

years of age, filled with a shivery blend of excitement and fear. She had always been fascinated by the water, from the time she had begun to dream of the glade and the pond. In her dreams the water had been soothing, welcoming, something beyond her waking experiences. She couldn't help but wonder as she left the dressing area and walked toward the sign directing her to the pool area, just how well she would adapt to a real body of water.

Diana arrived at the ladies' pool and watched the dark water that lapped gently against the steps as if inviting her in. Ignoring the sudden tremor of fear flowing through her, Diana lowered one foot into the water, then summoning her courage she placed her other foot onto the next step, letting the water close over it.

The water was warm, welcoming. She moved more quickly now, feeling the water inch up her legs as she stepped down, ducking her head as she passed beneath a walkway above and stopping only when she stood knee-deep in the pool beyond.

Diana stood still then, looking at the glass roof arching midnight blue above her. Ben must have turned a light on somewhere, for the windows facing the sea reflected a pale green glow. Lowering her gaze to look across the pool, she saw this light reflecting off the water in silvery crescents. The air was cool and moist, and although there was no breeze, she could feel some delicate movement over the uncovered portions of her skin.

A sudden shiver danced over Diana's arms. She crossed them beneath her breasts, shuddering slightly as she searched the glimmering ripples for some sight of Ben. Just as she began to wonder if she might be in the wrong pool, she spied him, a dark shadow in the water near a ladder far across the water's surface, a shadow moving away from her with barely a splash.

When he reached the other end of the pool he climbed a

ladder up to the deck separating the smaller pools from the larger L-shaped one beyond, then stood on the edge, facing her.

In the dim light she could see that his bathing costume was black like hers, but it appeared far more practical than the garment she was wearing. The top portion was similar to a woman's shift, the neck scooped low and the arms left bare. The light from the windows behind Ben created shadows on his shoulders and upper arms, shimmering on his skin and delineating his musculature. The bathing costume hung past his hips, ending just above the hem of the short black trunks that covered the upper half of his well-formed thighs.

Diana observed all this in the few moments Ben stood there, poised on the edge of the raised platform. A second later he dove into the water and disappeared from sight. Diana shivered again, this time with excitement. Ben's movements had been filled with grace and power as he appeared to float out over the water, hover like a seagull in a breeze, then plunge downward in an artful arc. He moved toward her rapidly, his arms curving in and out of the water with rhythmic precision.

Diana stood quietly in the water, her swimming dress floating around her as Ben cut through the pool toward her. When he came to a stop and stood in front of her, Diana asked, "Is it hard to learn to do that?"

Standing in waist-deep water, Ben pushed the wet hair out of his face. "Swimming? No, not at all."

"No—well, that too—but I meant diving. You made it look so easy."

"Anything is easy if you've been doing it long enough. Diving takes time, and practice. And first you have to learn to swim."

The mention of swimming made Diana's muscles tense again, but she nodded quickly. "Of course."

"Do you still want that lesson?" Ben studied Diana carefully. Her face looked so pale in the dim light, her eyes so very large and dark, shadowed with something that looked very much like fear. Perhaps he had misread that look of yearning this morning as she watched the swimmers, misunderstood the longing in her voice when she spoke of the times she'd tried to get her grandfather to let her try. "You don't have to, you know." He spoke in a gentle tone, one he had used with his younger sisters. "If you wish, you can simply relax in the warm water until I'm done. That should ease the soreness in those muscles."

He saw Diana straighten as he spoke. She gave her head a quick shake as he finished. "No, I *want* to swim. How do I start?"

"You start by getting accustomed to the water. That means you'll have to get wet. Come here, where the water is deeper."

Diana stepped forward slowly, her eyes on the water's surface, watching it rise slightly with each step, marveling at how familiar this seemed. She was experiencing the same sensations she had in the dream pool, the caress of the liquid slipping up her legs, the welcoming warmth, the feeling of buoyancy as the water rose above her waist.

Diana stopped walking when small waves began to touch her breasts, and lifted accusing eyes to Ben. He was in deeper water still, grinning at her in the dim light.

"You moved," she said.

Ben nodded. "Of course. You aren't all wet yet."

The water appeared suddenly to be very close to her face, far too close for comfort. In her mind she seemed to hold a memory of floating in the water, of an indescribable sense of freedom, but she knew that memory was from her dream, not from any waking ability that she possessed.

"Can I start my lesson here, where my feet can still touch the bottom?"

"Of course." Ben moved forward as he spoke and placed his hands on her shoulders. "But before we do anything else, you'll have to get used to having your face in the water. This frightens some people at first, but if you remember to take a deep breath before you submerge your head, then hold it until you come up, you'll be fine."

Ben paused and noticed her hesitation. "You are going to have to trust me, Diana. I promise not to make you do anything dangerous. When I tell you to, take a deep breath. Then, when I push on your shoulders, let yourself sink beneath the surface. Hold your breath for a couple of seconds, then come up for another breath. Do you understand?"

Diana fought off a shudder of fear and excitement as she nodded her agreement. Suddenly her entire body felt cold, except for where Ben's large hands rested on her shoulders. There a strange heat seemed to burn through the woolen material of her swimming dress. A little voice in her mind hinted that it would be wonderful to have those hands move down her body, to stop the chilling cold that gripped the rest of her.

"All right, breathe in."

It took a second for Diana's bemused mind to register what he had just said, and by that time, Ben's hands were pressing on her shoulders, forcing her down into the water. Just as the liquid reached her chin, Diana drew in a breath of air, then closed her mouth and her eyes as she allowed Ben to press her further downward.

Once beneath the water she tightened her lips as she remained submerged. Ben's fingers closed over her upper arms only a second later and pulled her up into the cool air. Diana opened her eyes, blinking at the sharp stinging sensation of the salt water streaming down her face. The taste of the sea tingled on her tongue as she took a deep breath.

"How was it?"

Diana shook her head. "I don't know. I wasn't under long enough."

"I didn't want to panic you the first time. Want to try again?"

Diana nodded, and they repeated the procedure. This time she took a deeper breath, and lowered herself into the water quickly in response to the pressure of Ben's hands on her shoulders. Once beneath the water, she concentrated on the new sensations, on the lightness of her body and the strange ringing sound that filled her ears. She felt something soft brush her arm, and her eyes flew open. The salt water burned as she noticed a strand of hair waving in the water in front of her. She closed her eyes again, fighting the urge to laugh at her skittish fears, and just as she found herself thinking about taking a breath, Ben pulled her to the surface.

She was vaguely aware that her wet hair nearly covered her face as she released her pent-up breath. Without thinking, she tried to pull fresh air into her lungs, only to find salty water mixed with it. Sputtering and laughing at the same time, she pushed her sodden hair back and opened her eyes to see Ben grinning down at her.

He suddenly looked very young, with his dark gold hair plastered to his forehead and his even teeth glinting in the dim light. The shadows softened the lines of his face and his smile lacked its habitual cynical twist.

"You look like a drowned kitten." He laughed out loud and Diana's laughter joined his.

"Well, that's not how I feel," she replied.

Ben's expression sobered a little as he leaned forward. "How do you feel?"

"Exhilarated," she answered, "and excited, and anxious to try more. What's next?"

Ben shook his head as he gazed down into her dancing eyes. Any hint of fear that might have been there earlier

had completely disappeared, along with the expression of
icy reserve she often wore.

Ben saw clearly the girl who had been robbed of a childhood by her selfish father. He thought of another life that
had been snuffed out, literally, by Daniel McKenzie's neglect, and his hatred for the man deepened, twisting like a
hot knife in his stomach.

"Ben, is something wrong?" Diana had apparently seen
Ben's expression change.

He shook his head, and eased his lips into a smile. "No,
nothing's wrong," he said. "I was just trying to figure out
exactly how to teach you the art of swimming. I've been
doing it for so long that it's become as natural as breathing.
It's something I don't think about; I just do it." He paused
a moment, then took Diana's hand and began leading her
toward the side of the pool. "I think I'll start off by teaching
you how to kick; then we can proceed to floating."

Ben found Diana to be an apt student, one who listened
to his directions carefully and followed them to the letter.
Holding onto the side of the pool with her legs stretched
out behind her, she mastered the flutter kick quickly once
he held her feet and showed her how to point her toes and
keep her legs straight.

Ben couldn't decide whether he was relieved or disappointed by Diana's easy aptitude. Her skin had felt like satin
beneath his fingers, the shapeliness of her calves promising
more delights hidden beneath the voluminous black skirt.
But such temptation was dangerous, he knew, even as a
tight knot of desire formed in his stomach—desire he knew
must be denied.

The next step, teaching her to float, made that knot twist
more tightly, as he held her lithe body only inches from
his. It became an exquisite torture to watch her stretch out
on her back, her black hair floating around her pale face,
her breasts rising and falling beneath the black fabric molded

to them. Following his instructions, she lay limp in his arms, captive to his slightest whim; more than once he found himself sorely tempted to lift her toward him rather than allow his arms to drop away as he had told her to expect.

Ben only managed to control these wayward desires by constantly reminding himself of the reason he was here at the Sutro Baths. He had come to capture Diana's father, and although Diana had obviously been wounded by her father's abandonment of her, there was still no guarantee that there was no connection between the two.

Fortunately, once Diana had mastered floating on her back, learning to do the same on her stomach took her no time at all. Ben was quite relieved to release her for the last time and watch her kick away from him, her hands outstretched, until she ran out of breath and had to surface in front of him.

"How did I do?"

Her words were half muffled by the thick shock of hair she was brushing out of her face as she stood in waist-high water. Ben grinned as he floated forward to reach her. "I don't think I can remember having a more apt pupil."

Diana felt a warm glow spread over her, then she cocked her head to one side and narrowed her eyes. "And just how many people have you taught to swim?"

"Several, actually. All of my sisters as well as several students at Oxford."

The cool air brushing over Diana's exposed arms raised goose bumps on her skin. She lowered herself into the warm water, amazed at how suddenly at ease she felt in his presence. She couldn't remember ever just being with a man, laughing and relaxing, not discussing geology or history. Before she could remind herself that she'd had good reasons for this, she found herself asking, "How did you come to attend university in England?"

Ben answered, "After my mother died, my father took

us over there. He went originally to study some new medical procedures, then was offered a position at a hospital in London.'' He stopped speaking abruptly. ''But that was a long time ago. How are you doing? I saw you shiver. Do you want to stop now?''

''No.'' Diana stood and shook her head so hard that a rope of hair flew around her shoulder and slapped Ben on the arm, twisting around the sculpted muscle like the tip of a whip. He released its gentle hold on him then looked over to Diana. Even in the dim light he could see her face blush a deep pink.

''You are going to have to do something about all that hair, young lady,'' he scolded mockingly. ''Next time you go swimming,'' he continued, ''put it in a braid or something, or it will drown one of us. I'm going to teach you the crawl stroke now, and show you how to breathe, but I must warn you, all that hair might make things difficult.''

At first Diana had no problem with her hair as she concentrated on learning how to stroke and turn her head to take a breath. It was the subtle touch of Ben's fingers on her arms, lightly guiding them in the correct motion, that disturbed her and threatened her concentration.

Still uncertain of her abilities, and disconcerted by the persistent tight ache in her lower stomach, Diana nodded when Ben asked her if she was ready to try putting everything she had learned together and actually swim.

Her first effort was a dismal failure. Her hair tangled around her face as she turned and tried to draw in air. Water filled her lungs, making her come to a sudden, choking stop. She stood in shallow water, coughing repeatedly for several moments, the salt water bitter on her tongue as she prepared to try again.

Before this attempt, however, she managed to pull the wet hair back and knot it around itself. Then she eased herself forward, determined to be successful. This attempt

ended almost as quickly, for she found that after the first
three strokes, she was sinking and her rhythm was off,
forcing her to stop and gasp for air.

"Relax."

Diana turned as Ben floated up to her and moved his arms
back and forth to keep himself afloat as he spoke again.
"You're trying too hard. You know how to float, so all you
have to do is kick lightly and stroke slowly and you'll have
it."

Diana nodded, then turned away from the wall of the
pool and stretched her arms forward as she eased herself
into the water. She let herself float a moment, then began
kicking, and finally moved her arms in the windmill motion
she had learned. She took three strokes, then four, then five.
Her chest expanded with the thrill of success. When her
lungs began to ache, she realized that she desperately needed
to breathe. Panic gripped her mind, causing her to forget
that she only had to turn her head to one side. She stopped
suddenly, lowering her feet to the bottom of the pool and
standing quickly to release the dead air in her lungs and
gasp in fresh. Ben's chuckle made her turn to where he
stood, his arm almost brushing hers.

"Very good." His expression held no hint of mockery.
"Just remember to breathe, and you'll have it down perfectly."

Diana prepared to ease into the water for another try, but
Ben reached out and grabbed her wrist.

"I think that's enough for one night," he said. "Look
at the gooseflesh on your arms. I think it's time you went
in to change."

Diana noticed the puckered skin on her forearms, and felt
it tighten further as a shiver rippled through her, originating
from the flesh covered by Ben's gentle grasp. As she bit
her lip to keep her teeth from chattering, she felt the sensitive
skin on her breasts tighten as well and saw her nipples

hardening into quite visible peaks beneath the clinging black bodice.

A wave of warmth suffused her face, and she lowered her upper body into the water and looked back up just in time to see Ben's eyes lift from her now submerged breasts to her eyes.

"I haven't gotten my swim in." His voice sounded even deeper than usual, with a husky quality she had only heard once before, the night he had kissed her in the Vesuvius room. "You go change, and meet me at the entrance to the ladies' dressing room. I won't be long."

With those words, Ben turned and swam toward the ladder at the deep end of the pool. Diana watched him cut smoothly through the water. She fought off the shivers as he reached the opposite end, climbed the ladder, then crossed the walkway to dive into the L-shaped pool beyond.

Diana sighed and turned toward the stairs leading to the dressing room. As she did so, a glimmer of light caught her eye, making her turn back. It was a reflection off the surface of the long slide on her left, angling into the larger pool.

The water at the deep end of the L-shaped pool was over twelve feet deep, Ben had told her. Diana couldn't take her eyes off the slide, thinking of the water beneath it, telling herself she didn't possess the ability yet to brave that depth, even as she stepped forward, already imagining herself flying down its shiny length. What she was planning was irrational, she knew, but she wasn't sure if she would ever get a chance like this again.

Carpe diem, Diana repeated silently to herself as she angled into the water, once again letting herself relax into a float. Then she began to swim, forcing herself to take long, slow strokes, and remembering to breathe. Once she reached the side of the pool, she clung to the lower portion of the platform and inched along, hand over hand, until she came to the ladder at the deep end.

Her sodden bathing suit almost prevented her from exiting the pool. As she ascended the ladder, the wet woolen fabric became heavier, threatening to pull her back into the pool. By the time she stood on the walkway, her breath was coming in ragged gasps, forcing her to take deep breaths as she bent down to wring some of the water out of her skirt.

Thus lightened, she found it much easier to go up the ladder to the top of the slide. A little voice began to whisper a warning in her mind as she mounted the twenty rungs. The part of Diana that considered herself a scientist and a scholar agreed with this warning, hissing that this action was insane. But the portion representing the young girl who had been denied such pleasures stubbornly tightened her lips and her resolve as she reached the top of the ladder, then climbed over to stretch her legs out in front of her.

The smooth slide flowed downward at a sharp angle beneath her, glimmering in the pale light from the windows. The water below shimmered, beckoning. Another warning against this foolishness whispered in her mind. A second later, a louder, masculine voice echoed through the cavernous building, telling her to stop.

Neither voice had any power over Diana. Responding to the child within, she grasped the borders of the metal slide and pulled with all her might. Her body shot forward. She found she was barely touching the metal as she flew down. The pool gaped black beneath her, like a huge rectangular pit, waiting to claim her. Her eyes widened and her heart pounded with belated fear.

Chapter Nine

THE POOL SHIMMERED and her fears disappeared as quickly as they had arisen. She sped down the slide, her chest expanding with the glorious sensation of flight. She felt as if she were a bird, diving toward the water like the gulls she had watched circling Seal Rocks. Cool air brushed by her with a soft whistling sound as she sped downward, faster and faster, until she crashed into the water, dropping like a stone into the cold liquid.

The frigid temperature stunned her after the warmth of the smaller pool, but after the first moment the sudden coldness was forgotten. Panic filled her like water pouring rapidly into a glass as she realized that she had failed to inhale deeply before plunging into the pool.

Diana opened her eyes and kept them open despite the sting of the salt water. Aware that her downward progress had slowed, she lifted her head to look up, spying the surface of the water above her, waving in the pale light like a rippling ceiling. Trying to ignore her already straining lungs, Diana started to kick.

She realized after a second that her kicking had only stopped her descent, not lifted her any nearer to the air her lungs were crying out for so desperately. For one moment her mind froze with fear, and her heart began to race. But she forced herself to think. Her legs were not the only means of propelling herself. She had her arms. That thought had barely shot through her mind before she raised her hands above her, then forced them down through the water to her sides.

Diana felt herself float upward. She stroked again, watching the waving ceiling above as her heart pounded harder and the pressure in her lungs became a sharp ache. She fought the urge to breathe in, and pushed more frantically at the water surrounding her, but this time as her hands moved down through the water, something grasped her right wrist.

Before she knew what was happening, she felt herself drawn swiftly upward through the water. The very second that she felt her face break the surface, her control shattered and she gasped in a lungful of cool, fresh air.

When she inhaled, water entered along with the air, and Diana could do nothing more than cough and sputter for several moments, aware of the arm around her waist, grateful for the support that kept her face out of the water. Once she had cleared her lungs, she realized that she was being dragged to the side of the pool. A glance to her right revealed Ben's frowning face as he used one hand to stroke through the water and the other to hold her afloat.

The scowl darkening his eyes brought a new sense of panic to Diana's mind. She was in for a scolding, she was sure.

She was no longer a little girl who had to do as she was told, forced to forego pleasures others took for granted. She had done what she wanted to do, and no one was going to make her feel guilty for her actions.

It was obvious that Ben was going to try, however. He grasped the side of the pool then he faced her, his anger clearly etched in the harsh lines of his face. Diana spoke before he could. "What did you grab me for? I was doing fine."

"No, you weren't." His words came out in a harsh, controlled tone. "You came damn close to drowning. I told you how deep the water was here. Whatever possessed you to pull such a childish stunt?"

Diana said nothing. She didn't have to, for Ben saw the answer in the half-abashed, half-defiant look in her wide eyes. He'd seen the same look often in the eyes of one of his younger sisters, and he knew without hearing Diana say the words that she had gone down that slide simply because it was something she wanted to do, probably some leftover desire from a childhood that had been devoid of such thrills.

Ben fought the sudden sympathy that filled his heart for that lonely child. A second later his features tightened again and his pulse raced with anger at the selfish father who had left her so he could follow his own ambitions, heedless of the harm he caused his daughter.

"Seize the moment." Diana's words were a mere whisper, drawing Ben's attention back to her face. The expression of defiance on her features had increased, once more reminding him of a rebellious child.

Despite his anger at her foolish and potentially dangerous action, Ben allowed himself to smile and whispered back, "Is that an excuse for almost drowning yourself, or an invitation?"

The stunned look on Diana's face told Ben that she recognized his reference to the words that had preceded his kiss the previous night. He watched her closely, seeing her full lips part. They were impossibly tempting, and he suddenly became aware that he still held her cradled lightly to him with one arm. Her body floated only inches from his, and as he thought of her supple form, imagining it pressed to his, he was sure he could feel a strange heat fill the water around them, and hear a voice urging him to pull her closer.

Diana's heart was full of conflicting emotions. She felt his arm tighten around her waist, drawing her toward him. She knew exactly what he was asking her, what he wanted to happen. She had seen desire in the eyes of a man before, though never before mixed with such a look of tenderness. She wondered a little about that as Ben's face drew nearer, realizing that her silence was in fact an answer of sorts.

Her lips softened automatically as Ben's mouth covered hers. He tasted of salt, and his lips felt like velvet as they moved lightly, gently at first, then with a deeper pressure that spoke of need and desire, and elicited those same reactions in her. His arm tightened around her waist. She felt their bodies meet, seem to meld, encouraging her to slide her hands up over his shoulders, to link them behind his neck, to draw herself even closer to his solid strength.

This was another of those things her protected youth had denied her. But in this case it was not her grandfather who had discouraged romance, but her own fears and her desire for independence. Even now, as her body grew warm in Ben's arms and her teeth parted to allow his tongue to enter her mouth, causing a strange heat to coil in the pit of her stomach, a cold voice hissed warnings of danger in her mind.

The pounding of blood in her ears drowned out those whispers as her body responded instinctively to Ben's caresses. She sighed against his lips as he splayed his fingers across the small of her back and pressed her to him, revealing the strength of his desire as it pulsed against her, changing her sigh to a soft moan that was trapped by the warm lips covering hers.

Diana felt her muscles relax completely. Her mind floated free of her body, noting with pleasure the warmth of the water surrounding her form, the heat where her body was pressed to Ben's; registering the touch of his fingers as they slipped beneath the skirt of her bathing costume to slide up her thigh, awakening an aching need deep within her.

A slow, pulsing warmth began to grow there, a sensation that possessed a will of its own. Diana felt her own will receding, being swept away in the force of these sensations. She felt powerless, lost, and suddenly afraid. Fear flooded her mind and stiffened her muscles, drawing her hands to the front of Ben's chest where she pushed, freeing her lips from his.

Ben was stunned for the moment by her abrupt move. Desire still pulsed through him, a need that urged him to lower his lips to her still parted ones, but when he looked into her eyes and saw the panic holding them open, he gathered the shreds of control remaining in him and simply continued to stare at her.

It was a struggle to think coherently, so clouded with passion was his brain, but as Ben's pulse returned to normal, he realized what a fool he had been. Granted, Diana McKenzie was tempting with her long, lean body, but she was also the daughter of the man he had come to trap and destroy. Any alliance between him and Diana was bound to be doomed, for it was obvious that Diana still harbored deep feelings for her father, despite the man's long absence and silence.

"Diana," he started, "I'm—"

"Please." She stopped him with a shake of her head, then moved back from his loosened grasp. "Let's not make this any worse with apologies or explanations," she went on. "It's late, and we both need rest in order to face the work we still have ahead of us. I want to change and return to the Heights to get some sleep."

With these words, Diana pushed herself back into a float and began to kick away from him; then she turned and began stroking smoothly and evenly toward the end of the pool. When she reached the shallow end, she turned back toward Ben, aware that her heart was filled with a wild blend of

emotion that mixed embarrassment over the way she had
so willingly accepted that kiss and pride in the fact that she
had just flawlessly executed everything Ben had taught her
about swimming.

Ben hadn't moved. She couldn't see his features, just his
face pale above the dark water. She called softly across the
pool, ''Thank you for the swimming lesson.''

With that she turned and began wading beneath the cement walkway. The air against her skin was suddenly very
cold, sending sharp, jolting shivers through her. She was
shaking badly when she reached the dressing area. As her
stiff fingers struggled to strip the sodden wool off her body,
she wondered just how much this reaction had to do with
the chill of the air and how much was a response to the
sudden ending of the warm embrace she had so recently
been wrapped in.

It's all for the best, she told herself. She had learned long
ago not to allow herself to become attracted to the men with
whom she worked and studied. She had become proud of
the skills she had developed in that area, of the ability to
deflect their longing looks without wounding their pride.

She was in control now, she told herself. The god Cupid
might have his arrows, but the goddess she had been named
for had been quite skilled with the bow as well, and imbued
with greater determination. As any student of mythology
knew, Eros had no dominion over the goddess of the hunt.
The goddess Diana had remained her own person, under
the power of none of the male deities, throughout eternity.

Diana's fingers slipped from the top button of her blouse
and another shiver shuddered through her as this last thought
crossed her mind. A spasm of fear gripped her, filling her
with a sense of emptiness that accompanied the thought of
an eternity of aloneness.

She frowned as she grasped the button anew and forced
it through the hole, mentally strengthening her resolve at

the same time. Remaining aloof and in control of her destiny was the only way to protect herself from the pain and longing that had haunted her childhood. She knew that as well as she knew the names of all the ancient gods and goddesses. And, she told herself as she drew on her coat, once she was launched in her career, she would be far too busy to notice whether she was alone or not.

Outside the ladies' dressing area, Ben was haunted by his own thoughts as he paced along the marble landing, berating himself for his earlier actions. He had warned himself against any involvement with Diana, even before he learned who her father was. His instant attraction to her had set off bells of alarm. True, he no longer believed her to be the cold, calculating woman he had first pegged her for, but it was her very vulnerability that made him regret his boldness in the pool.

Ben began walking away from the entrance to the ladies' dressing room. No, he corrected himself, regret wasn't the right word. How could any man fail to enjoy the pleasures he had tasted tonight? No, it was self-reproachment he felt, anger at himself for not seeing the danger of temptation before falling headlong into it and dragging Diana with him. She had suffered enough pain in her young life. Getting close to him would only bring her more.

He couldn't allow the desire he felt for her to interfere with the job he'd come to Sutro Heights to do. He knew Diana well enough now to recognize that behind the cool facade she assumed whenever her father's name arose lay the hope that perhaps the man's absence had been beyond his control, that he really did care for the daughter he had abandoned.

Daniel McKenzie was diabolically clever. He had managed to create an aura of respect while remaining a mystery. He hoped that Will was right, that Diana had kept those letters she had mentioned receiving from her father. If nothing else, they might at least shed some further light on the personality of the man he would be facing.

"Oh, you're still here."

Diana's quiet words made Ben spin around. Her wet hair, now twisted into a loose knot atop her head, gleamed blue-black in the dim light, framing a face that shone with the irridescent quality of fine, polished marble, and revealed just about the same amount of emotion as that cold stone. The return of her mask of control brought a strange tightness to his chest. Still, he smiled as he stepped out of the shadows.

"Of course I'm here," he said. "I have an agreement with Pete to see that the lights are out and everything is locked up whenever I stay late like this. Are you ready to go?"

Diana nodded. She grasped her skirt with both hands to lift it above her boots as she began ascending the steps next to him. She kept her eyes on the smooth marble as they rose to the arcade level, trying to ignore the feel of his hand riding lightly on the small of her back as he ushered her through the maze of exhibits.

The hint of chagrin Diana had seen on Ben's face moments ago haunted her. She had seen that same look in the pool, after she pulled away from his kiss. She was sure that he had been about to apologize for what had happened. She didn't want words of apology, especially since she realized she never should have allowed anything like that to happen. She just wanted to forget her foolish behavior and return their relationship to the one of mutual trust and respect between employer and employee that they had begun to forge before all these disturbing emotions surfaced.

She watched silently as Ben adjusted the apparatus that would lock the entryway door behind them and set the alarm that would ring up at the house if anyone were to try to break in during the night. The door shut with a click, and she turned and walked next to Ben as he started up the hill toward the entrance to the gardens.

Ben took Diana's hand as she turned onto the path leading to Sutro Heights' front door. Fear closed a firm hand over her heart, fear that Ben would pull her to him for another kiss, a deeper fear that she would go to him willingly. She tried to draw her hand away from his grasp, but his fingers tightened on her flesh as he whispered. "Let's go up the back way so we don't have to disturb anyone."

Diana nodded and let him guide her up the steep stone steps leading to the crenellated parapet above.

"It's a beautiful night."

Ben's hushed words made Diana stop and look up to find him looking out over the sea behind her. With his fingers still holding hers, she felt she had little choice but to see just what had captured his attention.

Beyond the dark silhouette formed by the roof of the Cliff House, the sea lay shimmering beneath a thin crescent moon that hung just above the horizon in the sapphire sky. It *was* a beautiful night, the kind that whispered of romance on the soft breath of the sea. For one moment, Diana felt herself growing warm as she imagined what would happen if Ben were to take her in his arms, and lower his lips to hers. The image had barely formed in her mind when her senses began to react, her lips parting and softening, her muscles tingling with waves of languid warmth.

"Diana," Ben began. The word was whispered in a low voice, a caress to her ears. Full-blown fear sprang to her heart, causing her chest to tighten in warning. The fantasy she had conjured up in her imagination could not come to pass. The feelings Ben awoke in her threatened the only power she possessed, the ability to remain remote and free of control. She started to step back, but before she could, Ben spoke again. "I want to talk about what happened in the pool. I feel an apology is in order."

Diana stiffened. She didn't want him to apologize, for if he did she would have to admit her own willing part in the passion that had flared between them. Her pride, and the fear coiling in her heart, would not stand for that. She shook her head.

"Well, you aren't going to get one," she said. She saw his surprise, but before he could question her, she went on. "I'm not one bit sorry for going down that slide. I know it was foolish of me to do such a thing when I'm not a strong swimmer yet, but I was willing to take that chance. I told you that I believe in living each day fully as it comes, searching for new experiences. So if I were to have come to grief, you would in no way have been responsible."

Her stiff stance, the way she had stepped back from him, revealed more clearly than any words that Diana McKenzie had no wish to discuss the desire they had shared.

Ben knew she was right, that his words of apology were best left unsaid. And yet he had this strange need to explain his actions, even though he wasn't sure he understood them himself. He opened his mouth to begin.

"Oh, there you two are."

Will Babcock's words floated across the parapet from the steps leading to the house. Ben watched Will approach, half-angry at the interruption, half-relieved that his friend's presence was most likely saving him from further embarrassing himself.

"I had hoped you might come back early tonight," Will said, "so that Diana could get some well-deserved rest." Will drew out a large watch, which he consulted. "It's after one-thirty, Ben. You're going to wear her out just like you did Brody."

Ben almost smiled at the reproach in the older man's voice. He felt Diana slip her wrist from his loose grasp as she stepped toward Will. "Don't blame Ben. We stopped working hours ago, but when he saw how stiff I was, he suggested that a swim in one of the warmer pools might help. So I took my first swimming lesson, and now I feel so relaxed that I know I'll fall asleep the moment my head hits the pillow. And I plan for that to happen very soon, so I shall say good night to you and to you, and head for my room.''

Ben stood next to Will in the center of the stone semi-circle, watching Diana's slim form glide away from them and disappear. When the soft click of the closing door echoed through the still night, Ben asked softly, ''Well, did you find the letters?''

''No.''

''Damn. I knew it was too much to hope that she had brought them with her.''

Will held up his right hand. ''We still don't know that. I never made it into her room, you see. Mr. Sutro was in a strange mood tonight, speaking about old accomplishments and people who have died. Emma warned us about these spells of his, remember? Anyway, by the time he was ready to retire, I was afraid to chance sneaking into Diana's room lest she come back while I was still in there. I'm sorry.''

Ben shook his head. ''No, don't be. I'd just as soon have a look at those letters myself, anyway. So . . . at lunchtime tomorrow I want you to take Diana down to the beach for a picnic. I'll slip into her room and see what I can learn.''

A bank of fog hovered above the ocean about a mile from shore, forming a thick, gray band between the pale blue sky and the green ocean, but not interfering at all with the sun warming the beach where Diana sat with Will the following afternoon.

Diana buried her bare toes more deeply in the warm sand as she let her eyelids fall shut; then she rested her elbows back against the plaid blanket and lifted her face to the sun.

The repeated roar of the waves crashing onto the shore blended with the warm air and her full stomach to make her drowsy, even as she told herself this was no time for a nap.

Although she had accomplished a fair amount of work on Vesuvius this morning, there was still a great deal of the mountain left to paint. Not only that, but Ben had mentioned that he wanted her to start work on a mosaic mural as soon as she was finished with the volcano. Just thinking of the tedious work involved in such an undertaking made her weary.

Also, she had slept poorly the night before. After she had gone to bed, her rest was disturbed by another dream of the goddess Diana, the glade, and the pool. It had begun much the same as the dreams she'd had on the train, with her aware that something was wrong as she approached her sanctuary. And again, once she had disrobed and stepped into the water, she had turned to see the man standing on the shore again. But this time as he stepped into the pond, she had not even tried to escape; she had simply stood in the center of the pool, paralyzed by the confusing emotions swirling through her.

And, as before, the dream had ended with the man taking her into his arms and kissing her. The sensation of warm lips and strong arms had been so powerful that even when she awoke with a start, she could still feel the man's touch.

"Don't let the sun mar that beautiful complexion of yours."

Will Babcock's gentle admonition made Diana obediently sit up so that her wide-brimmed straw hat once more shaded her face. The picnic lunch she had shared with the older man had been the perfect break in her day. As they munched on dainty sandwiches prepared by the chefs at the Cliff House, they had conversed easily, falling quickly into a relaxed banter that had brought laughter to her lips as the sea breeze brushed over them.

She found that she loved the ocean and everything about it: the salt air, the sounds of the gulls crying in the wind, the moist spray borne on the breeze, and the warmth of the sand beneath her feet. It had been Will who had suggested she remove not only her boots but her stockings as well, politely looking away as she did so.

But her hour in the sun was over. Diana gazed over the brilliant sea sparkling and frothing before her. Beyond the blue-green water the thick bank of fog formed a backdrop for the two sailing boats moving swiftly toward the Cliff House on her left, no doubt making for the safety of San Francisco Bay before the mist completely blanketed the sea. With a sigh, Diana reached for her boots.

"I suppose we should be getting back to the Baths," she said. "I think we've been gone more than the hour allotted us as it is. I can almost picture Ben staring at his pocket watch, whip in hand, as he waits for us."

Her playful smile froze when Ben's voice echoed deeply from behind her.

"Do you really think that I'm that difficult a taskmaster?"

_____ *Chapter Ten*

DIANA TURNED QUICKLY. Ben stood behind her at the edge of the plaid blanket, his dark gold hair ruffling in the breeze.

"Well, what else should the young lady think?" It was Will who spoke finally. "That speech you gave about time and work her first evening at Sutro Heights *was* rather stringent."

"You're right, I did sound like an ogre that evening. But I had no idea at that time how quickly Miss McKenzie could work, or how talented she was."

As Ben finished speaking he dropped slowly to his knees at the edge of the blanket, sitting back on his heels as he smiled at her. Diana felt her face grow warm despite the hat shading it from the sun as she found herself recalling those intimate moments she had shared with him in the warm waters of the darkened pool the night before.

She searched his face half-fearfully, half-hopefully, for some hint that his comment about her talent might refer to something beyond her artistic abilities. When she saw only straightforward admiration, she asked, "Then you feel secure that the exhibition will be completed by next Thursday?"

Ben nodded. "Unless some unforeseeable disaster visits us, we should be done with time to spare. In fact, I'm so confident about this that I've decided to take a midday break myself.''

''Oh.'' Diana reopened the picnic hamper. ''I wish we'd known. I'm afraid we've eaten everything we brought.''

''Not quite.'' Will reached into the basket and pulled out a shiny red apple and offered it to Ben.

''Well, this will be fine.'' Ben threw the apple lightly in the air, caught it, then took one bite as he winked down at his older friend.

''What I really need to do is stretch my legs. Sutro's engineer had me beneath the volcano room this morning showing me how he's progressing with the waterworks.'' Diana thought she saw him shudder slightly as he took a deep breath. ''It's mighty close quarters down there, and I'm in need of a dose of fresh air and a walk. Will you two join me?''

''Not I,'' Will replied as he shut the picnic basket. ''The quarryman is arriving today. He's delivering the rocks we're going to use to camouflage the barrels holding the trees in the Diana exhibit, as well as the slab of marble we're going to display the statue on. I'm to meet him in a half an hour. You two go on. I'll see that the blanket and basket get back where they belong.''

Ben's expression was a silent question and Diana wondered about the advisability of such a move. Several times that morning as she'd worked with her paints she had found herself remembering the undeniably pleasant, mind-numbing sensations that his kisses and caresses had stirred within her. Each time she had forced the thoughts away and fought the haunting physical memory of those moments.

She was not embarrassed by her response, only a little angry with herself. She had decided to limit all contact with Ben to purely businesslike interactions, but now, with the surf whispering behind her, the salty breeze ruffling the sleeves of her blouse, and the seagulls crying overhead, she found her resolve weakening. "I don't know," she said. "I still have quite a bit of work ahead of me."

"I have every confidence that you'll be done in time. If I didn't, I'd be cracking that whip this very minute."

The tickle of the sand beneath Diana's toes and the feel of the warm sun on her work-stiffened shoulders added their temptations to Ben's offer.

Moments later, dangling her boots by their laces, stockings tucked safely inside, Diana walked along the beach digging her heels into the soft sand. From time to time she watched a swell peak into a curl and crash into foaming disorder on the beach. As she walked she noticed the rippling patterns of dark sand on light on the shore beneath her feet, etched by waves that had slipped up during high tide. She was always aware of Ben Potter's smooth, long strides as he walked alongside her, munching on his apple.

The last bite of apple disappeared as Ben looked at Diana for the fifth time since starting down the beach in her company. The large straw hat she wore shaded her features, but it made little difference. If she wanted to hide her feelings from him, she would just fix her features in the porcelainlike mask of control that she assumed so easily.

Ben sighed. He wasn't quite sure why he'd insisted on this walk. After reading the letters Diana had saved from her father, seeing the care with which she had protected them in the velvet envelope, he'd felt a strange desire to talk to her about them, to attempt to reconcile the Daniel McKenzie he knew, arrogant and negligent employer, possible thief and murderer, with the man who had come off as a loving father in those letters.

Now he knew he couldn't do that, could not reveal that he had seen the unmistakable marks of tears on letters that had been folded and unfolded so often that some had torn in two. Diana deserved to deal with her father on her own, with no interference on his part, other than seeing that he did not cause her further pain.

Diana was laughing now, a light, lilting sound that drew his attention to her as she dodged a wave that had slipped up onto the shore.

"Watch out, Ben," she cried. "A sneaker wave is after you."

Ben saw that his boots were indeed in danger of being overrun by the moving water. He stepped away quickly to avoid the foamy edge of the wave, then looked up at Diana.

She stood in ankle-deep water, her divided skirt hitched halfway up her slender calves as water foamed about her ankles. She looked very young with her hair pulled loosely back and fastened at the nape of her neck, like a schoolgirl of perhaps fifteen. Loose tendrils of black hair tumbled past her cheeks, which were rounded above her smile and tinged with a delightful shade of pink.

"Am I in danger?" she teased. "Will told me these waves could sweep me out to sea."

Ben thought that if anything was going to sweep her anywhere it would be his arms, sweeping her off her feet and taking her someplace where she would be safe, away from the father she was waiting for, and the disappointment he feared she would face in that reunion. Instead, he answered.

"Not that one, Diana. But Will was right to tell you about those waves. Out on the cliffs they can be killers."

He looked toward the Cliff House perched high above the stretch of sand, while his body grew warm just thinking about being with Diana, alone, somewhere the shadow of Daniel McKenzie could not reach. But as far as he knew, that place didn't exist. He couldn't do any of the things he wanted to do with Diana, least of all pull her into another soul-stirring kiss like the one they'd shared the night before.

"I think we'd better go back now. As you said, we still have quite a lot of work to do."

Ben's gruff tone and abrupt manner confused Diana. She managed to nod her agreement; then she watched as he tossed his apple core into the center of a group of seagulls that had congregated on the beach. When he began walking, Diana stepped alongside of him, but she kept her eyes on the birds, watching them scramble in a flurry of feathers to claim the morsel. The victor flew away to a chorus of squawks and cries, and several gulls rose in the air to follow him. Diana saw that Ben appeared completely unaware of the birds' reaction to his little gift as he strode along.

Diana's face began to burn as she recalled the way she had laughed and pranced in the water, realizing how flirtatious her actions must have appeared. She glanced down at her toes, covered in damp sand, and imagined how unprofessional she must look, dangling her boots by their laces like a young girl half her age.

It feels wonderful, a small voice whispered. *It looks undignified*, came the reply, *unbecoming of a person who considers herself a scholar and a scientist*.

The muscles in Diana's shoulders protested as she straightened them and took a deep, steadying breath. She could not have Ben thinking she was trying to entice him in any way. She turned to him slowly, her face set in solemn lines, her voice carefully cool.

"Ben? Were you serious earlier when you complimented my abilities as an artist?" she asked.

"Of course." He looked down at her. "You're a very talented artist."

"Thank you." She gave him a brief nod. "But I wasn't searching for a compliment. I want to know if you would consider recommending my work."

Ben stared at her a moment, then narrowed his eyes. "To

someone like Professor Harrington, perhaps?''

Ben's sharp tone made Diana's jaw stiffen as she remembered his previous complaints about Professor Harrington. "Exactly," she replied. "I understand that we will all be dining with him and some of his associates tonight at the Cliff House."

"Yes, we will. And I suppose you plan to approach him to ask for a position with his next expedition?"

Ben's tone was openly hostile now. Diana frowned. "I believe I mentioned that he is part of the reason I came all the way out here. The professor spoke to my class last year, you see, and I was very impressed with his knowledge of Roman antiquities. Yes, I want to work for him."

"On a dig? You wouldn't last one week. The sun would raise a thousand blisters on that white skin of yours, and the dust—"

"We've discussed this before, I believe." Diana raised her voice to interrupt his speech. "I know all about the dust and the heat. Just because *you* don't enjoy fieldwork doesn't—"

"I never said I didn't like fieldwork." They had crossed the sand to stand near the road leading to the Cliff House. Several carriages filled with sunseekers rattled up the steep incline toward the popular summer attraction as Ben stopped and turned to Diana. "I miss it dreadfully."

Diana thought he was about to say more. Instead, he continued walking, his heels digging deep divots in the sand as Diana hurried to catch up with him.

They marched along in silence for several moments, then Ben's steps began to slow. "Don't misunderstand me. I enjoy my work at the museum. I find it infinitely satisfying to see that these items are preserved and displayed properly. But sometimes I do miss the excitement of a dig. Nothing can match the fever that runs through a company when a new find is uncovered."

"You can always go back into the field, can't you?" Diana asked.

As they reached the road, he turned to her. "It's very hard to be a member of a field crew when everyone knows you are unable to go into even the most open cave or tunnel."

Diana saw the fear hovering behind his scowl, and fought off a shiver as she remembered Will's words. Ben had been buried once, had almost died. She shook her head. "I'm sorry. I forgot. But it's not always necessary to work in enclosed areas. Many digs—"

"—are open pits," Ben finished. "I know. But you can't choose your sites and expect to keep any kind of respect." He shook his head. "It doesn't matter. As I said, I enjoy what I do. And don't worry about Harrington. I'll most certainly sing your praises to him tonight, if that is what you wish, but I don't want to discuss the matter any further."

With that Ben began to climb the steep road, leaving Diana to sit in the sand and don her stockings and boots before following him to the Baths, where Vesuvius awaited her ministrations.

Beneath the glittering chandeliers in one of the Cliff House's smaller banquet rooms, Diana smiled at Justin Harrington. Ben's earlier anger, and the sick, twisting feeling it had left in her stomach, were all but forgotten in the excitement of the moment.

She had dressed carefully for this dinner, donning a new gown of rose satin. The low neckline was trimmed with strings of pearls that rose and fell in a scallop design that continued across the edge of the short cap sleeves and the hem of the bell-shaped skirt.

The woman she had seen in her mirror up at Sutro Heights didn't look a thing like an archaeologist, and that was exactly as she had planned. The information she had assimilated in her university career would serve her in good stead once she obtained a position in her field, but she had decided that other skills, reluctantly acquired at the series of finishing schools her grandfather had forced her to attend, would be more useful in gaining the attention of the man she wanted to impress.

And she had been right in that assumption, for Professor Harrington had noticed her immediately. After Emma introduced them, the professor had spoken to Diana for several moments before dinner, then asked her to be his partner during the magnificent feast served up by the Cliff House kitchen. Diana had carefully bided her time, waiting until the third course to mention her involvement in the preparations for the Pompeii exhibit, then introducing her interest in archaeology.

Now, as they danced, the professor took up the topic again. "I must say, I wasn't even aware that Daniel McKenzie *had* a daughter, let alone one who yearned to follow in his footsteps."

The mention of her father made Diana's back straighten slightly, but she managed to keep her lips curving upward as she replied, "Well, to be honest, very few people are aware of this. My father and I haven't been close, you see. He has been busy pursuing the past, while I have been occupied with preparing myself for a career of my own."

"Ah, but your future will also involve the past. Is there any culture or time period that you particularly wish to investigate?"

Diana hesitated a moment. She was aware that, like her father, Justin Harrington had spent much of his career uncovering the roots of Roman culture. This was her main area of interest, too, but she was afraid that to state this would make her sound overeager, and place her on a par with other supplicants looking for a spot with his company.

"Well," she began, "I started out pursuing the same general areas as my father. However, his interest in ancient Rome has appeared to have narrowed down to a fascination with the little-known cult of Diana worship. I have found myself drawn toward the Greek roots underpinning the early Roman culture."

Harrington pulled Diana in a sharp twirl as the music floated through the room. "Interesting. I published a paper on just that subject not too long ago. Perhaps you are familiar with my theories regarding the sources of the myths created by the Greeks and adopted by the Romans?"

At Diana's answering nod the man began to discuss the dissertation he had published the previous year. Diana listened with half an ear as she reflected that if the man's secretary had indeed written the paper as Ben had suggested, Harrington would hardly be able to discuss it in such detail.

Even as she listened to the man's deep voice, Diana was aware of Ben standing by the wall opposite the bank of windows overlooking Seal Rock. She had been conscious of his eyes on her all evening, unable to forget the haunted look she'd seen in them this afternoon when he had spoken of his dread of closed-in places.

More than once during the afternoon she had wanted to go to him, to apologize for probing into an area that was none of her business, but she hadn't been able to find the words. Now, without willing it, she found herself looking at Ben, watching him lift a glass of amber liquid to his lips as he leaned against the wall papered in pale green and cream. He looked quite handsome in his formal black cutaway jacket. The stiff white collar of his pin-tucked shirt enhanced the sun-warmed color of his skin, and his deep frown accentuated the lines radiating from the corners of the dark eyes that she found so strangely attractive.

"I find it fascinating, don't you, that so many of the myths transfer from one culture to another with little to differentiate them other than the name of the deity?''

Harrington's question caught Diana's attention, and with a slight jerk of her head that she prayed was not obvious to the professor, she forced her attention back to his words.

Ben watched Diana whirl across the polished floor between the long rows of linen-draped tables. The pink satin dress clung to her slender waist and gently curving hips, then swung out behind her as she glided across the floor in the arms of a man he hated almost as deeply as Daniel McKenzie.

He noted the expression of rapt attention on Diana's features. She was obviously listening carefully to what the man was saying. Ben told himself that if the man were anyone other than Justin Harrington, he wouldn't feel so angry, or so frustrated.

He had only himself to blame, of course. After leaving Diana so abruptly on the beach, he should have tried to smooth things over with her. Instead, they had finished the afternoon working in studied silence. When he went in to see the almost completed volcano, he had only given her the faintest of praise. It was hardly surprising that she had avoided him once they reached the Cliff House.

Ben continued to watch Harrington, noting that at forty the man was still lean and fit. His angular face was tanned deeply, accenting the rugged edges softened only slightly by the deep lines fanning out from the corners of his eyes. His black hair glinted in the light of the many-faceted chandelier overhead, touched at the temples by a slight frost of silver that added to the distinguished appearance that so easily enthralled neophytes like Diana.

''Ben, we need to talk.'' The softly spoken words made Ben turn quickly to see Will standing next to him, his warm brown eyes narrowing behind his glasses. Ian stood to Will's left, red hair parted and carefully pomaded, his mustache twirled to sharp points.

Ben's lips twitched into a cynical smile. "What's there to talk about? The fact that the spider has caught another fly?"

Will turned to Ben quickly. "I don't think so. Diana is far too intelligent to be fooled by the likes of Harrington, at least for long."

"I'm not sure intelligence has anything to do with this. Diana has heard Harrington speak. You and I both know how mesmerizing he can be onstage. I've seen him work up society matrons to the point where they are ready and willing to follow him into the hills of Rome, practically begging to dirty their pampered hands in the search for the keys to the past."

Will added, "All offers, are, of course, declined."

"Of course. The only thing he wants from them is their money, which they obligingly hand over," Ben replied.

"Would he know whether Diana has money or not?"

"I doubt that matters to him. She is young and beautiful, a perfect audience for his charms." Ben's voice dropped to a harsh whisper. "And if you will notice, Harrington has assumed his stage persona. If Diana isn't careful, he will get anything he wants from her."

"Then we will have to arrange things so that she sees him for the charlatan he is, won't we?" Will snapped.

Ben almost smiled at Will's fierce tone. "I think that could be arranged," he replied. "Speaking as one who has been fooled by the professor, I think I can find a way to draw the veil of illusion away." He paused, his face clouded by a deep scowl. "I just hope I can manage this before Diana is hurt in any way."

"Speaking of Diana, did you find the letters?" Ian stepped forward as he spoke. Ben took a sip of bourbon and nodded. "Yes, and they were very interesting. Her father only wrote about every three months, in a small, cramped hand. Each letter was only about four pages long, but in those four pages Daniel McKenzie told his small daughter all about each dig he worked, about his successes and failures, and about his discoveries, both large and small.''

"Hence Diana's interest in archaeology," Will stated, then asked, "What about specifics? Was there anything about his interest in the mythology of the goddess Diana?''

"Only once. In his last letter McKenzie encouraged Diana to emulate the goddess she was named for, to be strong of will and spirit, and, of course, he referred to the small statue of Diana and the stag he was sending as her birthday present.'' Ben remembered the way the small figure had been arranged in the center of the desk, in a place of honor; then he went on. "It's strange. Daniel McKenzie is famous for the research he's done on this obscure deity; yet in the letters, McKenzie's interest in the goddess of the moon comes across as just that, an interest, not the obsessive devotion his latest papers have revealed.''

"Well, what I'm hearing from you, Potter, seems to give more weight to my theory, doesn't it?'' Ian asked.

"You mean that the thief we are after isn't Daniel McKenzie after all?''

"Yes. From what you've said tonight, my suspicions rest even more heavily on our friend Harrington.''

"Look, it's true that I've heard rumors of Harrington cheating his employees," Ben began, "and as much as I'd like to prove that Justin Harrington is involved in this, I—''

A jab from Will's right elbow made Ben stop speaking. In the silence following his half-uttered sentence he realized that the music had ended. He turned instinctively toward the man he had been discussing and saw that Diana and Harrington were indeed walking his way, but still safely out of earshot. As Ben looked at him, Harrington acknowledged his presence.

"Well, Potter, it's good to see you again. How is this Pompeii exhibit I've heard so much about coming along?"

"Well enough," Ben replied.

"I understand that Miss McKenzie has been working with you on several of the displays and that you are quite happy with her work. She was just telling me that she wishes to begin her apprenticeship in our field, so I'm anxious to see what she has done. I must say, if she is half as good an artist as she is a dancer, I will be most happy to consider taking her into my employ."

Ben looked at Diana, saw her cheeks turn pink, and felt a gripping fist close over his insides. "Since I've never danced with Miss McKenzie," he replied evenly, "I'm afraid I can't help you with that comparison. I will tell you that she is a very talented artist. That, combined with the degree she possesses in archaeology, should make her invaluable to any expedition."

Diana felt his warm words wash over her. She had worried about this moment, feared that Ben would refuse to give his recommendation of her to someone he so obviously disliked. Now she felt ashamed of herself for expecting such a mean-spirited response.

"I think you are right." Harrington's words brought Diana back from her guilty thoughts. She turned to the older man as he spoke again. "I'm impressed with the depth of knowledge she displayed in the short time we've conversed. Few men, and even fewer women, have the self-discipline to follow a career in our field of endeavor. Oh, many find the items we uncover fascinating, but for the most part they regard them as trinkets; they don't regard them as treasured keys into the secrets of the past. It's the same with Greek and Roman mythology. The myths are repeated as one might retell a fairy tale, without any comprehension of the powers they are dealing with."

Diana questioned, "Powers, Professor?"

"Oh, please, don't be so formal, my dear. All my colleagues address me as Justin, and I request that you do the same."

Diana controlled her features as she nodded, trying to hide the excitement bubbling up inside her. His colleague. Justin Harrington wanted *her* to address him as a colleague. Her head felt suddenly light as it occurred to her that this might very well mean that her wish for a job on his next dig would be granted, and she had to force herself to concentrate on his next words.

"Surely you are aware of the strong influences the ancient deities hold over us, even today? You are a perfect example of what I mean. Diana, the goddess whose name you bear, has obviously taken you in hand, molded you into the strong-willed person you are."

The excitement bubbling within Diana died as Harrington's words confused her. "Molded me?" Diana shook her head. "Influenced me, perhaps. I am aware that of all the goddesses, Diana had the most control over her life. This is a position I have aimed for also, but I am the one who has decided what to do with my life."

"Are you sure of that?" Harrington asked. "Think of the many instances in Greek and Roman mythology where humans thought they were in control of their destiny, when in actuality their lives were steered by the gods, whether it be Neptune stirring the seas or Aphrodite casting spells of love. Take yourself, for example. Jupiter gave his daughter Diana a gift of a bow and arrows, and encouraged her to use them. Your father gave you the gift of knowledge and the freedom to follow your own path."

Diana considered the man's words a moment, acknowledging the parallels he had outlined. A tiny chill raced down her spine as she considered the idea that her father's abandonment of her might have somehow been fated by the gods.

One second later the logical portion of her mind whispered that this was poppycock. Mythology was full of fascinating stories, used by early man to explain things he didn't understand. There was no such thing as fate. There were no avenging or rewarding gods on some distant mount watching her every move, helping or hindering her. It was up to each individual to make his or her own way in life.

But, she told herself, this was not the time to debate the professor's theory. There would be time for that later, once she was in his employ and had had a chance to prove her abilities as an archaeologist. So Diana replied, "Well, Prof— Justin, that is a very interesting notion. I shall have to give it more thought."

"And well you might. The goddess of the moon, for all her beauty and power, led a very lonely life, if you remember. She enjoyed great independence, yes, but at the cost of her—shall we say—more romantic side. If you will recall, the goddess frightened away or destroyed every man that attempted to get close to her. I would advise any young woman so obviously influenced by Diana to take care to nourish her softer side in order to avoid a similar fate."

Diana recalled the many times she had purposely discouraged the attentions of various men. Perhaps there was something to the man's theory, and she was destined to remain aloof from men, like her namesake. Avoiding romance had come so very easily to her; it had seemed only natural to her to spurn the attentions of the men who approached her, for she found their attitude of superiority rude and unappealing. Not until she met Ben had she—

Diana's mind stopped at the thought of Ben as a wave of warmth washed through her. Ben was different. In his presence she felt alive, supremely feminine. His kisses inflamed her, awoke emotions and sensations she had never known. And yet what had she done each time he had pulled her into his arms? She had pushed him away, because he threatened her sense of purpose.

"Harrington," Ben said with a shake of his head, "I can't believe you are still trying to sell that ridiculous theory of yours."

_____ *Chapter Eleven*

"THAT'S TYPICAL of you, Potter, to laugh at something just because it's beyond your understanding." Harrington looked wryly at Ben. "It's interesting, too, considering that I seem to remember a time when you found my theories most fascinating. I suppose that's what happens when you allow yourself to be locked up in a museum, dating and arranging artifacts instead of exploring on your own."

The professor's taunting words made Diana glance quickly at Ben. "Harrington, when I expressed interest in your hypothesis, you were promoting the idea that the Greek and Roman deities represent various personality types, that the myths were parables of sorts, created by the wiser men of the time to instruct the people. That is a far cry from your current position that these entities still exist on some plane, actually influencing individuals. Do you really expect thinking men and women to accept the idea that sheet-draped deities sit atop some cloud-enshrouded mountain and control the actions of the puny humans below?"

The tone of ridicule in Ben's voice echoed in the silence that followed his question. Diana watched the two men carefully, her muscles growing more taut as the two men glared at each other. Out of the corner of her eye, she saw Will turn and walk toward the dessert-laden table near the windows. When she saw Ian follow, her hands squeezed into impotent fists, frustrated by the knowledge that she could not escape as they had, nervous that the tension between Ben and Harrington would erupt into a major argument.

"Harrington. Come here a moment, will you?" Adolph Sutro's booming voice broke the strained silence. "Langstrom here wants to know more about that dig you have planned in the south of England."

Diana took a deep, relieved breath as the professor turned his head in Sutro's direction and nodded his intention to comply with his request. Then he said to Diana, "I hope you and I have a chance to speak again tonight. I would like to present my theories more clearly and to hear your thoughts on my concepts."

Diana turned to Ben as Harrington left and asked, "What in heaven's name made you do that?"

"Do what?"

"You know perfectly well what. You purposely started an argument with that man."

"Yes, I suppose I did." Slowly, he smiled. "The man is a pompous ass, and I can't seem to resist provoking him into a demonstration of that fact when the opportunity presents itself. Stick around; it should happen quite frequently."

Small lines fanned out from his gleaming dark eyes in a way that would normally have made Diana's knees weaken and her heart pound. Now her blood raced with growing anger. She had made it very clear how important it was that she make a good impression on Harrington. Instead of honoring this need, Ben had drawn the man into a senseless argument that had placed her in a very awkward position.

"I see," she said quietly. "Would you mind telling me just what makes him an ass?" She stared evenly into Ben's eyes as she spoke in a soft, chilling voice. "Is it because he happens to hold a different view about something than you do? For if that is the case, then I would say that you also resemble that maligned beast of burden.''

"If you are thinking that Harrington and I represent different sides of the same coin, you're wrong. As far as I'm concerned, the man can believe anything he wants. What I object to is the insufferably pretentious way he glories in using his intellectual aura to force his ideas on others and make them feel inferior.''

Ben paused. He cocked his head slightly. ''I don't understand why you are angry with me. I received the definite impression that you somehow objected to the idea that some goddess is controlling your life.''

Diana lifted her chin. ''Well, yes, but—''

''—but you don't want to jeopardize your chance at a job with him by admitting that,'' Ben broke in. ''Fine. I understand. Just be careful, though. I've found that when you compromise a position, even a little, the rest of your life can be threatened. If you don't watch yourself, you could find yourself beginning to accept his ideas.''

Diana found her anger fading as she acknowledged the truth in his words. She glanced down at the green and beige rug beneath her feet as she realized that despite her intellectual objections to Harrington's suggestions, something in his theory had struck a chord deep inside her, awakening certain fears she had tried to ignore.

''What is it, Diana?'' Ben's voice was deep and soft as he placed his hand under her chin and tilted her face up. He looked into her eyes for several seconds before he leaned toward her. ''What's wrong?''

Diana drew in a shaky breath. ''Nothing, really. You're right, of course. I don't believe that Jupiter is sitting atop a mountain hurling thunderbolts down at us in the form of everyday problems.''

''But?'' Ben's eyes narrowed, gazing into Diana's with

such intensity that she was certain he could read her thoughts.

She shrugged. "But I have to admit that his comparison of my life to that of Diana's does have some validity."

"Oh?"

The moment these words escaped her mouth, Diana regretted it. She searched her mind for a way to lightly explain them away, but with Ben standing so near her, filling her senses with his presence, she found it suddenly difficult to think at all. Finally she shrugged and forced a casual note into her reply. "It's just that I have always felt that I did have a strange connection with Diana. Other than the role she was purported to play as patroness of midwives and birth, Diana displayed few traditional feminine traits. Things like sewing and cooking have never interested me. I'd rather catch a fish than prepare it for dinner. I'm afraid that I really don't function well as a woman."

Diana felt her face grow warm as she spoke these last words.

"Since when?" he asked, his dark eyes glinting.

Diana's heart began to pound as she remembered the teasing light in his eyes the evening before in the Baths, where his kisses had stirred to life a female energy that she had never suspected existed within her. Not willing to admit this she tried to restate her thoughts. "Well, you see, I've always thought of myself as logical and practical. The more feminine sensibilities and responses seem to be lacking in my makeup."

Ben bent forward a few inches until his face was quite near Diana's and said, "Oh, I wouldn't say that at all. Certainly your artistic abilities indicate your sensitivity to beauty. And speaking from a more personal point of view, I would say your feminine reactions are very well developed. Those responses were most likely just waiting for the right circumstances in which to awaken."

Diana drew in a slow, shuddering breath. The room grew almost unbearably hot as unwanted emotions and strange physical reactions intermingled. Once more her hands curled into fists at her sides as she mustered shreds of self-control.

Her thoughts warred with the strange part of her mind that urged her to turn to Ben, to utilize the little-used arts of flirtation she had learned so long ago, and to incite the same spark in Ben that had caused him to pull her into his arms before.

Her only cogent thought was that she had to escape, to remove herself from Ben's presence, to find some room to breathe. This had always been her response to confusion— to seek solitude in which to order her thoughts. So, after taking a deep breath, she glanced at Ben and spoke abruptly.

"Ben, if you'll excuse me, I need to speak to Emma about several things. She mentioned that she and George would be leaving early tonight, and I just saw them step into the hallway. I want to catch her before they depart."

Why had he said those things to her? It was obvious that his words had embarrassed her, reminded her of something she wanted to forget. Moreover, what had passed between them the night before was an occurrence that he had vowed would not take place again. So why had he made such a blatant reference to it?

Because Diana McKenzie was an impossibly desirable woman, he answered himself. Her intelligence drew him to her almost as much as the rousing memory of her slender form sliding along his, warm water lapping about him; almost as much as the alluring feel of her lips parting to receive his kiss.

The muscles in his shoulders ached with sudden tension. None of this mattered. Until the situation with her father was settled, he told himself, the desire that flashed between them was potentially poison for Diana.

"Ben." The low, urgent voice made Ben turn. He looked

past Will's glasses into brown eyes dark with concern as the man spoke again. "Do you think starting an argument with Justin Harrington was the wise thing to do? Diana seems to be quite impressed with the man."

This was the second time in ten minutes that Ben had been questioned about his actions. Anger brought sharp words to Ben's lips, words he forced himself to bite back. Will was right, of course, as had been Diana, to point out his indiscretion. But at least he could try to explain to Will. "What would you have me do?" he asked. "Just stand by and let Diana fall under his influence the way Sarah did?"

Will shook his head. "Diana is more intelligent than that. Besides, as I told you before, Diana is not looking to go somewhere on the tailcoats of some man. She is looking for employment, not a champion."

"Perhaps." Ben shrugged. Diana was looking for a lot of things—a career, a father. What she wasn't looking for was the passion that had flared between the two of them. Yet, when he compared that danger to the disappointment he feared awaited her in her reunion with her father, and the peril he knew resided in employment with Justin Harrington, he had to say that an entanglement with him was the least threatening of the three.

"What did you say to her to make her run off like that?"

Will's question broke into Ben's thoughts. "Nothing. She went out into the hallway to talk to Emma about something."

Will replied, "No, she didn't. Emma is over in the corner, speaking with her husband."

Ben saw Emma deep in conversation with the large, portly gentleman with the light gray hair and beard who had been introduced to him earlier as Dr. George Merritt.

"Here." Ben handed his empty glass to Will. "I think I'd better see what Diana's up to."

Ben heard someone call his name as he strode across the

floor, but he didn't take his eyes off the door Diana had exited through. He stopped in the center of the darkly paneled hallway, and looked up one side and down the other but saw nothing except a light spilling out onto the patterned rug from the small window leading to the cloakroom. Ben crossed the hall, coming upon the uniformed attendant.

"Did you see a young woman out in the hall a few moments ago?" he asked. "She's tall and slender with black hair, wearing a pink dress trimmed with pearls."

The tiny woman dipped her head in a nervous nod. "Yes, sir. I just gave a coat to a young lady fitting that description not more than five minutes ago."

She opened her mouth to say more, but by that time Ben was halfway to the stairway at the end of the hall.

Billowing clouds of fog borne on gusts of salty air blew across the black road as Diana neared the entrance to the Sutro Baths. Her nearly frozen hands gripped the front edges of her black coat tightly, holding the collar around her neck in an attempt to keep out the mist swirling around her. The Cliff House lay not far behind her, but already a damp chill had settled into her bones that even her brisk steps had no power to warm.

Yet, despite the shivering sensation gripping her limbs, a deep heat burned in the lower regions of her stomach as the emotions ignited by Ben's words continued to swirl through her, clouding her thoughts despite the bracing air. She was only vaguely aware of the entrance to the Baths looming on her left until a clicking noise made her jump and stop in her tracks, then peer into the shadows under the peaked roof of the entryway. She could just make out the shadow of a man. She felt as if her heart stopped beating and didn't start again until the man stepped forward, one foot dragging slightly as he moved.

Diana's pent-up breath eased past her lips as she recognized the caretaker. "Pete," she whispered. When the man stopped in midstep, she went on quickly. "It's Miss McKenzie. I hope I didn't startle you."

"Oh, of course not." The tenor voice trembled only slightly. The man cleared his throat as he stepped forward. "I don't see many people out here at this time of night, of course."

"No, certainly not." Diana smiled. "Are you locking up for the night?"

"Yep. It's all ready for tomorrow. Floor swept, clean swimming costumes in place, and fresh water pumped into the pools. And, of course, the alarm is set."

As the watchman mentioned the pools, Diana was suddenly assailed by the image of the solitude that awaited in the warm water of the Baths. She took a step toward Pete as a plan formed in her mind, then spoke quickly to hush the voice that whispered against the folly of her scheme. "Well, I'm glad I caught you before you left. I was just discussing the opening of the exhibit that Ben and I are working on with Professor Harrington. The professor wanted to see the drawings we have of the layout. Ben left it in the volcano room and I offered to come fetch it, since the men are involved in complicated discussions of the upcoming festivities. Could you let me in so I can get them?"

"I can do more than that. I can escort you there and back again."

Diana's muscles tightened. That wasn't going to do at all. "Oh, that's not necessary. I know your wife is waiting for you. Ben showed me how to lock up from the inside and how to set the alarm, so if you just let me back in, I'll run in and out again. I promise to make sure that everything is secure when I leave."

She had stepped closer to Pete as she spoke and saw a worried expression etch deep wrinkles across his forehead. "Well, if you insist," he said slowly. "Myrtle did say she'd have a big beefsteak waiting for me, cooked rare just the way I like it. I keep an extra lantern just inside the door, so you don't need to switch on all the lights. I'll fetch the lamp for you and lock you in.''

Several moments later, as Pete handed her the glowing lantern, he narrowed his eyes at her. "Now, you're sure you know your way around, aren't you? Not afraid of gorillas chasing you?''

Diana grinned into his shining eyes. "No, Pete. I've made my peace with the creatures in here, and I've been in and out enough times to find my way. Now go on to your dinner, and don't worry about me.''

She walked toward the promenade deck, smiling as she heard the door shut behind her, followed by the rattling sound that told her Pete was checking to see that the lock had held. She took a deep breath, then released it slowly. She was safe now. Alone, where she could let her thoughts sort themselves out.

This feeling of security stayed with her in spite of the strange shadows cast by the lantern's light as it fell on the various plants and display cases she passed on her way to the broad marble staircase leading down to the Baths. When she reached the ladies' dressing area, she didn't even bother to turn on the light there, for she had decided that she was not going to burden herself with one of the heavy wool swimming dresses tonight.

Now that she was inside, Diana could feel the wine she had imbibed warming her blood, so that even when she removed her wool coat, her skin felt uncomfortably hot.

There was no one else in the building, no one to see her; therefore, she could see no reason why her movements should be hampered in any way. In the dim light she stripped down completely; then, after removing her chemise and stockings, she hesitated as she stared down at her pale flesh. With a sigh she stepped back into her knee-length drawers and slipped into her muslin corset cover, buttoning it quickly.

How long, she wondered as she held the lantern up and walked toward the entry to the pool, would a well-brought-up young lady continue to clothe herself for a swim if she were stranded alone on a deserted island?

Once Diana reached the entrance to the ladies' pool, she watched the shallow water lapping up onto the step below. The lantern's rays lit a narrow path of clear, translucent liquid, bordered by dark waters that beckoned her forward, urged her to place first one foot, then the other into the shifting liquid.

The warm water eased up over her calves as she passed beneath the cement walkway, sending the promise of further warmth flowing up through her. She paused to place the partially shuttered lantern on the edge of the walkway, making the water sparkle black and silver in the dim light.

The Baths were so large, and so very silent. Still, she had the strangest feeling that she was being watched.

A second later she shook away her fears. Pete wouldn't have left without checking every nook and cranny thoroughly, and she had distinctly heard him lock the door after him. She had the place to herself, and all the time she wished to relax in the warm, beckoning liquid. She smiled in anticipation as she stretched her hands out in front of her and leaned forward to slide into the water.

Up on the promenade deck, Ben stood at the railing and gazed at the pale form illuminated by the single light. He had been surprised and puzzled when he overtook Pete walking up the road toward the entrance to the Heights and learned that Diana was in here. Now he was simply stunned as he watched Diana's white arms arc in and out of the water as her slim, pale legs kicked up a tiny foam behind her.

Her slender curves glinted as she cut through the water,

and his earlier resolve regarding future contact with her faded in the face of the desire rushing through him. After watching her one more moment, he turned to make his way through the dark but familiar paths toward the entrance to the pool area, removing his jacket as he walked.

Diana was breathless and elated when she came up for air after her first swim across the center of the pool. She had been careful to stay in a depth that would allow her to touch the bottom, and now she stood in water that just covered her breasts. Pushing her hair out of her face, she dipped her head back into the water, then straightened, half closing her eyes as her hair streamed down over her shoulders to float around her like a dark cloud.

The deep end of the pool looked suddenly black and threatening beyond the reach of the lantern's weak rays, while the warm water surrounding Diana cushioned and supported her. She had become even more confident in her ability to swim, but for some reason she had no desire to venture into any deeper water. Instead, she leaned back and let herself float, her feet kicking ever so slightly, her hair caressing the arms she held out to her sides as Ben had taught her.

Her swim had cleared her mind somewhat, and now she found she could let her thoughts drift to the kisses she had shared with Ben without feeling threatened. She found that in a strange way these memories comforted her, took some of the sting out of Professor Harrington's hint that she was overly influenced by the goddess of the hunt, doomed to a path of loneliness.

Diana the goddess had possessed unerring aim, which seemed to be echoed in the ability of Diana the woman to determine her own goals and meet them. But never, in all the mythology of that goddess, was there ever a reference to the goddess allowing any man to have any influence over her.

There was no denying the effect Ben had on her, however. The warmth of his remembered caress lived in the water surrounding her, supporting her. Was this so very dangerous? Diana the goddess insisted on being worshipped, as did all the other Roman deities. Could not a mortal wish to be desired?

Diana let her feet drop to the bottom of the pool and stood in knee-deep water. It was heady wine in that cup Ben had coerced her to drink from, and she could no longer deny she wanted to taste more. She knew without much thought that there was no logic to this desire; it just was.

Diana prepared to stroke across the pool once more, when a slight motion made her stop so quickly that the swatch of hair flowing down over her left breast whipped in a semicircle, sending droplets of water into the pool as it circled around to her back.

Diana didn't move as she saw the form standing beneath the lantern, silhouetted against the light.

Cold shards of fear shot through her as she noticed the powerful shoulders and chest that tapered down to a narrow waist. As the figure began to walk toward her, the dim light glanced off his arm, revealing the hard curves of his muscles. A flash of pale skin at his hip caught Diana's eyes, and her indrawn breath hissed past her teeth as she realized that the man was completely unclothed.

"Diana."

Her name was spoken in a low voice. She recognized it immediately, but her panic only grew. She was not ready to see Ben yet, to be with him here, like this. Suddenly the desire she had only moments before acknowledged now filled her with terror.

Diana tried to swim away, and even as she did so, she knew what would happen next. Strong fingers closed over her wrist, halting her escape, and before she could draw a breath she felt herself pulled backward through the water. Strong arms encircled her waist, twisted her around, and set her on her feet in water that reached the tops of her thighs, forcing her to look up.

She knew there was no point in struggling. He was too strong, and her will was as weak as her trembling knees. Diana looked at Ben, and a deep ache grew within her as her breasts lightly touched his chest and her nipples hardened with desire. Yet when he placed his hands on her upper arms and bent toward her, fear and uncertainty made her muscles suddenly stiffen.

Ben felt the flesh beneath his fingers tighten. He was aware now that she was not naked, as he had assumed when he viewed her from above. But the thin, wet muslin plastered to her skin was nothing but a scant veil that accentuated rather than hid the charms of her pale curves.

He could feel his desire increase with every heartbeat, but the frightened look in Diana's eyes made him hesitate. When he recalled her worries that she lacked somehow in feminine charms, he wanted to laugh.

But he didn't. He was very aware how innocent she was in these matters, and although he had every intention of tutoring away this lack of knowledge, the teacher in him recognized a pupil that needed reassurance before proper attention could be given to her lessons.

And he wanted Diana's full attention. He lowered his eyebrows to a deep scowl and forced a harsh tone into his voice. "I thought I told you never to swim by yourself."

_____ Chapter Twelve

HIS DOMINEERING TONE, so similar to her grandfather's, penetrated the mixture of fear and surprise swirling through her brain, making her pull away from his grasp. She glared at him as she stepped back into deeper water. "You are not my guardian," she said. "I am free to make my own choices."

"Oh, and do you always make such foolish ones?"

Diana, peering through the dim light from the lantern, thought she saw Ben smile. Still, she eased herself back slightly, feeling the water slip up over her hips to lap at her waist. "There is nothing foolish about this swim. I have been very careful not to venture into the deep end."

Ben's eyes narrowed as he moved nearer. "I see. I suppose you didn't think that someone might find you here. Pete is very conscientious, you know, and he's been very protective of you ever since that first night you met. What if he had decided to come and check on you?"

He paused, then spoke again, his voice deeper, harsher. "Or suppose Pete had met someone other than me on the road looking for you? Would you like Will to see you unclothed, or Harrington, perhaps?"

All traces of a smile disappeared as Ben emphasized the professor's name. He stepped closer to Diana. She tried to move back, but his hand grasped her wrist, forcing her to stand her ground a scant two feet away from his suddenly threatening presence. She shook her head and swallowed before she could speak.

"I'm not unclothed."

She had hoped to sound defiant, but her words echoed with a childish petulance. Ben's fingers tightened around her wrist, and he remarked, "You might as well be."

His gaze dropped from hers. Diana saw him stare at her breasts. Aware that the water had rendered her muslin camisole nearly transparent, she felt an embarrassed blush rush through her, heating every inch of her skin. Anger followed in its wake—anger at herself for being caught in such a predicament, and far greater anger at Ben for behaving like something less than a gentleman by blatantly commenting.

She performed her next motion without conscious thought. She cupped her free hand and flung her arm up, splashing water into his face.

As he wiped the moisture from his face, Diana remembered the salt in the water, recalled it's sting, and felt immediate remorse from her action. "I'm sorry." She spoke in a rush. "I didn't—"

Her words were cut off as her mouth was filled with a wave of briny liquid. She sputtered against the bitter taste and the knowledge that she had somehow missed seeing Ben's arm move back to copy her action.

She found she wasn't at all angry. In fact, she felt the wildest desire to laugh, a desire she hid as she lifted her hand to her mouth to wipe away the excess water. Her eyes met Ben's, and saw them crinkle in the dim light. She saw the gleam of his white teeth as she let her hand drop back into the water and toss another handful of water toward him.

A wave of liquid rushed right back at her, and within moments she found herself engaged in a strange dance as she and Ben, still linked by his hand around her wrist, pulled against each other in a circular step, punctuated by the sounds of splashing water interspersed with choking laughter.

Everything stopped as they reached the side of the pool. They stood suddenly still, in water so deep that Diana had to stand on tiptoe to keep her head above the surface. She looked across at Ben. The muscular curves of his shoulders gleamed in the half-light. Silver droplets glistened on the hair covering his chest.

Diana's body responded immediately to the look of desire in Ben's eyes. A coiling heat twisted in the lower regions of her stomach and seeped into her every pore. She made no move to resist when Ben's free arm snaked around her waist and pulled her to him. Her soft lips parted as she recalled his earlier kisses. Yearning for more of them, she floated unhesitatingly across the scant distance. She allowed her free hand to glide up the rough mat of hair covering his chest and over the strong, smooth contours of his shoulders as his lips touched hers.

Their mouths were moist with the water from the pool, and their lips blended, sliding across each other in a deeply sensual kiss that intensified by the moment, rendering Diana weak and robbing her of the ability to do more than tighten her arm around the back of Ben's neck. She clung desperately to him as his tongue eased past her lips, filling her mouth with the taste of salt and the feel of rough velvet as it moved in and out in an arousing rhythm.

She wasn't aware that he had released her other wrist until she felt his thick hair between the fingers of her hand and realized that at some point she must have lifted it to the back of his head. It was only seconds later that she felt his free hand move over her buttocks in a worshipful caress that brought a slight moan to her throat.

That primitive sound sent a strange vibration pulsing

through Ben as his fingers sought the warmth of Diana's skin through the wet muslin covering her bottom. The rounded flesh filled his hand, but didn't satisfy his need to feel the silky softness he knew lay just beneath the fabric.

Relaxing the arm that held Diana to him, he slid his other hand around to the front of her cotton drawers, then slipped it up through the space separating her pantaloons from her camisole and eased his fingers up along her silky skin until the tips of his fingers touched the lower curve of her left breast.

At Ben's gentle touch Diana gasped against his mouth, then pressed her lips to his more firmly, encouraging him to gather her breast into his cupped fingers, letting her fullness fill his palm before he began slow, caressing motions that teased her nipple into a taut button.

When he found that the waist of her garment prevented him from moving his hand to the other breast, he withdrew his hand and began sliding the edge of the camisole upward, until both breasts were bared. Ben eased his hand over Diana's right breast as he continued to slant his lips over hers, then lifted his head and saw her midnight eyes open wide. He smiled into them before he spoke.

"I'm going to let go of you for a moment, so I can get your clothing out of the way. Just let yourself float in the water."

The words registered slowly in Diana's brain, and although one small part of her mind expressed a protest against Ben's plan, it was a very weak insurrection, easily suppressed by the yearning for further contact with Ben that sung through her body. The water supported her effortlessly as Ben released her, and she lifted her arms to let him draw the camisole over her head. She heard a slight slapping sound that announced its landing on the walkway, but before she could so much as glance in that direction, she felt Ben's

fingers at her waist, working to unfasten the string that held
her underdrawers up.

She looked down, but before she could protest, or decide
if she even wanted to, both his hands were slipping into the
waistband, curving over her hips to hold her buttocks firmly
in his cupped hands. Again she gasped as she was drawn
back toward Ben's body and her breasts were crushed to
his, but the sound was cut off as her mouth was captured
in another deep kiss.

Ben held Diana to him like that for several moments,
once more easing his tongue in and out of her mouth to the
rhythm of the desire pulsing against the apex of her thighs.
Her soft curves filled his hands as if they had been created
to do precisely that, and that thought sent his need for her
soaring to dangerous heights.

Realizing he needed to gain some measure of control,
Ben lifted his lips from Diana's, to trail them along the
edge of her jaw. He gently kissed the tender skin beneath
her ear, then nibbled down her neck, smiling slightly as he
felt her tremble against him. A moment later, she arched
against him, tilting her hips slightly, destroying the tiny
shreds of control he had gained.

Now it was Ben's body that trembled. He moved quickly
then, sliding Diana's drawers down her legs, his fingers
tingling over her satinlike skin. He held her to him with
one arm and grasped the material as it slipped off her pointed
toes, then tossed it toward the edge of the pool, not really
caring where it landed.

Diana heard the second slap of damp fabric against the
walkway. She was only aware of the strange twisting feeling
that had started in her stomach and had now moved down
to the area between her legs. When she had arched against
Ben, his arousal had pressed against her, both easing and
increasing the sense of pressure and need growing there.
She had tolerated being separated from him as he removed

the garment shielding her womanhood from him only because she, too, wished to discard that protection.

Enough of Diana's mind was working to be conscious of the inevitability of what was about to happen. She acknowledged that even if she were to suddenly decide that this was not a prudent action, it was too late to silence the aching desire Ben's kisses and caresses had awakened in her. When at last she was completely unclothed, she did not think to resist when Ben drew her back to him; rather, she let herself float forward, her muscles relaxed, letting the water support her as he had taught her.

Ben felt Diana's legs ease apart as he drew her to him. Still, he was unprepared for the jolt that ran through him when he felt his manhood glide over the tangle of her curls, and for the quickening that raced through him as he heard Diana's small gasp of pleasure. He lowered his mouth to hers, kissing her deeply, feeling his already aching need increase in the face of her answering kiss.

Diana tightened her arms around Ben's shoulders and pressed herself to him as emotions and passions swept through her with the force of a wave breaking upon the rocks. Any shred of control she might have retained had been swept away, leaving her clinging to Ben as the pressure between her legs grew, demanding something she could not name. She only knew that Ben held the answer to this, and when she felt him enter her, she did not pull back, not until she felt a tightening sensation that made her eyes open wide, and brought a strangled gasp to her lips.

Ben lifted his lips from hers to brush them with his reassuring words, ''Relax, Diana. Just relax.''

Diana recalled that he had used those same words during her swimming lesson. Slowly, she nodded. She took a deep breath. As she released it, she willed her muscles to soften, letting the warm water and Ben's arms support her even as she felt the pressure between her legs increase.

"Relax, love."

The hoarse words echoed in Diana's ears and she let her eyelids fall shut just as Ben's warm lips captured hers again as he slid further into her. The scientifically trained portion of her mind gave thanks for the warm water that aided Ben as he eased out, then in again, and slowly began to increase the pace of his thrusts.

That was Diana's last conscious thought before her body took over. She clung tightly to Ben as a wave of pleasure began to build to a powerful swell that urged her to move her hips rhythmically against his, matching his every move until she was fairly gasping with a strange, incomprehensible need. Unconsciously, she tightened her legs around Ben's waist, and bit her lip as sudden fear intruded on her desire.

She had no idea where Ben was taking her. She felt hopeless and needy in a way she had never wanted to feel. Yet she was powerless to stop this; her will was not strong enough to resist the pleasurable sensations that grew with each motion. She could only cling more tightly to Ben's strength as she felt a wave of heat crest with swift intensity, blotting her mind to all thought as the pleasure built further, then blossomed with an intense sensation that had her gasping against Ben's mouth as she felt his pleasure join hers.

A blend of physical satisfaction and emotional elation swirled through Diana as she slid her lips from Ben's and wrapped her arms around his neck. Ben's ragged breaths whispered past her ears as his arms tightened around her, emphasizing her vulnerability.

Sudden tears stung Diana's eyes as the veil of pleasure lifted from her benumbed mind, clearly revealing her recent actions. She felt no sense of shame, only fear, for she had allowed herself to do what she had vowed not to do.

She had opened herself to the pain of disappointment, of loss.

A part of her was thrilled with the knowledge that Ben Potter desired her, that he had taken pleasure from their joining. But only the night before, after he had kissed her in this very pool, he had seemed apologetic, almost embarrassed.

He probably feared that she would want a deeper entanglement, that she might try to trap him into the marriage Will said he so resisted. Of course she would do no such thing, she told herself. The only way to handle this situation was to enjoy the warmth still throbbing through her without confusing it with dangerous emotions.

When Ben eased away from her, Diana saw concern reflected in his face, confirming her fears about his reaction. She felt her heart twist again, and knew that the battle between mind and heart that she had fought for so long in her youth, a war she had believed she had won, had just begun again.

"You're shivering." Ben's voice was deep, and his tone reflected worry as he ran one hand down Diana's now shaking form. "Let's get you warmed up."

Diana found that her teeth had begun to chatter so badly that she couldn't speak—could only drop her head in a stiff nod. Although she longed to say something, to assure him that she would make no emotional demands, she could only cling tightly to him as he walked toward the shallow end of the pool. Once they reached the overhead walkway, Diana expected him to put her down. Instead, he shifted her form so that he could cradle her in one arm as he reached up to retrieve the lantern; then he ducked his head to go under the bridge toward the steps.

Once inside the dressing area Ben headed toward the ladies' dressing area. Diana managed to speak. "Ben, put me down. You can't go in there."

His chuckle echoed loudly down the hallway. "And who is here to tell me so?"

He stopped then, lifted the lantern to light the back wall, then walked toward the pile of thick white towels.

"Here." He lowered Diana to her feet. "Put this around you for a moment while I get a couple of these heated up."

Diana stood dripping onto the cold floor, her slender frame enfolded in a fluffy towel, while Ben slid two more out of the pile and opened a brass door in the wall. It clanged shut, and seconds later a hissing sound filled the room. Ben glanced at Diana and smiled. "It's a steam cabinet," he explained. "In a few moments we'll both have toasty warm towels to take away the chill."

Diana tried to return his smile, but her stiff lips could only twitch in reply. Moments later, after Ben had removed the towels from the cabinet, wrapped Diana tightly in the fluffy warmth of one, and draped his own shoulders with another, Diana felt her tense, shaking muscles begin to relax.

But inside, Diana continued to shiver as she looked at her bare feet. Her mind was a maze of conflicting thoughts until Ben cupped her chin in his hand and tilted her face toward his. "Something is bothering you, Diana," he said. "Did I hurt you?"

Diana's eyes widened as she shook her head. "No. No, you didn't."

"You're having regrets then. You think what we did was wrong?"

"No—yes." Diana stopped, trying to find a way to make it clear to Ben, and to herself, that what had passed between them had had no impact on her emotionally. She took a deep breath and met his gaze evenly. "No regrets, not in the way I think you mean. I . . ." She paused, then went on slowly. "I enjoyed what we did very much. But it *was* wrong. I'm afraid that I . . . I used you."

"You used me? In what way?"

Diana took a deep breath as she tried to gather the various strings of thought tangled in her mind. "I took advantage of what was happening between us to prove something to myself. To make it clear in my own mind that—"

Diana stopped speaking when Ben placed a gentle finger on her lips and finished the sentence for her. "That you are not fated to be some dried up spinster because your father named you for some goddess who is purported to have lived her days out alone?" He shook his head as he gazed down at her, the corners of his eyes crinkling as he smiled. "I thought I told you that Harrington's theory was poppycock."

There was a note of caring, a warm undertone that awoke a strange glow in her chest. Diana let herself imagine for one moment that Ben Potter might be falling in love with her. She had learned long ago the folly of living in a fantasy world. She hardened her heart against the warmth; then, to ease the tightening sensation in her chest, she took a deep breath before speaking. "I told you when we first met that I wasn't looking for a husband. I want you to know that is still true."

The sound of water dripping slowly onto the wet cement at their feet filled the silence. As Ben looked down at the slender woman in front of him, he felt a sudden rush of irrational anger at her words, an anger he controlled with difficulty.

"You have nothing to fear from me," he replied. "I decided long ago that love was only a myth, an excuse people use to justify tying their lives together. But, Diana"—he paused and narrowed his eyes—"that doesn't mean what we did was wrong. As a modern woman, one who is well equipped to take command of her life, there is no reason you should not approach lovemaking as the simple, uncomplicated pleasure I feel it was meant to be."

Diana stiffened. There it was, confirmation of her fears. Ben had obviously felt none of the tender, warm, and frightening emotions that had filled her as they clung together in the slowly fading warmth of their shared pleasure. Despite the ache in her heart, Diana replied, "You're right, of course. I think we'd best get dressed and return to the house. Mr. Sutro doesn't strike me as being at all modern in his thinking in these matters, and I would prefer that he did not know of our—"

Diana paused, searching for a word to describe what had passed between them that would not reveal her feelings "—association," Ben filled in.

"Yes." Diana went to the cubicle where she had left her clothes, drawing the towel more tightly around her as she walked. She was almost to the door when she turned, her eyes wide.

"Ben. My camisole and drawers. We left them by the pool."

A slow smile crept over his lips before he spoke. "I'll retrieve them, although I've half a mind to leave them there just to see Pete and the other workers worry over where they came from." He started for the door, speaking as he walked. "Your underthings will still be wet, so put on the rest of your clothes and meet me at the top of the stairs."

Diana found that it took her much longer than normal to dress. As each item slid over her flesh she was reminded of Ben's touch, and an enfeebling warmth surged through her, robbing her momentarily of the ability to move. By the time everything was buttoned, she found that she was shivering with a strange cold that seemed to have originated in the pit of her stomach and seeped into her bones.

The cold deepened as she held the lantern up to light her way to the stairs. She told herself that this had nothing to do with what had happened in the pools below, was in no way an indication that she was nervous about facing Ben again. Her mind fully accepted the idea that a woman could maintain a sensible relationship with a man she had been . . . intimate with.

However, her heart saw things differently. When Ben's tall frame stepped into the halo of the lamplight, her heart seemed to leap in her breast, then insisted on pounding rapidly in response to his wide smile gleaming in the darkness.

"Why don't you let me take the lantern?" he said as he reached for it. "You can carry this." He held out a small ball of damp muslin, which Diana took into her left hand as he took the lantern and spoke again. "I want to keep the light low so no one will see it and worry about thieves. Are you ready?"

Diana nodded, then followed him in silence. Not another word passed between them as they made their way through the cavernous room. He shuttered the lantern completely when they reached the front door. As Diana stood outside while Ben set the alarm and shut the door, the deep fog seeping through her thick coat made her shiver anew.

Ben turned the collar of his coat up against the cold, then reached over to do the same for Diana. With his hands resting on her shoulders, he said, "Well, we might be near frozen before we reach the house, but at least we know that in this fog we aren't likely to be spotted and start people asking questions."

Diana found that the easy camaraderie she had once felt in his presence existed no more, and as she walked silently next to him toward the house, a part of her mourned its passage and resented the tension she could sense growing between them.

The tension was even deeper the next day. Diana and Ben exchanged greetings at breakfast, but when she accompanied Ben and Will down to the Baths, she noticed that Ben said little, to her or to Will.

Later that morning, as Diana put the finishing touches on the bottom of the volcano, she told herself that Ben's distracted air had nothing to do with her. Although he claimed they were making good progress on the exhibit, there were still many things left unfinished that undoubtedly were worrying him.

Diana stood back to examine her finished project. If she had completed it yesterday she would have run down to the Diana chamber, where Ben was working, and brought him up to see it. She didn't feel she could do that now. She found herself thinking twice before anything she said, examining her actions before performing them, lest she give the impression that she saw Ben as anything more than her employer.

Holding a tray full of paints and brushes, Diana slowly descended the circular stairway to the shrine room, where the arched alcove awaited the same treatment she had given the volcano above. She heard a rattling sound from the door leading to the storage area, then froze on the bottom step as Ben stepped through it. He stopped, too, his eyes meeting hers immediately.

All morning he'd been fighting the urge to run up the steps to where she was working, pull her into his arms, and kiss her warm lips. The very strength of his desire frightened him. Now, as he found himself mesmerized by her midnight blue eyes, the curve of her cheek, the lure of her lips, that irrational need to keep himself from being swept into dangerous emotional depths increased.

After several seconds of silence, Ben forced himself to speak. "You're finished with Vesuvius?" When Diana nodded, he coerced his tight lips into a smile. "Well, there's more of the same work for you down here."

"This is going to require a slightly different technique

than I used on the volcano.'' Diana lifted her chin as she
turned to him. ''I will want to apply bolder strokes. I think
I'd best work on the interior of the cave, in some corner
that won't be noticed until I figure out how to get the effect
I want. Are you and Will done in there?''

Ben shook his head slowly. Diana's voice sounded tight;
her face was very pale. He wanted to cross the room and
pull her into his arms as he would a frightened child. Instead,
he forced himself to speak. ''I still have some plastering to
do in the left-hand corner. But you can start on the right if
you'd like.''

Once within the wide, low arch they worked close
together. Ben wielded his trowel slowly, trying to ignore
the chest-crushing tightness that always affected him in
tight places. More than once he looked at the arched
opening, as if to reassure himself, and in the process
caught a glimpse of Diana's slender form behind him.
Each time he told himself it was best to leave things as
they were.

Diana worked in her corner, trying to concentrate on
the correct blending and application of the paint, all the
while sharply aware of Ben's every move. No matter how
she tried, she could not ignore his presence, could not
prevent the strange warmth that rushed through her as
thoughts of the previous night insisted on flashing into her
mind.

The weakening heat that invaded her body with each
memory was accompanied by flashes of anger. Ben didn't
seem at all affected by the events of the night before, while
she found her arms growing so weak with remembered
desire that she had to lower them to her sides and lean
against the wall until her strength returned.

But slowly, after she began to layer the paint, adjusting
her technique to allow for the larger scale on which she
was working, she finally slipped into a creative haze that

blocked out her surroundings. Her sense of peace lasted several minutes, until she suddenly became aware that Ben was standing behind her, so close that his musky scent overpowered the smell of her paints. She tried to ignore him until his fingers gripped her wrist and held it tight.

Chapter Thirteen

"DIANA, why won't you look at me?"

Ben's voice echoed in the small cavelike area with a husky quality that made Diana's heart miss a beat. She swallowed, then cleared her throat. "What do you mean? I am looking at you."

She could hardly help doing so. His broad shoulders nearly filled the small area, trapping Diana in the corner. Her heart began to beat faster, to race as his frown deepened and he spoke again. "Now you are, but all morning you've barely glanced my way."

Diana couldn't deny the truth in this. Nor could she bring herself to admit the sudden sense of shyness and fear she felt in his presence. She lifted her shoulders in an exaggerated shrug. "I'm busy. And so are you. We still have an enormous amount of work to accomplish before the items arrive for the exhibition, or so you keep reminding me."

"So your silence has nothing to do with last night?"

Diana's shoulders tensed. She shook her head. "Of course not. I enjoyed last night. I always wondered what . . . sex was all about, beyond the clinical details, but I had no one to ask detailed questions about the subject, certainly not my grandfather. Now I understand."

"You make it sound as if last night is something you

have filed in your well-ordered mind under "new experiences." It is quite normal to have some emotional reaction to making love, you know."

He watched Diana closely as he said these last words. Her smooth pale features gave no clue to her feelings. He was angry at his words, at his thoughts, at the storm of emotions roiling through his stomach. Why had he assumed that the dark circles under her eyes suggested that she had spent as sleepless a night as he had? And just what was it about making love to Diana McKenzie that had caused him to lose sleep anyway?

He had been careful, ever since Sarah, to see that he never confused physical enjoyment between himself and a woman with the mythical emotion called love. But where Diana was concerned he found it nearly impossible to maintain that sense of distance. The thought that she might have found last night nothing more than an "interesting experience" made his hands form tight fists at his sides as she continued to gaze up at him.

"Of course I had an emotional reaction," she said at last. "It was . . ." Her eyelids dropped over her eyes a moment as she paused. ". . . Wonderful."

Diana forced herself to look back up at Ben. "Wonderful" was a woefully inadequate way to describe what she had experienced, both physically and emotionally, in his arms. But even if she could find the proper words, she knew she would never be able to utter them. Just the thought made her stomach tighten with fear. "It was even more exciting than the trip down the slide the night before."

Diana watched Ben's face closely. "Good," he said in a husky whisper. "You should enjoy it even more the second time."

Her arms hung helplessly at her sides and her legs fought the sudden weakness washing through them as she considered the meaning of Ben's words.

He wanted her again. She could see it in his eyes as they moved closer to hers, could feel it in his touch as he slid one hand around her waist. Diana gasped as Ben's mouth closed over hers. She knew that to permit the madness sweeping through her would only make the eventual pain and loneliness worse when he left her, but his kiss was so warm, his lips so compelling, and his caresses so wonderfully enervating that she allowed herself to be drawn closer to him. Without conscious thought she let her hands steal up over his shoulders, letting her fingers slide into his hair and urge him to kiss her more deeply, parting her lips to allow his tongue entrance, daring to meet its velvet touch.

Within mere seconds all her fears for the future were forgotten as Ben's arms tightened around her. His broad chest pressing against her breasts eased their aching need to be touched, and as his hand slid in a caress along her waist she felt her body grow warm and melt into his.

Diana's response fueled Ben's need for her, made him forget his surroundings, his misgivings about the emotions she unwittingly awoke in him, his suspicions regarding her father, everything but how she had felt the night before—warm and wet and silky.

The clothing that separated their bodies frustrated him as he let his hands roam up Diana's slender form. When Ben cupped his hands over her breasts, he could feel their heat beneath her muslin blouse and chemise. His palms tingled, yearning to feel naked skin, and so he smoothed his hands up, forcing himself to be content for the moment to cradle Diana's face as he slanted his mouth hungrily over hers. When he felt her slim fingers curl into his tousled locks, his hands moved again, almost of their own volition, his fingers tunneling deep into Diana's silken mane.

Desire throbbed through the blood that pounded loudly in his ears, blotting out all sound except for the soft moan that escaped Diana's throat. That was followed by a deeper tone, a sound he took to be an answering groan of his own, until a second later he heard someone call his name.

"Ben! Diana! Is anyone down here?"

Will Babcock's voice echoed loudly in the cavern. Ben felt Diana stiffen at the same time that his own muscles tensed, and he lifted his mouth from hers just as she pulled away. He still held her head in his hands, and for one long moment he looked down into her eyes, still dilated with passion. A second later he slid his hands from her cheeks in a quick caress then released her to step to the cave's opening.

"We're in here, Will."

Ben stepped through the archway as Will began to descend the curving stairway. "I'd like to see how it's coming."

Ben could see Diana struggling to straighten her clothes and smooth her rumpled hair. He suppressed a grin and turned back to Will. "Well, we really just got started here in the cave. Diana had to finish the volcano."

"Yes, I saw that. I went up there first. I have a little note to deliver to Diana."

Standing just within the cave, Diana gave her hair one final smoothing pat, then stepped out to smile at Will. "A note? Does Emma need me? She mentioned something yester—"

Diana broke off as Will shook his head. Something in the expression on his face made Diana shiver as a strange tingle rushed through her. She watched him reach into the breast pocket of his suit, and her heart began to pound wildly. *My father*, she thought. Somehow he had learned that she was here. Perhaps he had called the Sutros to apprise them of his arrival. Did he want to see her? Or was he writing to order her away?

The moment she saw the handwriting on the envelope, Diana knew that all her guesses were wrong. She reached forward, took the small white square, opened it, and drew forth a short note.

"It's from Professor Harrington." She knew her voice sounded flat as she lifted her head to look at Ben and Will. "He says that he is very interested in having me work for him, and that he wants to talk seriously about it as soon as possible."

The realization that this meant the culmination of her dreams brought some animation to her voice, and by the time she finished speaking it reflected the excitement bubbling within her. However, the men across from her demonstrated no immediate reaction to this news. After a silence that lasted several seconds, Ben's sharp tone split the air.

"I hope Harrington understands that 'as soon as possible' won't be for several days. We still have a lot of work to do here, and you've promised to help me get it done on time."

Ben's harsh words surprised Diana. "Well, of course I will, but—"

"But nothing. You have this entire cave to paint, as well as the murals upstairs that I mentioned earlier. When you're done with all that, I need you to paint the statues of the animals that will be arranged down here."

Diana was stunned by his sudden anger. "Well, perhaps I could ask the professor—"

"—to come interview you as you work?" Ben shook his head. "That would not only be unprofessional, it would be unacceptable from my point of view. I've watched you paint and have seen how much concentration it requires. I don't want you distracted."

Ben stood directly in front of Diana now. Her lips tightened. "What you don't want is for me to work for Justin Harrington."

"That's true. I know any number of archaeologists that I would be glad to recommend you to, and to whom I would be happy to vouch for your abilities. Not Harrington, however. I know him far too well. If you choose to go to work for him, you are asking for grief.''

Diana's jaw tightened. She knew all about grief. She also knew about overbearing men determined to protect her. Ben's words sounded so very much like something that her grandfather might have said that she almost laughed.

She didn't though. She frowned as her heart twisted in her chest. Ben was wrong about that special thing they had shared. There would be no second time. She might be able to survive the pain when their days together ended, but she could not risk letting him take control of her life, only to leave her directionless when he was gone. Slowly she straightened, her back stiff and tense.

''You're right. It would be unprofessional to speak with him while I'm working. However, I have no intention of forfeiting the chance to explore Roman ruins in England, which is the next dig Harrington is planning. Since you dislike him, I will of course not ask you for a letter of recommendation. However, I will write to Professor Harrington, explaining that my obligations here will prevent us from meeting until after the opening of the exhibit, and ask for an appointment at that time.''

With that she turned, slipping the note into the pocket of her skirt, and stepped into the cave where she picked up her fallen palette and brush. Doing her best to forget how the paint had come to be so smeared, she went back to work.

The next several days were torture for Diana. Each time she saw Ben she was tormented by memories of his kisses and caresses. She tried to avoid being near him as much as possible, even to the point of leaving the dinner table early to hurry back to the Baths to work in blessed solitude until she heard or sensed Ben somewhere else in the exhibit.

Ben seemed content with this arrangement. He rarely remained long in an area where Diana was working unless it was absolutely necessary. As the days went on, he worked longer and longer hours, remaining in the Baths after Diana had gone up to the house, where she would lay in bed and imagine him swimming in the darkness. As she tried to go to sleep, she found herself engaged in fantasies in which she joined him in the warm, buoyant water.

Her body ached to join him there, and her heart yearned for the sense of closeness it had experienced as he held her to him, their hearts pounding in unison, but her mind warned her against the foolishness of this. To her body's sorrow, her mind always won out. It was best to leave things just as they were.

The work on the exhibit moved along at a rapid pace, so quickly that on the day before the artifacts were due to arrive from the British Museum, everything had been completed, except for a few small areas that needed to be touched up on the mosaic Diana had completed the day before. Diana ate breakfast early and set out for the Baths, taking the long way down Palm Drive, and letting the sight of the statues peeping out through the lush summer foliage ease her mind. As she turned a corner, she saw Emma standing on the path, staring toward the spot in the foliage where Diana knew ''her'' statue stood.

''Emma, you're up at the Heights early today.''

The woman turned to Diana. ''Yes, Papa needs me to do a few things for him, some work on a report that he forgot was due. My husband had a light day planned, fortunately, so he agreed to see the few patients I had scheduled today.''

Diana lifted her brows. ''George must be a very thoughtful man.''

''Yes.'' Emma nodded. ''Practical too. I do the same

thing for him when he needs help. We are a team. Our life wouldn't work any other way.''

''No, I don't suppose it would. It must be wonderful, to be able to share a career with the man you love. You're very fortunate.''

As Diana spoke these words, she felt a wave of sudden sadness well up in her. She was surprised at the depth of the ache in her breast, for until this moment it had not occurred to her to look for such a thing. However, she had learned during the last week that the heart often possessed a knowledge that was hidden from the mind. Some part deep inside her had already considered the possibility of finding a partner for life, a man who could share her heart and her work. Diana knew that the seeds of this desire had been planted the first time Ben kissed her.

''Yes, I am a lucky woman.'' Emma's voice broke into Diana's thoughts. ''Being the daughter of Adolph Sutro prepared me well to make my way in the world, for my father expected much from all his children, boys and girls alike. However, coming from such an egalitarian upbringing, it was something of a shock to learn that most men don't look at things that way. I consider it something of a miracle to have found someone like George, secure enough in his own masculinity to love a woman as strong-willed as myself. Of course, I don't tell him that; I just act as if it's expected.''

''I understand completely,'' Diana said. ''It wouldn't do to let this go to his head.''

The women shared a moment of laughter, then Diana sighed. ''Well, I had better get down to the Baths and get to work.''

''And I'd better get up to the house. I should have had my carriage take me up, but I enjoy walking in the gardens before all the tourists arrive, so I had my driver drop me off at the gate. And I was richly rewarded. Look. An admirer has left some offerings for our goddess of the moon.''

Diana turned to stare at the statue of her namesake. Someone had placed a camellia in the hand that held the bow, entwined other flowers into a wreath that encircled the statue's head, and left a lily and a rose at her feet.

The sight had an immediate and disturbing effect on Diana, filling her with a strange emotion that made her want to laugh and cry at the same time as an odd shiver danced through her.

"How lovely. Does this happen often?"

"No, it doesn't. And just as well, too, because I know those flowers have come from our garden. As much as I hate to do so, I shall have to order one of the gardeners to remove them, lest other visitors see this and decide to copy the gesture. Well''—Emma took a step toward the house—''I may still be here at dinnertime. Perhaps I'll see you then. If not, I'll certainly be here for the opening of the exhibit on Friday.''

Diana didn't have any time to think of the statue again the rest of the day, as she took care of small details in the various exhibit areas. She was busy until late in the afternoon, when Ben declared that at last they were ready for the statues and other artifacts that would surely arrive the next day.

Diana recalled the concern that Ben's confident words had masked as she walked back to her room. The exhibition was to open in three days' time, and although all that remained was to place the artifacts and statues where they belonged, that would require at least one full day of work. He had expected the ship bearing these things to arrive today, but the last word from the wharf was not encouraging.

Diana's thoughts on this matter fled as she opened her door and noticed a flowery scent filling the room. On her desk, in front of her small statue of Diana, lay a pink camellia, a red rose, and a white calla lily. A wreath of flowers encircled the statue's base. Diana stepped toward the desk slowly, filled with the same tingling feeling she had experienced that morning, then stood in front of what looked like a small shrine. For no reason that Diana could identify, tears filled her eyes and streamed unchecked down her cheeks for several moments.

Finally she drew a shaking breath, wiped the moisture from her face, and shook her head. *This is ridiculous*, she told herself, *to react with such emotion over this sight*. It was a nice gesture, of course, and as she turned to dress for dinner she told herself to remember to thank Emma for having them sent to her room.

Emma was at dinner, as Diana had hoped, still in her shirtwaist and black skirt, making Diana feel very over-dressed, even though she wore a simple ivory gown. However, the heavy lace forming the high collar and stretching across the top of the bodice made it look quite formal, and made Diana feel almost dainty.

Perhaps it was the effect of the very feminine dress that made Diana less talkative than usual, and more attuned to the emotional state of those surrounding her. She was aware that Ben was preoccupied and tense, no doubt due to his concern for the as yet unseen artifacts.

However, Sutro seemed not to be worried about this when Will broached the subject. "If they don't arrive tomorrow, there will still be time on Thursday to arrange everything. In fact, even if the ship does come in tomorrow, I think the three of you should take the day off." Sutro paused to take a sip of wine, then smiled. "A friend of mine has a nice sailboat. I want you to take it out tomorrow, and sail around the bay. The sun and fresh air will revive your souls and your bodies."

Ben paused as he lifted a forkful of food and smiled at his host. "Thank you, but I don't think that would be wise. I want to get everything in place as early as possible."

"I understand. I am a man of action, too; one who likes things to be just so. But I do not think it would be wise for you to work with these precious items without reviving your weary spirits. Besides, you have Thursday to arrange your statues. So, it is settled. I will telephone my friend tonight to confirm these plans, and my driver will take you down to the pier tomorrow morning. You must remember to dress warmly."

With that he lifted his glass for another sip of wine, and Emma laughed and turned to Ben. "You have your orders. And I need to get home. I'll be back up Thursday evening for the party Papa has planned at the Cliff House." She turned to Diana. "Oh yes—Papa received another telegram from your father. He will be arriving that afternoon."

Diana's breath caught in her throat as she stared across the table at Emma. Her hands tightened into fists in her lap as she forced herself to speak. "Oh, wonderful. Thank you for telling me."

Emma grinned. "I've been reminding myself to do so all afternoon, and I didn't remember to tell you until just now. I hope you'll forgive me."

"Of course I will," Diana said. "I'm just as bad. I forgot to thank you for having those flowers sent to my room."

Emma looked puzzled. "What flowers?"

"The ones we saw on the statue this morning."

"They're in your room?" Emma asked. "How odd. The gardener told me at lunch that when he went to remove them from the statue, they had disappeared."

_____ *Chapter Fourteen*

"WHAT DO YOU MEAN, you aren't going with us?"

Ben stood in the shade of the weathered gray warehouse overlooking the boats in the small marina. A stiff breeze lifted his golden hair as he turned to Will.

"Just exactly that. I think it would be a good idea for you and Diana to spend some time together and straighten out whatever it is that has kept you so distant the last couple of days."

"The only thing that has put distance, as you call it, between Diana and myself is the amount of work we had to do."

"Oh? Then the fact that you don't look at each other anymore has nothing to do with my inadvertently interrupting your embrace the other day?"

The two men looked silently at each other for several moments; then Will smiled. "I should have apologized for intruding earlier, I suppose. I want to do that now, by giving you the chance to fix things with her."

Ben gazed down the long dock to where Diana stood by the sleek white and mahogany craft named the *Mary Malone*. The brim of Diana's straw hat hid her features, and her long, white dress flapped wildly in the breeze, hugging her slim legs, outlining the curve of her bottom. Ben shook his head, as much in response to the quick stirring of desire sweeping through him as to Will's offer.

"No. Things are best left as they are."

"It's best that you should both remain miserable?" Will's eyes narrowed. "I know you won't like hearing this, but I'm going to say it anyway. In many ways you can be a difficult man to read, but where it comes to Diana McKenzie your feelings are pathetically transparent. You are in love with her, and unless I miss my guess, Diana is in love with you."

Will's words kindled a warm glow in Ben's stomach. He denied the hope awakening in his breast with another shake of his head. "You're wrong. What you see is physical attraction only, a pull that Diana and I have agreed is best resisted."

"Oh? Well, perhaps that is wise. But does that mean you can't take her out for a day's relaxation?" Will glanced down to Diana's wind-ruffled form. "Other than meals and the time you have allowed her to sleep, she hasn't been outside the Baths at all." He turned back to Ben, his hazel eyes clouded with concern behind his glasses. "When I met Diana, her skin reminded me of marble, pale but lovely. Now her complexion has the lifeless color of bread dough."

Ben too had noticed Diana's pallor. In the last few days her skin had lost its translucent glow and grown pasty and drawn. But that didn't justify Will's plan to send the two of them off on some romantic voyage. "Fine," he said. "I'll concede that she needs fresh air. But I want you to come with us."

"No. One of us needs to be here when the items from the British Museum arrive. I know nothing about sailing a boat, and you do. Besides, as I said before, you and Diana need the time together. Perhaps out on the ocean you'll find the courage to tell her what I can see in your heart."

"There isn't much in my heart. You know that. And even

if there was, Diana McKenzie is off limits to me. Have you forgotten that I am here to help trap her father?''

"I am quite aware of the reason we are both here.'' Will's features hardened as he spoke. "I am also aware that we have an obligation to protect the items we are expecting, and if I want to do that I can't allow myself to be blinded by my desire to capture Daniel McKenzie. As much as I hate to admit this, it is possible that McKenzie isn't involved in these thefts after all.''

"You've been listening to Ian.''

Will smiled wryly. "When an inspector from Scotland Yard speaks, that's a good idea, especially if we wish to keep our jobs with the museum when this is over. LaPierre is arriving today, according to Sutro, and of course we are aware that Harrington is already on the scene. With Ian keeping an eye on things up at the Baths, I feel it's my duty to wait here in case the ship arrives today and see to it that everything makes it to the exhibit safely.

"I can't believe you are saying this. You and I know that the culprit can be no one other than McKenzie, unless in your years of tracking him you've misread—''

"I've misread nothing.'' Will's voice was a low growl. "I'm sure that McKenzie is the man behind all this. But I'm not about to put a million dollars worth of artifacts in jeopardy to support those beliefs. What if the man is secretly in San Francisco, even as we speak? It's possible he might suspect something and strike before the full moon this time. Have you considered that?

"Well, then.'' Will's voice softened. "If we do catch Daniel McKenzie stealing the statue of Diana, have you considered what effect that will have on his daughter? Diana is going to need someone to lean on. If you can't face your deeper feelings regarding that young woman, at least accept the fact that you and I are the only friends she has here. I'm in charge of security, so I will be the one who arrests her father, if he is the thief. And if this happens, she will most likely resent me. I think you should fix things between you so that she knows she has someone to turn to.''

Ben watched Diana as Will's next words echoed in his ears. ''Aside from all that, Ben, she's tired. Just seeing her father for the first time in so many years is certain to be quite an ordeal for her. A day in the sun and wind is just what she needs to rebuild her inner fortitude.''

These words reverberated in Ben's mind as his boots echoed on the wooden pier. ''I've some disappointing news for you,'' he started. ''Will isn't coming with us. Since he is the one responsible for the security surrounding the exhibit from the museum, he felt he should stay at the wharf in case the ship arrives today.''

Diana had been looking forward to a day of relaxation, anticipating the thrill of skirting over the waves like the sailboats she had watched glide across the water in front of the Heights. But she had counted on Will's presence, his easy joviality, to keep the atmosphere light and provide a buffer between her and Ben.

''You'll need to be careful stepping into the boat.'' Ben's words made Diana look up at him quickly as he continued. ''Sutro mentioned that the owner keeps several pairs of rubber-soled shoes aboard for guests to use. I'll look for them as soon as I get you settled.''

Ben held out his hand. Diana hesitated a moment before placing her hand in his, and tried to ignore the thrill that shot through her as his hand closed over hers. Carefully she stepped into the cockpit, lowered herself to one of the seats that ran the length of the little alcove, as directed, and sat patiently as Ben opened a small door and disappeared into what Diana surmised was the cabin Sutro had described, complete with a small stove, a table, and a bed.

Ben reappeared holding two pairs of flat canvas shoes that looked like large slippers. When Diana took them from him, their fingers touched. Once again a thousand pinpricks danced up her arm from the brief contact. She slipped her feet out of her heavy black boots. The sight of her toes, clad now only in dark stockings, made her feel suddenly vulnerable, as if far more of her were revealed to Ben's eyes than simply her feet.

She frowned at the silly feeling even as she put on the rubber-soled shoes, then stood to test their fit. "Oh, these are very comfortable. And sensible. Shoes should always feel like this."

"I doubt that they would pass muster in a ballroom, at least not as an acceptable item of fashion."

A wave of numbing desire washed through her. As her chest tightened and her body grew warm, her logical side ridiculed her weakness.

She noted how unattractive the wide, flat shoes appeared peaking beneath the hem of her lace-edged skirt. "I suppose you're right. It's a pity. They would make attending a ball at least physically less uncomfortable."

Ben stood, his boots in hand, then reached out for hers. She was careful during the exchange not to let her fingers touch his, but once he turned from her, she was unable to stop looking at his broad shoulders as they disappeared through the hatch.

Once inside the cabin, Ben released a deep breath, and leaned back against the wall. This was going to be even more difficult than he had imagined. It had been hard enough the last few days to keep himself from drawing Diana into his arms the few times they were alone, and kissing away the tension between them. But at least then he'd had plenty of work to distract him.

Now they were to be trapped together on a thirty-foot boat. The cockpit was small and if the merest brush of his fingers against hers, or the sight of her stocking-clad feet could send hot blood racing through his veins, what would happen in response to some deeper contact?

Nothing, his mind responded. Days ago he had sworn that nothing further would happen between the two of them, at least not until the situation with her father was resolved and he had sorted out his own emotions. However, he had promised Will that Diana would have a day of relaxation, a good time to revive her spirits. It would take some acting on his part, but he would keep that promise.

Diana sat in the cockpit, the wind tugging at the broad brim of her straw hat as she took in her surroundings. Up and down the pier other boats of various sizes bobbed and weaved, their masts tracing invisible circles in the blue sky above, making a high-pitched hum as the wind whipped around them.

The wind was brisk, but the sun on Diana's back was so warm that she welcomed the air brushing against her skin. She leaned back in her seat, feeling the tension disappear from her neck and a sense of relaxation melt into her muscles as she watched two seagulls circle above her.

"Don't get too comfortable, me hearty."

Ben's words made Diana blink and sit up straight as she turned to see him step out of the cabin. He had removed his jacket, rolled his sleeves up to his elbows, and tied a red bandana over his hair. His dark eyes narrowed as he leaned toward her.

"If you expect to sail with me, me fine friend, ye best be prepared to haul your weight. On your feet now, missy, and ready yourself to man the halyards."

Ben held his breath as he watched Diana stare mutely at him, then answered, "Aye, aye, sir." She saluted as she got to her feet, and he grinned.

Again Ben found himself bowing mentally to Will's wisdom. He'd been so careful the last few days to avoid Diana's presence that he hadn't noticed how the sparkle had disappeared from her eyes, nor how listless her reactions had become. He couldn't correct these things in the manner that Will obviously had in mind, but he did concur with the old man's assessment of Diana's impending reunion with her father. It was bound to be difficult for her to bridge the seventeen-year gap of contact. She would need every bit of the pluck and determination she had exhibited earlier, and his job today was to see that she recaptured these characteristics.

He watched her slim form sway as she stepped onto the deck, then turned to him, her hand on one of the lines stretching down from the masthead. "One thing, Captain," she said. "Just what is a halyard?"

By the time they had tacked out of the harbor under the power of the slender jib sail curving out over the bow, and rode onto the wide expanse of rippling water that filled San Francisco Bay, Diana knew the meaning of that term, as well as many others.

Now she stood next to the mast, admiring the city of San Francisco, noting the almost magical way it seemed to rise heavenward from the shore behind the boat, its buildings shimmering in the sun.

"All right, Diana." Ben's voice floated to her on the stiff breeze blowing into the bay from the ocean. "Hoist the sail."

Diana tightened her hands around the rope—*the halyard*, she reminded herself—and began to yank down with all her might. She was elated when the canvas laying on the boom began to rise, and increased her efforts. She tilted her head back to watch the top of the sail inch up along the slender spar, as the stiff white fabric flapped wildly in the breeze.

"Don't let it get away from you," Ben shouted from his place by the wheel in the stern. His voice rose over the snap of the canvas as it shuddered in the wind. Diana nodded as she clenched her fingers around the rough line and pulled tighter, happy when the wind filled the sail, making it billow smoothly away from her in a graceful curve. Satisfied with her performance, Diana secured the line to the cleat on the side of the mast as Ben had instructed, then turned toward him.

His look of approval sent such a powerful jolt rushing through Diana that her knees threatened to buckle and she was forced to wrap her arm around the mast for support.

"You did well, mate," Ben called up to her. "Come down into the cockpit now, for some well-deserved rest."

Diana nodded as strength returned to her legs and eased herself into the seat, facing away from the wind. She placed her hat back on her head, fastening it against the strength of the stiff breeze with a long hatpin. Ben had been right when he'd ordered her to remove it earlier. It definitely would have hampered her as she struggled to raise the sail, but now she needed its protection from the late-morning sun.

"That's a wise move." Ben glanced at her hat over the curved wheel. "Your nose and cheeks are already getting pink. The color looks good on you, but I wouldn't want you to get a burn."

She concentrated on the sail curving out in front of her, then gazed through the space between the boom and the deck, where she could see the blue-green water rising and falling in uneven swells. She watched the far shore, where the city of Oakland looked like a collection of toy buildings set on the edge of the bay.

Diana grew restless and turned her attention to California's Golden Gate, a wide stretch of blue-green water, stretched between two arms of land that rose to rolling promontories on either side. Diana could almost see the ships loaded with men bound for the goldfields of northern California passing through that gate, their sails billowing in the wind as they bounded over the whitecapped sea.

She took a deep breath of salt-scented air, feeling the tension that had knotted the muscles in her shoulders, as she fought with the sail, melt away.

"It's like magic, isn't it?"

"What's like magic?"

"The sun, the breeze, and the water. I always find that I look at things so differently when I'm out on a boat. I seem to view life in simpler terms." He paused. "Unfortunately, the feeling is like quicksilver; it disappears once I'm back on land, and I return to acting the ogre."

"You aren't an ogre . . . not all the time, anyway."

She eased herself deeper into the seat, letting the brim of her hat slip forward to cover her features as she rested her head on the wooden wall behind her. Diana listened to a voice whispering a warning in her mind against letting this renewed closeness go any farther. She shut her eyes, blocked out all thoughts, and let her body relax to the magic of the motion of the sailboat as it rose and fell over the gentle waves.

"Diana, wake up. You have work to do."

Diana tried to respond but couldn't.

"Hey there, matey." The deep voice fairly boomed this time. Her eyes flew open as she straightened to a sitting position and pushed her hat back. "Up on deck with you and trim that mainsail. We're pulling into port."

Diana got to her feet slowly, then checked to see San Francisco still behind them. "Into port? The city is back there."

Ben shook his head. "Will gave me the name of a restaurant that Sutro told him about in a town named Tiburon on the opposite side of the bay. We're almost there now, so hop to."

"We must tell Mr. Sutro how lovely this place is, and thank him for his suggestion." Diana sighed as she gazed

out the window by their table. The Seafarer's Inn was located on a small rise above the harbor. The window looked
eastward, revealing a small bay dotted with sailboats. "It's
a wonderful place for a relaxing lunch."

"Yes," he said. "The view is wonderful and the food
is good and plentiful. Are you sure you won't have anything
else to eat?"

Diana drew her lower lip between her teeth and shook
her head. "No, I think I'm quite satisfied now."

"Well, I think the proprietor will be glad to hear that. I
think he would probably like to have something left to serve
his dinner crowd. Will would be thrilled to see you eat so
much at one meal."

Diana felt her face begin to grow warm. "Look here,
Ben Potter. I didn't see you leave anything on your plate
either."

"You're right. Didn't anyone tell you that sailing works
up a powerful hunger?"

"The only thing I ever heard about sailing was that it
was a dangerous and foolish thing to do." Diana paused,
then went on to explain. "My grandfather felt that man
belonged on solid ground, you see. Of course, when I
pointed out that he wouldn't be living in the country he
loved so much if his ancestors had felt that way, he always
managed to change the subject."

Ben watched Diana's face take on a wry expression.
"Your grandfather must have been a difficult man to grow
up with."

"Sometimes." Diana shrugged. "He loved me very
much, though. I always knew that, and although we argued
more and more as I grew older, I realized that he never tried
to deny me anything out of spite or hard-heartedness."

"He just wanted to protect you."

Ben was aware that his husky tone had reflected his own

desire to prevent harm, whether it be physical or emotional, from affecting the woman across from him.

"I know," she said. "And as frustrated as I was by the endless restrictions he tried to place on me; I was always grateful that he cared so much." Again she paused, but this time her frown showed no sign of levity. "Unfortunately, he could never understand that to keep someone from growing, from reaching their full potential, is the cruelest thing you can do, especially to someone you profess to love."

Diana stood as she finished speaking, sighing deeply before she went on. "I think it's time we started back, don't you?"

Ben opened the folder containing the bill for their lunch. He stared at the amount at the bottom of the slip of paper for several moments before reaching into his pockets to withdraw enough money to cover the bill, an amount equal to a week's salary. As he placed the folder in its silver tray he noted Diana's shocked expression.

"Well, that's a lesson. Don't let a millionaire suggest a restaurant unless you've just come into an inheritance yourself." Ben grinned at Diana as he finished speaking, then reached over to the arrangement of fresh flowers on the table. He plucked an enormous pink rose out of the center and handed it to her.

Diana opened her mouth, but before she could speak, their waiter came forward to ask if they had enjoyed the meal. It wasn't until they were outside and walking down the path toward the small harbor that Diana had a chance to thank Ben for the flower.

"You can add it to the other offerings to the goddess of the moon."

Ben regretted the words the moment he uttered them. He tried not to glance at Diana, but when she planted her feet in the dirt path and grabbed Ben's arm, he had little choice but to turn toward her.

"It was you," she said.

"What was me?" he asked, feigning surprise.

"The flowers to the goddess. The ones Emma and I found on the statue in the garden yesterday morning." Diana's excited tone told Ben that his attempt had been unsuccessful. "You placed them on the statue in the garden," she went on, "and then had them moved to my room."

"Well, you're half-right," he replied. "I have no idea who placed them on the statue in the gardens. The first I learned of that was when I overheard Emma discussing their removal with one of the gardeners on my way out of the house. When I passed the statue, some strange mood came over me. I removed them and took them to one of the maids with orders to arrange them near the small copy of the statue in your room."

Again Ben realized his mistake. Diana had mentioned the statue, but had never told him that she had set it out in her room. Before Diana could begin wondering how he could know about it, he turned and began walking down the hill. When she joined him, he spoke again, barely glancing at her. "Emma mentioned you had a replica of the statue in your room. I thought the flowers would make a good peace offering."

"Peace offering?"

"Sure. You must admit I've pushed you rather hard this last week. You've borne it very well, too. I'll have no trouble at all recommending you for a position on a dig."

Diana received these words with a mixture of heart-expanding pride and disturbing doubt. "Ben, have you been testing me?"

She watched him closely. This time the surprised expression on his face appeared completely genuine. "No, I wasn't." He stopped as they reached the dock. "I needed that work done and done well. But if I *had* been testing you, I can tell you that you would have passed with honors."

Diana found her throat suddenly too tight to allow her to speak. As she gazed up at Ben she saw the warmth in his dark eyes deepen. He looked at her and she felt her lips part. Her heart began to pound as his fingers grasped over her upper arms and began to pull her toward him.

A second later Ben captured her lips in an urgent, hungry kiss as he crushed her to him in a strong embrace. The ache in Diana's throat tightened as she realized just how badly she had wanted to be in his arms again, to kiss him, to feel the strange melting warmth that both frightened and thrilled her.

Their lips met again and again, until Ben lifted his head from Diana's and stared into her eyes. *I want you.* The words were unspoken, yet they seemed to echo loudly in the air around them. Diana found herself thinking of the ship's small cabin, lying there with Ben, making love to the rhythm of the ocean.

The hungry look on Ben's face intensified, but instead of kissing her again, he released her from his embrace, only to capture her hand and begin leading her quickly toward the small harbor.

Diana's heart pounded as she followed him along the narrow pier, her mind so full of hopes and fears that she didn't notice he had slowed his pace, and almost ran into him when he came to a sudden stop, just before they had reached the end of the dock where the *Mary Malone* was tied.

"What's wrong?" Diana came around to stand at Ben's side, but she saw the answer before his one-word reply.

"Fog."

The arm of the peninsula near them was shrouded in a deep gray mist, and when she tried to see across the bay, she found that she could hardly make out San Francisco through the dense wall of mist moving slowly over the water's surface.

"Get in the boat." Ben's voice was all business. "We'll have to hurry if we want to get back to the city while we can still see."

Diana had her doubts about the feasibility of Ben's plan, but there was no point in discussing the matter. They didn't bother to don the rubber-soled shoes this time; they just removed their boots and socks, and went to work in their bare feet. Within minutes they had maneuvered out of their mooring and headed the sailboat toward San Francisco.

After raising the sail and watching it fill with the brisk wind, Diana began to believe that they would indeed be able to cross the bay before the fog grew too thick. Shivering, she dropped down into the cockpit and took a seat near the wheel, watching the mist move slowly in front of them. It seemed to grow thicker by the moment. For several beats of her heart the city would be lost in a shroud of gray, only to appear again, dimmer each time.

"*Damn.*"

The explosive word turned Diana's head toward Ben. "We aren't going to make it?"

He shook his head. "Not this way. It's too dangerous to attempt to cross the open water in this. A larger boat would be on top of us before the crew saw us. I'm going to have to turn eastward and sail along that edge of the bay. I'll need you to help me turn her about, so listen carefully."

Diana did exactly as he told her. She was careful to duck as the boom swung around, then held her breath as the sail fluttered impotently in the wind for a moment. Relief filled her as the breeze caught, filling the white canvas, and they again began moving quickly across the now choppy water.

Ben had her take the wheel then, instructing her to keep the ship straight as he took charge of the sails. Diana's hands tightened over the smooth wood, fighting its pull, her heart sinking as she watched Ben coax more speed from the little boat, only to have the moving wall of fog keep pace.

The mist rushed over them even as the port of Oakland came into sight, and within moments they were trapped in a wooly gray cavern whose walls seemed to move ever inward. Leaving the jib up to keep them moving, Ben dropped the mainsail and lashed it to the boom as Diana tried to maintain their course.

"We should be nearing the entrance to the harbor soon," Ben shouted back over his shoulder. "Hold on a second longer, and I'll come take the wheel from you."

As Ben finished speaking, he gave one last jerk to the line he was tying off, then jumped into the cockpit in front of the wheel. Diana peered past him, into the gloom, wondering just how thick it could possibly get, when she noticed a darker shadow of gray looming through the mist.

"Ben, I can see someth—"

Diana broke off, her eyes widening as the shadow took shape. It was not the outline of a dock or a pier, but that of a widebodied fishing boat, riding low in the water and headed directly for them.

_____ *Chapter Fifteen*

DIANA'S HANDS closed convulsively over the wheel as every muscle in her body tightened. "Ben!" She forced the words past her frozen lips. "There's a ship coming at us. A ship dead ahead!"

She saw Ben spin around to look over the bow, then pivot back. "Turn the wheel, Diana. Hard to port!"

He spoke even as he stepped onto the deck on the starboard side of the cockpit. Diana felt her muscles relax slightly with the knowledge that in seconds he would come around to take the wheel from her. With some of the tension removed, she was able to do as Ben had ordered, and she quickly turned the wheel.

For several moments nothing happened, except that the large vessel in front of them continued to close the gap between them. Then the *Mary Malone* responded. Diana watched the bow swing to her right. The sailboat continued to drift forward as the larger, heavier ship approached, but when Diana squinted she could see that the crafts were no longer on a collision course.

As she checked the distance separating the two crafts, she noticed something move across her line of vision. The wave of relief that had swept through her became a terrifying undertow of fear as she realized that the ship's sudden mo-

tion had sent the boom swinging out, then back toward Ben.
Even before she could open her mouth to scream a warning,
the heavy beam crashed into Ben, and as Diana turned and
watched in horror, she saw the boom sweep him off the
deck and into the ocean.

She wasn't aware that she had screamed until her cry
echoed back to her from the wall of fog. The sound broke
the spell that seemed to hold her frozen to the spot. She
took one step toward the side of the boat where Ben had
disappeared. The moment she lifted her hands from the
wheel, she felt it begin to rotate back to its original position.
She saw that just that small shift had the *Mary Malone*
drifting back toward the fishing boat.

Diana's heart raced, but she closed her hands over the
wheel and gave it another turn to the left. She grabbed the
line coiled at her feet and wrapped the rope around several
of the wheel's spokes.

The moment she finished tying a knot that she knew no
sailor would recognize, Diana leapt onto the deck where
Ben had stood, and holding onto one of the lines, she
searched the water for signs of him. The fog surrounded
the small ship like cotton encasing a piece of jewelry. She
could see no sign of Ben, either alongside the sailboat, or
in the area directly behind her. Nothing moved on the gray-
green surface of the bay except a few shreds of mist snaking
over the gentle swells.

"Ben!" Diana called his name at the top of her voice,
then listened for an answer, or a splash, anything that might
direct her to his position.

After several seconds she did hear an answering call, but
it came from the front of the ship—a voice hailing, "Ahoy!"
She ignored the cry for a moment, squinting desperately
into the dense fog until it occurred to her that the fishing
vessel would be full of able-bodied men who could un-

doubtedly swim faster than she could. She looked toward the larger boat, and this hope died.

The ship wasn't as close to the *Mary Malone* as she had expected. If she waited for help it could be too late. Something had obviously happened to incapacitate Ben. He was a strong swimmer; he should be alongside the slow-moving sailboat by now, demanding angrily to be helped back aboard.

This knowledge filled Diana with a cold, sinking fear. Ignoring the second hail echoing across the water from the fishing boat, Diana scanned the water behind the little ship again, every muscle quivering with concentration as she peered through the wall of gray. The fog seemed to shift, to part, and her narrowed eyes tightened further as she caught sight of a spot of white seeping through the mist behind the boat. For one second she was sure she saw something moving, waving. The next moment she saw only a curtain of gray again.

Diana didn't hesitate another moment. She leapt off the ship, taking a huge gulp of air as her feet touched the water; then, as soon as the water closed over her head, she kicked to the surface and began stroking toward the floating blur that had caught her eye.

The icy water and her swift strokes nearly robbed Diana of her breath. She was gasping for air, shivering against the cold water as her legs fought the pull of her long skirts. Panic ripped through her as she grasped the form floating face downward and flipped it over. Ben's eyelids flickered open and shut as Diana shifted him onto his back and cradled his head with one arm.

Before Diana could do anything else, she heard a voice shouting through the mist again, "Ahoy!" She glanced behind her as she tried to support Ben's head, and saw the fishing boat pull up alongside the *Mary Malone*. A bulky figure dressed in a yellow slicker stood in the stern of the wider ship, a figure who looked for all the world like a savior to Diana as she shouted, "Over here. In the water."

Remembering how difficult it was to see in the foggy gloom, she lifted one arm above her head and shouted again, "Here. Please hurry."

Diana's pounding heart quickened as she saw the man nod and begin to remove his slicker as the ship slid past the sailboat. When she saw him bend to remove his shoes, she almost sobbed with relief. She turned to look down at the face of the man she was holding just above the surface, and gasped.

Ben's eyelids no longer flickered, but rested half-shut in a face that had paled to a shade of white that nearly matched his shirt. The only color in his skin was a bluish tinge edging his lips.

Diana felt a terror so deep that she didn't turn at the splashing that announced the approach of the fisherman. Despair replaced fear, leaving her with barely enough strength to continue to kick her feet and keep her arm beneath the inert head of the man she loved.

Diana huddled on the narrow cot, shivering within the heavy folds of the enormous blue wool jacket one of the sailors had slipped around her shoulders. She studied the still form in the bed across from hers, her intertwined fingers squeezing convulsively as she watched Ben's eyelids flicker. She drew a quick, shaky breath a second later when Ben opened his eyes and stared across the small cabin at her.

"Hello," she said softly.

Ben let his gaze slide from Diana's to roam around the small room for a moment. He stared at the open porthole above his cot before he finally moved, slowly easing himself onto his elbow and turning to face Diana once more. Diana slid onto the floor between the bunks, coming to rest on her knees as his eyes met hers again, narrowing with pain.

"Does your head hurt?"

"Yes." Ben lifted his hand to the back of his head, then winced again. "I remember the boom hitting my knees, but how . . ."

"You were thrown backward as you fell. I think your head must have struck the side of the boat."

"I remember now. It was hurting like hell by the time I landed in the water. I was dizzy, and I vaguely recall trying to tread water, waiting for my mind to clear." He paused, then looked directly into Diana's eyes. "I remember seeing you standing on the deck at the back of the ship. You jumped into the water, didn't you?"

Diana nodded. "You were floating facedown when I found you. Apparently you had slipped into unconsciousness and swallowed half the bay."

Anticipating his next question, Diana spoke again. "We were pulled out of the water by the men on the fishing boat—the one we almost collided with. They hauled you aboard their ship, and by the time I was pulled up, you were lying facedown on the deck and some huge man was pounding on your back, forcing the water from your lungs."

Ben flexed one shoulder, then winced. "So that's why I feel as if someone's taken a large stick to me." Ben paused, then shook his head slowly. "Water wasn't the only thing that came up, was it?"

Diana bit her lip, then answered. "No, I'm afraid you lost that very expensive lunch as well. However, since you traded it for your life, I would say you've been amply compensated."

Ben's answering smile was weak. "The *Mary Malone*? What happened to her?"

"She's being taken care of. Once Captain Quilici saw that you weren't going to die, he ordered his boat to turn about and chase ours. Before I followed you into the water, I managed to secure the wheel, so she continued to drift forward in a fairly straight line. The fishermen were able to locate her and transfer some of their men to her deck to sail her into port. The captain was down here a little while ago to check on you and told me that we should be docking soon.''

Slowly Ben reached out and ran his forefinger along her cheek, a caress that sent instant warmth seeping into Diana's still tense muscles. ''You've done very well, matey,'' he said huskily.

Ben's words brought a small smile to her lips and a twisting sensation to her heart. ''I had little choice,'' she replied. ''And to be honest, if the fishermen hadn't helped us, we would both be beneath the surface of the bay by now. I really doubt that I could have hauled you back aboard our boat by myself, and I certainly wouldn't have known what to do about all that water you swallowed if I had. The crew members acted like perfect saviors, other than trying to force brandy down your throat after they'd brought you down here. I'm sure they were trying to help, but I was once told by a doctor that strong spirits should be withheld from someone who is unconscious due to a head injury.''

''I see. Tell me, did this authority say anything against allowing the near victim to kiss his rescuer?''

''No.'' Diana stared at Ben for a moment, then said, ''But I'm too angry at you to allow that at the moment.''

''Angry?''

''Yes.'' Diana lifted her chin slightly. ''After all, weren't you the one who warned me against going swimming all alone?''

Despite the damp hair straggling past her face like shreds of tangled black silk and the bulky jacket encasing her slender form, she looked arrogantly certain of herself, almost regal, as she gazed across at him with an amused glint lighting the dregs of worry in her eyes.

He reached for her as he pushed himself into a sitting position, shifting his body so that he sat on the edge of the cot. His hand closed over her wrist and he smiled as she moved toward him with only the slightest pull of his arm. His eyes never left hers as he lowered his head. Then his lips closed gently over hers.

Their kiss deepened to an urgent meeting of tongues. Ben took Diana into his arms, pulling her up into his lap as her hands slid up over his chest and clasped behind his neck. He drew her closer to him with his left arm as his right hand slid up over the damp muslin of her bodice to close over one full breast, his lips slanting across hers again and again, letting the glow of desire flow through him, warming away the last of the memories of those moments before he lost consciousness, moments filled with fear that he would die without having told Diana McKenzie that he loved her.

Ben was vaguely aware of a creaking sound, but was unmindful of it until a deep voice echoed in the cabin. "We have docked. Perhaps it would be best if you were to continue this aboard your own ship."

Diana pulled her borrowed coat closer to her as she accompanied Ben through Oakland's fog-enshrouded streets, trying not to blush as she remembered the wide grin lifting Captain Quilici's dark mustache as she turned from Ben's kiss. She shook her head as she recalled the next moments, filled with embarrassed conversation as she introduced the captain to Ben.

After thanking the captain and his men, Ben had decided that it was far too cold for them to spend the night in the small cabin of the *Mary Malone*. They located the slip where the sailboat was moored, then retrieved their boots and Ben's jacket. Diana took a few moments to brush her hair and twist it into some semblance of style before they started for the hotel the captain had recommended.

"I think that must be it."

Ben's hand squeezed Diana's as a large building came into view. Through the deep mist Diana could make out a three-story structure, bordered at either end by twin turrets, giving the hotel the appearance of a mystical castle.

They stopped by the short, wide stairway leading up to the recessed entrance and read the sign that had captured Ben's attention. Single rooms could be obtained for the price of six dollars a night, and suites went for nine.

"Diana." Ben's concerned tone drew Diana's eyes to his. "I only have enough money for one room. That very expensive lunch left me with only ten dollars to my name."

Diana stared at him a moment. The embarrassed concern almost made her laugh. Instead, she shrugged as she spoke. "That's not a problem, Ben. You have enough for a suite. That will give us two rooms."

Diana felt a little warmth seep into her arms moments later as she stood in the mahogany-paneled lobby, her feet cushioned by a red and gold patterned carpet. On the other side of a tall, wide desk carved of the same dark wood sat a portly gentleman with black hair and a wide mustache that curled up at the edges of his pursed lips as he examined the two people before him.

"I believe we do have a suite available, but I'm afraid I must insist on advance payment."

"Of course." Ben turned to Diana as he reached into his breast pocket. "See, dear, our luck is improving." Diana saw Ben give her a quick wink. "I know this isn't exactly how we had planned to spend our wedding night, but this is a very fine hotel."

Ben handed the desk clerk the ten dollar bill. The man took it slowly, as he asked, "Your wedding night?"

"Yes. I'm afraid it doesn't look like we're getting off to a very promising start. A friend of ours lent us a sailboat for our honeymoon, you see. After the ceremony this morning in San Francisco, we set off across the bay, planning to stay at the Seafarer's Inn for several days. But we didn't get even halfway across before the fog rolled in and we had to hurry for the nearest port.''

The desk clerk replied, ''You're right. That is hardly the way to start one's honeymoon.''

''That's not the worst of it.'' Diana stepped forward. ''We almost ran into another ship in the fog, and in trying to avoid a collision we capsized and fell into the bay. I shudder to think of what would have happened if Captain Quilici had not pulled us out.''

Diana did shudder as she finished speaking, and was pleased to see the desk clerk's expression soften further. ''Angelo Quilici? He sent you here then, did he?'' The man smiled at her as he reached behind him to grasp what looked like a very thick rope. He brought his hand around to his mouth and Diana could see that he held a funnel-shaped device.

''Millie.'' He spoke loudly into the mouthpiece. ''I have a couple coming up to 318. Please see to it that fires are burning on the hearths in both the parlor and the bedroom; then order tubs and hot water for each of our guests.''

''Millie is the maid in charge of the third floor,'' he explained as he let the cord fall back into place, then reached over to ring a bell. ''My name is Walford. I want you to let me know if we can get you anything at all. I hope ordering the baths was not presumptuous of me, but you both look chilled to the bone. Now, I see that you have no luggage. I take it this was lost in your little accident?''

He paused while Diana and Ben nodded, then went on. ''Well, we shall provide you with some nice robes. Give your wet things to the maid and we'll restore them the best we can. Oh, and a nice dinner comes with the price of a suite. Please use the telephone to ring down and order it when you're ready. We shall do our best to see that your stay is as comfortable as the circumstances will allow.''

As Walford finished speaking, a young man dressed in black trousers and a short red jacket appeared and was instructed to show Diana and Ben to their suite. He led them to an ornate wrought-iron elevator that lifted them smoothly up the three floors. Grateful that she hadn't been forced to climb three flights of stairs on legs that had begun to shake slightly from the effects of the last several hours, Diana stepped into the room and immediately lowered herself into an armchair covered in dark blue brocade.

Diana heard none of Ben's conversation with the bellboy as she noticed the walls papered in stripes of navy blue and deep gold. The carpet was patterned in the same colors and velvet curtains in a shade as dark as night covered the windows on either side of the oak-mantled fireplace.

Flames had just begun to dance along the thick logs sitting on the grate, flames that held Diana's attention, encouraging her to get to her feet and cross the rug to stand before the hearth, her slender hands outstretched, searching for warmth.

Real warmth finally seeped into Diana's form as she sunk deeper into the tub. She had washed her hair and every portion of her body with the hot water, there before the fireplace in the suite's bedroom, and now she rested her head against the curved edge of the full-sized tub. Bright flames crackled within the ornate oak mantlepiece framing the fireplace.

The warm robe that Walford had promised, made of white terry cloth, awaited Diana on a chair at the foot of her tub, but she ignored it as she turned her thoughts to Ben—most likely lounging in his own tub on the other side of that door—wondering if his skin glowed as hers did.

This thought conjured up a vision of Ben's face as he lay

in the bay, white and so very cold-looking. Diana shivered despite the warm water surrounding her.

Another memory, less chilling but no less vivid, filled her mind, making her recall the moments she had watched Ben's face in the cabin of the fishing boat, waiting for him to regain consciousness. As the time moved slowly by, Diana had been forced to reexamine her actions of the last several weeks. The hypocrisy of her behavior had struck her sharply, as she recalled how she had turned from the warmth Ben's arms offered, forcing him away at every chance for no more substantial reason than her fear that he would eventually abandon her.

Diana shifted in the tub, recalling how she had boasted of her vow to live life as it came, to "seize the day."

The knowledge that she had betrayed her deepest conviction, that she had lost entire days that could have been spent in joy instead of strife, filled her eyes with tears. She lifted a damp hand to wipe them away, leaving her cheeks even wetter. She reached over for the towel hanging on the rack attached to the edge of the tub and pressed it to her face.

She sighed as she released the rough material, then started when she saw the tall figure filling the doorway opposite her.

Ben wore a thick white robe that matched the one waiting for Diana; it was belted loosely around his waist. The thick hair on his chest glistened in the light from the overhead chandelier. Diana's heart raced.

There could be no more running from fate, she thought. Today's events had shown her clearly that she loved this man. Acknowledging this to herself filled her with fear, for she didn't know how she would bear it if he didn't feel the same way. But even if their time together was fated to be short, she had to take each day, each moment, as it came.

She would hug the memories to her against whatever pain the future might hold.

She grasped the edge of the tub with both hands for support, then slowly rose out of the water, letting it flow down over her curves as she stood naked and unprotected in front of him.

Chapter Sixteen

BEN'S HEART POUNDED. He'd never really had a chance to gaze at her unclothed body before. His breath caught in his throat as he marveled at the perfection before him, at the slender lines sculpted into high breasts above a slender waist that curved into narrow hips. He gazed at the glistening liquid gliding down her slender form, making her skin glimmer like polished alabaster in the firelight.

His loins tightened with instant desire, but he found he couldn't move a muscle; he could only lean against the door frame for several moments, stunned by the force of the passion racing through his blood and pounding in his ears, reducing to faint whispers the well-considered thoughts that had run through his mind moments before he opened the door.

The events of the day had revealed much to him, exposing as much about Diana's feelings as they had about his own. As he came to recognize her fear of being abandoned again, he saw a reflection of his own reluctance to risk his heart. His betrayal at the hand of the fair Sarah had scarred him as deeply as Daniel McKenzie's desertion had wounded Diana.

But just as Diana was not cut from the same cloth as the cool young woman who had hurt him so deeply, he was not the kind of man who would leave someone he loved without an explanation. Yet, circumstances had almost forced him to do just that, to slip out of Diana's life without telling her just what she meant to him, how her cool beauty sent white heat surging through him at the mere thought of her, how her insistence of independence made him want to smile and draw her to him, to keep her there always.

Even as he placed his hand on the brass doorknob, Ben had warned himself that with time to reflect over the day, Diana might once more have retreated into her protective shell, that she would reject his offer of love. Still, he had twisted the knob with determination, knowing that if he had come upon a moment worthy of seizing, this was it.

He had expected to meet resistance when he entered the room. To see Diana standing before him, her eyes shining with welcome and challenge, made him feel as weak as a sail that had lost hold of the wind. His breath caught in his throat as she lifted one slender leg to step over the rim of the tub. He watched the curve of her hip gleam in the firelight as she brought the other leg out; then, finding new strength pulsing through him, he strode across the room, loosening the belt of his robe and shrugging out of it just before he reached her.

He lowered his mouth to capture her softly parted lips as he took her into his arms, letting his fingers explore her curves, silken with moisture, as he drew her against his body. The same breathless need he had felt earlier in the cabin of the fishing boat lent a similar urgency to his kisses, and yet as much as he longed to lose himself in her, he controlled his every move, wanting to savor the glory of each moment he held her in his arms.

Diana sighed against Ben's mouth as she felt his hands cup her buttocks to lift her into the air. She continued to answer his deep kisses as he turned and carried her across the room, easing her onto the satin bed-coverlet, and followed her down to its smooth surface.

She welcomed the weight of his body on hers, the feel of his knee sliding between her legs, the warmth of his stomach pressed to hers, the velvet strength of his masculinity caressing her inner thigh. His power and vitality surrounded her, and as she thought of how that vibrant life had almost been taken from her, she tightened her arms around his waist and increased the pressure of her lips on his.

Desire coiled tightly in her stomach and seeped down like molten fire to the area between her thighs. She was aware of an urgent need to cradle his strength within her, to confirm life and passion and everything that was Benjamin Potter. At the same time she wanted to savor every kiss, to revel in every caress, to truly experience both his lust and his love.

Tears filled Diana's eyes as the last word floated into her passion-drugged mind. Despite all her efforts, it had been impossible to keep emotion out of her relationship with this man. It had vibrated between them from the very beginning, whether it be anger or distrust or desire. All her attempts to protect her heart against pain had been pointless, for she was helplessly in love with this man, and if the future were to bring her pain, she knew that the joy of this moment in his arms would be worth any amount of suffering she might have to face.

Diana moaned softly as Ben rolled partially onto his side and eased his hand firmly up over her ivory skin to cup her exposed breast. He was aware of the other breast moving against his chest as Diana shifted in pleasured reaction to his caress. A jolt of desire shot through him like a burning brand. His body urged him to move, to slide into the opening that lay so close, but he resisted, determined to luxuriate in each kiss, each touch that passed between him and the woman he held in his arms.

Yet, as he kissed Diana deeply, his tongue in her mouth, he felt her arch against him. The softness of her tongue met his as she rolled toward him, and the tips of her breasts seared his chest, further enflaming his need for her. He slid his hand down, over the curve of her hips, then angled in to tease the curls between her legs.

Diana moaned again as Ben touched her. Passion and need became a throbbing heat beneath his hand. Her hips twisted beneath his, bringing her thigh into deeper contact with his desire, and she was rewarded with a deep groan that rumbled in Ben's throat as he removed his hand and eased himself back onto her.

This time she issued no gasp when he slid into her; instead, she released a gratified sigh against his lips. As he moved slowly in and out of her, she adjusted the shifting of her hips to that rhythm, content for the moment to savor the feel of each stroke, though her body cried out for release from the building pressure.

Ben controlled his movements in spite of the demanding desire raging within him until Diana's deep, urgent kisses and the occasional soft mewling sounds he heard escape her throat told him she felt the same desperate need. He lifted his mouth from hers then, placed his hands on the bed, and pushed himself upward, watching her face as he pressed into her.

Diana's eyes opened, midnight blue and wide with desire. He increased the rhythm and depth of his thrusts. Her head lolled slightly to one side as she arched against him. Her features tightened, then her eyes opened wide again and she reached for his shoulders, pulling him down to her as he felt her grow tight around him. He was only vaguely aware of her continuing pulses as his own pleasure reached its climax, spilling into her repeatedly as he clung to her even tighter than he had tried to cling to life earlier that day.

Diana lay beneath Ben, cradled between his warmth and

the soft bed. It seemed to spin beneath her as she tried to control her rapid breathing. She tightened her hold on Ben's waist in an attempt to control the dizzying sensation. Ben's head was tucked in the crook of her neck, his warm breath washing over her skin in an uneven rhythm that matched her own ragged breathing, punctuated every few moments by the tiniest of kisses dropped onto her shoulder.

When Ben finally moved, it was to lift his head. Then, trapping her head in the warm clasp of his hands, he lowered his lips to hers in another bruising kiss.

Long moments later, when Ben lifted his mouth from hers, Diana drew in a shuddering breath.

"Diana . . . I love you."

Ben's words seeped slowly into Diana's passion-drugged mind. Her heart rate dropped and for several slow beats she could only stare up at him mutely, turning his words over and over in her mind until their meaning grew clear. The message registered in her heart at the same moment, filling her chest with a dazzling burst of joy so intense it was almost painful. Her eyes filled with tears and her throat tightened, almost choking back her reply.

"I love you, Ben."

Deep silence filled the room, broken only by the soft crackling of the fire. Ben searched his mind for more words, thinking there should be so much more to say. But he felt Diana knew without him saying it that she need never again fear abandonment. She had his heart in her hands now— his life and his protection.

"Are you hungry?" he whispered at last.

Diana replied by choking on a combination of tears and laughter as she nodded. "I'm starving. Call down to Walford and order our dinner. Ask for an extra one for me."

Ben grinned as he sat up and reached for the slender black upright telephone sitting on the lace-covered table next to the bed. "We can't afford to pay for anything extra, remember? But I'll see that you get plenty to eat."

The food that arrived twenty minutes later was beautifully prepared and plentiful enough to feed several hungry people. Wrapped once more in their robes, Ben and Diana sat at the small table in front of the parlor fire, serving themselves from an array of dishes and tureens under silver covers. In companionable silence they worked their way through a delicate cream of broccoli soup, a perfectly broiled rack of lamb, and several vegetable dishes that included sliced red potatoes served with a delicate cheese sauce.

As Ben poured coffee into dainty china cups, Diana happily noticed the dishes mounded with chocolate mousse.

"Does that expression mean that you have had enough to eat, or that you are enjoying the anticipation of your dessert?"

"Neither. I was just remembering how I used to want to take my dessert to bed with me. Grandfather thought that was terribly decadent, not to mention messy, so of course it was forbidden."

"So who's stopping you now?" Ben picked up his cup and saucer with one hand and his bowl and spoon with the other, then stood and stared expectantly at Diana.

Diana could hardly suppress her desire to giggle as she picked up her dessert and followed Ben to the other room. As if they had discussed it beforehand, they both went to opposite sides of the bed and placed their burdens on the side tables as they turned down the covers. Diana gave the top sheet an extra smoothing pat, then glanced across to see Ben shrug out of his robe before he slid into bed. This time one small giggle did escape her throat as she copied him, then drew her dessert into bed with her and took a bite of the rich chocolate.

"Mmmm."

"I take it you're enjoying your dessert."

Diana nodded as she closed her mouth over another spoonful.

"Can I have a taste?"

Diana leaned away from him. "You have your own."

"I wasn't talking about the mousse."

Diana glanced at him again, then found her gaze held by the hunger in his dark eyes. Suddenly, the dessert had lost its allure. She let him take her dish and spoon from her suddenly numb fingers, then melted into his arms as he turned back to draw her to him.

Their lips met in a deep kiss that shifted from gentle to desperate to deeply passionate, reflecting the day's kaleidoscope of emotions. Desire flashed through them like a jolt of lightning. As their bodies met between the cool sheets, they surrendered to the urgency of their desire.

Diana was not content to allow Ben to move slowly this time. As his arms tightened around her, she leaned forward, forcing him onto his back. She kissed him deeply, then lifted her head to study his reaction to her boldness.

"You want to lead this time, do you?"

His words rumbled out of his chest, his eyes dark with an unspoken challenge. Diana lowered her lips to capture his, slid her tongue past them, and smiled even while she continued to kiss him. He groaned his pleasure and tightened his arms around her.

Desire sprung to life as her leg brushed against his throbbing strength. Slowly she eased her parted legs down until his manhood rested at the apex of her parted thighs. She tilted her hips back and forth, teasing them both into urgent moans; then she positioned herself and shifted back, letting him glide into her.

She tried to arch against him as she had before, but found that in this new position the action didn't produce the desired effect. Pressing down on Ben's chest, she sat up, still holding him in her, then lifted herself up and down against him,

smiling at the sensations coursing through her and the pleasure on Ben's face as they reached the pinnacle of their
pleasure together.

Diana lay within the warm curve of Ben's arms, her head
resting on his chest where she could listen to the strong
beating of his heart. She felt him drop a kiss on her brow;
then she shifted to look up into his eyes.

Ben's lazy smile filled her with warm joy. She returned
it, then sighed as she snuggled next to him and let contented
sleep wash over her.

The sun danced on the relatively still waters as the *Mary
Malone* floated into her home mooring after an uneventful
sail across the bay from Oakland in the early-morning light.
Within minutes, Ben and Diana, working together, had
everything tied down and secured, ready to leave the sailboat
as they had found her the day before. After handing Diana
onto the pier beside him, Ben looked back at the ship and
smiled.

Diana's face was lifted to his, her cheeks glowing and
pink, her blue eyes glinting with joy and a sense of security.
Ben leaned over, planning to drop a quick kiss on her lips,
only to let his mouth linger and slide over hers for several
long moments. When he lifted his head at last it was with
deep-felt reluctance.

"We'd better go," he whispered. "We need to find a
carriage to take us up to the Heights."

Diana let him take her hand, and walked next to him
down the pier.

"Ben." She stopped, her hand tightening on his, forcing
him to turn and look down at her as she went on. "What
will Emma and her father be thinking?"

"About our night together? Well, not that it's any of
their—"

"No." Diana interrupted him with an impatient shake of

her head. "They must have been worried when we didn't return. And what about Will?"

"I telephoned the house last evening from the hotel, before I got into my bath. I explained to Will what had happened, and in case you're feeling a little shy about things, I made it clear that we were in *separate* rooms. Will sounded quite relieved. He seems to have developed a rather paternal attitude toward you."

As if Ben's mention of Will Babcock had conjured up the man, Will's unmistakable voice echoed down the dock. "Benjamin, you've arrived. How perfect."

Diana walked into the welcoming arms he held wide for her. "I'm very glad you are safe, young woman." Will's voice was soft in her ear; then he grasped her upper arms as he stepped back from her and spoke in a louder voice. "Well, I hear I have you to thank for saving this ungrateful boy's life. You have my undying gratitude. The artifacts have arrived and I need his help."

"They're here?"

As Ben stepped forward, Will dropped his hands from Diana's shoulders and turned to the younger man. "They arrived late yesterday, along with the fog and Simon. You remember the young bear of a fellow that normally works in the Egyptian area at the museum. I made him stay aboard the ship last night, since it was too late to unload, and too risky in the fog. This morning everything was transferred to two wagons. I left Simon and the drivers standing guard while I came looking for you on the off chance you'd come in. So, come along. Simon can ride in one wagon, and the three of us can go in the other and plot out our day's work as we go."

Within the narrow walls of the delivery wagon, Diana sat wedged between crates and barrels, listening to Ben and Will go over the list of items that had been delivered, making the final decisions about where they would be displayed. As she relaxed against the curved sides of a large wooden barrel, she made mental notes so that she could help with the unloading and the arrangement of the artifacts within the exhibit area.

Ben and Will were still talking when the van pulled to a stop, but then Will turned to take Diana's hand to guide her down the folding steps.

"Diana, I can't believe what a fool I am. I meant to tell you right away. Your father arrived last night, earlier than expected. Sutro informed him that you were here."

Diana's body tensed immediately. "I imagine that my father was surprised to learn this."

Will nodded. It was on the tip of Diana's tongue to ask if her father had appeared at all pleased at the news, but she changed her mind and instead asked, "Which crates did you want me to start unloading?"

"We don't need you to work here today, Diana," Ben said. "Between Ian, Simon, Will, and myself, we can see to all this. You're free to go on up to the house."

Diana didn't know which upset her more—the thought of the man waiting up at the house for her, or Ben's cool dismissal of her offer to help. It was this last that she responded to, lifting her chin and narrowing her eyes as she looked up at him. "I know how to handle these items, Ben. You don't have to worry about me trying to lift anything too heavy, or doing any other foolish things that would place the artifacts in danger."

Ben reached over to place his hand gently on her shoulder. "I know that. I also know you must want to freshen up before you face your father."

The pressure of Ben's fingers on Diana's shoulder banished her anger, leaving in its wake a feeling of panic at the thought of her father waiting up at Sutro Heights. She bit the inside of her lip and told herself it was best to get this meeting over with now, before the house was filled with tonight's preopening guests.

Diana decided that it was just as well that her father had not been at the house when she came up from the Baths earlier. She had needed some time alone to gather her thoughts about this meeting, so she had spent the day in her room, even having her lunch delivered to her.

The nap she had taken had restored her courage, and the long bath she had indulged in before dressing had eased away most of the tension in her body, except for the twisting and fluttering sensation in her stomach.

Gazing into the mirror, Diana saw a young woman who appeared confidently garbed in a pale gray dress that had been carefully altered in Philadelphia to emphasize her slender figure. The neckline, trimmed in a lacy design of jet black, skimmed the upper swells of her breasts, and the same decoration dotted the slender bands draped over her shoulders.

Teardrop crystals glittered in her ears, and her smooth, black hair had been swept up into a thick cloud framing her face. Diana told herself to smile—it was time to seize the moment, the moment she had been waiting for all these years. She straightened her shoulders, then turned toward the door, reminding herself to take this evening one step at a time.

She was not expecting Daniel McKenzie to greet her with deep affection, she reminded herself. If he had any feelings for her he surely would have written to her or searched her out long ago. She just wanted a reasonable explanation for the rift, so that she could put that chapter of her life firmly behind her.

Diana stood at the top of the stairs, listening to the murmuring voices below. She took a deep breath, reminding herself that Ben would be near, that his presence would give her strength if her own should fail, and she started down the steps.

She stopped as she reached the bottom, peered into the parlor and saw a room full of strangers. Her lips curved into a nervous smile and she almost laughed out loud. She still had no idea if she would recognize her father. Her one distinct memory was of a tall, thin, bearded man wearing dusty khaki clothes, holding her plump three-year-old hand as he showed her how to gently brush dust away from a half-uncovered shard of pottery.

"Diana!"

A familiar deep voice caught Diana's attention, and she turned to see Adolph Sutro standing by a bank of windows. His white hair shimmered in the well-lit room, and his small black eyes held hers as he called out again. "Come here. I've someone you should meet."

Diana's hand tightened on the banister as she slowly shifted her attention to the man standing next to Sutro. She saw a figure dressed in a black cutaway jacket over a startlingly white shirt. The man was tall and lean. His medium brown hair was streaked with white, as was the full beard framing his narrow face.

Diana took a deep breath, then forced herself to cross the room, telling herself as she neared the two men that this was not necessarily her father; he could be any of a number of people Mayor Sutro might want to introduce her to, a member of the city council that he was always complaining about, for instance.

"Diana McKenzie," Sutro began as she reached his side. "May I have the pleasure of introducing you to Daniel McKenzie."

His eyes were the same pale, golden brown she remembered from her childhood. But those eyes had always glimmered with warmth and humor. The eyes now revealed no trace of any emotion at all, and when the man spoke, his voice was also devoid of expression.

"Hello, Diana," he said. "I was quite surprised to learn of your presence. May I ask what brings you here to San Francisco?"

_____ *Chapter Seventeen*

DANIEL MCKENZIE'S QUESTION seemed to hang in the air. Diana was aware that Sutro had moved away, leaving her to study the bearded man before her, searching for a sign of welcome in his eyes and finding only the cool, inquiring glance of a stranger.

"I came here for the same reason you did." Diana was surprised at how composed her voice sounded. Some inner portion of her mind reacted with pride at her self-control as she went on evenly, "I never lost the interest in archaeology that you instilled in me, so when I learned about the exhibit scheduled to appear at the Sutro Baths, I knew I had to see it. Besides, I saw it as an opportunity to meet with people who might help me with my career."

"Oh?"

She stiffened and answered quickly. "Yes. I have been speaking with Professor Justin Harrington about accompanying him on his next dig."

"And you really think that Harrington would be interested in taking on an untrained—"

"*Not* untrained," Diana broke in. "I have a degree in the subject, and—"

"—and she is a gifted artist as well."

Diana pivoted around as Ben's voice finished her state-

253

ment, then watched him as he went on. "Diana has been helping us with the Pompeii exhibit. She has quite a knack for reproducing artwork. I believe that her talent, along with her knowledge of antiquities, will make her a very valuable addition to any dig."

Ben was aware that Diana was watching him closely and he noticed the wounded expression in her wide blue eyes.

If he hadn't seen that, Ben would have thought Diana's father's attitude hadn't bothered her at all. He had only heard the last of their conversation as he approached the pair, but even from across the room McKenzie's stiff stance and the way Diana was twisting her hands together behind her back had told him that this was hardly the reunion she had hoped for. Hearing the remote manner in which McKenzie questioned the daughter he hadn't seen for seventeen years had made Ben want to grab the stiff lapels of the man's dinner jacket and shake fear into his eyes—any emotion besides the cool expression with which he regarded his daughter.

But now that Ben saw the tight control that Diana had over her feelings, he reigned in his anger, turned back to her father, and forced a tight smile to his lips. "I'm sorry. In my enthusiasm for Diana's work I forgot my manners. My name is Benjamin Potter. And you, sir?"

Some emotion—recognition or wariness or both—flickered on McKenzie's face. "Benjamin Potter, of the British Museum?"

"Yes."

"I see. I'm pleased to make your acquaintance. I am Daniel McKenzie."

If this man was indeed behind the robbery attempt and the murder at the British Museum six months earlier, he would be watching for a trap. Ben had no intention of giving anything away.

"Diana's father? Well, this *is* an occasion. I am pleased

to have at last made your acquaintance, sir.'' Ben stretched his hand out, grasping the one McKenzie had offered, and coerced a pleasant tone into his next words. ''I'm sure you are aware that you are something of a legend in the world of archaeology. I believe I have been looking forward to your arrival almost as much as your daughter has.''

''Well, I must say, I was very surprised to learn she was here. I'm gratified to hear that she is doing well, of course, and, quite frankly, I'm relieved to find she had other reasons for coming all the way out here than simply to see me.'' He paused and turned to Diana. ''I hope you understand that my schedule is quite full. I doubt we will have much time for socializing. I only plan on being here until Sunday.''

Ben stopped the angry words churning in his mind as he watched Diana draw a quick breath before she spoke. ''No, I didn't suppose we would have time to do much more than exchange greetings. As I mentioned, my main purpose for coming out here was to obtain a position with Professor Harrington. He's indicated that he may hire me, but I've been so busy with the preparations for the exhibit that he and I have had very little time to speak. If I hope to accompany him on his next dig, I must make sure he and I have a long talk.''

McKenzie nodded. ''Tell me, what does your grandfather think of all this?''

Diana was aware of another twinge of pain in her chest. It was obvious that her father had in no way concerned himself with her life for any period of time. However, she was also conscious of a feeling of numbness spreading throughout her body that enabled her to answer him evenly. ''I'm surprised you asked. I don't ever recall you caring a thing for what Grandfather thought before. To answer your question, Grandfather never approved of my studies, but when he saw how determined I was, he paid for my school-

ing. He passed away last year, shortly before I started my
last year at the university.''

Diana's last words were swallowed up by the loud clang
of a bell, which was followed by Sutro's announcement that
dinner was ready to be served in the dining room. Without
another glance at the tall, bearded man she had come so far
to see, Diana turned and let Ben escort her to the dining
room.

An hour and a half after taking her seat at the long, linen-
covered table beneath the sparkling chandelier, Diana
viewed with disinterest the chocolate-covered eclair that had
just been placed in front of her. She had been able to eat
very little of the sumptuous meal, feeling like one of the
mechanized dolls she'd watched at the Musée Mécanique
in the Baths, politely lifting her fork to her mouth over and
over without any thought to what she was eating.

She was aware that Ben sat across from her, but she had
only let her eyes meet his once. The look of sympathy in
those dark depths had slipped under her defenses, awakening
the emotions she had been carefully keeping at bay.

She kept her eyes lowered, and forced herself to concentrate on Adolph Sutro's voice. Her host sat at the head
of the table, near Diana, where he indulged his insatiable
curiosity by questioning her father on the subject of mythology.

Each time her father's voice reached her ears, Diana was
aware of a strange chill seeping into her bones and of a knot
twisting more tightly in her stomach. Each bite of the beautifully prepared but tasteless food added to her discomfort.
In an attempt to distract herself from the pain, she concentrated on the voices of the others.

Jean-Paul LaPierre, a small man with heavily pomaded
blonde hair, spoke across the table to Professor Harrington.
''Well, I will be anxious to see that vase, Harrington. I
know you are aware of my collection, so I shall not insult

you by pretending indifference to the item." Diana turned
to see LaPierre smile broadly as he finished. "I only hope
that you will have consideration for my pocketbook as a
reciprocal favor."

Harrington returned the smile. "We shall see, my friend.
Etruscan vases dating back to 500 BC are hardly a common
item, so such things command uncommon prices. But we
are old friends, so I am certain that we can come to some
equitable arrangement."

"*Bon.*" LaPierre nodded, then glanced at Ben. "I just
hope I did not err in discussing this in front of Professor
Potter. I fear he may desire the article for the British Museum and bid against me."

"Don't worry." Ben picked up his wine glass. "I'm not
on a buying trip, and as far as I know the museum isn't
interested in another Etruscan vase."

Harrington turned to Ben. "You might change your mind,
Potter, when you see this one." A hint of arrogance echoed
in the professor's voice, causing Diana to glance sharply at
him as he went on. "It's in nearly perfect condition. We
found it last year in a dig near Rome in what had apparently
been a storeroom. The vase was wrapped in straw and
packed in a small crate. The crate had been broken from
the weight of the surrounding dirt, but the vase was untouched. I was fortunate to get the item as partial payment
for heading the dig."

"It sounds like a wonderful find," Ben responded, then
took a sip of wine, and swallowed before he spoke again.
"I'd like to see it. But as I said, I'm not on a buying trip,
so don't expect me to help you drive up the price and
bankrupt poor LaPierre here."

"So the rumors are true then?" Harrington asked. "The
museum has no funds left since purchasing the statue of
Diana from the museum in Naples last year?"

Ben watched the wine he had sent swirling around in his

glass. "I wouldn't really know about that. The financial committee doesn't take me into its confidence."

"If the price I heard quoted is correct, your museum received a bargain on the statue regardless of how high a price others might consider it." Daniel McKenzie's voice drew everyone's attention down the table—including that of the reluctant Diana.

"I saw it in February," he went on, "when you opened your display in London. As you know, I have made something of a career searching out artifacts associated with that particular deity. That statue is the finest example of an expression of Diana's combined roles as mistress of the moon and goddess of the hunt that I have ever seen."

Diana heard Harrington's voice rumbling in reply, but his words faded to an indistinct murmur, drowned out by the loud ringing sound in her ears. The warmth and interest she had heard in her father's voice when he spoke of this statue, as opposed to his cool tone he used when speaking to her earlier, had pierced her heart with a dagger so slim that it had darted past all her defenses. She sat unmoving until she noticed that the people around her were all standing. She looked up to find Ben frowning at her.

"We're going into the other room, Diana," he said. "Harrington has brought some photographic slides that Sutro would like us to view."

Diana nodded and got to her feet slowly. Sutro was fascinated with photography. During more than one evening she had heard him order one of the servants to set up his projector as she and Ben left for the Baths. It occurred to her that if she wanted to work for Harrington, she should display an interest in his work, but she was even more conscious of the anger and grief that had grown within her, and of her rapidly deteriorating control over these emotions.

As Diana exited the dining room she noticed that a crowd had formed in the doorway to the large parlor. Taking advantage of the confusion, she stepped rapidly toward the stairs, then hurried up, holding her breath until she reached the top step.

Her bedroom door had barely clicked shut behind her before she uttered a wrenching sob. Diana crossed her arms tightly over her chest, as if trying to contain the emotion stored there. She would not cry, she told herself. She had promised herself long ago never to allow the pain of her father's desertion to touch her again, never to let pain and yearning have any place in her life.

Diana held her breath in an attempt to gain control over the agitated rise and fall of her chest. The pressure eased slightly and a second later she moved through the dimly lit room to her desk and placed an unerring hand around the small metal figure there.

The stag's antlers bit into her palm as Diana turned, exited her room, then stood at the top of the steps. Harrington's voice drifted up the stairwell. "Here you can see the evidence of years of neglect."

His next words were less distinct, and as he continued to speak, Diana tiptoed down the stairs and hurried out the door and up the stone steps to the parapet at the edge of the cliff.

Ben had positioned himself at the back of the parlor, one eye on the shadowy pictures projected onto a large screen, and the other on the hallway. When Diana's slim figure darted by, he edged toward the door. Moments later, certain that the other occupants of the room were concentrating on the images before them, Ben slipped out and followed her.

As Ben reached the top of the steps a strong wind caught the tails of his dinner jacket. They flapped behind him as he caught sight of the slim figure standing at the low wall. As he watched, Diana turned and gazed at him. Then he was at her side.

He reached for her hands, but found them closed tightly over something. "What's that?" he asked.

Diana shook her head. "Nothing."

Ben saw her fingers tighten. He placed his hands over Diana's and gently pried her fingers open to reveal the small statue he had noticed in her room. Again his eyes sought hers. "What are you doing with this up here?"

Ben had expected to see grief or anger reflected on her features. Instead he saw only indifference. "I was going to throw it into the ocean," she replied.

She had retreated into her protective shell again. Ben knew how to deal with her anger, but this complete absence of emotion puzzled him. Recalling how he'd once dealt with his younger sisters, he forced a light tone to his voice as he spoke. "Well, you must have a very good arm then. I don't think *I* can throw that far."

"That's what I decided. I'm afraid that if I threw it from here it would only land on the road below us, perhaps on the unsuspecting head of some poor soul leaving the Cliff House." She paused, then went on in a voice tight with suppressed emotion. "This silly statue has caused enough grief for me. I wouldn't want it to do the same for anyone else."

Ben reached over, placed his hands over hers, and eased the figurine away from her. He lifted it up, positioning it between his eyes and Diana's. The light from the nearly full moon above glittered on the antlers of the stag as he spoke again. "This little thing? It looks harmless enough to me."

"Harmless? I suppose you're right. Unfortunately, I wasn't perceptive enough to see it for the mere trinket it is." Her voice trembled despite her cool tone as she continued. "Instead, I made a fool of myself, holding onto that all these years, treasuring it when it meant absolutely nothing. You saw my father tonight—heard him speak to me.

I'm a stranger to him. I stopped being real for him years ago. The only Diana in his life exists in myths and statues like that one.''

Diana glared at the object in Ben's hand. He dropped it into his coat pocket as he lifted his other hand up and slid his fingers over Diana's jaw. "That sort of thing happens to men like your father," he said. "Men who devote their lives to one particular thing suddenly find that it has captured them. I hope you won't mind my saying that I think men like that are utter fools.''

He watched the anger slowly fade from Diana's eyes— saw her lips tremble slightly, then tighten. Before she could gain control again, slip into that shell of hers, he placed his arms around her and pulled her to him.

"Cry, Diana. You'll feel better, darling.''

For a moment after Ben spoke Diana was completely motionless in his arms, as stiff and unmoving as if she had actually turned into a statue herself. Ben began to fear that he'd said and done the wrong thing until he felt her begin to shake and heard her heartwrenching sobs.

Ben held her for several minutes, tightening his arms around her slender frame as it shuddered, until finally he felt her relax against him and heard her muffled voice ask, "Ben, do you have a handkerchief I could borrow?''

Moments later Diana stepped out of the circle of his arms and dabbed the white fabric at the corners of her eyes. "Thank you," she whispered. "I'm afraid that wasn't very professional of me.''

Ben placed gentle fingers beneath her chin and nudged her face toward him. "I thought you and I had gone beyond that. Have you already forgotten last night?''

Diana's eyes widened and she shook her head. "No, Ben. I'll never forget last night.''

The warmth in her voice and the soft shimmer of her eyes brought a smile to Ben's lips. "Then don't worry about hiding your emotions in front of me. Besides, this isn't a professional matter; it's a personal one.''

Diana shook her head. ''Not any longer. If Daniel McKenzie wishes to treat me as simply an old acquaintance, one he obviously cares little for, it's fine with me. I realize now that I never really knew him. I created a . . . a myth about him, a story about a father who loved and wanted me, but who had somehow been robbed of all memory of my existence. It had no more basis in reality than did the stories about Zeus, Apollo, or any of the others. A myth can't hurt me.''

Ben looked at her pale features, now blotchy and puffed from her tears. He hoped she was right, that her father's indifference had broken the bond that might have come between the two of them if he were to prove McKenzie was a thief and a murderer.

This thought, the idea that something might destroy the connection he had forged with this woman, awoke a fierce sort of anger that Ben had never known he could possess. Along with the fury came a compelling need to feel Diana once more in his arms.

Ben lowered his mouth to hers, to claim her lips in a deep, possessive kiss as he drew her body to his. His hands glided over the satin of her dress, easing over her curves. He smiled against her mouth as he heard a soft moan escape her lips.

''To your right is the observatory I told you about, Professor McKenzie.''

Adolph Sutro's voice echoed across the parapet floor. Diana and Ben broke apart and turned to see two figures come to a stop at the top of the steps leading up from the house. Sutro continued to speak. ''Tomorrow, after the ceremony at the Baths, I shall take you up and let you see my view in the daylight. But for now, let me show you how the sea looks at night from my battlement up—''

He stopped speaking as he spied Diana and Ben, now standing respectably apart. "Mr. Sutro is not exaggerating. It's a magnificent view. And the air is wonderful up here, if a little chilly at times. I was just telling your daughter she should have put on a coat before coming out."

Diana stepped forward. "I got very warm suddenly in the house, probably because of all the visitors." She rubbed her hands over her arms. "The cool air felt good at first, but now I think I'd better get back inside. Good night, Mr. Sutro, Ben, . . . Father."

That night, beneath the satin covers, the grove once more called to Diana in her dreams. As Diana walked beneath the naked branches made silver by the moonlight, garbed in her short tunic, she became aware of a growing sense of unease, a disturbing mood that was stronger than those in her previous visits.

The foliage was gone from the trees; the moss covering the ground had dried up. It crackled beneath her sandals as she stepped forward. The nearer she drew to the pond, the greater her fear grew. Her heart raced as she stared ahead, then pounded loudly as she caught a glimpse of the cypresses that encircled her sanctuary.

They were all dead—tall skeletons formed of narrow branches that managed to maintain their spirelike shape. Diana tried to slow her footsteps, but found she could not. Some force made her continue forward, until she stepped within the sinister circle.

It was here that Diana stopped. The pond was gone. In front of her lay a deep bowl formed of hard gray earth that lay fissured and puckered in the moonlight.

An emotion deeper than terror chilled her flesh and her pounding heart. Diana tried to turn, but could not. Instead she found herself drawn forward. Her sandaled feet sank into the dry earth as she stepped into the vile hole that had once been filled with life-giving water, until she stood in the center, her very bones trembling.

Diana stood there for several moments, suddenly conscious of another presence. She pivoted quickly. On the edge of the dried pool stood a tall, powerful figure cloaked in black. A hood covered his head, shadowing his face as he began walking toward her, his larger feet stepping into the depressions her footsteps had left, obliterating her tracks.

Diana stared at the shadows beneath the hood as he approached, ordering the moon to cast its light upon the shrouded features. When the man came closer, her command was answered, and her heart leapt with joy as she recognized the dark eyes and deep golden hair gleaming in the moon's pale light.

A second later, the joy turned to pain as the man took another step and his features changed. The eyes became lighter, and the bone structure became more narrow, partially obliterated by a dark beard streaked with silver.

Diana shook her head and tried to back away. The thin lips smiled. The smile widened, until the lips and beard surrounding it disappeared, leaving a wicked grin. The eyes grew larger and darker until they became empty sockets in the skeleton of a face. Diana opened her mouth and screamed.

Shreds of Diana's nightmare continued to haunt her the following morning as she stood at the rear of the shifting crowd separating her from the model of Pompeii and Vesuvius.

The opening of the exhibit was going well, but she was too tired to take much pleasure in the success. She had awoken just before dawn, a scream still echoing in her ears, and had been too cowardly to go back to sleep. Now, she tried to concentrate on Ben's voice as he explained how the demonstration was going to work.

The once familiar room seemed alien to her, filled as it was with the first crowd of the day to see the display. But Diana was aware of another reason for the tension gripping her shoulders. Even as she watched the volcano she had worked so long to complete, she was conscious of her father's presence.

He stood several feet away, but she refused to look at him. She was still stunned and confused by his actions of this morning, when he had approached her the moment she came down the stairs and asked her to join him at the breakfast table. Her father's warm tone and sudden questions about her aspirations as an archaeologist had stunned Diana so completely that it had been difficult to answer his questions about her education and experience in the field.

Daniel McKenzie seemed to be a completely different man this morning, leading the conversation rather than forcing the others at the table to draw him out as he had the night before. Diana saw a puzzled frown on Emma's face that indicated that she had noticed this change in Diana's father as well. She found herself wishing that Will or Ben were there to see this, but they had gone down to the Baths to supervise last-minute arrangements in the exhibit.

"Well, I think it is time we went down to the Baths." Sutro's voice boomed down the table, the signal for everyone to rise and exit through the front door, where several carriages waited to take them to the exhibit. Although Diana would have preferred to walk, which would have given her some time to ponder this strange change, she found herself seated in a carriage with her father, Jean-Paul LaPierre and Professor Harrington.

Her father's actions had grown more and more perplexing as the morning went on. During the opening ceremonies Diana was aware that he was watching her, and now, as the crowd exclaimed over the demonstration of Pompeii's destruction, he had edged his way over to stand at her side.

"I need to speak with you, Diana."

Diana found herself glancing at her father, asking herself if she wanted to speak to *him*. The crowd's applause saved her from replying, and a moment later everyone was instructed to turn and exit down the steps to the last portion of the exhibition. Diana was relieved to find that in following these directions, the crowd separated her and her father.

She took a deep breath, attempting to calm the deep-seated dread of speaking to him. She had no desire to awaken the explosive emotions that had surfaced the night before. She wanted to forget about past hurts, to concentrate on the future; so when she reached the bottom of the spiral staircase, she found a spot near the front of the crowd and prayed her father was somewhere at the back.

The appreciative murmurs of those around her drew Diana's attention to the shrine area. A hush fell over the crowd a moment later when the main lights were switched off, leaving the glimmer of the stars and the round moon in the painted sky above to cast a dim, shimmering light. A shiver of anticipation danced up Diana's spine.

"Welcome to the shrine of Diana," a melodious female voice began. "This display is a reproduction of the sanctuary dedicated to the Roman goddess of the moon that was situated at Aricia, an area south of Rome. To this shrine came her worshipers: hunters asking for the goddess to guide their arrows, young girls seeking the goddess's protection, and expectant mothers petitioning Diana for her help in their coming births."

The voice stopped speaking and the curtain parted to reveal a statue, three feet in height, formed of pure white marble. The slender feminine form was garbed in the short tunic Diana was accustomed to seeing on representations of the goddess. She wore a quiver strapped to her back, filled with silver arrows. The curved bow was also silver, as was the crescent moon on her forehead.

Diana's heart raced, then the voice spoke again. "This statue was uncovered recently in Pompeii. It was in the courtyard of a large home that had been completely engulfed by the ash that blanketed the city that fateful day. Ironically, it was this very ash that protected the silver paint, and preserved the statue in its original glory. The statue normally resides in the British Museum, which has graciously sent it here on loan for this exhibit.

Just before the voice faded, Diana recognized it as Emma's. She stood to one side until the last person stepped toward the exit and the blue curtain again dropped into place. Diana continued to stand there, the image of the goddess still vibrant in her mind, as the lights came on. She was aware that she should leave, that she was expected to join Ben in one of the banquet rooms upstairs, but she didn't move until a deep voice made her turn abruptly.

"You have done a wonderful job here, Daughter."

Diana's muscles tightened as she faced her father. His thin lips curved into a smile as he spoke again. "Sutro tells me you are responsible for the display in the room above, as well as much of the shrine down here."

Diana glanced around the room. "I painted the arch and the cave to look like they are made of stone. Ben and Will did everything else."

Her father stepped forward. "You are a very modest young woman. I should have expected that. You inherited your mother's artistic talents; it shouldn't be surprising that you have her humility."

The mention of her mother sent a cold shiver down Diana's back. "I remember little about my mother, other than what my grandfather told me. Believe me, I have never been accused of humility. I simply state things as they are."

"Ah." Her father nodded. "Blunt should be the word, I suppose. I suppose that means you're like him, then, your grandfather. Again, not surprising. Still, you look just like her.''

There was a gentleness to his voice that made Diana relax slightly. ''I know. There were pictures of Mother all over the house.'' There was something different about him today, less stiff, more approachable. Perhaps it was the mention of his dead wife that had brought this about. Perhaps he had not forgotten *her* in his obsession with an obscure Roman goddess.

A deep ache twisted in Diana's chest. She had promised herself just last night not to allow this man to hurt her again.

''We should be going now.'' Diana was aware of the frosty tone in her voice. ''I believe you are expected to deliver a talk at the luncheon.'' As she finished speaking, she stepped past him, heading for the arched exit.

''Diana, I need to talk to you.''

Her father's voice made her steps falter, but she forced herself to continue walking.

''I just want to know one thing,'' he said. Anger and hurt resounded in the raised voice. ''What made you change your mind after all these years about seeing me again?''

_____ *Chapter Eighteen*

DIANA CAME TO an abrupt stop. "What are you talking about?"

"That's interesting. In one breath you profess to state things as they are, and in the next you pretend not to understand when I confront you with your rejection of me."

Diana could only shake her head. "*I* rejected you? That is preposterous. I have been the one waiting for years and years to hear from you, watching for letters that never arrived, hoping for just one word from you to let me know you even remembered my existence."

"That's not true. I wrote again and again, but never received any answer from—" He stopped speaking abruptly. "Diana, do you recall the last letter I sent you?"

The intense query in his eyes made Diana take a step back. Something about his watchful gaze flustered her, and brought a defensive stiffening to her spine. "I certainly do. I received it on the day of my twelfth birthday. You were supposed to be arriving for the party Grandfather had planned for me, and all my friends were at last going to meet my famous father. Instead, I received a small statue of Diana, and yet another empty promise that you would come home 'sometime soon.'"

She closed her lips tightly over the quiver in her voice.

"Diana, how can I describe the pain I felt writing that letter to you? Or how many times I have regretted my actions? Back then it had seemed imperative that I take the opportunity that had been offered to me. Heading a dig at Pompeii was my lifelong dream." He shook his head, and his eyes seemed to grow more bright as he stepped toward her. "Had I known that you would have been unable to forgive me for missing that party, I would have chosen differently. But that wasn't the letter I was speaking of."

Slowly Diana shook her head. "There was no other letter. And yes, I was hurt and disappointed when I learned you couldn't be there that day, but even though I was only twelve I *understood* why you had to go to Pompeii. What I didn't understand was why you never wrote to me after that."

"Oh, my God." The words came out slowly as his eyes widened. "Are you saying you never received any of my letters?"

Diana's heart slowed to a dull thud as she numbly shook her head.

"I wrote to you the moment I arrived in Pompeii. I'm sure I posted it. I suppose I can't be positive about that one. I . . . I had a run-in with one of the men I was working with, a Peter Vicini, shortly after I arrived in Pompeii. He ran off with a statue he discovered and—"

Diana held up her hand to stop him as she said, "I know. You followed him and were very ill after that. I often used to imagine that your illness had caused you to forget me."

"No!" McKenzie took another step toward Diana. "I never forgot you. As soon as I recovered from the effects of the sun and lack of food and water enough to hold a pen, I wrote to you, saying I would be coming home, to Philadelphia, to complete my recovery. But you never wrote back, so I went to a hospital in Paris."

Diana's heart twisted. "I couldn't reply. I never received any letter like that."

"What a fool I am. All these years I have imagined that you hated me. Fueled by my feelings of guilt I have imagined that because I had disappointed you that day, you never wanted to see me again."

Diana stepped forward, her heart twisting as she shook her head. "No, that's not true. I—"

"What is it, Diana? Did you say those things, in anger and disappointment, to your grandfather, perhaps?"

Diana took a quick, shaky breath. "I don't know. I can't remember exactly what I said when I received your letter, only that I tried to keep from crying because it always made Grandfather angry to see me hurt in any way."

"I see. Perhaps, after all these years, I understand what must have happened."

The deep sadness in her father's voice made Diana look at him sharply as he went on. "I have been such a fool. I should have expected something like that after all the trouble Leland Robbins gave me when I was courting your mother, and later, after we were married."

His words made Diana stiffen once again. "Grandfather? You think he—"

"—kept my letters from you?" He nodded. "Yes, but probably not out of spite toward me. He was very protective of you, wasn't he?"

Diana managed to nod as her mind reeled. All these years, all this pain, just because her grandfather wanted to protect her? Yes, that was just like him, to keep her from something she wanted because it appeared harmful in his eyes. Diana took another step toward her father, her lips trembling. "I thought you'd forgotten me, or that the goddess Diana meant more to you than I did."

Diana's throat closed over her last words.

"Professor?"

A polite, masculine voice broke the emotionally charged silence. Diana turned to see Ian MacRogers standing beneath the exit's archway, his hair glinting red-gold in the dim light.

"Yes, what is it?" Her father's words were spoken in a choked voice as he drew a handkerchief from his breast pocket.

"They're waiting for you in the banquet hall. You are to address the assembly, remember?"

"I think someone else will have to take my place. I have something more important to see to at the moment."

Diana saw at last the warmth and caring she had yearned for. Her heart filled with emotion, yet she managed to control her voice as she smiled and spoke past the lump in her throat. "We'll have time to talk later, Father. Besides, I have never heard one of your famous speeches. As an archaeologist I must insist you deliver it as planned."

Diana decided that the applause rippling through the banquet hall at the end of her father's speech was best described as polite. Although she could feel Ben's presence across the table from her, she found she couldn't bear to look at him just yet. Her feelings about her father were still a tangled ball of emotion that needed sorting out. Ben had only been exposed to the man he had met last night, a man who was hiding old wounds behind a cool facade. Ben was very much like her grandfather. She had a strong feeling that he would warn her against the sudden warming between her father and herself.

As the clapping dwindled and died, Diana dropped her hands to her lap and watched them smooth imaginary wrinkles out of the impeccably pressed linen napkin. She had to admit that she had her own misgivings about her father's story, but at the same time, she couldn't forget the hope she had glimpsed in the man's eyes as he squeezed her hand before striding up to the podium.

On a more impersonal note, the archaeologist in her was

fighting disappointment in Daniel McKenzie's speech.
When Justin Harrington turned to her from the seat next to
hers and cleared his throat, she instinctively tensed.

"Your father certainly has led an interesting life, my dear,
chasing after the goddess of the moon," he said. "I must
admit, though, that I would feel stilted if I restricted my
interests as he has."

Her fingers tightened into fists as she forced herself to
control her defensive reaction to his implied criticism of her
father. "Well, I suppose that is the beauty of our field.
There is still so much to be uncovered about past cultures
and civilizations that there is room for those searching out
the large picture as well as those enchanted by only one
portion. My father has obviously delved very deeply into
his area of interest. And I must say, despite my own studies
in mythology, I wasn't aware how many goddesses similar
to Diana have existed in other cultures."

"Well, it is my opinion that such similarities are mere
coincidence. Of course, I agree that Diana was modeled
after the Greek goddess Artemis, but knowing how ancient
the Greek culture is, I find it highly unreasonable to think
that Artemis was patterned after some older deity."

"You'll have to ask my father about that, I'm afraid.
This is the first I've been aware of this particular line of
study on his part."

"I'm not surprised at that." Jean-Paul LaPierre's voice
drew Diana's attention across the table, where the Frenchman sat between Will and Ben. "Other than announcing a
particularly interesting find now and again, your father has
kept rather to himself, especially these last five years. He
appears to have abandoned fieldwork to concentrate on the
intellectual and emotional sources of the early Roman culture. And speaking of early Roman culture"—he turned to
Harrington—"when am I going to get a chance to see that
Etruscan vase you have been teasing me with?"

"This evening, if you would like. Sutro expressed a desire to see it as well, so I had Josephs go down to fetch it from the vault in my ship."

"Sutro? Why, you swine. Leave it to you to draw the interest of a millionaire when you know I am short of funds."

"And leave it to you to pretend to be destitute." Harrington shook his head and smiled widely. "I have no heart, LaPierre. Don't imagine for one moment that you can get my treasure at a good price by engaging my sympathy for your light pockets."

The Frenchman replied, "One can always try. So, you say I can see this treasure this evening?"

"Yes. It will be in the study at five P.M. If you are interested, we should be able to strike a deal before supper is served. Then we can toast each other for a good exchange."

"I don't think so. I never make such quick decisions on matters of this importance."

"Then you will miss out on what could be the centerpiece of your collection, my friend. You have only today and tomorrow to decide. In two days I sail for England." He stopped and turned to Diana. "You can be ready to sail that soon, can't you?"

Diana nearly choked on the sip of coffee she had just taken. "In two days? The newspaper clipping I have stated that you are to be here for the two weeks of the exhibit. Professor Harrington, I—"

"You are to call me Justin," he broke in. "Remember? As to the article, I'm afraid I've had to change my plans. I'm sorry not to have told you of this sooner, but every time you and I have begun to discuss your employment with me, we have been interrupted. I do need your services, Diana. I am sorry that I cannot offer you a dig in Italy, but we will be working in areas of England that have relinquished some interesting evidence of early Roman occupancy to date, and I feel certain I can uncover even more."

As Diana considered these words, she heard a chair scrape loudly against the floor. She saw that Ben had pushed himself back from the table.

"You won't need to worry about tools, you know," Harrington went on. "But I will need your answer soon, so that I can make arrangements for a berth aboard my ship."

Diana tried to sort her thoughts, to behave like a professional. "Well," she began. "I did bring my heavy work boots with me, but I lack several items that—"

"—that you can pick up in our brief stop in New York, or when we arrive in London," Harrington finished with a warm smile. "What is most important is that you bring your artistic ability and the willingness to work that you've displayed here. That is, of course, if you are still interested in becoming an archaeologist."

Diana's mind was racing. This was what she had hoped—no—prayed for. But the timing was so very terribly bad. Only an hour ago her entire life had been turned upside down. She had so many things she wanted to discuss with her father, so many years to live over with him.

And then there was Ben. So many things remained unsaid between them, things that could not be rushed. She coaxed a small smile to her lips as she spoke to Harrington. "I need to think about your offer, Prof— Justin. I will give you my answer this evening."

At that moment everyone around them stood, signaling the end of the luncheon. As Diana got to her feet, her eyes met Ben's. His face was an emotionless mask. Realizing how much she needed to speak with him, she hurried around the table, struggling through the knot of people, only to find, when she reached the other side, that Ben was nowhere in sight.

She noticed three men speaking to her father, jotting down his words in the small notebooks they held. Diana looked around the room one more time, searching for a certain broad-shouldered figure, then nearly jumped when Will Babcock's voice echoed nearby. "Are you looking for Ben?"

"Yes."

"He went down to the volcano area, to make sure everything is still working properly. I'm on my way down now, to relieve Simon in the temple room so he can get something to eat. Shall we walk together?"

Neither of them spoke as they made their way through the crowded exhibition area. Diana's mind was swirling with the things she had learned, the opportunity that had been offered to her, and the decisions she faced as she preceded Will up the steps to the entry to the temple. Just as they entered, the older man touched her hand.

"Everything will work out, Diana."

"I hope so. My life has all of a sudden become extremely complicated."

Will patted her on the shoulder.

Diana sighed as she stepped into the corridor leading to the volcano room. A week ago everything had seemed so simple. She was on her own and knew exactly what she wanted to do. Now, not only did her father seem to want a place in her life, but she found her heart bound to a man who had given her a great deal of pleasure, and wonderfully warm words, but no plans for the future.

And suddenly Diana knew that what she wanted more than anything was a future with this man. She had never before thought of marriage with anything but scorn, but that was before she had seen how Emma and George had managed to combine their lives and their careers, before she had come to know how wonderful love could feel.

The door to the volcano room glided forward silently.

Diana stood within the opening, her heart pounding as she saw Ben's broad back. His hands rested on the barrier surrounding the miniature town of Pompeii, hands that were so strong, yet so gentle.

He didn't move, he just looked down at the small houses and streets, the little world Diana had brought to life. She wished she could read his thoughts at that moment. There was still so much left unsaid between them, so much room for misunderstanding.

"I'm surprised to see you." His voice was flat—as expressionless as his face. "I thought you would be up at the house, packing."

Diana felt her shoulders tense. She had expected opposition from Ben, but she had hoped he would at least try to understand how important this job was to her, and perhaps even share her excitement. She took a deep breath before speaking. "I have some thinking to do before I consider packing."

"What's to think about?" He lifted his shoulders in a shrug. "This is what you wanted, isn't it? To be off on a dig somewhere."

"Yes, it's exactly what I wanted, a week ago. Now . . ." She shook her head, then crossed the room to watch the last of the water drain from the city. "Now I'm confused. My father spoke to me again this morning. Things are different."

"Different? In what way?"

"In every way. He thought *I* had stopped writing to him. He wrote to me time and time again, and never received a response. All these years he has believed that I hated him for disappointing me so often, while I thought he had forgotten about me. We think that my grandfather must have destroyed his letters as they arrived."

"That's the most cockeyed story I've ever heard." Ben grabbed Diana's shoulders so suddenly that she jumped.

"Why would your grandfather do such a thing?"

The anger in Ben's eyes stunned Diana. "Because he hated to see me hurt in any way. You see, when my father failed to show up for my birthday, I was heartbroken. Grandfather had never liked my father, anyway. I think he must have decided to protect me from any more disappointment."

"So your father just left it at unanswered letters. He didn't come to your grandfather's house, ask you why you were angry, beg your forgiveness?"

Ben's sarcastic tone angered Diana. "I don't know. My father and I were interrupted before we could discuss each of the last ten years. Perhaps he just gave up when he didn't hear from me, and devoted his life to his research."

"And you believe this story?"

Diana wasn't sure what she believed. She only knew she had seen tears in Daniel McKenzie's eyes, and before she dismissed his tale she would need to speak to him further.

The thought that he had been in as much pain as she had over the years brought a defensive stiffening to her spine as she responded to Ben's question. "I believe the part about the letters. It sounds crazy, I know. But you weren't there when we were speaking—you didn't see the wounded look in my father's eyes when he spoke of how hurt he was by my apparent rejection of him. I recognize that look. I've seen it hundreds of times in my own eyes."

"So, now he wants to make up for lost time."

The deep distrust in his voice vibrated in tune with the doubts that Diana had been trying to deny. She twisted her shoulders to break his grasp, then stepped away from him. "I don't know what he wants. I told you, we had to come up to the luncheon before we could really talk much."

Diana paused. All the decisions she faced seemed to crowd around her, making her shake her head. Her next words came out softly; she sounded lost. "This is all so unfair. I have so much to think about, and no time in which to do it."

"I received the impression that you had decided to go with Harrington."

Decided? She had decided nothing. All the demands placed on her made Diana feel like a rabbit cornered by a pack of hounds. Her growing confusion and frustration lent a note of panic to her voice. "I don't *know*."

"Then just tell Harrington no. There will be other opportunities to get the kind of work you are looking for. You are talented. You'll find another archaeologist who will hire you."

Diana shook her head. "As an artist, perhaps. Justin has assured me he will have me actually working the dig as well as just drawing what someone else uncovers."

"Diana, tell him no. Justin Harrington is not—not the kind of man you want to work for. Leaving with him would be the biggest mistake of your life. I can't let you do it."

The harsh, commanding edge to Ben's words hit Diana like a slap. She had come looking for him, thinking that there were so many things she wanted to talk to him about, so many unsaid words between them.

She had been wrong to expect him to understand. She had been wrong about so much, especially about Ben Potter. He had said he loved her, but what he had meant by those words was that he could claim the right to decide her future.

Deep inside, Diana could feel a shaft of resistance form and harden. Long ago, she had decided never to let emotion rule her life. Ben was the kind of man who would demand that she do just that.

Her mind whirled with angry words, words that wilted and faded without warning, leaving her to shake her head again as she stepped back from the touch that she once had found comforting. Whatever had flared to life between her and this man was only a trap. She found that there was, after all, very little to be said.

Chapter Nineteen

"I TOLD YOU when we met that I decided long ago to always make my own decisions," Diana said. "I had some things I wanted to discuss with you, but since you prefer to issue orders, I think I shall work them out myself."

With that she walked out, pulling the door shut behind her. Ben's stomach twisted as he recalled his dictatorial words. He hadn't planned on ordering her about. He had counted on her taking up the argument, opening the door to discussion, and in doing so, clearing her mind of the sentimental hopes that were clouding it.

He had handled things badly; he had spoken rashly. But there was so much at stake. The impossible story she had recounted about her father's "pain" had angered him beyond belief. It was obviously pure fabrication. Diana was sure to see through this, no matter how good an actor Daniel McKenzie was, given time. But as Diana had said, time was the problem. There was so little of it.

An attempt to steal the statue would be made within the next two days. Until this moment Ben had sincerely believed that it was best that Diana not know about the suspicions hovering over her father's head. Something was going to happen soon. If Daniel McKenzie wasn't the thief and murderer he and Will were waiting for, LaPierre or Harrington was. All three men had made it clear that they would only be in town until Monday. Before that time, one of them would attempt to steal the statue, and no matter which of the three was involved, Diana needed to be warned.

Ben strode to the door and pulled it open. He couldn't let Diana face the demands both Harrington and McKenzie were placing on her without some tools with which to guide her. As he strode down the corridor, he searched his mind for the right words to approach her with, words that would not elicit further anger and make her doubt his story.

"Ben!"

Will Babcock's voice put a halt to Ben's rapid steps when he was halfway through the temple room.

"Where are you going in such a hurry?"

"After Diana. Did she come through here?"

Will looked at Ben closely. "Yes, a few moments ago. She looked upset."

"She was. As usual, I said the wrong thing." He felt Will's hand on his arm, but kept his eyes directed to the confusion of people, plants, and exhibits below them, searching for Diana.

"And so you are going to run after her and correct what you said." A hint of amusement in Will's voice made Ben turn around. "What are you planning on telling her?"

"Everything, I suppose. The rumors about her father. And all about Harrington and Sarah. Anything I can think of that will make her realize how dangerous these men are."

"I don't think that would be a good idea."

"Why the hell not? I thought you said she should be told about Sarah."

"I still think she should. But I don't think the story should come from you, at least not now. I doubt, given the mood she appeared to be in, that she will be inclined to listen logically to anything you have to say."

"Then how—"

"I'll talk to her." Will let his gaze sweep the room below as he went on. "She trusts me. Right now I am the only one who hasn't made some sort of demand on her. I see her now, going into the engine room. She must be on her way to the cliffs. You stay here till Ian and Simon return from lunch."

Before Ben could speak, Will began hurrying down the steps. Ben took one step toward the stairs, planning on following Will, then remembered the treasures that needed guarding. With a sigh he turned and walked into the temple room.

Diana could hear her gasping breaths echo off the rocky walls in the tunnel, keeping time to the crunch of sand beneath her hurrying feet. Anger and confusion pulsed with each rapid beat of her heart as she reached the end of the dark passageway. Her racing feet came to a stop as she stepped out into the sunlight. She regarded the crescent-shaped stretch of beach below, before she climbed the cliff where she had first picnicked with Ben and Will just over a week before.

She stood at the top of the cliff, gazing at the ocean through eyes filmed with tears. Ben had been a stranger to her that day. In the space of a week she thought she had come to know him. She had certainly come to trust him.

Sudden fury at her own naïveté brought her hands up to her eyes to rub away her tears. She had warned herself against giving her heart to anyone. She had no one but herself to blame for the pain she was feeling now, and it was up to her to unravel the tangled web of her life and move beyond the pain.

The wind whipped her skirt about her ankles. Diana watched as a large wave crashed onto the face of the cliff, sending white foam spraying into the air. The drops fell like rain around Diana, and as they hissed and crackled at her feet, she discovered that suddenly the answer to all her questions appeared as clear as the blue sky above.

Four years ago she had claimed the saying *carpe diem* for her battle cry. After doing her grandfather's bidding all her life, she had stood up to him and demanded to be allowed to study archaeology at a university. Once she had won that battle she had vowed never to allow herself to be dictated to again. Now was the time to renew that vow.

She could not go with her father, even though it pained her to think that he had been as miserable as she had all these years. Ben's sarcastic remarks had at least made her see that it had been in her father's power to remedy the situation if he had so chosen. He had been an adult. He could have come to Philadelphia and demanded she speak to him. She, however, had been truly powerless. It should not have been necessary for her to search him out. If he wanted to deepen the relationship, it was up to him to make the next move, to prove his sincerity by following her to England.

For that was where she was going. It had become clear to her when Justin Harrington spoke at the university last year that he was the archaeologist she wanted to work with. That was the destiny she had come here searching for. Ben knew this. If he truly cared for her he would not try to stand in her way.

If he truly cared for her he would ask her to marry him and work with her on building a life together.

"Diana!"

The shout startled her. She pivoted to see Will cresting the path behind her. As he stepped toward her, she noticed that his face had taken on a ruddy glow, and that he seemed to be having trouble breathing. Diana hurried over to him.

"Will, are you all right?"

He took a deep breath, then another before he spoke.

"Yes, I'm fine." He looked into her eyes, then touched her cheek. "But what about you? I thought you told me that you never cried."

Diana moved away from his gentle touch and looked back at the sea. "I guess I should have said rarely instead of never. But you don't have to worry. I'm all right now."

"You are? Five minutes up here and everything is straightened out?"

"Yes. Once I put everything into perspective, I saw that I really had no choice."

"You are going with Harrington."

It wasn't a question; it was a statement issued in a tired, pained voice that touched the doubts still lingering in Diana's mind. Fearing she would be cast back into the swirling waters of indecision if she thought about this any further, she straightened her shoulders. "Yes. Don't try to talk me out of it."

"I would never do that." The smile framed by Will's beard had a tired, ragged look as he spoke again. "This is a decision only you can make. But don't you agree that before you make up your mind it's best to learn everything possible about all sides of the matter?"

Diana nodded. "Of course. That's just what I was doing, weighing my options. I've known for at least a year that Justin Harrington is the archaeologist I want to work with. The speech I heard him give last year fascinated me, as did the research papers he has published. I haven't just come to this willy-nilly; I—"

"You only have part of the story," Will said firmly. "Harrington's reputation as a scholar is solid. You know little about the man, however."

Diana frowned. "What do I care what he is like as a man? I am only interested in what he can teach me."

"There are some lessons that are best left unlearned, Diana." Will's voice had taken on a harsh tone. "Justin

Harrington has always been a perfect gentleman around you, has he not?''

Diana answered emphatically. "Yes, always."

"You've never noticed him looking at you with a particularly hungry expression in his eyes?''

Diana's voice reflected her shock as she replied, "Absolutely not."

"Well, I have. I've seen his eyes follow you, roaming up and down your body, and I am here to tell you that he is not interested in your talents as an artist, nor in teaching you anything other than how to respond to his spell.''

Will's words sounded preposterous. "What are you talking about, his spell?''

"You heard him speak about the goddesses of Rome and Greece as if they still existed. He trades on that belief, slowly weaving mythology and emotion into a web in which he traps eager young females. This sounds outrageous and melodramatic, I know. But I've seen him do it, and so has Ben.''

The mention of Ben made Diana's shoulders stiffen. She shrugged and lifted her chin as she asked archly, "So why didn't he tell me this instead of simply forbidding me to go?''

"Because all of this sounds too melodramatic to be believed. We both hoped you'd see this on your own, and—'' Will held up a hand to silence Diana when she opened her mouth to protest. "We both believed you would see through him, given time. But aside from all this, Ben still finds it difficult to talk rationally about Justin Harrington.

"He has firsthand knowledge of the man's tricks, you see. Ten years ago, when Ben was on his first dig, working for Justin Harrington, he was as excited about the prospect as you are. Then Ben's fiancée was drawn into Harrington's web.''

Will's words sent a sharp pain shooting through Diana's chest. She couldn't decide whether it was due to jealousy at the thought of Ben loving someone else, or sympathy for the pain he must have felt at losing this love. She suspected it was a little of each.

"Sarah wasn't as strong-willed as you are," Will went on. "Until her husband died, everything in life had come quite easily, you see. She was small, and delicate, and had the combination of waif-like innocence and sensuality that makes even the most intelligent of men long to play the role of willing slave. She had managed to marry quite well, to a man twice her age and far above her social rank, but at his death everything went to a son from his first wife. Sarah lost status immediately. Ben had no social standing either, but I believe Sarah recognized Ben as the kind of man who would sacrifice everything to take care of someone he loved. It was also obvious that she was entranced by the world of archaeology, drawn to the romance of the search for lost secrets with no appreciation for the work it involved."

Will paused as Diana saw the reasons behind some of Ben's attitudes toward her career become clear. She was about to protest that she was nothing like this woman, but Will spoke first. "Perhaps everything would have worked out had she stayed in London. But she insisted on visiting Ben on a dig in the south of France where he was working as Harrington's first assistant.

"I had been working for the man for a year, so I was familiar with his tactics with women. The moment I heard him tell Sarah that she had the soul of Aphrodite and shared that goddess's need to move from one intense experience to the next, I knew there was bound to be trouble.

"In the month that I had been working with Ben I had come to like the boy a great deal, so I tried to warn him. He laughed at my concerns and told me that I should try to keep out of the sun. But two weeks later Sarah broke off their engagement, and told him she was in love with Harrington.''

Gone was Diana's need to protest the difference between herself and this woman. Her heart ached for the pain that Ben must have felt, and her mind whirled with questions about his reaction to this treachery. "Will," she said quietly, "what did Ben do?"

"What could he do? He left the dig and went to England. I went with him. He obtained a position with the British Museum and worked so long and hard that he received a promotion after only six months. That's not the end of the story, of course. Shortly after his promotion, Ben received a letter from Sarah, apologizing for what had happened. It seems that Harrington had left her in France when he moved on to his next dig. She wrote in the most heartwrenching prose of how much she regretted having hurt Ben, and of her fears of returning to England and facing the scandal of her relationship with Harrington. Not one week later Sarah's brother came to tell Ben that Sarah was dead. She had fallen from the ship she was traveling on and drowned. Ben has always wondered just how accidental that fall was.''

The wind whistled over the rocks and a wave crashed onto the cliff as Diana stared up at Will for several moments. "Tell me something, Will," she said at last. "Do you think that instead of warning Ben against Harrington, if you had cautioned Sarah against trusting this man, that it would have made any difference?

"Think hard before you answer. Consider Sarah's personality, this need of hers to have someone take care of her that you mentioned and the craving for excitement that Harrington saw in her.''

"No, she wouldn't have listened.''

"Of course not. Harrington tried that goddess story with me too, you'll remember. I'll admit that a bit of it struck a chord at first, for I have used Diana as a model of sorts in my life. But ruled by her?'' She shook her head. ''That's a bunch of tripe. Believe me, I am safe from Harrington. Still, this information does place a different slant on things, so I will have to think more deeply on the matter before I make my final decision.''

She placed her hand on Will's shoulder. ''Thank you for telling me all this, and for being so concerned. I'm going to my room now. I need to be alone. I hope you understand.''

As she turned to go, Will grabbed her hand. ''Diana, I want to talk to you about your father.''

''Don't worry. I've decided that regardless of where I go from here, if Daniel McKenzie wishes to truly be a father to me as he hinted, he will have to follow me. I won't trail after him like a needy puppy.''

With those words, Diana drew her hand from Will's, turned, and walked toward the tunnel, conscious of the man's warm, worried eyes following her as she descended the path.

Despite everything Diana had to think about, by the time she reached her room she found that she was suddenly too weary to do anything but remove her boots and lay down on the satin coverlet. She let her eyes close, planning on a short rest to clear her mind. Images, some sharp, others shadowy, swirled through her mind, and when she opened her eyes she found that she had been asleep for over an hour.

A sense of urgency brought her to a sitting position so quickly that she had to sit quietly a second before her head quit spinning. The clock sitting on the small bedside table told her that she would have to hurry if she wanted a chance to speak to Ben before dinner was served.

And she did want to speak to Ben. For somehow as she slept, all the jumbled pieces of her life had fallen into a

clear pattern, and she knew exactly what she wanted to say
to him.

Will's story had explained several things to her about Ben
Potter. In a sense, it was almost like looking into a mirror,
for now it was clear that Ben had also suffered the pain of
being abandoned. Knowing about Sarah made so many
things clear to her: Ben's need to protect her, his anger at
her resistance, even his reluctance to speak of a future with
her.

She could not force him in that area—would not even
attempt it. But she had to make him understand her need
to fulfill her dreams. She had to make him see that her
decision to work for Harrington was not a way to desert
him and what had begun to blossom between them. Somehow she had to find the words to get Ben to realize that
going to England on this dig, bringing her close to London,
would give them both time to finish healing from past
wounds before they had to decide on the future.

Diana changed quickly into her dark blue satin dress, her
mind sorting out the words she would use in her meeting
with Ben. Nothing sounded right. Her hands trembled as
she arranged her hair, then tightened into fists as she stared
at the reflection in the mirror and told herself what a ninny
she was being.

Still, her heart beat rapidly and her cheeks glowed with
excitement. No matter how muddled her explanation, she
was determined to somehow make Ben understand, make
him see as she did that fate had handed them a gift, the gift
of time and proximity. The dig was less than a day's train
ride from London. She could visit Ben at the museum, and
he could come down to see her, both of them pursuing their
careers until he was ready to entrust her with his heart on
a permanent basis.

When Diana reached the bottom of the stairs she saw
Emma, resplendent in a low-cut gown made of striped silver

and rose taffeta. Emma came over to take Diana's hands in hers. "There you are, Diana! I haven't had a chance to tell you what a perfectly marvelous job you did on the exhibit."

"Thank you, Emma." Diana smiled. "And since I can only take credit for executing someone else's design, I guess it's permissible for me to say that I think the whole thing is wonderful. It's a shame it will only last a couple of weeks."

"Oh, don't worry. Papa's already talking about ordering copies of the statues and making them a permanent fixture in the Baths. And speaking of my father, have you seen him?"

"No. I'm looking for Ben. But if I happen to come across your father in my search, I'll be glad to tell him you're looking for him."

"Ben's in the study with LaPierre and Harrington. I thought Papa would be with them, but none of them have seen him, either. I guess I'll try the observatory."

Emma turned swiftly, her dress swishing loudly as she walked away. Diana took a deep breath and crossed the narrow hall toward the study door that Emma had pointed to. It was unfortunate that Ben wasn't alone. She wanted a chance to clear the air with him before she was forced to reveal her decision regarding Harrington's job offer.

Somehow she would have to get Ben away from the others. Perhaps she could make him believe that there was something wrong down at the Baths. With that plan in mind, she pushed the door inward.

"Ben?" Diana stepped into a room lined with stuffed bookshelves, white statues, and busts. In the center of the room was an oval table, where three men turned solemn faces to her, with three pairs of eyes narrowed in anger. Diana paused on the threshold. "Oh, I'm sorry. I didn't mean to interrupt. I'll—"

"Come in, Diana."

Ben's sharp tone surprised her, and his angry scowl made her step quickly in and shut the door behind her as Harrington spoke. "Yes, do, Diana. We need another expert here, and I think you shall serve splendidly."

Ben asked, "How familiar are you with Etruscan culture?"

"I'm fairly well versed in the subject, between my studies at the university and reading every paper the professor here has written on it."

She saw both Ben and Harrington frown. "All right," Ben said. "Then would you mind coming over here and looking at this vase?"

As Diana stepped forward, LaPierre moved, revealing a black item about eight inches high sitting on the center of the table. She could see a bas-relief carving running around the center of the vase.

"Go ahead, Diana." Ben's voice echoed loudly in the expectant silence. "Pick it up and look at it closely."

Diana reached for the vase. With gentle fingers, she turned it around to look at each side.

"I believe this is what is known as a *bucchero* vase. The shape and design is Greek. The Etruscans were greatly influenced by the Greeks." Diana glanced at Ben, who nodded; then at Harrington, who smiled. She took a deep breath and continued her inspection. "The carving of a large horse and several small buildings seems to represent the story of the seige of Troy. It is a beautiful example of Etruscan pottery."

"Yes it is, my dear." Harrington's voice sounded strained. "However, Benjamin here refuses to authenticate it."

Diana turned to Ben. "Why?"

His dark eyes met hers. "It's not of the time period that Harrington claims. He says it is from the sixth century BC."

Diana looked back at the vase in her hand. She knew that

Etruscan items were difficult to date, for the artists used the same designs repeatedly over many centuries. "How can you be sure?"

"It is relatively easy. I'm sure that once you look closer, you'll agree with me. Here."

As Diana reached out to take the round magnifying glass Ben offered her, Harrington spoke again. "Yes, Diana, study the vase closely. I explained to you how well it was packed, which accounts for its excellent, almost modern appearance. But look at the material it is made from and at the carving itself. If you have examined other artifacts from this time period you are sure to see the similarity."

Diana placed the glass between her eyes and the vase and scrutinized its surface. Then Ben pointed to what appeared to be a small rope-like design running beneath the carving.

"Forget the material it's made from," he said. "What can you see there?"

Again Diana studied the vase, squinting as she adjusted the magnifying glass; then she gasped.

"It's not just a design; it's letters."

"Can you read what it says?"

Diana concentrated on the characters. They were formed in the manner of the Greeks and there were no spaces to indicate the separation of words, but soon a pattern emerged. Slowly she turned the vase as she translated, "It says, 'I fear the Greeks even when they bring gifts.' It's from Virgil's *Aeneid*."

"Very good."

Diana looked up and saw with surprise that Harrington's features had frozen into a stiff mask.

"And what language is that written in?"

Ben's question brought a frown to Diana's lips. "Latin, of course. The Etruscan language is still something of a mystery. A few scholars have managed to decipher a word here and there, but—"

Diana stopped speaking in midsentence. Her eyes widened as she stared at Ben. He continued, "But a sixth century BC Etruscan vase would not bear a Latin inscription. An artifact from a later period might, since the Etruscans did rule Rome in the fifth century BC. I would say this must be first century BC or later." Ben turned to Harrington. "Since we all know that Virgil died in 19 BC, it is impossible for this vase to be as old as you claim, or to be worth the inflated price you have offered to LaPierre."

Harrington got to his feet. "I must apologize. I obviously made a mistake."

"Mistake?" The Frenchman leapt to his feet, sending his chair crashing into the bookcase behind him. "You were trying to steal from me!"

"No." Harrington shook his head. "No. I would never do such a thing. It was an honest mistake. It could have been made by anyone."

"Anyone but you, Harrington," Ben interjected. "You're an expert on the Etruscans. At least you claim to be. Are you trying to say now that you aren't?"

"I'm not saying any such thing," he replied stiffly. "If you and LaPierre prefer to think I am capable of such fraud, that is your right. You will have a damned hard time proving it, though."

Harrington opened the door and stalked out.

"Filthy liar. Rotten cheat." LaPierre's shout echoed out the open door; then he too hurried out of the room.

Diana looked at the black vase she cradled in her hands. Harrington was all that Ben and Will had warned against and more. A fraud. And she had almost aligned herself with him. He would have been found out sooner or later, even if Ben hadn't happened to be on hand in this case, and if she had connected her name to Harrington's, her name would have been besmirched, her career ruined. Only fate, and Ben, had saved her from her own blind self-assurance.

So now what was she going to do? Any future relationship with her father depended on his actions. Any future relationship with Ben was cast in shadows. She no longer had any prospect of a job, and the sense of purpose that had guided her life was sinking in the wave of self-doubt washing over her.

_____ Chapter Twenty

DIANA STILL HELD the vase in her hands, and when Ben placed his fingers over hers, he noticed that her flesh was as cold as marble. He removed the artifact from her hands and placed it on the desk.

"Diana." Ben barely whispered her name, yet she started as if he had shouted at her. She stared past him. Ben reached out and took her hand in his. He wanted to draw her to him, to gather her into his arms and ease her out of her stunned state of mind. But he checked the impulse, waiting and watching, certain that at any moment she would shake away the confused expression and brush off his efforts to comfort her.

A moment later the door opened and Will's voice echoed in the silence. "Ben, everyone is assembled in the dining room for dinner. We're waiting for you and Diana to join us."

Will stood in the half-open door, his glasses winking in the light as he gazed at Diana. "Fine," Ben replied. "We'll come along as soon as Diana is ready."

As he finished speaking, Diana twisted away from him and walked silently past Will into the hallway.

"What's wrong with her, Ben?"

"I'm not sure." Ben sighed. "Remember that vase Harrington was trying to sell to LaPierre?"

"Etruscan?"

"That's the one. It was a fake. Well, perhaps that's too strong a word. It isn't from the time period Harrington claimed, and there is no way he could have been ignorant of that."

"I see. So Ian was right; the man is a thief, of sorts. And Diana knows this?"

"Yes. I figured that this would upset her, but I expected her to react with anger, not look like some lost waif."

"She has just seen all her plans for her future destroyed, Ben. She must feel like a ship without a rudder. I told her about Sarah and Harrington, but that apparently didn't prepare her for this. And why should it? Frankly, *I'm* surprised by this development."

"Well, Ian did warn us, and we tried to warn Diana. Perhaps if there hadn't been so much going on, she would have listened. I don't know whether or not she told you, but her father approached her earlier today. He has her half-convinced that his years of neglect were due to some kind of misunderstanding."

Will grabbed Ben's arm. "She didn't say a word about this to me. What's the story?"

Ben gave him a brief summary of what Diana had told him about the letters her grandfather supposedly withheld from her. "I don't have any details," he continued, "but apparently McKenzie did a good job of convincing her of this."

"Well, *I* don't believe it."

Ben almost smiled at the fierce note in Will's voice. "Neither do I. And I'm not sure Diana really does, in her heart of hearts. However, we don't have time to debate this now; we're late getting to dinner as it is. Just one more thing." His expression grew serious. "We know that the last two crimes have been committed on the night of the full moon. That's tomorrow night. I want to be sure Diana isn't around tomorrow evening. I want you to arrange for Emma to take her to San Francisco tomorrow, and keep her overnight.''

Will nodded as the two men walked into the dining room.

Diana was aware of Ben and Will's arrival the moment they entered the room, although no one commented on their tardiness. In fact, no one spoke at all. They just lifted their spoons and began to eat the rich clam chowder in front of them. After her third spoonful of the warm, thick liquid, Diana finally began to notice the taste and texture of her food as the others spoke.

Nothing was said regarding the absence of Professor Harrington. Sutro began speaking to the members of society that he had invited to dinner, exclaiming in a strained voice over the success of the opening of the exhibit. After the first few moments of this, Diana found that she was actually able to smile and reply politely when he complimented Ben, Will, and herself.

As the first course was removed, to be replaced by baked salmon drizzled with an inviting-looking sauce, her interest in her surroundings had revived enough to glance around the table, noting several city dignitaries that she had been introduced to earlier. No doubt some of them admired her, she thought. They probably believed in the picture of an intelligent and capable woman that Sutro's words painted of her.

They were wrong, of course. She was a fool, and had proved it many times over in the past day. Emma sat at the opposite end of the table with Diana's father at her side. He was talking in a low monotone. Diana heard him discussing the shrine exhibit, and saw Emma attempting to disguise her boredom as the man's voice droned on.

Diana concentrated as her father's words drifted down

the table. His voice was nothing like the one she remembered from her childhood, warm and rich, as he read a book of Roman myths to her.

It wasn't the same voice, because he wasn't the same man. The thought almost made Diana drop her fork. She placed it on the plate slowly, her stomach coiling tighter as she recalled the conversation she'd had with her father that morning. She realized that there had been a false note in his words, but she had refused to listen to what her instincts knew to be true, just as she had refused to believe that Justin Harrington could have been lying about that vase.

Her father had changed radically during their long separation. Perhaps this had come about because of the death of his wife. It was possible that only his wife's love had kept him rooted in reality, and with her passing his fixation with Diana the goddess had taken over his life.

"I always knew that Diana would grow up to be an exceptional young woman." Daniel McKenzie's voice echoed with a hint of the warmth in his voice Diana had only moments before decided she would never hear again. She looked at him quickly. Then he spoke again. "After all, she is so very much like her mother."

Diana was too stunned to form a reply. Emma's voice interrupted the silence. "Well, having seen a picture of Diana's mother, I must say that the resemblance *is* quite remarkable. I suppose that it shouldn't be surprising that they shared personality traits as well."

Diana wanted to make it clear that any similarity between herself and her mother rested in appearances only. She had heard her grandfather remark a thousand times on their differences, citing in particular how reticent and obedient his daughter had been, except for choosing Daniel McKenzie for her husband.

But that wasn't something she could say with all these people around. "I really don't have enough of a memory of my mother to attest to any similarity between our personalities. Mama died when I was quite young.''

An uncomfortable silence followed, until at last LaPierre spoke, broaching a subject that had heretofore been ignored—Justin Harrington and how he was to be punished for attempting to defraud him.

Justin Harrington was not a subject Diana wanted to hear about at that moment. She didn't want to think about her father, but she couldn't seem to help it. The look he'd just given her had sent a strange cold shiver slithering up her spine that both puzzled and frightened her.

She managed to take two bites of her raspberry ice. It slipped down her throat, easing the tightness, and the sweet taste counteracted the bitter flavor caused by her thoughts.

She had been wrong to think she could bridge the distance between herself and her father. It was obvious he lived in some fantasy world, cut off from reality. She had been wrong about Harrington, too; about so many things.

As these thoughts swirled through her mind, she felt the confusion that had blanketed her sensations earlier threaten to cloud her mental faculties. Diana knew she had to resist its paralyzing grasp. She needed to be alone, to think.

Moments later, when everyone rose to make their way to the parlor, she slipped out the front door. Cool, moist air surrounded her as she walked beneath the eucalyptus trees, heading toward the conservatory and the front gate beyond.

The pungent scent of the long, slender eucalyptus leaves blended with the tangy air from the sea as the sounds of the surf and the wind in the trees formed a soft sigh. The sky above was a deep blue, the nearly full moon shown brightly, and its light reflected off the white statuary dotting the dark lawn, giving them the look of ghostly figures gliding among the foliage.

Diana walked more slowly as she neared the front gate.

Without any conscious plan, she stopped by the small slope at the statue of Diana. The tall figure, proud and self-confident, glowed as if the light of the moon were actually emanating from the goddess herself.

Her soul felt every bit as empty as those blank, white orbs. For years she had focused on two goals: finding her father and becoming an archaeologist in her own right. Seize the day, she had told herself. Instead, she had seized a lie, for Daniel McKenzie was nothing like the father she remembered, and the man who she believed held the key to her future as an archaeologist was a fraud.

An ache started deep in her chest as Diana studied the symbol of feminine strength in front of her. Her hands tightened into fists as she fought the tears that threatened for the second time that day. She must not allow them to come, she thought, for they would be the final sign of the weakness she so abhorred and feared.

Several feet away, Ben stood beneath a large palm tree. The thick fronds far above his head rustled in the breeze as he saw Diana standing in front of the statue, noting how small and helpless she looked in comparison to the goddess towering atop her rock pedestal.

Something about the way Diana had moved after dinner, slowly and without apparent direction, had compelled him to follow her, choosing to risk her ire at invading her privacy over the chance of letting her meet with an accident.

He knew he'd made the right choice. She moved as if she were in a dream, fairly drifting down the path. He longed to cross the distance that separated them, to offer her the comfort of his arms, even as he reminded himself how resistant she could be to such overtures.

The sound of a deep, shattering sob put an end to Ben's indecision. He sprinted across the road, reaching her side just as she lifted a hand to her mouth in a vain attempt to smother back another. Without hesitating a second, he gathered her to him, folding his arms around her as she stiffened.

He lay his cheek atop her head, trying to think of something to say that might ease her pain. When no words would come he lifted a hand to the back of her neck and began slowly kneading the taut muscles. Another sob burst from her tense form, followed by another; then, as Diana began to shudder with the force of her anguish, he felt her arms steal around his waist and her form grow limp within his embrace.

Her emotional storm stopped slowly, easing into occasional gasps, until finally he felt strength steal back into Diana's muscles. A moment later she straightened. She leaned away from him, not attempting to move out of his grasp, but just far enough to lift her head and look up into his eyes.

Ben almost gasped at the despair he saw in her grief-ravaged face. Gone was the proud, determined woman he'd come to know so well. In her place stood a lost child. His heart lurched. He placed one hand on her cheek and smoothed his thumb along her tears.

"Diana," he said, "I'll help you get a position with one of my colleagues. I promise you."

Diana's features tightened slightly. "No. You were right. I would never last on a dig. I thought I was strong, capable, but I'm just a weak, emotional woman after all."

Ben shook his head. "You're tired from hours of work that would have left most men exhausted, and you have had a day full of surprises on top of that. What did you think you were—an all-powerful goddess like this one here? You aren't. You're human, and you are in desperate need of some rest."

Diana's eyes glistened in the moonlight. A half-sob, half-gasp escaped her lips, and Ben's heart twisted again with the need to comfort her. He lowered his head and placed gentle lips on hers, then closed his mouth over hers to capture another sob.

Diana shut her eyes as she rocked toward his strong form and felt the hot tears trickle out onto her cheeks; then she tightened her arms around Ben's waist as her sorrow receded in the face of the sudden desire coursing through her. As Ben's lips continued to move over hers, Diana gave in to the force of his growing passion, welcomed the feel of his body pressing against hers, found herself willing to surrender completely to the sensations stirring to life that promised pleasures along with a state of mental oblivion.

Ben's arms closed about her. One hand slid down, caressing the curve of her buttocks, bringing a moan to her lips. His gentle touch shifted down to her thighs and in one swift motion he lifted her up. Diana heard the rustle of bushes and opened her eyes as she felt herself being lowered to the ground.

They were in a small clearing behind the statue, veiled from sight by the surrounding shrubbery. The moon shimmered above them, set in a sapphire blue sky as Ben's mouth once more closed over hers.

The force of Ben's kiss burned through her, caught her up in a wave of desire that left her with only enough strength to hold onto his shoulders as he kissed and caressed her. She was barely aware that he was removing her clothes, hardly conscious of her feeble efforts to help him remove his shirt and pants. But once she lay beneath him on the soft moss, she was fully alive to the feel of his warm flesh against hers, to the urgent need growing between them.

Later, as Diana lay beneath Ben, her legs entwined with his, she found that she felt light, so weightless that she was afraid she would float away if he were to move off her. She nuzzled her face into his shoulder and eased her arms around his neck as she released a deep, satisfied sigh.

Diana's warm breath blew across Ben's shoulder, bringing one side of his lips up in a half-smile even as his brows lowered into a frown. Something about the lovemaking they had just shared struck him as different; something had been missing. The heavy, warm feeling in his limbs argued with that thought, and he shook away the frown, telling himself he was imagining things.

"Diana," he whispered.

"Yes?" He could barely hear her voice.

"It's time we got you back to the house. You are very tired."

"Yes, I am."

Ben noted the spiritless note to her voice. "I don't think you should sleep out here, lovely as it is," he said.

"No, Ben. You're right."

Ben shifted into a sitting position, pulling Diana with him to cradle her in his lap. Her head lolled softly on his shoulder, her thick, dark hair tumbling down around them as he looked down into her eyes. They were as dark as the night sky, wide with what he hoped was the aftermath of spent desire. He dropped a light kiss on her nose, then spoke. "I want you to get a good night's sleep. I don't want you to rise before noon tomorrow, do you understand?"

"I understand."

"Good. The staff will have orders not to disturb you until that time. Will and I have to go into the city early in the morning, to accompany Harrington to the authorities. We'd like you to join us there for dinner at the Palace Hotel."

"Is that an order too?"

"It is. Will is arranging for Emma to take you into town with her tomorrow, after you've had a late breakfast. She'll show you around and perhaps you can shop for some new clothes. And speaking of clothes, as much as I enjoy looking at your naked figure in the moonlight, I think we'd better get dressed and return to the house.

Diana's sigh floated in the air. "I suppose you're right."

* * *

An hour later, Ben stood at the window in his room, watching the moonlight dance in a narrow arc over the dark waters of the ocean. His body was still heavy with spent passion, flushed from the warmth of Diana's response to his lovemaking. His heart still beat rapidly when he thought back to her unrestrained surrender, but now that he considered her behavior he found a twinge of doubt worming its way into his mind.

It was unlike Diana to be so yielding. Even the first time they had made love, she had made shy attempts to become an equal participant. The pleasure he had shared with her tonight had blinded him to her uncharacteristic compliancy, and he found that he missed the slight fight for control that had spiced their earlier encounters.

He wasn't totally comfortable with Diana's easy acquiescence to his orders, either. That was totally unlike her. He recalled how weary she had looked when he left her at her room. It was possible she had simply been too tired to respond with her usual wit, or perhaps too sated by their lovemaking.

This last thought made Ben happy; he liked the knowledge that he pleased her. When he answered a knock on the door, Will stepped in and Ben asked, "Is everything set?"

Will nodded. "Emma will take Diana shopping and sightseeing for several hours tomorrow. I told Emma that you and I will meet them at the Palace Hotel for dinner, and I included Emma's husband in the invitation. I figure we can call the restaurant and leave a message with some excuse for our absence, insisting that they dine without us. We'll also request that Diana be allowed to spend the night with the Merritts."

"It should work. You didn't give Emma any hint that Diana might be in danger, did you?"

"No. For one thing, I couldn't speak privately with

Emma. Besides, I doubt that there really is any danger. I'd just feel better if Diana were somewhere else tomorrow night."

"You know, we really can't be sure something won't happen sooner—tonight, for example."

"Of course we can't. Which is why you and I will take turns alternating guard duty with Ian and Simon both tonight and tomorrow. You are due to relieve Simon even as we speak."

Ben removed his jacket from the back of a chair. "What about Pete?"

"He should be safe. He leaves at eleven, and our thief has been striking after midnight. I've assigned Simon to keep an eye on him just in case the fiend decides to move before that, though. I really don't think that anything will happen tonight, you know."

"I almost wish it would. Patience has never been a virtue of mine. And tonight I know that Diana is safe. She looked tired enough to fall asleep on her feet when I took her to her room."

"Where did you two disappear to this evening, anyway? Her father wanted to talk to her."

"We went to the garden. Diana needed to be away from everyone."

"But not away from you?"

Ben felt his face grow warm. "She needed someone. We . . . have an understanding."

"I hope that understanding includes wedding bells."

"We haven't discussed it."

"Why not?"

Ben was conscious of muscles tightening across his shoulders. "Diana is rather resistant to the idea of marriage. She doesn't like being told what to do, remember?"

"She only needs to know three things: that you love her,

that you won't leave her, and that you won't prevent her from being who she needs to be.''

"Why are you telling me this?"

"Because after tomorrow night, Diana is going to need someone to watch over her interests, to act in her father's place. Not that he's done much of a job till now.''

"I don't think it would be possible for me to act like her father.'' He opened the door and stepped into the hall.

"Breakfast is served, sleepyhead.''

The soft voice seeped into Diana's dozing mind. Slowly she opened her eyes to see Emma standing by her bed, holding a tray. Diana tried to sit up. Her body felt heavy, her muscles stiff, and it was an effort to push herself onto one elbow.

"I'm sorry,'' she said. "It's very late, isn't it? I should have been up hours ago.''

"No, you shouldn't have. You were under orders to sleep in this morning, remember?'' Emma spoke briskly as she placed the tray on the table next to the bed. Diana finally pulled herself into a sitting position and had just begun to swing her legs over the side of the bed when a gentle hand arrested her motion.

"Breakfast in bed this morning. Doctor's orders. You've been overworking yourself. I should have seen that and ordered you to get some rest earlier.''

"Tell me, do you ever give yourself such advice?'' Diana asked.

"Rarely. Of course, I believe strongly that it's healthiest to lead a full, busy life. But now and then even I overdo things and have to force myself to rest a little. You should count yourself lucky. I'm only insisting you stay in bed a few moments longer. If I were a male doctor, you'd be abed for two days at least. Here now, scoot back and get those legs under the covers so I can put this tray in front of you.''

Diana obeyed the order; then, as the tray was placed over her lap she looked up. ''I'm still to go into town with you, aren't I?''

''Yes. It's all arranged. However, after I spoke to Will last night I remembered that I have several patients to see this afternoon, so I can't show you around San Francisco as I would like. But that may work out for the best anyway. Your father is coming with us.''

The muscles in Diana's outstretched legs tensed as she raised her eyes to Emma. ''Oh?''

Emma looked concerned. ''That's all right, isn't it? He asked about you this morning, and when I mentioned that my work was going to interfere with my plans to give you a tour of the city, he asked if he could escort you. I assumed you would want to spend some time with him, since he will be leaving tomorrow.''

''Yes, I suppose I should do that.'' The words had barely passed Diana's lips before she glanced up at Emma and spoke again. ''That probably sounded horrible to you. It certainly sounded very undaughterly to my ears.'' She shook her head. ''I don't know what is wrong with me. I have longed to see my father for so many years, and now I find I am counting the hours until he's gone.''

''Diana, that is hardly something to blame yourself for.'' Emma took a deep breath. ''I hope you will forgive me for being blunt, but when your father was speaking to me last night I could only think of two things. First, that Daniel McKenzie is very cold, and second, that he's a . . . well, a pompous ass.''

''So I wasn't the only one who noticed?''

''Hardly.''

Diana's laughter died just as quickly as it started, and her senses once again grew dull. ''But he *is* my father, and he did seem sincere in his sorrow yesterday for all the years we've been apart. I suppose it's only right to spend some time with him before he leaves."

"People sometimes hide behind false masks. Perhaps in the time you have together you'll find the man you remembered buried deep in that conceited facade."

Diana replied, "Perhaps."

Chapter Twenty-one

"I INSIST on buying it for you, Diana. It's not every night that I get to dine with my daughter in a magnificent hotel like the Palace. I want you to have something special to wear."

Diana stood next to her father in front of a shop on Kearny Street, which had a flowing white silk gown hanging on the dressmaker's form in the window. Yes, this would be a special occasion, she supposed; most likely the last such dinner they shared. She hadn't yet told him that she had no intention of leaving with him the following day, for she wasn't sure how he would react. She wanted to enjoy this evening, to make some part of their reunion a happy one.

And this dress *was* perfect for the occasion. The designer had taken the classic lines of a Roman costume and modeled it into a beautiful gown. The neckline dipped in front, and the flowing silk draped over the shoulders to form loose sleeves that ended at the elbow. A simple length of silver-gray rope was tied at the waist, letting the fabric flow in smooth lines to the floor.

"Please, Diana. Let me do this one thing for you."

She couldn't say that his eyes were pleading with her, but they held a sincere expression of desire that made her nod despite the unreasonable sense of doubt that gnawed at her stomach.

"Fine." He led her toward the front door. "I suppose you should try it on, but I can tell by looking at you that it will fit perfectly. We'll have it wrapped up and you can change into it when we reach Emma's office. We'll look for shoes on the way there."

Her father wouldn't need to shop for himself. As usual, he was faultlessly garbed in a well-tailored black suit with a gray silk vest and tie. On his head sat a black derby banded with a gray ribbon.

And his manners had been just as impeccable. He had accompanied Diana on a cable car ride up Nob Hill, where she had ogled the enormous mansions overlooking the city, then agreed to a tour of Chinatown. There, they found themselves surrounded by figures in trousers and tunics of brilliantly colored silk. The singsong voices of the inhabitants and the fragrances wafting into the streets from restaurants and herb shops made Diana feel as if she had been suddenly transported out of San Francisco and into some Oriental port.

They had talked quite a bit, too, but her father had done most of the speaking. From time to time during the day her father had alluded to various digs he had commanded, and had spoken of the different artifacts he had uncovered. At those times his eyes had glinted and his features had taken on a softer mood, like that of a man remembering a lover.

This very expression lit his face now as they walked toward Emma's office on Montgomery Street and he spoke of Aricia, Italy, the site of the main shrine dedicated to Diana.

"You can feel the goddess's influence so very strongly in that spot," he said. "Especially at night, with the moon shining above. The animals come out—owls in the trees, squirrels and rabbits on the ground, a fox in the bushes—

as if they sense that Diana will protect them from any alien presence."

He stopped in the middle of the street and turned to Diana, ignoring the carriages rattling by on either side of them. "You must go there with me. It can be arranged. We can work a dig there, together. Not that there is much left to be uncovered, but you should experience the site." He paused and grasped her wrist. "Come with me. After dinner we can return to Sutro's home and pack your bags so that you can leave with me tomorrow."

Diana's feelings were in turmoil, her heart pounding slowly as her mind played with visions of this magical place. Then, into the picture of the glade he had described, a dark shape moved into the shadows, a familiar form of a man with golden hair, dark eyes, and warm, welcoming arms.

For years she had prayed for just such an invitation from her father. Now, when her heart was in need of unhurried time to unravel the tangled strings of her life, he wanted to force her into a decision.

Her jaw tightened. She was prepared to refuse his request, but before she could speak, he placed a hand on her shoulder. "I'm sorry," he said. "I can't expect you to agree to a request like that so quickly. Let's go have a nice quiet dinner with your friends. We can discuss the matter later this evening."

Diana agreed as the anger melted from her limbs. She let him take her elbow to guide her across the street, then walked silently at her father's side as they made their way to Emma's office.

Diana felt strange asking Emma if she could change into her new dress when Emma was wearing a simple white shirtwaist and a dark blue skirt, but Emma surprised her by pulling open a closet filled with an assortment of clothes. "George and I enjoy going to the theater," she explained, "but we usually find we are both working until almost

curtain time. So we've learned to keep a few things here
for emergencies. George is meeting us at the Palace, by the
way.''

The two women dressed quickly, Diana in her white gown
and simple silver slippers, Emma in a dress of deep wine
silk. Diana's father helped them into the waiting carriage,
and as the vehicle rocked behind the chestnut mare, Diana
told Emma about her sight-seeing.

As they neared their destination, Emma pointed out the
Palace Hotel as it loomed in front of them. Diana fell silent
as she spied a building that occupied a full city block and
rose seven stories high. The carriage pulled into an opening
in one wall, to enter a circular drive in the very center of
the hotel. Her father disembarked and handed down first
Emma, then Diana. As soon as she was safely on the ground,
she drew her hand away.

The interior of the hotel was just as impressive: richly
decorated with red, cream, and black patterned carpets on
the floor and gilt-framed pictures lining the walls in between
lacy potted palms. Diana walked silently next to her father
as Emma led them to an ornate wrought-iron elevator that
took them up to the restaurant. Dr. George Merritt was
waiting, his large frame dwarfing one of the palms framing
the entrance. He stepped toward them, a folded piece of
paper in his hand.

''Ben called the maître d' about fifteen minutes ago,'' he
said as he handed the paper to his wife. ''The fellow wrote
down the messages. Apparently Ben and Will are going to
be delayed. They asked if we would see that Diana has a
nice meal, and requested she stay the night with us.'' He
addressed Diana. ''There was a separate message from Babcock for you. I haven't read that. I only open messages sent
to my *wife* from another man.

Diana took the small piece of paper. ''He says, 'Be a

good girl and eat all your vegetables.' '' She looked up. "Will worries that I don't eat enough."

Will would not have worried had he been at the table that evening. Dinner was a marvelous feast. Diana ate her fill, despite the fact that the decision her father had asked her to make hovered at the back of her mind like a nagging ghost. Conversation flowed easily, too, with Emma and George bantering back and forth about their patients. Everything was fine until Diana was sipping her coffee and she heard her father clear his throat.

"Well." Her father placed his cup into his saucer as he smiled across the table at the two doctors. "It's very nice of you to offer to have Diana spend the night with you. However, she and I have several things to discuss, and precious little time left to do so." He turned to Emma. "I hope you don't mind, but I would like to take my daughter back to Sutro Heights tonight, where Diana can make her decision."

Diana already knew what her answer would be, but she didn't want to risk making everyone uncomfortable by announcing this in public, so when Emma turned an inquiring glance her way, Diana nodded. "I think that will be the best plan," she said.

It was on the tip of her tongue to say that there would be plenty of time in the two weeks of the exhibit's run to spend with Emma and George. She caught herself and smiled. "If Ben and Will catch up to you tonight, please be sure to tell Will that I ate everything that was served to me."

It was nearly ten o'clock when her father hired a carriage for their return ride, and it was obvious that the driver didn't relish a trip out to Sutro's property at such an hour. The bills her father slipped into the man's gloved fingers seemed to ease the driver's concern somewhat, and soon they were rattling through the brightly lit city.

For the most part, the ride was a silent one. Diana was grateful for her father's distracted air, for it gave her a chance to frame the words she would use to refuse his offer of a trip to Italy. She had been concentrating so hard on her speech that she jumped when her father leaned out the open window and shouted for the driver to stop.

He sat back in his seat as the vehicle slowed. "We're almost to the gates leading to Sutro's garden, but I'm not ready to go up to the house. I'd like to visit the statue of Diana in the Baths one more time, wouldn't you? I think it would be nice to walk from here, and get another taste of the salt air."

"Well . . . I suppose." Diana frowned. "But I'm not sure about visiting the Baths. If Pete is still there, we can get in. Otherwise you'll have to wait till tomorrow morning."

Her father nodded as the carriage stopped, then opened the door and stepped out. Diana felt her flesh contract as he handed her down. As before, she drew her fingers out of his grasp as soon as she touched the ground, then looked at the Baths, lying dark before them except for the glint of moonlight on the glass roof. She stood breathing in the scent of the ocean, shivering a little as the moist air penetrated her wool coat, until her father took her arm and began to guide her gently down the hill.

Again, neither spoke. Their path was well lit by the huge, round moon shining above. When they reached the entrance to the Baths, they found the door unlocked. Before Diana could suggest that her father knock loudly on the door to attract Pete's attention, he grasped the ornate knob and pulled the door open.

Diana stepped in, then glanced around. "Pete?" she called. "It's Diana."

She stopped. A dim light shown ahead, moonlight seeping

through the glass onto the promenade deck. She peered ahead, listening for the shuffling sound of the watchman's steps. Instead she heard the door close softly behind her, followed by the soft click of the lock slipping into place.

Diana began walking through the entry hall, raising her voice to call Pete's name. When a hand grasped her wrist, she whirled to find her father's eyes glinting down at her.

"I don't think he can hear you, Diana." He spoke in a soft, chilling whisper.

"Of course he can. His hearing is just—"

Her father cut off her words with a frown and a painful tightening of his fingers over her wrist. He pointed to a dark shadow in the corner on the floor. "Believe me, Diana. He cannot hear a thing."

Diana moved, her father still grasping her hand, until she could see that two forms lay on the floor. She recognized the first as Will's assistant, Ian. His red pomaded hair gleamed brightly in the dark, as did his wide, staring eyes. Diana gasped, then glanced at the other limp figure, dressed in the familiar rumpled uniform. Her eyes widened as she stared at the still features of the night watchman.

The clock on the mantle in Sutro's parlor ticked quietly. Ben glanced up from the *San Francisco Chronicle* to check its ornate hands. Eleven-thirty, and no indication that McKenzie had returned yet. His gaze shifted across the room, where Will and LaPierre sat facing each other over a chessboard.

LaPierre seemed oblivious to the time, as did Will. Ben knew better. His friend was no doubt just as tense as he was, attempting to disguise the fact that he was listening, as Ben was, for the crunch of wheels on the driveway out beyond the window, or the ring of the telephone.

Ian and Simon were in the Baths, Simon standing guard in the exhibit area, Ian stationed near the telephone in the entryway. Ben wanted to be down there with them, but he and Will had decided it would allay any suspicions the thief might have if it looked like they were unconcerned.

Ben was still sure that McKenzie was their man, but he agreed that they couldn't count on his instinct. Harrington had left early that morning, but he could easily come back, since LaPierre had decided that there was little point in taking his charge of attempted fraud to the authorities.

LaPierre himself appeared relaxed. He gave no hint that he was anxious to retire or in any other way escape the company of Ben and Will. Ben knew that didn't mean a thing. Whoever had committed the previous thefts was far too clever to show their hand in such an obvious manner.

The high-pitched ringing of the telephone out in the hall made Ben jump slightly. He made a great deal of noise turning the page of the newspaper to cover his startled motion, then looked up when a uniformed maid appeared at the door to the room.

"Professor Potter? There is a telephone call for you."

He rose and followed the small woman quickly.

"Yes?"

"Ben?" Emma's voice crackled across the line. "I called to tell Diana that she left her day clothes in my carriage, but the maid said she isn't there."

"No, she isn't. She was supposed to be with you."

"I know, but her father convinced her to return to the Heights with him tonight. They left over an hour ago, so they should be arriving at any moment. Will you give her my message?"

Ben's mind was racing so fast that the last question barely registered in his mind. Finally he said, "Yes, I will. Goodnight, Emma."

He hung up as he placed the telephone back on the table before him, then turned to stride back into the parlor. When Ben reached Will's side, the man looked up quickly.

"That was Emma. Diana and her father supposedly left the city over an hour ago."

Will rose to his feet, ignoring LaPierre's indignant gasp and the chess pieces rolling off the table. "Let's get down to the Baths. Now."

"She's coming round, sir."

Diana heard a deep voice penetrating the darkness of her mind. It was familiar and yet different at the same time. But the identity of the speaker was not what caused her confusion. It was the hard surface that she lay on—so cold that it had leeched the warmth from her body.

She shivered, then forced her eyes open. Her vision was clouded, revealing only a dark shape curving over her. She tried to lift her hand to her eyes, to brush away the cobwebs that seemed to blur her vision, but her arm would not move.

Diana closed her eyes again, aware of a sense of heaviness to her muscles that resisted her mental command. Yet, through the numbness of her wrists she thought she could feel the presence of something more, something tight that grasped her wrists and prevented any motion.

"Diana, open your eyes."

She knew that voice. It was her father. He spoke to her in a commanding voice. He could not order her about in that way. His simple purchase of a new dress had not earned him that right.

Determined to tell him this, Diana opened her eyes and saw a knife poised a foot or so above her chest. The sight of the sharp point gleaming in the dim light made her gasp.

Her father hovered behind the blade. A dim light illuminated thin lips forming a tight smile. "Ah, back to the land of the living, are you? At least for the moment."

A thousand questions raced through Diana's mind, becoming a tangle of words that hovered on her speechless tongue as she glanced at the knife again, and then back at her father.

"You don't understand what is happening, do you?"

Diana shook her head.

"Well, look around, see where you are. You should be able to hazard a guess."

Diana tried to sit up. Again her muscles would not obey. She managed to lift her head to see that her hands were tied in front of her, and that she was bound by ropes to the slab of granite where the statue of Diana was supposed to be standing. Before her neck muscles grew tired, she caught a glimpse of her bare feet, and beyond them, the statue of Diana sitting on the floor just outside the archway.

She let her head rest on the stone altar again, letting her eyes move from side to side, soaking in the familiar curves of the shrine area of the exhibit as if they might somehow tell her why she was there. The plaster walls told her nothing. They simply reflected the lights of the false moon and stars, mocking her with the appearance of real stone. Then a huge shadow darkened the painted surface. Diana twisted her head until she found the source of this shadow, a tall man with pale brown hair. She had only seen him twice before, but she immediately recognized Simon, the man who had accompanied the artifacts on the boat from England.

None of this made sense. Diana saw her father had straightened, but he still grasped the knife tightly, as if ready to plunge it downward at any moment. His smile appeared to be wider.

"I can see you haven't guessed," he said. "Well, that is not too surprising, for what I have planned is really a variation of my own, not an exact reenactment of the old ritual."

Diana shook her head in confusion, but this time she was able to give voice to her question. "What ritual?"

"Oh, surely you recall the stories of Aricia, how the old priest must be killed by the new one, as an offering of sorts to the more bloodthirsty aspects of the goddess of the hunt. I have repeated that ritual two times now as I have collected certain images of Diana. The first one represented Diana as the huntress, very similar to the statue in the garden. The other is of Diana, goddess of the moon, stars and a moon wreathing her head. This one"—he pointed to the statue at the foot of the slab—"combines both aspects, and completes the set. I plan to take them to Aricia, where they belong, where they can be viewed in their proper place, where the goddess can once again be worshiped as she should. Since you obviously have no desire to accompany me, you shall serve as the last sacrifice."

Diana could see no hint of madness. His voice was as calm as if he were giving a lecture on the construction of Roman roads instead of hinting at something as deadly as human sacrifice.

Diana didn't want to hear any more about his plans. The knife held over her heart and the ropes binding her told her all too plainly what they were. It was also clear that in spite of the picture of sanity he presented, the man's actions revealed that he had somehow lost touch with reality. Her only hope lay in reasoning with him, reminding him that this was no longer ancient Rome, and she was no priestess.

"Father," she began. Her voice tightened over the word, but she forced herself to continue. "I do remember the tales of Aricia now, of the battles of the priests. But the sacrifice offered was of a small animal, never of humans. And Diana is the protector of young women, remember. She would not be pleased if you were to offer my life up to her."

Her father leaned closer, his lips tight, his eyes narrowing. "You are mistaken on several points, my dear. Diana is not the protector of young women; she is the protector of virgins. Simon here told me all about the night you spent in

Oakland with Potter. And last evening, after dinner, I followed you two—saw you slip into the bushes behind the statue of Diana in Sutro's garden. Both the goddess and I are aware that you are *not* a virgin; therefore, you are no longer under her protection."

He paused, then leaned closer to her, his eyes glinting in the half-dark as his lips eased into another smile. "Also, I am not your father."

Chapter Twenty-two

BEN WHIRLED AWAY from the exit archway and flattened himself against the wall outside the shrine as McKenzie's words floated through the opening. Burned in his mind was an image of Diana, lying helpless beneath the shimmering blade, as McKenzie stood over her and Simon's huge form stood guard.

He turned toward Will, expecting to see the man's features reflect the surprise he was feeling. Instead, the moonlight sifting through the glass ceiling revealed Will's small smile, as if McKenzie's words confirmed some long-standing suspicion.

LaPierre stood behind Will. He had surmised that Diana was in trouble, and had insisted on coming with Ben and Will. They had explained their suspicions on the way down. Now, with a wave of his hand, Ben motioned for Will and LaPierre to ease back from the opening. Once they were several feet away he spoke to them in a whisper that was barely louder than a breath. "Stay here. I'm going to go up to the volcano room and let myself down the ladder to the storage level. Listen for my call, then go for whichever man is closest."

The stakes were high. They had spared a moment to examine the bodies in the entryway. Ian was dead, and

Pete's breathing had been ominously shallow.

A second later Will nodded his agreement to the plan. Immediately Ben moved away, quietly skirting the mock hill until he reached the stairs leading up to the temple room. He stopped then, bending down to remove his boots before he started up the wooden stairs, testing each step for a hint of a telltale creak before he put his full weight on it.

Once he slipped into the temple room he was able to move more swiftly. By the time he reached the end of the corridor and stepped into the volcano room, his heart was racing and his breath was coming in quick gasps. He opened the narrow storeroom door, stepped in, and stood at the top of the ladder, forcing his breathing to slow and listening to the deep voice rise from below.

"So you have heard of Peter Vicini? And like the others, you thought me dead. It has been such a wonderful ruse. Your father and I were good friends, you see, for the first two weeks of the dig at any rate. He told me all about his life, all about the little daughter he hadn't seen in so many years. He was writing a letter to you, but I never knew if it was sent off, until you told me you had never received any message from Pompeii.''

The voice stopped. There was a moment of silence, then the man spoke again. "That has caused me quite a little bit of worry over the last years. You see, toward the end of the second week your father was becoming less and less friendly toward me. All in all, I guess things worked out for the best, thanks to the goddess.''

A dry chuckle followed these words. Ben silently groaned as the soft laughter floated up through the opening. Ben began to slowly descend to the storage area below as the man who had identified himself as Peter Vicini began speaking again.

"Speaking of the goddess you were named for, that was what had drawn your father and me together in the first place. However, his interest in Diana was only of an academic sort; he did not share my devotion to her. And so he had to die.''

''You killed my father?''

The anger in Diana's voice cheered Ben. Gone was the complacent tone that had concerned him last night. She was alert, and if he knew Diana, ready to fight for her life.

Ben reached the bottom of the stairs and felt the walls of the small room begin to crowd around him. Sweat moistened his brow and he found it difficult to draw a breath. Forcing the contracting walls out of his mind, he concentrated on the knife gleaming in Vicini's hand.

Diana was watching the knife as well, her heart pounding with an erratic rhythm. But beneath the fear burned a growing anger at this man who held her helpless, whose lips had twisted into an evil smile in response to her question.

''No, Diana,'' Vicini said quietly. ''I did not kill him. I imagine the mountain did that for me. It was such a needless death, you know. I only wanted what was mine, a very small statue of Diana that I had uncovered. As head of the dig, your father demanded that it be handed over to the museum funding the expedition. That was unfair. I was willing to take the statue in lieu of pay, but he refused and so we fought. I fled, and your fool of a father followed me into the hills, where I managed to elude him. When I surfaced again in nearby Naples, half-dead myself, I learned that he had not come out of the mountains. The opportunity was too good to pass up. Your father and I were of the same build and coloring, so I continued to let my beard grow and waited until everyone connected with that dig left the area. It was then that I reappeared, claiming to be Daniel McKenzie. No one ever doubted me.''

''Not even a daughter who had only vague memories of her father.'' Diana's voice echoed her bitterness. ''Still, you must have been very unhappy to learn of my presence here.''

"Very. It took me a while to decide how to deal with you. Fortunately, your father had spoken of you, your mother, and your grandfather often, so I had quite a bit of information stored in my memory. I think you'll admit that my approach was very effective.''

She replied coldly, "For awhile.''

"Ah yes. I suppose I made some mistakes. I gather, for example, that you are nothing like your mother, other than in appearance. Well, I am sorry that you would not agree to accompany me to Aricia. You would serve as a perfect priestess at Diana's shrine. With you I could bring alive the old beliefs. Never fear, however; I shall find one more willing, thus more worthy of the honor. For you, honor will be found in serving as the supreme sacrifice, a fallen virgin, offered upon Diana's own altar.''

Diana watched as Vicini's hand tightened on the hilt of the knife as he raised his arm. Suddenly she heard a deep voice roar, "Will, *now*."

Vicini's face registered complete disbelief for one second, then his features twisted with rage. He swiveled around just as a figure hurtled toward him from the shadows beyond. Vicini slashed his knife downward and Diana's heart leapt to her throat as she saw the blade rushing toward Ben.

Ben's forearm blocked the knife's descent as he reached for Vicini's throat with his other hand. She watched in helpless frustration as the man evaded Ben's grasp, whirling away only to turn back and begin to approach, brandishing the knife as he closed in on Ben.

"You double-dealing snake.''

Diana jumped as Will's strained voice echoed in the room. She heard a scuffling sound to her left, and twisted around to see Simon and Will locked together against the cave walls. Simon was so much larger and so much younger than

Will that Diana's heart grew cold with dread. She strained against her bonds, but the ropes only gave a mocking creak as they held her tied to the slab.

Will is going to be killed, she thought. She twisted around, searching for Ben, but he wasn't in any more of a position to help the older man than she was.

Ben was backing away from the ever advancing Vicini, his dark eyes on the knife that waved menacingly from side to side in front of him. Again Diana struggled in vain against the grip of the ropes as she saw Ben come to a stop against the wall and Vicini continue to move forward.

Once more the blade gleamed as it arced in the air toward Ben's chest. His right hand shot forward to grasp Vicini's forearm; then Ben swung the man around and smashed his hand against the wall.

The knife fell, then clattered across the floor to stop with a clank as it hit one of the stones supporting the slab Diana lay on. Neither man turned to look for it. Locked hand to hand, Ben and Vicini continued to struggle, with Diana watching every move, not shifting a muscle, until a loud popping sound split the air.

Diana jumped so violently that the ropes bruised her chest. Both Ben and Vicini froze, neither of them relaxing his hold on the other. Diana heard a heavy object fall to the ground. She turned her head, her heart frozen with dread, until she spied Simon's still form on the floor and the bright badge of red spreading across his chest. Out of the corner of her eye she caught a glimpse of Will.

Then the sound of a shot echoed right above her head. Her body jerked even more sharply. A second later she saw Will wheel away, and heard him cry out softly as he crashed against the wall behind him and slid to the floor.

Diana saw the trickle of blood coursing down the side of his face. Her heart sunk when Vicini spoke. ''Well, La-

Pierre, that first shot was hardly on target. I do hope you will be careful this time.''

Diana pulled her eyes away from Will's motionless form. Directly above she saw an arm holding a black pistol. She glanced at the face of the Frenchman, standing a little behind her head, and felt her body grow cold with fear. The bored, amiable expression she had always associated with LaPierre was gone. His face was set in a cold mask.

''That's it. Aim carefully now.''

She realized that Ben's position, pinning Vicini to the wall, now made his broad back a perfect target.

Diana screamed out Ben's name at the exact moment he moved to one side. A second later the gun fired again, and Diana saw Ben reel from the force of the bullet, lifting his hand to his shoulder as he fell backward. A loud crack split the silence as his head hit one of the large boulders, then he slumped onto his side, his bloodstained hand lying limply on the floor.

''Get me the knife, LaPierre.'' Vicini's harsh voice woke Diana from her stunned state. She turned to him as he approached the altar. His eyes glittered. Diana was aware of the Frenchman's position on her right. His sleeve brushed her arm as he stood. Diana watched the knife, then shuddered as the man handed it to Vicini.

''My friend,'' LaPierre said, ''we must hurry. The tide changes quickly.''

''I am aware of the need for haste.'' Vicini's words were clipped. ''I have unfinished business to attend to.''

Diana didn't look at the man's face this time. She kept her eyes on the gleaming blade as it drew closer. She tightened her jaw and swallowed the whimper cowering in her throat, refusing to give this man the satisfaction of seeing her fear.

The tip of the weapon hovered over her heart for a moment, then lowered slowly, slicing the ropes that lay across her chest before rising into the air once more. Again Diana tensed, preparing for death, but this time the descending blade attacked the bonds holding her legs to the slab.

"I have changed my mind, Diana." Vicini's face hovered over hers. "I think there has been enough blood spilled here to satisfy the goddess on her special day. I shall save your sacrifice for another time, when it can be performed properly, without the need to rush."

Diana tried to move, to roll away from him, but the moment she shifted in that direction, his thin fingers closed over her wrist. In a move so swift she could barely follow it, he grabbed her by the waist, then lifted her in his arms, cradling her like a father might carry a small child. His grasp, however, was not parental. His fingers bit into her right arm, pinning her bound hands uselessly in front of her. When Diana struggled against him, he tightened his hold, squeezing her against him so hard that she gasped with pain as he turned to the Frenchman.

"You carry the statue," he said, "and follow me."

"And what of my bounty?" LaPierre gestured toward a collection of vases and small artifacts Diana recognized from the Pompeii rooms above.

"They are not important. I must have that statue, however, and I cannot carry both Dianas. Do as I ask and I will see that you are amply compensated."

Diana held her breath, willing LaPierre to refuse, hoping she would be left down here, free to get help for Ben and Will, praying they weren't already beyond help.

The Frenchman hesitated then lifted his shoulders and retrieved the statue of Diana. Vicini's voice echoed over Diana's head. "Let's go. The boat will be looking for us."

Diana saw the arched exit loom in front of them; the next moment they were weaving through display cases and potted plants.

* * *

Ben regained consciousness just in time to see Vicini's booted feet disappear out the exit. He tried to raise himself up, but a burning pain shot through his shoulder. He rolled to the other side, then stood quickly—too quickly. For one sickening moment the world seemed to whirl and dip, and he was afraid he would fall again but a moment later the world righted itself.

Ben turned toward the exit. His uncertain steps took him across the room in a zigzag pattern, but he forced himself to keep moving until he stood beneath the tall palm on the other side of the arch. His head began to swim again, and although he was not as dizzy as before, he placed his hand on the rough trunk of the tree and stood still for several seconds.

Just as he lifted his foot to start forward he heard a door shut. The sound didn't come from the entrance in front of him, but from his left.

The steam room. Ben turned and began moving again. His shoulder continued to throb, but by the time he reached the steam room door his legs were able to carry him along at a good pace. He made his way through the familiar pipes with no difficulty, and when he stepped outside, the sea breeze cleared his mind completely.

He knew which way they must have gone, but his gaze scanned the sides of the cliff rising before him anyway. The full moon reflected off the rough surface, forming dark shadows, but none of these moved. His eyes came to rest on the semicircle cut into the side of the rock. There was no doubt in his mind that Diana had been taken through that.

For one second he contemplated climbing the cliff as he had the day he picnicked there with Will and Diana, but he knew how long that would take. His stomach twisted as he took a deep breath and forced himself to cross the narrow cement walkway toward that long, dark tunnel.

Each step that took him nearer to the passageway increased his dread. Even before he stepped beneath the arch he could feel the familiar weakness sap his strength. He tried to think of Diana as he moved into the black opening, of the danger she faced if he couldn't get to her, but his fear prevented him from drawing the breath he needed. He heard voices echo down the tunnel, but the buzzing in his ears was too loud for him to understand the words.

Diana grew hopeful when Vicini called out to the man exiting the tunnel in front of them. "Wait, LaPierre. Give me the statue, and you take this Diana."

The Frenchman turned as Vicini stepped into the moonlight. His pale hair and features contrasted sharply with the gray rocks behind him. "Don't be ridiculous, Vicini. We don't have any time to waste. The tide is rising. If we do not hurry, the waves at the end of the rock will prevent the men from getting close enough to make the transfer. Besides, what if the girl breaks away?"

"Then shoot her." The man's voice was a low growl in her ears as he stepped toward LaPierre and relaxed the arm that had been gripping her knees. The other arm tightened around her, holding her so tight she could barely breathe. "She is expendable. That statue is not. I want it in my possession, where I know it is safe."

"Now!" Vicini shouted. The Frenchman stepped forward, placing the statue in Vicini's outstretched arm.

Diana tensed, watching for an opportunity to break away when she was transferred into the other man's arms, but LaPierre grasped her just as tightly, holding her in the same manner as Vicini had. She didn't move as she was carried up the path leading to where she had picnicked with Ben and Will, aware that if she threw her captor off balance both of them would fall against the craggy rocks rising on either side of them. But as soon as he began to pick his way over the shadowy surface, she began to squirm.

"Oh, a woman with fight," LaPierre panted in her ear as he tightened his hold on her. "Magnifique. Perhaps I can talk Peter into holding an orgy before the sacrifice. That might compensate, in part at least, for the treasures I was forced to leave behind because of you."

Diana's blood froze in her veins. She shivered, then anger coursed through her, bringing with it a determination to free herself from these men, even if it meant dying there upon the rocks. It was far better than what she faced if she allowed them to take her with them.

She saw that they were almost at the edge of the cliff. She could hear Vicini calling something out, most likely an order to the boat that was to be waiting for them. Twisting her head around she saw a large rowboat about thirty feet out, rising beneath a large swell. A second later, the wave slammed into the rocks, drenching them with it's spray.

Diana almost laughed. "You *are* insane, Vicini. You'll never get to that boat."

His white teeth flashed as he snarled, "You are wrong, Diana. My men are well trained for this sort of thing. They have judged the tide here, and the ocean in general. They tell me that waves come in sets of seven, growing progressively larger, then receding to start over again. They will time the swells, move in after the last big one so that we can jump on board, then row back to safety before the next large wave arrives. That, apparently, was the seventh wave. Look, the boat is moving in now."

With these words he gazed out to sea. One pale hand slid down the marble arm of the figure he held like a lover's caress. Diana's stomach lurched. She took a deep breath, using the expanding of her chest to test LaPierre's grip on her. It was looser than before, but still tight enough to prevent her from wiggling away.

Frustration and fear grew as she studied the man holding

her. His head was turned so that he could gaze out at the boat like Vicini. She stared at his ear for one second before making her move, jerking her head toward it and clamping it between her teeth.

Her action had the exact result she had hoped for. LaPierre screamed, loosening his hold on her as he reached for his ear. The moment Diana's arm was free of his crushing fingers she lifted her hands to his chest. She pushed away from him at the same moment that she opened her mouth to release his ear.

Sharp rocks stabbed into Diana's derriere when she landed, sending shards of pain up her spine. She rolled to one side and tried to stand, but her back refused to straighten. She forced herself to take one step, then another, before she stumbled and fell to the ground, this time breaking her fall with her bound hands.

"Shoot her."

Vicini's voice echoed over the sound of another wave slapping the face of the cliff. In the hissing silence of the retreating water, Diana turned, half-lying, half-sitting, to stare at the black object LaPierre was leveling at her. She heard a whistling sound, followed by a shout, then saw the Frenchman's arm jerk upward as if it had been pulled by some imaginary string, and the pistol fly into the air.

LaPierre didn't even try to reach for the gun. The strange look in his eyes made her turn to see Ben rushing forward. His left arm hung limply at his side, but his right arm he held cocked, a large rock cupped in his palm. A second later, he released the stone. Diana heard the familiar whistling sound as it passed over her, then a dull thud and a gasp. She twisted around just in time to see LaPierre stagger back, totter at the edge of the cliff as he waved his arms wildly, then fall backward with a cry that echoed in the sudden stillness.

Quickly, Ben removed the rope that bound her wrists and

then she followed his gaze to where Vicini stood at the edge of the cliff. The boat was still some ten feet away, but five pairs of oars working in clocklike precision eased it closer by the moment.

Then, as Diana watched, she saw a huge swell lift the craft high into the air, slip beneath it, then continue to grow as it curled forward. A cry caught in her throat. She shifted her gaze to the man holding the statue and saw Vicini take one step back, then another. But before he could move again, the wall of water broke, sweeping down on him in a curtain of foaming white.

The wave receded just as quickly, leaving the edge of the cliff empty. Diana heard a muffled shout echo from the boat, glanced in that direction, and saw oars moving in a disorganized frenzy as the frothing backwash chased the craft.

In the bright moonlight she saw a mixture of horror and satisfaction reflected on Ben's features. They stared at each other for a long, silent moment. Foam bubbled and whispered on the broken surface beneath their bare feet as they stepped gingerly over to the spot where Vicini had disappeared.

He then led her back to the point where LaPierre had fallen, with the same result. There was no sign of any body, alive or dead. The sea crashed onto the rocks again, and Ben stepped back, pulling Diana with him.

When he pulled her toward him, Diana went eagerly, parting her lips to taste the salt on his as their mouths met in a savage kiss borne of receding fear and mutual need. When the kiss ended Diana clung to Ben's shoulders as he tightened his arms around her and eased his lips from hers, holding her close, her head on his shoulder. She shivered despite the warmth of his body pressed against hers as the icy air licked her damp skin. Another wave crashed against the rocks, making her flinch and long for the safety and relative warmth of the Baths. That was when she remembered.

"Ben." She lifted her mouth toward his ear and raised her voice to be heard over the sounds of the surf. "What about Will?"

Ben stiffened away from her, grabbed her hand, and without a word, began leading her back across the rocky plateau. They made slow, painful progress. By the time they reached the bottom of the trail, Diana felt as if she had just walked across a bed of nails.

Ben paused at the mouth of the tunnel and turned to Diana. "Can you run?" he asked.

Diana nodded.

"Good," he said. "That's the only way I can make it through. Ready?"

Diana recalled the haunted look she had seen on his face when he had talked of his fear of closed-in places. She saw Ben take a deep breath before tightening his hand on her wrist and stepping forward. As they passed through the dark tunnel she kept up with his loping stride. The echoes of their ragged breaths led them down the long passageway until they were greeted with moonlight and the sounds of the sea on the other side.

Two men, one tall and heavy, the other short and slight, also greeted them. The two men had apparently just crossed the cement divider from the back of the Baths. They shifted their rifles from their shoulders to aim them at Diana and Ben. Diana felt Ben stiffen and she stood frozen at his side.

"Professor Potter, is that you?" the tall one asked as they drew nearer.

"It sure as hell is," he replied. "Johnson? What are you doing with a rifle instead of a rake?"

Diana recognized the men as two of the gardeners she'd seen working on Sutro's property as they shifted their weapons back to their shoulders. "Miss Emma sent us," the shorter one replied. "Said there was some trouble out here."

"There was, but it's over now. How did Emma know?" Ben queried.

"She didn't say. She called us up to the house just a few minutes ago. She couldn't talk a lot. She was working on some man in the parlor."

Ben turned to Diana. "Will." They hurried past the gardeners, ignoring the men's worried questions.

Ben's impatient knock on the front door of Sutro Heights was answered by a small maid. She retreated behind the door as Ben and Diana hurried toward the murmuring voices in the parlor.

They stopped just inside the threshold, looking at the man stretched out on the couch and the woman wrapping gauze around his head.

Emma brought the material around and reached for the white tape Will held out to her. "Well, hello."

"Hello, yourself." Ben's voice held a muted quality as he stepped into the room. "What are—? How did—?"

"Why am I here?" Emma finished for him. "Because your tone of voice on the telephone was so very strange-sounding, and because I was concerned that Diana hadn't arrived yet. I thought about that a moment, then rang back, only to be told by one of the servants that you and Will had rushed out of the house shortly after my call. I could hardly just stay home after hearing that."

"Sorry I couldn't follow you two. When I regained consciousness, the only other person in the shrine room was poor Simon." Will shook his head slightly. "He's dead, of course. I can't imagine what made him take up with Vicini and LaPierre, and of course we'll never know now. Anyway I made my way to the front of the Baths just in time to find Pete coming around."

"Yes, and I arrived just in time to greet Will and Pete as they stumbled into the house," Emma broke in. "I sent

Pete home not ten minutes ago. He had been rendered unconscious by some kind of ether, and is suffering no ill effects. Will is another story.

"So, which of you shall I see to next? Both of you appear to be bleeding onto the carpet," Emma remarked.

Diana saw how Ben's blood had soaked his sleeve. She looked down to see drops of red dripping onto the gold and beige carpet, then gasped as she noticed the dark stains spreading out from both of their feet.

"Oh, we're ruining it." Diana headed for the wooden floor bordering the carpet, pulling Ben with her. Emma rose and walked toward them.

"Don't worry about that, or the furniture. Father can replace those things. He finds it difficult to replace people he likes, however, so come in here and let me see to those wounds."

She urged Ben into one of the overstuffed chairs, then motioned for Diana to sit in the other. She called for Matilda, then stepped over to Ben and without ceremony ripped the sleeve right off his shirt.

"Ah, a bullet wound," she said as she leaned forward. "It cut a nasty furrow in your skin, but I should have no trouble closing it up. I'll give you something to ease the pain first, though."

Emma glanced up as the petite maid entered the room. "We will need several basins of water, strips of sheeting, and a bottle of my father's best brandy."

The maid nodded as she left. Emma walked over to the couch and patted a silent, thoughtful-looking Will on the shoulder, then bent to remove a syringe and vial from the black bag on the floor. She kept her eyes on the syringe as she drew liquid from the inverted vial.

"This will sting a little, but it will numb the area for a while so I can work on it." She paused to jab the needle into Ben's shoulder, then went on speaking in a musing tone, almost as if she were talking to herself. "Actually, Papa *should* replace some of this furniture. I think I'll suggest a trip to Europe to him when his term as mayor ends. I've already convinced him not to run again, and I must say he gave in rather easily. He'll never get the rest he obviously needs here. Shopping in Europe will be just the thing. He can pick out some more statues and rugs and buy books to his heart's content."

The love and concern in Emma's voice reminded Diana suddenly of what she had learned about her own father this evening. For several moments she heard none of the conversation in the room and noticed no movement until a little maid knelt in front of her and began gently washing her bloody feet. As the woman dabbed at the cuts on her soles, Diana winced at the sharp pain as she heard Emma ask Will if he would like some brandy.

"Yes," he replied, "I would. And then, if it's not too much trouble, I would like someone to fetch something from my room. It's a small cigar box at the back of the top drawer of the dresser, beneath the socks."

Emma issued an order to the manservant standing at the door. "Would you see to that, Jacobs? Also, please bring a clean shirt down from Professor Potter's room." She turned to Matilda. "I need you to get a warm dressing gown for Miss McKenzie, and some soft slippers."

By the time the servants returned to the room, Diana's feet had been bathed and Emma had finished stitching up the jagged wound on Ben's shoulder. Diana stood on a white towel as she was helped into her dressing gown. She watched Will ease himself into a sitting position and take a deep drink of the brandy he was handed. Then he shook his head as Jacobs brought him the cigar box.

"That is for Miss McKenzie. Please take it over to her."

Emma had just bent down and lifted one of Diana's feet

to begin bandaging it. Diana took the box, then looked questioningly at Will.

"Open it, Diana."

Diana studied the faded red label on the lid a moment, then slowly raised it and saw the stack of yellowed envelopes. She focused on the writing, large and childish and sharply familiar, then read the name of Daniel McKenzie.

"These are mine," she breathed. "They are letters I sent to my father, years ago. Where . . . ? How . . . ?"

Diana's heart pounded as a thousand little clues fell into place, like pieces of a puzzle fitting together to form a picture. "Father?" she breathed.

Chapter Twenty-three

A LONG MOMENT of silence came on the heels of Diana's one-word question. Will stiffened up to a full sitting position as he shook his head. "No, I am not your father, Diana. However, I would be more than proud if it were so."

The lovely fantasy Diana had just formed crumbled, leaving her feeling more lost than ever and totally confused. "But the letters. How did you happen to have them?"

Will sighed. "I worked with your father in several different locations. I think he mentioned me in some of your earlier letters. I went by the name of Billy Bascombe then."

She remembered her father writing about someone with that name, telling her how the young man's sense of humor kept things light on the digs.

"I arrived at Pompeii several weeks after the dig had gotten underway," he said. "When I got there, the camp was buzzing with the news of the altercation between your father and Vicini and their disappearance. I was told that they had both been missing for three weeks and were presumed dead. This box, filled with letters, was with your father's things. Knowing how very much you meant to him, I took them, with every intention of bringing them to you, along with some kind of explanation for your father's disappearance."

Will shifted, turning to face Diana more squarely as he went on. "Then I heard that your father had surfaced in Naples, that he was in a hospital, suffering from exhaustion. I hurried to see him, but was denied admittance. The doctor in charge of the case said that Daniel was still weak from his experience. The man refused to allow me to see him, stating that his patient was confused and in need of rest."

"Like a fool, I let the matter lie and went back to the dig until the season was over. The next thing I knew, Daniel McKenzie was giving a speech at the Sorbonne. I went to Paris, and after listening for ten minutes I knew that the man up there was not the man I had known."

He looked into Diana's eyes. "Your father had a special way of blending his excitement for his subject with dry facts that kept his audience completely enthralled. This man, although he looked like Daniel, sounded all wrong. In his discussion of the Diana myth he shifted from near irrational conjecture to a dry scholarly tone that left the audience completely confused."

"Didn't you do anything about it? Tell anyone?"

"I certainly did. I was positive the man speaking had to be Peter Vicini. I told this to several people, but by this time they were completely fooled, far too convinced that they had the great Daniel McKenzie in their midst to listen to me. So, how could I come to you and tell you of your father's death when the world believed him alive? I'm sorry."

Diana quickly said, "Don't apologize. I know now, and that's all that matters."

Diana's voice thickened as she spoke these last words. She gazed at the swollen bundles surrounding her feet, then clutched the box containing the letters to her breast as she eased herself out of the chair and spoke softly. "I think I should go to bed now, providing Emma feels we will all survive our wounds."

Emma spoke as she wound more gauze around Ben's arm. "Yes. Jacobs and one of the other men will see that Will gets to his room. I can't promise that any of you will get much sleep tonight. I'm afraid your wounds will throb a bit, but I guarantee you'll all survive the night." She paused. "Do you want Matilda to help you up the stairs, Diana?"

"I can make it on my own."

Twenty minutes later, Ben stood in front of the door to Diana's room. As Emma had promised, his shoulder had begun to throb, and his feet ached. When he thought about it, there wasn't a portion of his anatomy that wasn't sore to one degree or another, but the physical pain paled before the twisting ache in his chest as he recalled watching Diana hobble across the floor, then step gingerly up the stairs, one hand on the banister, the other cradling the cigar box full of letters to her heart.

He remembered her words, "I can make it on my own." He knew she would not welcome his intrusion into her sorrow, but he knew with equal certainty that if he allowed her to battle her way through this alone she would emerge with her shell so firmly intact that she would never let another person close to her again.

The doorknob twisted silently in his hand. Diana stood near the corner of the room in front of the windows, holding the sheer undercurtains aside to gaze at the night. He let the door close behind him and braced himself for an angry greeting.

Diana looked like a very young girl dressed in her high-necked nightdress, with her hair falling from a center part to frame her pale face. The light from the window obscured the expression on her features.

"The last letter, you know, the one Vicini said my father was writing to me in Pompeii? It was at the bottom of th

box. I wonder if Will knew that.'' She sighed. ''I guess it
doesn't matter now, except it's good to know that my father
was thinking about me. All these years, I half-hated my
father for abandoning me. And all that time he was dead,
perfectly blameless.''

Ben placed gentle hands on her shoulders. ''You couldn't
have known that, Diana.''

One tear trickled down her cheek. ''I should have. I had
his letters. Ben, you should read them; just one would tell
you how much he cared for me.''

Ben considered telling her that he *had* read the letters.
He would some day, he knew, but now was not the time.
Instead he spoke in a soothing voice. ''Diana, he did leave
you with your grandfather for six years without visiting.''

Diana opened her mouth as if to protest his words, but
Ben lifted a hand to stop her as he spoke again. ''I'm sure
that your father thought this was necessary. But I am equally
as sure that before he died, he regretted those lost opportunities. I don't think he would blame you at all for the
bitter thoughts you've had over the years. I do, however,
think that the time for regrets and recriminations is past.
You need to remember the love he gave you, and to move
forward. Isn't that what this trip was all about?''

She took a deep breath. ''That's right. I came to put the
past to rest, to begin my career.'' She paused as she released
a long, slow breath. ''So, I guess I start applying for positions as an artist with archaeologists tomorrow.''

Ben let his hands slide down her slender arms to grasp
her hands in his. ''That won't be necessary, Diana. I have
a couple of positions I'd like to offer you. With Simon
gone, I will need someone with your expertise at the museum. He regularly went out to various digs to authenticate
items that were to be donated to the museum.''

''No, I don't think that will do at all. I don't see how

we could work together, when it's obvious that you don't trust me. If you did, you would have—"

"—told you about our suspicions regarding the man calling himself Daniel McKenzie." Ben spoke rapidly as he tightened his hold on her hands. "I know. That was wrong of both Will and me. At first, we couldn't be sure that you were not connected with the man somehow. I thought he was really your father, remember; I had no idea about Will's suspicions regarding the man's true identity. Later, we kept silent in order to protect you. And it backfired on us. I'll never make that mistake again, Diana. I promise. Please, come work with me."

He watched Diana carefully. He held his breath, hoping this moment of indecision would work in his favor. A second later she shook her head. "No," she said. "I think it would be best if I found work on my own."

Ben's shoulders slumped as he watched Diana's features set into firm lines and realized there was no point in bringing up the other offer he had in mind. He told himself that after all she had been through, Diana didn't need him pressuring her into making a decision that would affect the rest of her life. As a sigh slipped past his lips, he released her hands and stepped back.

Ben's action, slight as it was, startled Diana. Her suddenly freed fingers felt cold. The chill spread throughout her body as she watched him back away. Why had she refused his offer? Pride? Anger because he had tried to protect her? He had admitted he was wrong, something she knew was difficult for Ben Potter to do. What kind of a fool was she to pass up a position with the British Museum over such petty, emotional issues? Was she or was she not a person capable of separating personal and professional matters?

Diana opened her mouth, then shut it as something Ben had said brought a quick frown to her brow. He had mentioned something about a *couple* of positions.

Diana's heart began to race. She told herself she was being foolish to think that the other position might be involve something more intimate than archaeology. But she might never know, if she didn't ask, if she let him back out of her room, if she never let him see into her heart.

The silence was broken by the sound of Ben's bandaged foot on the floor. Diana stiffened. "*Carpe diem,*" she whispered.

Ben paused and glanced at her sharply. "What did you say?"

"I said, I want to make a counteroffer."

"A counteroffer?"

"Yes. To your offer of employment." Diana paused. Her heart raced as she tried to put her feelings into words, then she took a deep breath and continued. "I don't think it would be good for your . . . reputation at the museum if we were to work together as things stand."

"For *my* reputation?"

"Yes. I . . . I find it very difficult to control my . . . emotions around you. It would not be good for your career if rumors start circulating about our . . . association."

"I see," he said. "Does your counteroffer have something to do with these prospective rumors?"

This was the moment. It was now, or possibly never. Diana clasped her hands behind her back. "Yes. I can only work for you if you agree to marry me."

Ben didn't say a word, nor did he move a muscle or even an eyelash for a period of several moments. Diana watched him, her heart beating faster with each second that passed.

"Yes, Diana. I'll marry you."

Diana leaned toward him as he curved his right arm around her waist, lifting her face to his to receive a kiss that began gently and tentatively, then increased in intensity as their hearts pounded in unison. When Ben lifted his head to take a long, shuddering breath, Diana let her eyes drift open.

"The proper thing for me to do at this moment would be to sweep you into my arms and carry you over to the bed. Unfortunately, I don't think that will be possible. Do you suppose you could walk over?"

Diana smiled, then took Ben's hand to lead him to the side of the bed. She moved to the center of the satin coverlet, then turned to see him dropping the shirt he'd removed. Her body grew warm and languid as she watched him strip off his pants, then turn and place a knee on the bed.

She went to him eagerly as he pulled her under him, but when she looked up at the face hovering over hers, she saw him wince. Her body was ready to welcome him; desire pulsed through her as his weight pressed down on her, but the pain on his face made her place a restraining hand on his chest as he leaned forward, his lips already parting.

"Your arm, Ben," she whispered. "Perhaps we'd better wait until—"

A quick shake of his head stopped her words. "Don't worry about my arm," he whispered. "Seize the moment, remember?"

Ben's lips closed over Diana's in a kiss that held both searing passion and the promise that whatever the future held, they would see it through, together, seizing each day it came.